Scruffy

Books by Paul Gallico

PAUL GALLICO

Scruffy

A DIVERSION

Garden City, N.Y., 1962

DOUBLEDAY & COMPANY, INC.

813.54
G 135

42993
July, 1962

Old Gibraltar hands will, no doubt, amuse themselves trying to identify the characters in this book and associate them with persons living they have known. This pastime I must hasten to inform them and all others so disposed will be a waste of energy since never during the war was I within a thousand miles of Gibraltar, and thus was unable to base my characters upon any persons dwelling or in office there at the time.

There is only one demonstrable fact in this otherwise total work of fiction and that is that on the 25th August 1944 the Prime Minister, Winston Churchill, caused a signal to be sent expressing his anxiety over disquieting rumours concerning the welfare of the Barbary apes in Gibraltar and the wish that they should not be allowed to die out. And on the 8th September of the same year a second directive was despatched to the effect that every effort should be made to restore the establishment of the apes to the number of twenty-four, and that this should be maintained thereafter.

So much for truth. All that follows is nothing but the wildest imagination.

P.W.G.

Chapter 1

INTRODUCING SCRUFFY

The telephone rang in the narrow, crowded office in the Old
Queen's Gate Headquarters of the 3rd Coast Regiment, Royal
Artillery, Gibraltar. It was a humid, hazy August morning. The
flyblown calendar on the wall confirmed that it was the fifth day
of the eighth month of the year 1939, and the dial of the wrist
watch on the arm of the pleasant-looking young officer who
emerged from a huge pile of documents littering his desk said that
it was ten minutes past ten.

The officer, who was in shorts and open-necked khaki shirt, was
of medium height, with a frank, open face and a pair of gay blue
eyes, which at times could reflect the most startling innocence,
excitement, and enthusiasm.

He picked up the insistently shrilling instrument and said,
"Captain Bailey speaking."

The voice at the other end of the line said, "Hello, sir. Lovejoy
here."

The Captain said somewhat testily, "Yes, yes, Lovejoy. What is
it?" Ordinarily he would not have been so short with his right-
hand man, the invaluable Gunner Lovejoy, Keeper of the Apes,
but at that moment he was busy concocting an official letter
which, when it reached its destination through all its official channels, he hoped would soften the heart of the Colonial Secretary
to the point where he would not only increase the amount of
funds available for the daily food allowance for the Rock apes but
would also do something about the monkey-nuts situation. This
was a simple problem controlled by the laws of supply and de-
mand. They were out of monkey nuts on the Rock, and the price
of them from both French and Spanish Africa had shot up beyond
the Captain's budget.

The reason that this was a concern of Captain Timothy Bailey, Royal Artillery, was that in addition to his myriad other duties in connection with commanding anti-aircraft batteries, the job of Officer in Charge of Apes had been wished on him. This position carried with it no kudos, no perks, no medal at the end of it, not even so much as a "Well done!" from anyone.

From time immemorial, or ever since the British had taken over and held the Rock, and with it the responsibility for the simian packs that infested its upper reaches and every so often came swarming down to raid the town like a gang of destructive hooligans, the method for choosing the OIC Apes had been for the Brigadier to make testy noises in his throat and, with a look of distaste upon his features that he should have to concern himself with such a matter, run a finger down his list of officers and select the one least likely to squawk or make a nuisance of himself over the appointment.

From the point of view of Brigadier J. W. Gaskell, D.S.O., M.C., O.B.E., Captain Timothy Bailey had been the ideal choice. The young officer had a record of good conduct, respect for his superiors, no bad habits, and total absorption in the labours assigned to him. He appeared to have no time-wasting hobbies, to be of a serious turn of mind and eager to please.

"Yes, yes, Lovejoy," repeated Captain Bailey. "What is it?" And then added, "Are you drunk or sober?"

"Sober, sir," reported Lovejoy, and from the earnestness and timbre of his voice the Captain knew that this was so. "Sorry to disturb you, sir, but he's off again."

"Oh Lord," groaned the Captain, "how long ago?"

"Half an hour."

"Why didn't you stop him?"

"I tried to, sir—but you know how he is."

"Then why didn't you call me earlier?"

"I couldn't, sir—I've just got back from first aid."

A throb of sympathy ran through Captain Bailey and softened his voice. "Oh I say—are you O.K.?"

"Yes, sir."

"Whereabouts?"

"The usual place, sir—the hand."

A proverb rose to the top of Captain Bailey's brain and went floating about there. It said, "Don't bite the hand that feeds you." The point was that the ape, Harold, otherwise known as Scruffy, always did bite any hand that fed him. Yet somehow this managed to be a part of the perverted charm of the beast and the spell he had contrived to cast over both of them.

"Poor old chap," Captain Bailey repeated. "Hadn't you better be having a drink?"

"I've been thinking about that, sir—but I thought it best to call you first."

"Quite right," Captain Bailey agreed. "Where are you calling from?"

"St. Michael's Hut. I came back here after the M.O. fixed me up. I thought perhaps the old bas—pardon me, sir—I mean, Scruffy might've come back. But he hasn't. I reckon he's well on his way now. You ought to be hearing from the C.R.A. within a couple of hours."

Captain Bailey said, "Blast! Well, thanks for warning me. By the way, what started him off this time?"

"Well, sir," explained the voice at the other end of the line, and Captain Bailey in his mind's eye could see Lovejoy scrunched up like a goblin in the narrow confines of St. Michael's Hut, the little gazebo not far from Prince Ferdinand's Battery, where the apes hung out.

"Well, sir, you know how Scruffy is about his scoff—when he wants monkey nuts there's no two ways about it. It was carrots this morning. He takes one look at them, picks up the biggest, and lets go for me 'ead."

Captain Bailey's sporting sense momentarily got the better of him and he asked, "Did he hit you?"

Gunner Lovejoy replied with what almost amounted to pride, "He ain't never missed yet."

"Yes, of course," Captain Bailey said. "And then?"

"He knew I'd fetch 'im one on his ruddy ar—— Beg pardon, sir—I mean he knew I'd take measures if I caught him, so he called me a dirty name and went off down to the car park."

Captain Bailey shuddered and said, "Oh dear. Were there any cars there?"

Gunner Lovejoy said, "Yes sir—three."

The Captain shuddered again and said, "Tourists?"

"Yes, sir."

"Well?"

"The usual, sir. He had the windscreen wipers off quick as a wink. You know he loves the rubber off'n them. Caviar, that's what it is to 'im."

"Yes, yes," the Captain assented, "I know. Any other damage?"

The Gunner's voice grew a shade less confident as it said, "I have the list 'ere, sir. Shall I read it out to you?"

A trifle wearily the Captain said, "Yes, I suppose you might as well." He took a fresh sheet of notepaper and poised his pencil.

"Binoculars, one pair, Zeiss, size eight by fourteen, value thirty-eight pounds, belonging to a gentleman named Schlummer staying at the Rock Hotel," the Gunner read off.

"What happened to 'em?" queried the Captain.

"Bunged them over the edge," replied Lovejoy. "There wouldn't be much left of them. The drop is seven hundred foot there."

"Go on," said the Captain.

"One camera, Ansco Reflex Automatic, three-five lens, fifteen unexposed films in magazine, value forty pounds, property likewise Mr. Schlummer."

"What happened to that?" asked the Captain.

"Same thing, sir."

"He didn't like this fellow, Schlummer, did he?" the Captain suggested.

"That's right, sir. You might almost say as what he 'ad a point there."

"German type, eh? Is that the lot?"

"No, no, sir," the Gunner replied cheerfully. "One hat, lady's, sir, with violets on, property of a Miss Sacking, staying at the Bristol, value three guineas."

"Good Lord!" exclaimed the Captain. "What happened to that?"

"Tore it up, sir. He didn't like it. It wasn't all that bad."

"Yes. Go on."

"One purse, lady's, brown leather, chain and clasp broken, contents spilled, money blown over cliff, owner Mrs. Pritchard, likewise staying at Hotel Bristol. Damages and value of money claimed at fourteen pounds ten shillings."

The Captain noted down the details of the sum and realised that he was sweating slightly. The ape had really been on the rampage.

The Gunner was reading again: "One teddy bear, child's toy, property of Master Leonard Sletch, father and mother Mr. and Mrs. R. J. Sletch, at Hotel Victoria. Damages claimed to value of——"

The Captain interrupted with a bitter laugh. "That one at least oughtn't to cost much."

There was a moment's silence from the other end of the telephone, and then Lovejoy said, "Well, you see, the trouble was, sir, the kid wouldn't let go of it."

"Oh Lord," breathed Captain Bailey, "don't tell me——?"

"Yes, sir, he did. But the medical officer's fixed the kid up, and he'll be all right. It wasn't much of a bite—just caught 'im on the end of the finger. But they're claiming their nipper will be maimed for life."

A sudden wave of anger passed over Tim and he shouted into the telephone, "Dammit all, Lovejoy—what the devil were you doing all this time? Didn't you have any balloons on you?"

"No, sir—sorry. Not a one on me person. You know how it is with the budget, sir."

"Damn and blast the budget!" Tim shouted. "If you'd come and told me you hadn't any I'd have bought you some out of my own pocket. We can't have this sort of thing going on."

This part of the conversation, which would have sounded utterly lunatic to an outsider, was a reference to the fact that the irritable Harold, or Scruffy, who feared nothing living on earth—not man nor beast, not lightning, thunder, hell, or high water—was subject to the thrall of but one thing, a child's toy rubber balloon. When Gunner Lovejoy, in extremes of emergency, pro-

duced one of these in red, blue, green, or yellow, and blew it up to
the point where explosion was threatened, it reduced Scruffy
temporarily to a wretched, cowering, quivering, panic-stricken
mass of fur. In this state he could be handled and remained
tractable for a period of twenty-four hours before his nerves began
to recover and he became his old, unpleasant self again. This was
a secret shared between Gunner Lovejoy and Tim Bailey and was
resorted to only in the case of genuine emergencies.

Lovejoy repeated, "Sorry, sir."

"What started him off after that?" demanded Tim. "I should
have thought he'd had a lovely morning. Pleased as punch. Cost
the Government over a hundred quid. I'd say he could have
retired on that. You say he's off to town? Why——?"

The Gunner said, "He caught a look at hisself in the wing
mirror of one of the cars, sir."

It was now the Captain's turn to fall silent for a moment at his
end of the telephone. Then, in a more subdued voice, he said,
"Oh."

"You know how that sets 'im off, sir," the Gunner was saying,
his voice suddenly smarmy with sharing a confidence. "He hates
the sight of hisself. He hates me, he hates you, he hates everybody,
but worst of all he seems to hate hisself."

"Did he break it off?" Tim asked.

"He broke them *all* off," amended the Gunner. "Six! They were
the several properties of Mr. and Mrs.——"

"All right, all right—never mind. You can give me those later.
Anyway, thanks for letting me know."

The Gunner said, "If you should be needing me later, sir, I'll
be——"

"In the Admiral Nelson," the Captain concluded for him, and
then added almost absent-mindedly, "Have one for me, too,"
and hung up.

He sat there for a moment looking down upon the list of
destruction and knew that with Scruffy on the loose and headed
for town, this was just the beginning. Yet somehow there was
really no anger in his heart against the animal, and actually the
beginning of a smile was fighting its way to the corners of his

mouth. He then looked at his own thumbs, one of which bore one, and the other two, whitening cicatrices, mementos of Harold —Scruffy. The smile did not disappear—in fact, it settled there, for the truth was that deep down in his heart of hearts Captain Timothy Bailey had a sneaking affection for the brute; he was so damnably and magnificently consistent and unregeneratedly naughty.

While this conversation was going on, the subject thereof, the notable Scruffy, largest, oldest, toughest, and most disagreeable Barbary ape inhabiting Gibraltar, was making his way down to the town via the remains of that spine of stone and brickwork known as King Charles V Wall. The ruins climbed straight up from below, almost like a ladder, constituting a convenient short cut for the ape population when they decided to pay a visit to the city in search of goodies and entertainment. In this instance, Scruffy was both hungry and bored as well as irritated.

Scruffy was one of the ugliest specimens of magot, scientifically known as *macaca silvana simia*, the African tail-less macaque, or Barbary ape, ever domiciled on the Rock, and likewise one of the largest specimens. He was the size of a full-grown boxer dog, but twice as strong and ten times as destructive, his fur greyish, reddish brown, the hair rather thick and somewhat wavy. His black face was illuminated by a pair of golden-brown eyes brimming with meanness and shining forth malevolently from beneath cavernous brows. Large tufts of hair stood up from his ears. He was pure monkey, and yet he contrived likewise to look like a lot of people one knew, and disliked.

Scruffy's body was thickset, his hindquarters heavy, so that at times he resembled a fat Arctic explorer in a fur suit several sizes too large for him. He had a set of murderous canine teeth, a jaw like a steel trap, and was further armed with ten strong nails set into black paws at the end of powerful and muscular arms.

He was grumpy, wary, unfriendly, suspicious, irritable, bad tempered, and vengeful. He was wily as a Red Indian, as treacherous as a snake, and withal brave. He was one four-footed mass of animated vices, unleavened by a single thing that a human might consider a virtue—unless the humans were a pair of odd ones like Gunner John Lovejoy and Captain Timothy Bailey. Each loved and admired Scruffy in his own way, and for his own reasons; the former because he recognised the monkey in rebellion against a world in which he had not asked to be put, and because he felt, without knowing it, the tragedy of the basic loneliness of the animal.

Scruffy's first port of call was at a back street behind Prince Edward Road, where the wall came to an end. Here he made his way to the red tiled roof of a small cottage and for a few moments sat scratching himself contemplatively and letting ideas float up into his head.

It is the considered opinion of zoologists, anthropologists, and scientists that primates cannot and do not think, though they would have encountered a stiff argument from Gunner Lovejoy and Captain Bailey on the subject, but obviously some mental process must be involved when a beast who has been sitting comfortably pleasuring his nerves by scratching itches suddenly ceases and commences to de-tile a roof.

The scientists are insistent that primates are neither able to go back into the past beyond remembering perhaps where food was accustomed to be buried during a series of experiments, nor project themselves into the future, such as deciding: "I think if the weather is fine tomorrow I'll go down to town, but if it's raining, I'll stay home and let Annette, my favourite female, get on with a bit of grooming up my fur."

There then remains the present, and if Scruffy was denied the past and anticipating the future, his evil mind was a whizzer when it came to deciding what he would do now, or at any given instant. Thus his wicked, intelligent eyes coming to rest upon the tiling of the roof noted one that was slightly damaged and loose. At once his prying fingers completed the job and quite naturally loosened the one next to it.

Scruffy had a dozen off before the householder, hearing the noise, came forth and began jumping up and down with rage and shouting in Gibraltese Spanish.

Since the householder was down on the street level and Scruffy was up out of his reach, the shouts of anger were no concern of his, except to arouse in him a feeling of satisfaction, but he now discovered that the flat roofing tiles when thrown sailed beautifully, almost like the flight of those wretched creatures, birds.

Scruffy now busied himself with the interesting and exciting task of making tile birds, while, drawn by the shouts of the irate householder, a crowd began to gather in the street. The ape, who in addition to his formidable list of vices was a ham, enjoyed nothing better than witnesses. He filled the air with whizzing red birds, and when one crashed into a wall and splintered it gave him another idea. Below him and a little to the right, mounted on a black and white pole, was the attractive glass globe of a street lamp.

It took him three tile birds to get the range and the hang of it, and then he sent the fourth crashing deliciously through it, shattering the globe into a thousand pieces.

Two of those thin Gibraltar policemen arrived, their narrow, sallow Spanish features and figures looking, as usual, out of place in the costume of the London bobby, rather as though they had been caught coming home in daylight from a fancy-dress ball. They were understandably and righteously wroth at this destruction of public property, drew batons, and prepared to mount to the roof and do something about the situation.

Again proving that when it came to the present Scruffy had all his mental buttons, he now decided that there had been sufficient entertainment for a first stop, and, with a leap, a bound, a hop, and a swing of his strong arms, and in spite of having to do without the assistance that every other monkey could claim, a fifth limb in the shape of a tail, Scruffy was three telegraph poles and five houses away from the scene.

The policemen made a note of damages and called their Sergeant. The Sergeant notified the Lieutenant, who had a word with the Inspector, who picked up the phone and dialled Fortress Headquarters to ask to speak to the Brigadier.

The Chaplain to the Brigade of Royal Artillery stationed in Gibraltar, probably because of the nature of his calling, had been awarded quarters in a charming cottage not far from the French

Consulate, in a grove of pepper and eucalyptus trees, but his pride and joy was his vegetable garden at the back. There was a Garden Club at Gibraltar, and the Chaplain was one of the fiercest competitors for the tiny, practically infinitesimal cups awarded for prize specimens. It had been an extraordinarily good spring, with just enough rain, and the Chaplain's vegetables were in fine fettle. His leeks were bursting from the ground like tree trunks, his carrot tops were lush and green; sturdy long green runner beans hung from the bean poles, tomatoes as big as grapefruit were ripening in the sun. The Chaplain's garden contained at least half a dozen firsts, and probably twice as many seconds and thirds, assuring him sufficient points for the Grand Championship trophy, which was about the size of an egg cup.

Scruffy had never been in that direction before, and so he did not know of this paradise. Whim, fancy, and luck took him thither on that wonderful day, and it was like a starving man who finds himself suddenly seated at a Lucullan banquet and bidden to eat his fill. Nobody had bade Scruffy, but this was beside the point.

When the Chaplain, finally roused from labours in his study by noises off, went out and stared aghast at his garden, it was all over. The tomato vines were down, the fruit trampled to a pulp, beans and peas were uprooted, ravished leeks strewed the ground, the tops had been torn off the carrots, tender courgettes shattered, the grape arbour denuded, and the place left a shambles. He was just in time to see the greyish-brown rear end of the depredator retire into a tree. When the Chaplain approached the tree, Scruffy spat out a mouthful at him and departed.

The Chaplain went and dialled the private number of the Brigadier. By the time he had got through to him there was very little, if any, Christian charity in his heart.

If the Chaplain had been proud of his vegetable garden, the librarian of the Garrison Library was equally proud of the orange tree in the lovely floral glade surrounding the building, and the golden oranges that hung thereon. Actually on his way to another part of the town, Scruffy had only paused in the orange tree for an instant to catch his breath and rest himself. For the moment he had neither mischief nor gluttony on his mind, but unfortunately the librarian had no way of knowing this. He saw only the largest and ugliest of the magots which an inscrutable Government insisted upon fostering on the Rock perched in his tree. No diplomat, and certainly no connoisseur of the vagaries of *macaca silvana simia*, the librarian picked up a large, smooth pebble from his gravel walk and shied it at the ape.

Thinking apparatus or none, one thing that Scruffy could get was an idea when it was presented to him. He therefore deliberately and methodically detached each orange from its stem and fired it at the head of the librarian. After three direct hits, the unhappy custodian of Gibraltar's culture retreated into the library. Scruffy raised his sights and continued the bombardment, splattering the fruit up against the doors and windows of the building. When there were no more oranges on the tree he continued on his way, feeling rested and refreshed by the incident. The librarian made for the telephone.

The Surveyor attached to the Colonial Secretary's office lived in a neat two-storey house not far from Ragged Staff Gates. It being then eleven o'clock of the morning of a working day, the Surveyor was out dutifully somewhere around Europa Point surveying, the children were at the beach with their nanny, and Mrs. Surveyor was out shopping. Like a good and careful housewife, she had locked the front door and the back door and closed the ground-floor windows. However, a window in the second storey was open to admit fresh air into the bedroom.

If there was anything Scruffy loved, it was an inside job. On his rooftop way across town to turn more of the unimaginable future into the delectable present, the open window beckoned him like a lodestone. He went down the drainpipe, pausing only a moment to detach a loose piece of the rain gutter and throw it down into the street, and then entered the Surveyor's bedroom. The bed looked inviting, so he got into it, uncovering in the process the Surveyor's red and white striped flannel pyjamas, the design and colour of which irritated Scruffy, so he shredded them and threw the remains out the window.

Encountering his ugly mug in the mirror of Madame Surveyor's dressing table, he was reduced to the usual state of fury and, pick-

ing up a chair, whanged it into the mirror, thus causing himself
to disappear. This may not have been a feat of memory, but it was
certainly practical.

He went sniffing through the dressing table, opened a bottle of
expensive scent and drank the contents, spilled powder and got it
all over his face and up his nose, bringing on a sneezing fit. The
ticking of an ormolu bedroom clock annoyed him, so he stopped
it the only way he knew how—by pounding it on the floor until
its innards came out.

He then turned his attention to the cupboards, which he
opened. The clothing that disturbed him either by its texture or
colour he rendered into strips, but for some reason fell in love
with a pair of the Surveyor's checked golfing trousers. These he
flung over his shoulder and went to the window just as the
Surveyor's wife, returning from shopping with her baskets laden,
looked up to see a brown-furred, white-faced fiend from hell with
her husband's golfing trousers wrapped around his neck staring at
her.

The scream she emitted was heard at the dockyards a mile
away.

Scruffy retired from the scene the same way he had come—up
the rain spout and over the roofs—still bearing the trousers.

Shaking, the Surveyor's wife went into the house and called the
Colonial Secretary's secretary and dusted him off on the subject
of the famous Rock apes. The buck then passed from one telephone to another until it ended in the lap of the Colonial Secretary himself, who said bitterly to his assistant, "When you can get
through to Brigadier Gaskell, call me—and don't stop trying until
you do."

There was not a great deal left of Scruffy's happy morning on
the town. As time was getting short and he liked to be back up on
the hill and into his favourite olive tree for his siesta before midday, he went through three flower beds, disrupted education at
the Grammar School by giving a performance of gymnastics and
acrobatics on the flying rings and other playground equipment,
then, having thoroughly digested his meal, went off and relieved
himself in a fresh-water catchment, where he was observed by the

Chief Water Engineer, whose life was wrapped up in providing adequate and sanitary water for the people and the garrison of Gibraltar. Next to the Governor, Colonial Secretary, and Military Commander, his job was the most important on the post, and the rocket he loosed at the C.R.A. when he got through to him really finished the job of boiling over the Brigadier.

Since all of his telephone lines were tied up and apparently would remain so until the ape on the loose left town, the Brigadier summoned his Staff Captain and snarled, "Get over to Old Queen's Gate H.Q. and find young Bailey. I want him brought here immediately." Unspoken but implicit in the glare of the Brigadier's eyes and the choleric crimson of his countenance was the phrase, "Dead or alive."

Chapter 2

THE BRIGADIER IS NOT AMUSED

The Brigadier was a tall, florid man, whose mouth beneath a short military moustache was set in lines of permanent exasperation engendered by having to deal with young officers and rankers sent out these days who were simply not a patch on what soldiers had been in his own youth.

His life had been dedicated to the service of the guns of the Royal Artillery, but now that he had reached General Officer status and Brigade Command he was not sure to what purpose. He had during his career dutifully blown up and dismembered an adequate number of human beings designated as enemies but whom he had never seen, since the range was rarely less than two thousand yards: he had himself suffered punctures of his hide. On his chest the fruit salad of ribbons contained the requisite decorations testifying to his courage and understanding of comportment consistent with the furthering of a military career. He was a thoroughly conscientious officer who had become set in the routine of trying to get on with things with men he considered inadequate for the job and administering his command with as little trouble as possible.

Trouble was what Brigadier Gaskell hated, personal trouble, military trouble, trouble with superiors, trouble with inferiors, trouble at home, trouble on the post, and, above all, trouble with politicians, civil servants, and civilians. Trouble was what he had on his hands now, trouble which would have repercussions quite possibly in the office of the Colonial Secretary, the Governor, Whitehall, and—one never knew—might even spark a nasty-minded question or two in Parliament, and which could have been avoided if a young nitwit of a Captain delegated to do the job had discharged his duties properly and kept his filthy beasts up at Queen's Gate and Middle Hill where they belonged, instead of pestering him with requests for cages, sprays, concrete floorings, increase in food allowances, and other damned coddlings of the foul creatures.

Well, young Bailey was for it now, and Brigadier Gaskell, who had somewhat more imagination than usually associated with a soldier, relished the state that Captain Bailey would be in as Captain Quennel, his Staff Captain, marched him over to receive his chewing up. He would know that he was for the daddy of all rockets.

Thus the C.R.A. was totally unprepared for the bustling, eager entrance of this officer, the engaging and friendly innocence of his blue eyes, and the unsettling expression of pleasure and enthusiasm on his countenance. He had under his arm a large manila file, apparently filled with documents, and as he came through the door his fingers were already delving into it and bringing forth typewritten sheets and other pages covered with what appeared to be rough drawings and figures.

So startled was the Brigadier by this breezy and whirlwind entrance, when his imagination had promised him a pale and shaking creature standing craven and trembling on the carpet, that he failed immediately to touch off the blast, as he had intended, with the crash of his fist onto his desk and a shout of, "Goddamn it, Bailey—once and for all . . . ! ! !"

Instead he took the Captain's crisply delivered salute and remained seated behind his desk, staring open-mouthed and unbelieving, listening to him say: "It's frightfully decent of you to give me this time, sir. I know how busy you are, but I've got everything in shape, I think, so that you can practically take it in at a glance. . . ."

The papers were out of the file and spread on the desk before him, and, in spite of what was pent up inside, the Brigadier could not help but find his fire-and-brimstone-shouting glance momentarily distracted to them, so that at one instant he found himself staring at what seemed to be a drawing of a large and primitive bear trap, the next at a list of names—"Joyce, Mary, Helen, Phyllis, Peter, Albert, Harold, Marjorie, Daisy, Penelope, Oswald,

Jeremiah"—then again more drawings which looked like refrigerator coils, and other sheets drawn up most intriguingly in the form recognised as used for genealogies and lines of descent from ancient families.

Staff Captain Quennel found himself staring down at the papers, too, thus unwittingly drawing upon himself the explosion the C.R.A. had been saving up for the Captain.

"What the devil are you standing there gazing at, Quennel?" he shouted, causing the Staff Captain to pale beneath his tan.

Tim, who had produced a pencil, now pointed with it to one of the drawings and said, "I think probably my trap, sir. The way it works, sir, is—you put the banana here, with a nylon thread attached to it."

The Brigadier was beginning to recover his lost poise and said with a cold and repressed menace, "Captain Bailey, do you realise——?"

"I know it isn't exactly sporting, sir," Captain Bailey continued, "but he picks up the banana, pulling the thread which is tied to this support here, dragging it out from under—down comes the cage, and there you are."

"CAPTAIN BAILEY!" At last the C.R.A. had gathered his forces for the shout he had meant to emit at the very first. "Do you realise why I have sent for you?"

Tim did, and wondered how long he could continue to conceal the fact from the Brigadier. It had worked well so far and was quite probably worth another try, but he also knew that there was such a thing as goading a man beyond the limits of containment. He said, "Yes, sir—to go over the things that need to be done for the apes."

Brigadier Gaskell's fists clenched and unclenched. Then he said, "Do you see that telephone, Captain Bailey?"

"Yes, sir."

"Do you know that that telephone has been ringing constantly for the last two hours?"

"No, sir."

"Well it has. And during those two hours I have been compelled to listen to a list of complaints of depredations by a filthy brute that is supposed to be your responsibility to keep under control—gardens torn up, orange trees knocked down, gutters demolished, roofs torn off houses, the Surveyor's trousers——" There was a slight movement on the part of the Staff Captain, and the Brigadier's fury was again distracted to that unfortunate young man. "Captain Quennel," he said icily, "if you laugh, you may consider your military career at an end." He returned to Tim. "——homes invaded, catchments fouled—I'm surprised there's anything of the town left standing."

Tim's voice suddenly went low and was filled with sympathy. He said, "I know, sir—and that's not all."

"W-what?" The Brigadier here found his mind and senses reeling. "W-what's not all?"

"Of what's happened," Tim explained. "It started earlier up at the Queen's Gate car park. Gunner Lovejoy is bringing down the list of claims, but I've heard some of them, and I don't anticipate too much trouble. The chap who had his camera and binoculars smashed had obviously been teasing the animal. I think we can deal with him, sir. As for the child that was bitten——"

"*Child that was bitten?*" repeated the Brigadier in tones of mingled fury, despair, and disbelief.

"If he had used his nut and let go the teddy bear, it wouldn't have occurred." Tim's voice suddenly grew confiding and conciliatory. "The whole thing wouldn't have happened, sir, if some attention had been paid to my memo of ten days ago on the peanut situation. It all ties in with what I had to say about the shocking lack of monkey nuts—— You see, he does like his peanuts, and I think if you will consult the order issued on March 28, 1932, by the Secretariat on behalf of the Government, you will find he is entitled to them as a part of the regular rations."

The Brigadier at this point could do nothing more than stare helplessly.

"Now, the other part of my plan," continued Tim, "—it's all written down and set out here—is for better control of civilian molestation and unauthorized feeding of the apes in the town. Suggested: that further signs be posted on Southport Gates, Waterport Gates, Casemates Gates, Trafalgar Cemetery, the Post

Office, and the apes' den, warning civilians and Army personnel
against feeding and enticing the apes; increasing the amount of
the fine for violations; and above all, sir, jacking up the police to
do their duty and arrest violators. If the apes didn't know they
could cadge monkey nuts from the townspeople, they'd never
come down. If I were you, I'd have the Police Commissioner in
and give him a real rocket."

The Brigadier took a long, deep breath, and then two more,
since murder was not his idea of bringing to a close an honourable,
if undistinguished, military career. Then he said, "Captain Bailey,
am I to understand that you are presuming to offer me advice?"

"No, sir—except, of course, where the apes are concerned——"

"You know it all."

Tim tried to look modest. "Well, sir, I have made a study of the
job since I took it over a year or so ago, and I must say I've
learned a good deal."

Brigadier Gaskell found suddenly that his massive choler and
temper had evaporated, almost as though he had held it in too
long. Now that he had use for it, it was no longer there. To his
Staff Captain he said, "Thank you, Captain Quennel, you may
go," and after his departure said quietly enough, "Sit down,
Captain Bailey, and let's have a word together."

Tim stopped perspiring internally and gave a mental "Whew!"
It looked as though he were about to get away with it, and he
even harboured notions, now that he appeared to have talked the
Brigadier out of his rage, of putting over some of the pet ideas
for the comfort and happiness of his apes that he had been working on for so long.

"Bailey," the Brigadier asked with almost an air of amiability,
"do you know why I put you into the job of Officer in Charge of
Apes?"

Tim was always one to repay amiability with the like. "Well, no,
sir," he said with what he hoped was an agreeable expression,
"not really."

"I selected you," interrupted the Brigadier, and then pronounced each word of the following sentence separately, "because—I—didn't—want—any—trouble."

"Trouble, sir?"

"Trouble! Trouble with those seeping apes. Bailey, you may or may not realise it, but this is a military outpost of the Empire. If war comes, as it most likely will, I shall be called upon to defend it. I have things to do, Bailey. You may be too young to realise it, but the command of a Brigade of Royal Artillery is complicated and arduous. For God knows why, the Government has seen fit to encumber me with the further responsibility of a pack of foul and undisciplined monkeys. I am to keep track of their numbers, look after their welfare, write reports, and otherwise waste my time on this pack of repulsive slobs."

Tim thought it wise to remain silent at this point, and did so.

"That same Government in its benevolence," continued the Brigadier, "has seen fit to permit me to delegate authority by appointing an OIC, or Officer in Charge of Apes." The Brigadier's fists suddenly clenched again, his jaw muscles tightened, and he hissed, "That's you, Bailey, isn't it?"

"Yes, indeed, sir, and I've tried——"

"Who asked you to try?" the C.R.A. cut in. "Who asked you to make a career out of those filthy beasts? When I asked Old Nosey Peeb—that is to say, Colonel Peebles—for a recommendation for an OIC Apes I said I wanted a young chap who could be trusted to carry on in the tradition of his predecessors. 'Right,' said Colonel Peebles, 'I have just the man for you, young Bailey. Just sent to us; enthusiastic and seems to like animals. Always picking up strays of one kind or another. Good record. Doesn't give his superiors any trouble.' That's why I picked you for this important job. And you know what I expect of you?"

"Well——" began Tim.

"No 'wells,' if you please," the Brigadier retorted. "Two reports a year on births, deaths, number of apes in each pack, and no trouble. I expected you to work out your own way of keeping the beggars out of town, and if they persisted in coming down, well— I gather even the young men of today haven't quite forgotten how to handle a rifle or a sporting gun."

Tim could not keep the horror from showing on his countenance. "What, sir," he cried, "you mean——?"

The Brigadier regarded him evenly and then said grimly, "One of the things we expect from our young officers is initiative. Well, and what did I get?"

"Well, if I may say so, sir," began Tim, and could not keep his eyes from looking in the direction of the papers he had laid out on the Brigadier's desk.

Crash! went the Brigadier's fist on them. "Bumph!" he shouted. "Bloody, all-fired, eternal bumph! You've buried me in bumph. Every time I come to my desk in the morning there's some bumph from you suggesting this, suggesting that, demanding this, that, or the other, using me as a messenger boy or postal station to pass along your nonsensical notions to the Colonial Secretary or the Governor, filling my head that ought to be kept clear for the men of my Brigade with monkey nuts, oatmeal, carrots, onions, or whatever you're trying to cadge—concreting of shelters, building of cages, installation of salt-water system for cleaning and cooling of cages, reduction of rat colony——" He interrupted his list with another violent bang of his fist. "Goddamn it, if you want to reduce the rat colony, why don't you get a pea shooter and go out and do it yourself? Do you want to see what I've had to put up with since you took over, Captain Bailey?" He pressed a button and, when the Senior Warrant Officer appeared, said, "Get me Captain Bailey's file, and Major Patterson's, too, while you're at it."

The chief clerk returned carrying a stack of six bulging manila envelopes and one small, thin one, which he deposited side by side on the Brigadier's desk.

"Look at that, Bailey," the Brigadier said. He picked up the thin envelope and said, "Why the devil can't you be like your predecessor, Major Patterson? There you are—two reports a year: so many born, so many died, to hell with them, and there's an end to it."

Tim looked down with distaste at his predecessor's file. "He didn't love them, sir," he said. "What I found out was: it isn't just a tally job—they need love and attention. You see, in a way, they're sort of like us."

The Brigadier's absent temper returned again. "What's that?"

he yelled. "Are you trying to tell me that——?" He shut off what would have been Tim's elucidation with another crash of his fist. "Do you know what's been the matter with those animals since you've taken over? They're filthy, rotten spoiled, that's what they are."

Here he came to the point that he had really been meaning to make and jabbed a finger at Tim. "Let me tell you something, young man," he said, "the Colonial Secretary is sick and tired of you and your bumph, the Governor is sick and tired of you and your bumph, and [crash] most important, I am sick and tired of it. And what's more, you've become the town bore on the subject. People avoid you. Or hadn't you noticed?"

The Brigadier choked off another reply that Tim would have made and said, "That's how it is, young man. And now I'll tell you what we're going to do. First of all we'll cut out the bumph. I don't want to see another communication from you for the next six weeks. Then you keep that confounded ape out of this town. The next time he comes down I'll shoot him myself. And just to help you along and fire you with diligence and enthusiasm, hereafter all damage to personal property perpetrated by any of your bloody monkeys comes out of your pay. Thank you, Captain Bailey; that will be all."

Somehow Tim found himself headed for the door.

"And take this bumph with you," the Brigadier shouted.

Tim went back, collected it, stuffed it into his file, saluted without really having his heart in it, and went out. There was no enthusiasm left in him. For the first time he felt genuinely crushed.

Chapter 3

WHAT OIC APES MEANS

Emerging from the Brigadier's office, Tim, with his file pressed to his side, his head sunk in moody reflection, wondered whether what the Brigadier had said was true. He rather thought it might be. And, if so, then it wanted a bit of thinking about and sorting out. He climbed into his car and drove out of the town along Willis Road, past the ruins of the old Moorish castle and upwards into Queen's Road towards the village of the apes.

On the way he passed through Theatre Royal Square where the Admiral Nelson was located and where he was sure Lovejoy was to be found. For an instant he wished that protocol didn't forbid him joining the Gunner for a drink, for Tim was in need of the sympathetic company of a kindred soul, even though he knew that much of what had happened at the car park could be laid at the Gunner's door.

There was in the Gunner, Tim thought, a faint "Bolshie" streak, similar to the large one which manifested itself in Scruffy. The Gunner was anti-people and in particular anti-civilians. For instance there were signs up all over the area warning tourists that the apes were wild animals and would react violently to sudden movements and sounds. These signs forbade them to stroke and handle the apes and advised them further that they frequently carried away such articles as cameras and handbags. If they chose to disregard these signs, which invariably they did, that was no business of the Gunner's. Furthermore, Lovejoy, who understood the apes, their ways and their moods better than they did themselves, always knew well in advance when there was going to be an incident. At such times he would wander nonchalantly over to the rail guarding the precipice, throw a leg over, light a cigarette, and contentedly wait for it to happen. When taken to task by Tim for this callous attitude towards the appendages and property of human beings, Lovejoy would reply, "They can read, can't they, sir? You can't tell 'em anything—it's the only way they'll ever learn." Perhaps it was just as well he couldn't see the Gunner at that moment.

Tim's car climbed steadily up the narrow road lined on both sides with dusty olive trees, fig and locust beans, and the prickly pear cacti with their oval, spiny leaves.

He came to the concrete square protected by a railing just below Prince Ferdinand's Battery, the playground of the apes, from which there was the splendid and much photographed view of the town and harbour of Gibraltar spread out below. To the left across the Straits on a clear day Mount Atlas would loom, but not in the haze and sticky humidity of August.

Plainly visible were the harbour installations with their forests of cranes, the dockyards, where a destroyer or two nestled, and the basins of the dry docks. Immediately below, seen through the flat tops of the pine trees clinging to the side of the hill and the royal palms lining the streets, were blocks of apartment buildings, the rooftops of the town, and the line of Main Street cutting its way through the centre. Across the bay the white town of Algeciras glittered in the sun.

This was Gibraltar—the lock on the door to the Mediterranean, and to which his country held the key. He and all the rest of the members of his Artillery Brigade were a part of that key, which in time of emergency must very swiftly be turned in that lock, shutting off ingress and exit to the Mediterranean to all but the friendly. What the devil, then, was he doing messing about with a pack of apes?

He drove onto the concrete facing the sea, from whence a two-funnel passenger liner was steaming into port to discharge its load of tourists, and sat there to think things out. He was alone, since it was the lunch hour and there were no trippers about— not entirely alone, though, for a small apelet with sad eyes and an old man's face, whose mother was probably snoozing some-where near by, swung itself up the side of the car and into his lap.

"Hello, chum," Tim said. "Where's your mum?"

The apelet gazed up at him for a moment, liked the tone of his voice, and threw its arms about him and cuddled to his chest, clutching and pressing his face close to Tim's khaki shirt.

Tim scratched and stroked the small, furry head and, as always, felt the essential loneliness of these creatures and the mystery of affliction that seemed to lie deep within their eyes. No child could have demonstrated the need for closeness, warmth, and affection more vividly than the apelet which clung to him now, and yet it was an animal entering upon the threshold of life. Was this the tragedy—that they had just missed being people—and was that good or bad? And how could one be thrust into contact with these creatures and not be aware of the calamity that had befallen them when the law of natural selection had left them behind?

Tim Bailey, who had grown up as an average young man and officer, who had never really cared greatly about anything, had suddenly found an avocation in the care and study of these caricatures of human beings.

He had been resigned at first when he had been stuck with the job of OIC Apes. This was the Army; he was the new boy in the garrison and gathered that was about what one might expect.

But the strange plight of the monkey had laid hold of Captain Bailey, engaged his sympathies and touched his heart and turned what had originally started out as another army chore to be endured until it could be passed to another victim into an interest and a project in which he threw himself with all the enthusiasm of youth and a sunny nature, with the result that he was not only a trial to his superiors but in a short time had evolved into a kind of Regiment character, an "Oh-God-here-comes-Bailey—we're-going-to-have-to-hear-about-his-flipping-apes" sort of thing.

The small figure had begun to chew the middle button of his shirt and almost had it off. "Ahem," said Tim. "You know who and what I am, I trust? Officer in Charge of Apes, and a blinking nuisance to everybody." He pried open the small teeth and rescued his button. "Officer in charge of you, my fine fellow. As His Majesty's representative and your personal and private Captain detailed to look after your wants I direct that you return to

your dear old mum and chew on her for a while." He detached
the apelet from his person, turned it around, gave it a spank on its
bottom, and sent it on its way. Then he climbed out of the car
himself, went to the railing and stood looking down at the pano-
rama of the city.

He thought back to the beginning of it all, when he had been
summoned to the Brigadier's office to meet a Major Patterson who
had been posted home. "Captain Bailey," the Brigadier had said,
"this is Major Patterson, who is leaving us. Among other things
he's been our Officer in Charge of Apes. Done a damn fine job.
I've been looking for someone I can entrust with his duties, and in
whom I can have confidence. The Rock apes have been the
responsibility of the Royal Artillery since 1806—a traditional matter—important post, in a way. I suggest you go along with the
Major to his office and he'll give you the form. Glad you decided
to take it on, Bailey. Well, that will be all, gentlemen."

Tim hadn't decided to take it on; in fact, he hadn't opened his
mouth during the entire interview, but like so many things in
army life it seemed to be settled, and he went along with the
Major to his office, where Patterson turned out a file of records
on papers and official correspondence going back apparently to
1921.

Patterson had said, "There's nothing to it, Bailey. The fact of
the matter is that they're a pack of filthy, bad-tempered brutes,
and the further you keep away from them the better for you and
the better for them. There's a clot by the name of Gunner Lovejoy looks after them and does all the dirty work—dim bulb, and
half an ape himself—which is probably why he gets on with the
middens. You can leave it all to him. Every six months you bung
in a report to the old man which says: "All present and accounted
for." Or if one of the little bastards got himself shredded in a
brawl, you write, "Regretfully announce the passing of Mona, or
Kathleen, or Pat, or whatever the stinker's name is. Please omit
flowers." And that's that. Well, good luck, old man. And—ah—
you might watch out for an old tusker by the name of Harold,
better known as Scruffy—he's been known to give a bit of trouble

at times. If he comes at you, get your back to a wall and let fly with a good kick to you-know-where."

Tim was remembering the first day he had come up there to pay a visit to his charges and see what it was all about.

He had driven by himself up to this so-called ape village located by Prince Ferdinand's Battery, which was no more than an area of some flat rocks where the apes came at their feeding time. Some previous administration had erected a kind of structure of poles and bars on which the apes could swing and entertain themselves and, incidentally, the visitors.

But that was all. There was no shelter of any kind against inclement weather, no place where a sick monkey could be isolated, or mothers with young babies could be protected from the savagery of the males and the danger of the brawls that sometimes involved the entire packs.

There had been only one ape there at the time, sitting on the wall, the rest of the pack being off in the trees down the road somewhere. He was a young male who perhaps was not feeling very well, for when Tim arrived, instead of scampering off or coming over to beg, he had just remained sitting there. Tim remembered now, as sharply as though it had been yesterday and not over a year ago, the way the beast had turned its head and looked at him, and the ineffable and penetrating sadness in its eyes which had struck home to his heart more powerfully than anything he could remember.

So strong had been the emotions of pity and awe in the presence of this monkey that he had sat down on an outcropping of rock and studied the ape. Equally motionless the ape had regarded him. And thus they had remained for perhaps five minutes in silent contemplation, these two who had once had a common ancestor and now were separated forever by eons of time and evolution.

Thoughts which never before would have troubled the mind of young Bailey now racketed through his head. One of them was: "Why you and not I?" What cosmic accident had decreed that he, Timothy Bailey, should be sitting clad in the uniform of an officer of His Majesty's Royal Artillery, a unit dedicated to the

long-distance piecemeal dismemberment of his fellow man, looking upon a miserable caricature of himself, instead of vice versa?

A wisp of his education floated through his stream of consciousness, a recollection that it all had something to do with the thumb;
man had been made from monkey by the mobility of his thumb.
Tim had looked at his own broad, stubby, capable ones and
shuddered slightly.

He had seen many of the apes before, scampering and mischief-
ing about the town, but had never paid any close attention to
them. Now everything was different; he was OIC, Officer in
Charge of Apes, and whether the position was nonsensical or
useless, the fact was it existed. It was a regimental tradition, it had
continuity, and inescapably as of that moment he was it. Now
for the first time he was looking into and behind the eyes of one
of these creatures and was feeling himself extraordinarily moved
by what he saw there.

What had it been? Disappointment—loneliness—regret—old,
old echoes of a past that one could not remember or wholly grasp,
but which left one sad and dispirited as when the residue of an
unhappy dream remains with one long after waking? Or was it a
compendium of all of these?

Tim had looked into the misery that seemed to lie behind the
golden-brown eyes of this monkey and suddenly found himself
tormented by a whole host of questions that formulated themselves in his mind. *"You just missed it, didn't you? Yet you almost
made it! Why? Was it your fault? Was it anyone's fault? Or anyone's design? Who decreed that you should be monkey and I
should be man? You were so very close to it at one time, weren't
you? And then something happened and now you can't think or
reason, or remember or look forward. You sit and scratch and
pick bits of dried skin, and eat and fight and eliminate and
procreate, and that's the sum of it. You look like us. You can
even get up and walk like us, and that's as far as it goes."*

Was this, Tim had wondered, the original Adam ejected from
the Garden of Eden and now gazing longingly out of those unhappy eyes at the riches and treasures within that garden forever
denied them?

As a boy, dogs, cats, birds, mice had been casual pets and he cared for them, but this was something different again, this silent, unhappy creature who with its fellows had been entrusted to his care. Upon that care would depend whether they would go hungry or fed, be wet or dry when the rains came or the Levanter shrouded the Rock, be healed in sickness or left to suffer, survive or die.

The Brigadier had sloughed off a job he obviously considered futile and absurd, but in this moment Tim knew that it devolved upon him as to whether these victims of Nature were comfortable or not. And in that same instant he had inwardly voiced the determination that, by God, since the Brigadier had seen fit to nominate him Officer in Charge of Apes, he was going to be just that.

The Timothy Bailey who had descended from the heights and returned thoughtfully to his office that first day was not the same one who an hour or so before had ascended the side of the Rock to the village of the apes.

Becoming an expert on the subject of macaques, however, proved to be more difficult than Tim had anticipated. To begin with, in accordance with the geographical distribution of monkeys, they had no business being where they were. Apes (the macaques were really not apes at all, but a tail-less species of the dog monkey, Tim learned) were simply not indigenous to Europe. Histories of the Gibraltar apes there were none, and such theories as had been propounded by the oldest inhabitants, whom Tim consulted, were pretty far-fetched.

One of them was that at one time Africa and Europe were joined, making the Mediterranean an inland lake, and the apes were descendants of those who crossed over from Africa at the time. But this made no sense to Tim's logical mind, since in that case the monkeys would have spread throughout all the coastal regions of southern Spain where climate and flora were no different than at Gibraltar.

Another was that some kind of tunnel existed under the Straits between Africa and the European mainland, terminating in St. Michael's Caves, the entrance to whose impressive underground cathedrals was halfway up the side of the Rock. Tim found this to be poppycock.

Most sensible of the presumptions was that during the Moorish occupation of the promontory then known as Jebel Tarik the beasts had been brought over in dhows by Moorish traders. The animals found the place to their liking and began to breed.

Books on monkeys by famous zoologists and anthropologists for which Tim sent away to London proved equally unenlightening. There appeared to be endless chapters entitled "Menstrual Cycle and Behaviour," and "Sexual Periodicity," which depressed him beyond words and shed no light whatsoever upon his immediate problems. Professors wrote books on the mentality and sociological organisation of apes, or their aptitude for learning how to get at bits of food hung or buried beyond their reach, but none of them had got around to explaining how a monkey felt about things, which was what had concerned Tim from the beginning, and even more so now with Scruffy, the Problem Child, on his hands.

From the regimental point of view, the Royal Artillery's concern over apes was buried in dry archives and was not fruitful, but in the course of his investigation Tim ran across one bit of archaic gossip which somehow seemed to link the apes with the presence of the British and their regiments. This was to the effect that if and when the apes ever died out completely, or left the Rock, the British would be driven from Gibraltar.

Since this cheerful little curse was not exactly friendly, it was no great feat of deduction for Tim to conclude that it must have been devised originally by Britain's enemies.

To maintain foothold on this extraordinary piece of real estate, the British had fought the Spanish, the French, and the Dutch. Which of these nations had fostered this happy slogan was not clear, but what interested Tim was the extent to which it had persisted in modern times, and even to this day on the Rock. He thought that in all probability it had been kept alive by the Spaniards, who for all of their politeness and seeming friendliness had never forgiven the British for pre-empting a piece of their territory to sit athwart the Mediterranean.

Tim wondered whether this way was why the responsibility for the apes had been handed over to a regiment quartered there and the Government actually provided an allowance for their maintenance. The apes not only appeared to be backed by tradition but seemed to be looked upon as mascots to an alien race occupying an alien territory. Tim was charmed to find the British Government involved in this kind of superstition.

In the end his real foundation of ape lore, knowledge, and eventually experience Tim acquired from Gunner Lovejoy.

Still smarting from the strips that had been torn off him by the Brigadier, Tim's thoughts now turned to the Gunner and the strange partnership he had formed with him. The first meeting which had taken place in Tim's office had been what one might have expected and had yielded little.

The Gunner with that inevitable suspicion and cunning with which a ranker encounters his new officer for the first time was wary and close-mouthed, restricting himself to "Yes, sir, No, sir," and "Very good, sir." In the main it had been obvious to Tim that Lovejoy had been trying to make out what his predecessor, Major Patterson, had told him. Furthermore, he had been anxiously estimating how much Tim intended to interfere with his way of life. The interview had ended with the Gunner apparently satisfied, saying, "Just you leave everything to me, sir," and taking his dismissal with alacrity.

Strange, Tim thought, how much, how very much more he now knew about Gunner Lovejoy.

Physically Gunner Lovejoy of His Majesty's Royal Artillery was small, just a half an inch over minimum requirements for height. He had the agility acquired from years of nipping round corners or popping into doorways to avoid meetings with sergeants or officers, who invariably had work for him to do. He was fortyish, with a mop of ginger-coloured hair which was usually down over his eyes or sticking out in untidy wisps from his Gunner's field service cap. His face was seamed and leathery and small, with a button nose, and perhaps it was the slightly flaring nostrils which led Scruffy to the belief that John Lovejoy was really one of them. Lightish-coloured blue eyes were deep-set in the weathered countenance, eyes that could mirror innocence, when innocence was wanted, but mostly reflected that cunning resulting from years of scrimshanking in the Army, ducking responsibility and anything which looked like hard work or interference with the pleasures of private life.

Actually as a regular in charge of apes, a post he had filled with distinction for twenty years, Gunner Lovejoy from time to time worked far harder and longer and weirder hours than any of his colleagues in Anti-Aircraft Battery 5.

But the point was that they were hours of his own choosing and in a field where he was the unquestioned specialist. In his denims and khaki jacket he was the most unsoldierly specimen on the Rock, and when compelled to appear in regulation uniform not much better, since he contrived somehow to make it look ill-fitting and too large for him. It had been twenty years since Gunner Lovejoy had fired a round from a fieldpiece, or so much as laid a hand clutching a polishing cloth to muzzle or breechblock of anti-aircraft guns. Instead he had made himself indispensable to a series of OIC Apes and had remained through practically three generations of apes, feeding, guarding, and nannying them.

He was attendant at births, marriages, and deaths; he rooted them out from under culverts or plucked them out of trees; he guarded the infant apelets from jealous members of the pack; he broke up savage and vicious battles, often too late to avoid a fatality; he nursed them in illness and when necessary gave them what-for in health. He knew every quirk of their mischievous little minds and every trick of which they were capable.

Tim understood that the Gunner's anthropomorphic attitude toward his charges was quite natural. He saw in them a kind of third-class and wholly underprivileged people, since Lovejoy's opinion of the human race was very low. Reflecting upon this, the thought struck Tim that there was no reason why this anthropomorphism should be a one-way street, and it was quite possible that Scruffy and the rest of the pack regarded their keeper as only another and larger species of tail-less monkey.

However, the facts were that if there was anything in the world the Gunner loved, it was his apes; he was devoted to them and in

particular to the bad boy of the pack, the intransigent and practically uncontrollable Scruffy. Something of Scruffy, Tim felt, was
present in Gunner Lovejoy. He, too, was in constant rebellion
against life as he had found it, or as it had been inexorably welded
about him. And the reason he probably loved and admired Scruffy
so greatly was that the monkey got away with it all.

From the time of the sheer accident by which the Gunner as a
boy of twenty had been commanded to feed and take on the
responsiblity of the two packs of apes resident on the Rock,
known as the Middle Hill and the Queen's Gate packs, Lovejoy
had seen at once his opportunity for avoiding all the onerous
duties connected with servicing His Majesty's hardware, as well as
indulging in his preference for animals over the human species. As
a result, whenever the question of his transfer to other climes had
come up in accordance with army bureaucracy and custom, the
screams of the resident OIC Apes who leaned upon him had
always served to postpone such transfer.

Tim remembered that after his first meeting with the Gunner
there had followed a period of cautious eyeing of and sparring
with one another, during which time Lovejoy, as he became aware
of Tim's interest in the apes, gradually warmed to him. But it was
when he discovered in Tim the growing affection approaching his
own for the intractable Scruffy that the Gunner had relaxed, let
down his hair, and become Tim's staunch friend and ally.

And it was during this period that Tim discovered that Lovejoy,
far from being the racketeer he had suspected who would pocket
the Government's food allowance for his charges or steal and sell
their rations, frequently spent his own pence in monkey nuts and
fruits for his own favourites. To further their feeding and well-
being he stole rapaciously from both the Sergeants' and Officers'
Messes. He pinched medical supplies from the infirmary and straw,
hay, and an occasional blanket from Stores, all this to his direct
and simple mind being less complicated than going through
channels. He was in fact, Tim concluded, a kind of Robin Hood
who stole from the people to give to the monkeys.

Eventually Tim was to establish the Gunner as the most sensitive, sympathetic, and logical of all the bolsheviks. Lovejoy went

one step further in his concept of carrying on the class warfare and started with the apes entrusted to his care.

This cleared up the mystery of small peculations which had encumbered Tim's records, accounts, and supplies, but also opened his eyes to the needs of the apes. It did not matter that Tim's was the Tory and feudal approach; the aims of himself and Gunner Lovejoy were identical, and the alliance was formed.

With it Tim cheerfully took on all of the Gunner's liabilities—his disinterest in matters military, his slovenliness and partiality to strong beers. None of this mattered in the face of the Gunner's genuine devotion to these beasts. This was what counted with Tim.

As for Lovejoy, it was all just too good to be true. He had found not only a kindred soul who understood him but also a powerful patron to stand as a buffer between himself and the Powers when his failings had brewed up a mess of trouble. Twenty-four hours after the Entente Cordiale had been closed between them, the Captain had secured the Gunner his Lance Bombardier's stripes. The further fact that the Gunner had lost them twenty-four hours afterwards, owing to the magnitude of the celebration he had staged, was beside the point. No one could expect miracles.

Part of the treaty read that the Gunner should give up his pilfering even in a good cause, while Captain Bailey would inaugurate a campaign to acquire all that was necessary for the comfort, if not a bit of luxury, of the apes by means of appeals to the authorities through proper channels. That these might fail, and that eventually both of them would return to the logic and efficiency of the Sherwood Forest method they could not foresee. But thus began the unprecedented bombardment of the Government of the United Kingdom with correspondence from the OIC Apes, Gibraltar.

At first it appeared as though Tim were about to make progress by leaps and bounds through sheer shock and surprise and the Brigadier's unfamiliarity with the whole subject. Confronted with letters on his desk in the proper form and headed, APES; NECESSITY OF CAGES FOR, or APES FEMALE; STRAW FOR COMFORT OF, or even APES; SUGGESTIONS FOR SALT-WATER COOLING SYSTEM FOR CAGES

WHEN CONSTRUCTED, and which all began properly with, "May I respectfully call to your attention, sir, the need. . . ." or, "It is respectfully requested in the interests of the ape colony Gibraltar that. . . ." The Brigadier, who had other problems on his mind, and assuming that this was normal procedure for a new OIC taking over, ordered these requests stamped "Approved" and forwarded on to the Colonial Secretariat.

This department not wishing to stir up a rather notoriously cantankerous Brigadier likewise put on an "Approved" seal and sent them along out of their ken, the damage ultimately winding up in the Controller's office.

One immediate result was that the menus of the monkeys were augmented with imports of fresh foodstuffs until they offered almost the variety to be found *à la carte* at the Savoy. The apes grew fat and almost contented, and Lovejoy as the Santa Claus who distributed all this largesse, was in his element. Tim looked forward to the day when the men and material he had ordered would arrive and begin the construction of dens, rookeries, cages, and proper shelter for his charges.

This idyll persisted until a yell emanated from Whitehall which could have been heard on the Rock without benefit of cable or wireless. Who the devil was Captain Timothy L. Bailey, OIC Apes, and what in blazes was he trying to do—bankrupt the Empire?

Like seismographic impulses, shock waves went forth from London and crashed up against the Rock. They brought about a series of recriminations which washed down from the Governor to the Colonial Secretary, the Assistant Colonial Secretary, the Brigadier, and finally Tim, who was treated to his first course of Brigade Headquarters fizzing blue temper, of which the details remained vague but the upshot definite. All the bloody nonsense was to stop; the apes were to go back on their original rations. No new building was to be undertaken, and Captain Timothy Bailey was to watch himself if he did not wish suddenly to find himself assigned to the hottest station in India or Aden.

Only one exchange remained vivid in Tim's memory, for it had blown the Brigadier to new altitudes of choler never before scaled by man. It had come when the C.R.A. had demanded, "Can you give me any reason for your actions? Can you give me one single, solitary reason for this senseless and wasteful expenditure of Government funds on a pack of filthy, verminous, ill-tempered brutes, the lot of which ought to be shot and dumped into the sea?"

It was a challenge which could not go unanswered but unfortunately nothing came into the Captain's head at that moment but the tale of the superstition connected with the British being driven from Gibraltar should the apes ever die out and leave the Rock.

"The British leave the Rock! The British be driven from Gibraltar if—if——!"

"Yes, sir," said Tim.

It was at this point that the Brigadier's temper made its celebrated ascent into the stratosphere. So tremendous was the blow-up that word of it reached the ears of Lovejoy even before Tim arrived back at the office to impart the news.

"I say, sir," said the Gunner, "I hear it was a snorter."

"It was that, Lovejoy," Tim assented. "We're going to have to lie low for a while, but at least we've got them thinking apes. How much groundnuts have we on hand?"

"About a hundredweight, sir."

"Well, that will last a couple of months, anyway," said Tim philosophically, "and by that time they'll have cooled off."

"Then you're not quitting, sir?" Lovejoy asked in amazement.

"Hell, no," said Tim, "we've just begun."

The Gunner was so impressed by this that he could do no more than raise his right hand to his forehead in the snappiest salute he had rendered in the last twenty years and reverently breathe the word, "sir!"

But with the eventual giving out of the monkey nuts and other fancy greens and silage, and Tim's immediate failure to wangle more out of the authorities, began the intransigence of Scruffy.

It was Scruffy who was the stumbling block to Tim's far-reaching and grandiose plans for the apes. Often when he had some little improvement in the set-up for them lined up, Scruffy would go on a raid and ruin the pitch, and there was even a time when Tim

SCRUFFY

found himself fighting tooth and nail and lobbying day and night against the-ape-Scruffy-ought-to-be-shot movement which had powerful adherents in army, navy, and civil circles. Then surely it had only been precedent that had saved Scruffy. The shooting of an ape was something which had never been done before.

Chapter 4

FELICITY

So had run the thoughts and recollections of young Captain Bailey as he stood leaning on the rail and looking out over the town shimmering in the summer heat haze. He became aware of a slight movement next to him, turned and saw the object of his deliberations seated on a rock near by regarding him malevolently.

"Oh, it's you, you clot," said Captain Bailey, for at that moment his thoughts had managed to put him out of sorts with the beast who was messing up his plans to create the best of all possible worlds for the worst of all possible monkeys. "Why the hell don't you behave yourself? Don't you realise you're spoiling it for everyone? What I ought to do is catch you and give you a damn good hiding."

Scruffy said nothing, but kept regarding Tim balefully. And, as always when he became angry with this creature, Tim grew repentant. He said, "Sorry, old boy, I didn't mean it. I oughtn't to have said that. Had a trying session with the old Brig. Forget it, will you?"

As always, the concentrated fury and hatred in Scruffy's eyes moved Tim to do something to win him. He reached into a side pocket and produced a peanut, a small supply of which he always carried, held it up and said, "All right then, come over here and have one on me."

The animal lifted his head slightly to make sure what it was Tim was holding out to him, then rose and with deliberation he marched over to Tim on all fours, reached up with his left paw, and took the peanut. With his right paw he seized hold of Tim's wrist and quietly and firmly bit him in the hand. The blood spurted forth. Scruffy gave a tremendous leap which moved him ten yards away, where he turned his immediate attention to the monkey nut. Tim let out a yell and a rich army curse which was topped by a feminine scream.

"Oh! The nasty thing! I saw him do it."

Startled, Tim looked up and saw a small car drawn up by the concrete platform, with a fat girl at the wheel.

She wasn't really stout, Tim observed upon second glance, but only rather plump, as though the baby fat had not yet entirely been melted away. The tanned arms at the steering wheel had dimples at both the elbows and the wrists and there was somewhat too much flesh on the oval of her face. Tim's thought was that if she were to thin down she might possibly be quite good-looking. Even so, he was struck by the clarity and brilliance of her eyes, which were the colour of aquamarine and were now filled with sympathy. The roundness of her face made her nose seem slightly too small, if delectable, but the mouth was firm and full of character. All this was surmounted by a twist of short-cut, unruly hair the colour of wild honey.

"Oh," said Tim, "I didn't know—I do beg your pardon."

"That's quite all right," said the girl, and hers was a soft voice that fell pleasantly upon the ears. "I should have said worse myself. He did it deliberately. Why don't you go and give him a kick?"

It was almost automatic for Tim to spring to Scruffy's defence. He said, "It wasn't his fault."

The girl said severely, "Oh yes it was. He planned it. I saw him making up his mind to do it two minutes ago. Look at your poor hand!"

Tim did. His life's gore was welling from two holes and dripping to the ground.

"Shall I do it up for you?" she asked.

Tim felt embarrassed at having a fuss made over him. "It's all right," he said. "It's nothing. It stops after a bit."

Ten yards away, Scruffy was jumping up and down on all fours and coughing, which meant that he was delighted with what he had accomplished and felt he ought to be rewarded with more monkey nuts. So habitual was the performance that before Tim knew what he was doing he plunged his uninjured hand into his pocket, withdrew a half dozen or so nuts, and threw them to the ape, who collected them and bared his fangs once more.

"Oh, you men!" said the girl, and got out of her car, opening her handbag and shaking her head. She produced a clean handkerchief and said, "I do it very well. I've had first-aid training. And then you ought to have it cauterised. I'm sure that thing is poisonous."

As she came over, Tim thought she must be twenty-one or two. A girl that old ought not to be quite so chubby, and yet once one had been caught up in her eyes it did not seem to matter—in fact, one quite forgot everything else, everything except, of course, one's problems. Her touch was gentle, her hair and clothes smelled of fresh air and sunlight. She wiped away the blood, examined the two holes with clinical and enthusiastic interest, and then deftly and efficiently bound his wounds.

"There," said the girl. "Now," and she motioned with a bob of her sunny head in the direction of Scruffy, who was gorging himself, "aren't you going to do anything about him?"

"No," Tim replied. "Thank you." And then suddenly, as a wholly new idea came in answer to this question of Scruffy's behaviour which had so long been plaguing him, he said, "I say, do you know what? I've just had a thought—do you suppose it could be because he hasn't any tail?"

This query, if one wanted to make something out of it, could go to show how a single sentence carelessly uttered can sometimes change entire lives, and even the course of history, for the young girl had already begun to wend her way back to her vehicle, convinced that there was no present, and certainly no future, in any young man so tame and spiritless as to let himself be shredded by an ungrateful beast upon whom he had just conferred a favour, without offering so much as a cuff, pinch, or tweak in retaliation. He had seemed a nice-looking boy, but she was not in the habit of collecting saints. However, his remark stopped her in mid-air, so to speak, with her foot on the running board. "What?" she said. "Because who hasn't got a tail?"

"Old Scruff over there. By jove, do you know, I think I've got it.

She came walking back slowly. "Hasn't he one?" she asked. "I hadn't noticed."

Tim said, "No? I'll show you." He then called out, "Hoy—Scruffy. Come here old boy," knowing full well that the animal would do just the opposite, which indeed he did, turning his back at the summons and elevating his buttocks into their faces.

"There you are," said Tim.

"I don't see what that has to do with it," the girl said, "or why it should make him bite you just after you had presented him with a lovely monkey nut."

Tim already saw himself preparing a monograph upon the subject and submitting it to the Zoological Society and being possibly rewarded with an F.Z.S. after his name. "Frustration," he said. "Disappointment, frightful feeling of inferiority. Not one thing or the other, don't you see? Social and physical liability. Bound to prey on his mind and cause him to have a bilious outlook on the world. Every other monkey has a tail. Uses it to swing from or pick up small objects. Rounds him out. Dogs have tails; cats have tails—and here's poor old Scruff going around without one. Debasing and humiliating. The kind of thing you can't get away from. Always imagining people are talking behind their hands even when they're not."

It was not so much the theory as the earnestness and satisfaction of the young man with his idea which now began to interest the girl. She had returned all the way from her car and now stood beside him, not quite reaching up to his shoulder, and looking at Scruffy, who, having shown his contempt for them, had now reversed his position and was sitting with his canines bared.

"How did he lose it?" she asked. "Caught it in a door—or did someone cut it off to get even?"

"No, no—of course not. He simply hasn't got one—none of them have. It's that kind of monkey. They are known as macaques, but those are the only tail-less ones."

The girl frowned in slight bewilderment. "You mean none of them have any tails? Are they all then as nasty as that one?"

"Oh no," said Tim, again swift to spring to the defence of his

charge, "only old Scruff there is something special in that department."

A look of triumph fired the charmingly chubby countenance of
the girl. "Oh-ho," she cried, "so then it's not because he hasn't a
tail. If the others haven't got one either and are sweet about it;
it's just because he's a nasty, surly, bad-tempered, mean old——"

She stopped suddenly in mid-description. "Oh dear," the girl
continued in genuine sympathy and contrition. "I've spoiled your
perfectly beautiful idea, haven't I?"

"That's quite all right," Tim said, even though his F.Z.S. had
gone a-glimmering.

"Oh dear," the girl repeated, "you care about him, don't you?"

Tim nodded and said, "One can't help it. He's so extraordinarily
and consistently wicked. It's something like having a very naughty
child—you feel that somewhere there must be a little bit of good
in it, if only you could get at it. Nothing on this earth ought
to be that absolutely and completely useless and destructive. There
must be some reason——"

The girl shook her head slowly and said, "He's just plain
bad——"

A female ape appeared out of a tree with an apelet clinging to
her back. Scruffy gave a cough of rage and let fly a cuff that swept
the apelet off the mother's back and into the dust of the road.
He then took a bite at the female's flank, sending her shrieking
down the road.

The girl watched the performance with her grave eyes and
murmured, "Sweet."

Tim said, "He's never cared for her a great deal."

The girl asked, "Do you come up here often to visit him?"

Tim replied, "Well—yes, in a way. You see, I'm Officer in
Charge. I'm OIC Apes."

The girl now turned her gaze upon him in full astonishment
and said, "I beg your pardon—you're what?"

Tim said, "Officer in Charge of Apes. Forgive me, I should have
introduced myself—and you've been so kind. My name is Tim
Bailey."

The girl was still regarding him with utter disbelief and amazement. She said, "Do you mean to tell me that the Royal Artillery actually appoints a Captain on active service to a post called Officer of Apes?"

Tim bristled perceptibly. "I do. The care of the Barbary apes of Gibraltar has been a tradition of the Royal Artillery for over a hundred and thirty years."

Again a wave of contrition and extraordinary tenderness came into the face of the girl. "Oh dear, I *am* sorry. I didn't mean—— Of course—— But you see, I didn't know. We're Navy. I mean I've just come out here to join my parents." And she repeated again, "Oh dear—I am making such a muddle of this. I've hurt your feelings, and I didn't mean to. I'm Felicity French. We live at the Mount—and after you've been so sweet about that nasty— I mean your friend. Do forgive me."

"Please, please," Tim said, "that's quite all right. I assure you I don't mind a bit. Quite a few people think it's odd." In his mind a brief addition of two and two making four had taken place: the Mount and the name of French, and the fact that he was conversing, obviously, with the daughter of Admiral Sir Richard French, Flag Officer, and Second-in-Command of the Rock. He turned to her suddenly as a new idea entered his head and asked, "Had you ever thought what it must be like to be a monkey—I mean chaps like these who live where there are people?"

Felicity replied, "No, I hadn't." She went over and sat on the rail. Scruffy, having finished his peanuts, loped off; the mother ape returned, presented her rear end to her offspring, who climbed aboard her back and clung to her.

"There you are," said Tim. "What kind of a future is there in store for that little thing?" He went over to it, plucked it from its mother's back, and let it hang from one of his fingers. He said, "That's the girl, Adele—show the lady some of your tricks." He placed the apelet onto his palm, where she did a neat handstand.

Felicity applauded. "Oh good!" and then asked, "Do they all have names?"

"Of course," Tim replied. "I name them when they're six months old and it looks as though they're going to make it. But there again you have it—what's the good of having a name if you can't make use of it, like signing cheques or writing to your pals? What's this little creature got to look forward to but being bitten to pieces in a fight, or dying of pneumonia when a Levanter moves in? That's the kind of thing I'm trying to stop."

"Tell me about it," Felicity said, and knew not what she did.

Tim looked at her swiftly for an instant to see whether she was serious or having a pull at his leg, for recently everyone had been avoiding him, and it was less than an hour ago that the Brigadier had referred to him as the town bore on the subject of apes. "Do you really mean it?"

Felicity said, "Yes, please," and now suspected that she might be in for something of a session. "You wouldn't have a cigarette on you, would you?"

"Yes, of course. How very rude of me." He offered her one from his case and lit it. She inhaled the smoke gratefully, folded her hands, and waited.

After a moment's mental floundering, Tim said, "You see, they're all so lonely. Even though they have their own friends and families here, they're lonely inside—and disappointed. It's as though whoever made us had tried things out with them first and then cast them aside. But there they are."

And from this earnest beginning he launched into the full narrative of his arrival on the Rock, his being made OIC, and his suddenly awakened interest in the Barbary apes entrusted to his care.

He talked and talked and talked, did Captain Bailey, the story, for the first time, falling upon willing ears, pouring from him in a seemingly endless torrent. Felicity listened without interruption, smoking quietly and never seeming to take her grave, sweet eyes from his face. Much of what he was saying was unintelligible to her—statistics and logistics, measurements and complicated mechanical devices for protecting and controlling the apes, but through the story that he told, somehow never involving himself or his disappointments directly, there emerged the picture of a good, kind, and loving man in whose make-up there appeared more than the usual shred of tenderness and gentleness allotted to men and concern for fellow creatures on the earth other than himself and his kind. And this picture went straight to the heart of Felicity and touched her.

Tim talked on. He told her about Lovejoy, the stickiness of bureaucracy, its sole concern with statistics and entries on the right side of the ledger, and the difficulty of getting its administrators to see or even consider the human—or rather, the animal —side of the question. With laughter directed at himself, he revealed the latest blow-up of the Brigadier which had sent him along up to the apes' village to do some soul-searching, concluding with, "I suppose the Brig has got more to worry about than monkeys—and old Scruff did tear up the town. Wait until the C.R.A. gets the list of damage he did up here before starting below."

Tim ran down a bit at that point, and in the hiatus Felicity said firmly, "I think he's horrid. You're not appreciated."

"Oh, it isn't that," Tim said, "I don't mind—I've never had quite so much fun or been so interested in anything—it's for *them*, don't you see, that I get discouraged and a little low sometimes. Nobody seems to care about them really but Gunner Lovejoy and myself."

"I do!" Felicity heard herself cry with a fierceness that astonished her. "I do now since you've told me about them. I think they're sweet." She was rewarded by a look of gratitude and worship combined that poured from Tim's eyes. "And you're not to become discouraged," Felicity added firmly. "Supposing something happened and they all went away—they'd change their tune then soon enough."

"Yes," Tim said eagerly, "do you think so? Well, of course there'd never be any chance of that happening."

"What we ought to do," Felicity said, and now she was frowning again from the intensity of her concentration on the subject, "is think up something which would call everybody's attention to the wonderful work you're doing." Her face became suddenly exquisitely illuminated with the idea that had smitten her. "I've got it!" she cried. "You wouldn't have one without a name, would you?"

Tim reflected. "Well, yes, as a matter of fact we have. There's

one just about the age of that little creature there that Lovejoy
and I were going to name—but it's a she."

The two aquamarines in Felicity's countenance were now lus-
trous with excitement. "Splendid!" she said. "You write to the
King and tell him you'd like to name the new apelet Elizabeth
after the Princess."

Shock went through Captain Bailey in waves. "What?" he
cried. "Write to the King? Why, I'd be court-mar——"

"Nonsense," said Felicity. "Anyone can write to the King as long
as they don't threaten him. It's not as though you were going
over anyone's head. After all, you are OIC Apes, aren't you—and
they're in your charge, aren't they—and you do have to find names
for them, don't you—and he is your King, isn't he? Then why
can't you tell him what you'd like to do?"

"Do you know what," said Tim, "that's absolutely brilliant!
Do you think the Princess would like it?"

"Certainly," Felicity replied firmly, "She'd be thrilled. She may
be a princess, but don't forget she's a thirteen-year-old girl, too—
and she'd want a picture of it to put up in her room."

"I could send one along."

"That's a good idea," said Felicity. "And what's more, you must
do it at once. Then perhaps you won't be bullied by that nasty
Brigadier any longer."

She looked at her watch and said, "Goodness, I've kept you too
long from your work. I had no idea it was so late. It's been so
nice meeting you. Do let me know what happens after you've
written to the King." She rose from the railing, offered him a
cool hand with firm pressure, and said, "Good-bye then," went
to her car and drove off.

Tim stood looking after her, filled with the wonderful sensation
of having found an ally. "What a funny kid," he said to himself.
Scruffy appeared on the concrete platform, bounced up and down
on all fours, coughed and cursed. "What a jolly good kid," Captain
Bailey said aloud. And then, addressing the big macaque: "You
wouldn't care to take a bite out of the other hand, would you,
chum?"

One might consider it not exactly fair to suggest that the fate
of the British Empire, which meant the fate of the then free world
as well, was influenced by the fact that Felicity French, the
daughter of the Admiral commanding the naval base at Gibraltar,
had met an unknown, impoverished, and unspectacular Captain
of Artillery who was further handicapped by holding down the
doubtful post of Officer in Charge of Apes.

Yet it is true that the threads of life twist, turn, cross, and knot
sometimes seemingly so unconnected with events they are due to
affect that it is not even possible to trace them back. The fact
remains that Felicity, who was a good driver and thoughtful and
polite as well, set in motion a train of consequences when she
came close to knocking down an individual, a Gibraltarian by
the name of Alfonso T. Ramirez, with the fender of her car.

Entering Main Street from Library Street on her way back to
the Mount, she was only half looking where she was going and not
at all thinking what she was doing. Her mind was taken up with
the young man she had met, the quality of his smile, and the
charm of his concentration on and affection for some rather nasty
brutes.

And thus she came to within a hairsbreadth of running down
the man named Ramirez who was a third of the way across the
street within a safety area where it was neither legal nor sporting
to kill a pedestrian. All rights of the situation belonged to Ramirez.

Young and healthy, Felicity's reflexes were quick enough. She
tramped on the brakes and twisted the wheel hard right, and the
strange-looking little man with the thick-lensed spectacles and
the *en brosse*, short, stand-up haircut which so ill became his
squat, dumpy figure felt no more than the breeze of her left
wing passing his person.

Because she was so frightened of what she had almost done,
Felicity cried out involuntarily, "Oh, why don't you look where
you're going?"

Then she realised that it was all her fault and that not only had
she been driving dangerously but had been inexcusably rude, and
she cried contritely, "Oh dear me, I am so sorry, it was all my
fault."

Felicity had jarred the car to a halt midway on the crossing so that the individual she had so nearly erased was standing peering in at her, his face white and then flushed, level with her even though she was sitting down. Behind his thick lenses his eyes were pale and angry. His mouth was shaped like the small letter *o*.

The awful thing was that it didn't seem to be able to give vent to his indignation. Whatever was bottled up inside of him—fright or wrath he couldn't get it out. He swelled up like a balloon, the little *o* of his mouth working furiously and silently. Felicity thought suddenly of the grotesque figure in the Michelin tyre advertisements and the relief from panic led her to commit another unintentional rudeness.

She couldn't help herself; she giggled.

There was no point in remaining there forever on the crosswalk, traffic piling up behind her, so she tittered nervously, said once again, "I'm sorry," and drove on, leaving behind her a vain and misanthropic little man swollen by sufficient cubic centimetres of superiority complex to fly a dirigible, who had been laughed at by a girl of an alien race.

For Felicity it was an episode quickly forgotten; for Mr. Ramirez it was the beginning of an unfortunate day of humiliations, the end of which was to confirm him as an implacable enemy of Great Britain and all her people.

Arrived home at the flower-trellised Georgian mansion which served as the Navy's home for its Flag Officer at Gibraltar, Felicity abandoned her car in the gravel forecourt and went banging happily through the house with all the joy and energy of her twenty-two years.

Eventually her ebullience washed over her mother, who was working on a piece of tapestry by the big picture window in the drawing room that overlooked the sea and the dockyard. Lady French had started her first piece of tapestry at the time she had married young Lieutenant French, as an occupation eminently fitted to a sailor's wife and the daughter of a baronet, while her sailor husband was away at sea. The habit formed was never broken, and the Admiral was once said to have confided in a convivial moment that when Lady French slept her fingers still continued the movements of running needle and wool through the holes of the pattern.

Felicity's chubbiness did not stem from her but from her father. Lady French was tall, slender, and cool. Her hair was still golden; she had been a great beauty. When she had married, the consensus was that she had thrown herself away. But now she was Lady French, and an Admiral's wife, so it actually had worked out all for the best. Still, it might not have done, and she had a quiet determination that her daughter, Felicity, should not expose herself to the same hazard. She was glad she had her come out to the Rock for the summer. In one sense it was a small, narrow, tight-fitting community, but as a navy and colonial base it was full of eligible young men of good families on the threshold of important careers.

Lady French looked up from completing a stitch and said, "Felicity darling, must you make so much noise? You know, you aren't sixteen any more. In fact, you'll have to be thinking very soon of——"

"Getting married," Felicity completed for her, for this was one she had heard before. "I think of it all of the time, Mummy. Guess what! I've just met the nicest man. Maybe I could marry him."

Lady French was startled by this announcement, for she never knew when her daughter was joking. But ladies, in the lexicon of the Admiral's wife, did not show emotion. She disciplined herself with three more stitches before she replied, "Really, dear? How very nice. Is it anyone we know?"

Felicity's lovely clear eyes were bent upon her mother with an expression of quizzical tenderness. She replied, "Captain Bailey."

Lady French sent the blunted needle four more times through and back, drawing the piece of red wool after it while she assessed rapidly the information her daughter had revealed. Like all mothers she felt that every young man her daughter met was a potential husband. A Captain was starting close to the top indeed; at the same time it posed another problem. "My dear," she said, "isn't the company of a Captain a little bit old for you?" She lifted her own beautiful golden head and looked out across the town to the mole. There was nothing there but a pair of destroyers already tied up for a fortnight, a naval collier, and a couple of rusty freighters plus the cruise ship. A puzzled frown now appeared upon her own handsome brow and she murmured, "*Captain* Bailey? Is there any ship in now with a Captain Bailey?"

Felicity struggled and won the battle to keep the corners of her mouth from twitching. She felt somehow that she ought to say, "Hang onto your needlework, Mum—this is going to be a real snorter." But she refrained, and instead said demurely, "Captain Timothy Bailey of the Royal Artillery, Mother. Army."

The tapestry needle was blunt, but Lady French still managed to run it into the end of her finger. She then let fly a good round navy swear word she had learned from her husband. Thereupon as she sucked at the drop of blood that appeared on her finger the lady inside Lady French scored one more imperishable triumph. She said quite quietly: "Oh no, Felicity—not Army, surely?"

Felicity said, "Yes, Mother—Army."

Lady French then asked, "Who is he?" Three words which in these circumstances constituted a three-page questionnaire and included such vital items as: What is his family? Who is his father? What was his mother's maiden name? What, if any, armorial bearings? Have they any money? What schools did he attend? Is he at the very least the General's A.D.C. and headed for Staff College?

Felicity thought that she might as well complete the job, since her mother was really bearing up wonderfully. She said, "He's OIC—Officer in Charge of Apes."

Lady French was sometimes afflicted by the tortures of sinus and found that smelling salts offered a certain relief. She now laid down her tapestry, opened her nearby handbag, took out the bottle of smelling salts, removed the stopper, and took two deep whiffs that brought tears to her eyes. By the time she had wiped them away she was able to speak. "Well, I wouldn't mention this young man to your father if I were you. You know how he feels about the Army. He's in a state anyway—the Brigadier is coming for dinner tonight. We're dressing, of course. Do try to do your hair nicely for once, Felicity. I don't think your father likes the Brigadier very much—he never lets him get a word in edgeways —it's Army, Army, Army, when he comes."

And indeed it was so at the dinner party that night. The Admiral never did get to hold forth, for the Brigadier was loaded to the back of his teeth with narrative anent the depredations committed by one of those confounded Rock apes, a creature by the name of Scruffy, who had invaded the town that day and wrought enough damage as might well cause an investigating committee from Parliament to descend upon them.

It was apes this, and apes that, filthy destructive beasts, and gradually through the Brigadier's fulminations the name of Captain Bailey surfaced. Impudent, time-wasting young cub. Just the useless type of officer they were sending out these days. The name of Scruffy receded into the background and that of Captain Timothy Bailey took over. It seemed that everything that was wrong with, on, in, around, and about Gibraltar might now safely be laid at the door of a congenital idiot named Bailey.

Lady French paled beneath her make-up, but never once wavered in the elegant and delicate dissection of the portion of fish upon her plate. She did, however, manage to throw one glance of anguish at her daughter, who sat at the opposite side next to the Brigadier's handsome young Staff Captain, to whom she was paying not the slightest attention. She had done the best she could with her unruly hair and had plastered it down with water, but now it was drying and beginning to stick up. Her attention was bent upon the Brigadier. She was drinking in every word he was saying, and absolutely glowing with pride and happiness.

Lady French suddenly felt she didn't care for any more fish.

Chapter 5

SCRUFFY LIFTS A SCALP

Infuriated by having been laughed at by a young English girl as
well as shaken by his narrow escape, Mr. Ramirez felt the need of
a drink and continued on his way to a pub, the Admiral Nelson,
where he often stopped for a beer on his way home, there to
encounter his second humiliation of the day.

It was always a lonely beer he had in the Admiral Nelson since
no one ever asked him to join up or opened conversation with him.
Even strangers who came into the pub in search of companion-
ship as well as drink would not bother to pass the time of day with
the unprepossessing little man with the thick lenses, pasty, un-
healthy-looking skin, squat body, and shoebrush haircut.

It was about his usual hour, just past six o'clock, when Ramirez
entered the bar, which had not yet begun to fill up, although at
one end he saw Gunner Lovejoy.

Ramirez knew the Gunner by sight. Everyone on the Rock knew
Gunner Lovejoy, Keeper of the Apes. The Gunner on the other
hand, particularly when he was having a drink, saw no one.

This particular evening Ramirez felt the need of some kind of
companionship or human contact to the point where, unfortunately, he chose to force himself upon the Gunner, who was on his
third monkey juice, a revolting potion he had invented himself. It
was Guinness's stout, laced with a dash of lime juice. It did
something for him.

As Ramirez entered, Lovejoy turned his head at the noise to see
who had arrived, looked directly at and through Ramirez as though
he were not there, although they had both been frequenting the
same bar at the same hour for years.

Lovejoy had already turned away when Ramirez spoke to the

sun-tanned area that was the back of the Gunner's neck between the collar and his tunic and his artilleryman's cap.

"Would you care to have a drink, Sergeant?" he asked politely enough.

Lovejoy, who was neither a sergeant nor a bombardier but a plain gunner, turned slowly and examined Ramirez, becoming aware of him as for the first time and was not pleased with what he saw. He came close to articulating his thoughts, which were *"Cor, what rock did you crawl out from under?"*

He didn't like civilians anyway and was particularly hostile to any type who tried to curry favour with him miscalling his rank, or rather lack of rank.

He hesitated but for only a moment. The hesitation had been caused by the fact that he was thirsty, he was alone, pay day was two days away, and a free drink was a free drink. But as he looked Ramirez up and down he was unable to keep his lip from curling or the expression upon his face as of one looking at a toad. It was an expression which Gunner Lovejoy reserved in general for civilians, but this man in addition to being non-military actually resembled that unhappy amphibian.

Lovejoy wiped his mouth with the back of his hand and replied, "I never drink with civilians," turned his back, pulled his last half crown from his pocket, slapped it on to the bar, and said, "Another of the same, Joe," and thereby drove another nail into what might become the coffin of the British Empire.

That day Alfonso T. Ramirez, having been almost run down and killed and then laughed at by the rich daughter of the English, had now been spurned by the poorest of the same nation and the lowest in grade of service. The little mouth again formed into a small and angry o and he turned, went out of the bar, and set off to keep his appointment with the ultimate and final encounter.

Mr. Ramirez who was some forty years of age and an expert employed in the Optical Repairs Department of the Navy Yard where he engaged upon the finest and most delicate precision work on range finders, telescopes, etc., was the possessor of two secrets, one of them safely and securely buried, the other unfortunately somewhat more vulnerable.

The one that was to remain secure from prying eyes, even through the most severe wartime security check, had to do with his middle initial. Alfonso T. Ramirez was his name, and if you asked him what the *T* stood for he would have told you Tomaso for good St. Thomas and so indeed it was inscribed upon his birth certificate. For Ramirez was a Gibraltarian born and bred upon the Rock from a line of Gibraltarians. At some time in the past, of course, the Ramirezes must have moved to the Rock from the Spanish mainland, but they had been Gibraltarians for generations and had assimilated all characteristics of that curiously hybrid people, as well as embracing British customs, drinks, licensing laws, police, and their singular way of driving on the left-hand side of the road.

And such a one was Alfonso T. Ramirez. His well-kept secret was that the *T* actually didn't stand for Tomaso, but for Treugang, a name as German as the *Nibelungenring*. And at heart Mr. Ramirez was a Nazi.

On his mother's side there had been a great-great-grandmother, a von Waltz, from Koenigsberg in East Prussia, and this had led his mother secretly to christen him Alfonso Treugang Ramirez, though officially as a good Catholic she had endowed him with the middle name of a saint. But outside of Ramirez's home no one ever knew of this, for then Ramirez was ashamed of the name and hated it, and eventually it was dropped.

But in the middle life, with the rise of Hitler to power and the propaganda attendant upon the theory of the master race, Ramirez had reason to remember that there was German blood in his veins and quite suddenly to become secretly and vengefully proud of it.

No blame could attach to Ramirez for being a misanthropic, lonely, despicable little man. Nothing had ever favoured him. From a fat, unwholesome-looking child with a pasty skin, he grew into an unwholesome-looking adult with short arms and legs and a round head that sat almost directly upon his shoulders. He resembled a slug. He had a harsh voice and an unpleasant and repellent manner. Nobody liked him.

Ramirez lived alone in two rooms off Calle Mendoza, where

he cooked his own meals on a single electric hot plate, and had no friends, although there were plenty of neighbours.

While Gibraltarians are normal and cheerful, friendly and most hospitable people, Mr. Ramirez had been at war with the world for too many years and it showed. He didn't like children, he didn't like animals, and he didn't like his neighbours.

Now for the last few years he had been buoyed up by a secret satisfaction, the philosophy of the Nazis. It didn't matter how you looked or what people thought of you; if the blood of the master race flowed in your veins, then you were a master man. And he followed the career of the little Austrian housepainter, no beauty himself, with passionate fascination. Some of these magic corpuscles were locked into his system and made him one of them.

It was none other than Scruffy who climaxed that catastrophic day by penetrating and exposing the second secret of Mr. Alfonso T. for Treugang Ramirez.

Scruffy's siesta could last anywhere between two and three hours, depending upon the heat of the day and how active he had been in the morning. At five-thirty that hot afternoon he awakened, yawned, stretched, scratched himself, and proceeded to confound the scientists, learned men, and animal psychologists by remembering that he had had a bang-up time that morning. Simultaneously he also knew by the automatic timer that he carried in his stomach, or somewhere within his unprepossessing person, that it was an hour past his feeding time. He therefore went off at a skip and a jump to Prince Ferdinand's Battery to find that the Gunner had already delivered their rations and that in Scruffy's absence the pack had disposed of most of them. He took a desultory nibble at a carrot end lying on the ground, then chucked it at the tin sign warning tourists not to feed the apes, scored a ringing bull's-eye, and was off. The need for food and the recollection of what fun he had had a short time ago decided him to return to town.

He reached King Charles V Wall and descended at a speed that could truly be compared to that of lightning, without ever seeming to try and with a kind of gliding motion that made his great body seem to flow along the stones as though he were skimming over the surface without touching it at all.

He arrived at the foot of the wall just as Treugang Ramirez emerged from the Admiral Nelson.

There was still the width of the town separating the two and so each, unaware of the other, proceeded inexorably towards their encounter.

The street where Ramirez lived was in that part of the old town close to the towering cliff of the Rock where the houses looked as though they had been built helter-skelter upon one another. It was a kind of monkey paradise since there were clotheslines and clothespoles crisscrossing the thoroughfare, and affixed to one of the cornices of a building was a traffic sign, surmounted by a triangle.

Arrived there, Scruffy found that this triangle suited him admirably. He wedged his thick body into it. There is no doubt that any picture looks better framed and Scruffy was no exception; it gave him a kind of patriarchal elder-statesman look, and he sat there letting himself be admired.

It was not usual for an ape to appear so far to the north of the town and thus Scruffy was able to assemble more of a crowd of the curious than he usually attracted. Men, women, and children came out from their stone and stucco dwellings and stood looking up at Scruffy.

Ramirez now came striding into this picture still smarting from the snub delivered to him by Gunner Lovejoy. He found a crowd gathered around, blocking the entrance to his domicile, children leaping up and down and pointing, women carrying babies in their arms, men stretching their necks, and above his head a large and ugly Barbary ape framed in the crossroads sign.

Ramirez paused for an instant to look up. The small mouth pursed into an expression of distaste; the pasty white brow beneath the fine upstanding haircut knitted in a frown. He uttered an exclamation of disgust which sounded like "Pfeugh" and commenced to thrust his way through the crowd of children and grownups barring the way to his door.

One would not say that Scruffy understood the word "Pfeugh," but he did feel that a jarring note had suddenly marred the harmony of the pleasant sensation he had been creating. Also since he was an animal, he was equipped with that sharp instinct which at once recognised that the newcomer was unquestionably one of those who differed from the rest of the human pack, and he felt the hostility of the others towards him. Vicariously it excited him and started adrenalins discharging into his blood stream. This called for action, and with wonderful accuracy he swooped from his frame onto the shoulders of Ramirez. To steady himself he anchored ten strong fingers, at the end of which were ten equally powerful black claws, in Ramirez's hair.

Even so, if the unfortunate little man had kept his head or had been less irritated by prior events, the debacle might have been averted. Something would have distracted Scruffy and he would have abandoned his perch for another shoulder, or returned to his picture frame. But, at last, all the pent-up fury which had not been able to escape through the o of his mouth now did so in one large yell followed by a torrent of combined Spanish and English expletive. With this he raised his two stubby arms and punched Scruffy in the flanks.

This was war, and Scruffy liked nothing better. With a glad cough indicative of accepting the challenge, he dug in hard with his toes and with all the strength of his powerful body yanked with both hands, and the next moment found himself, for the first time in his life, off balance as not only Ramirez's hair, but apparently his entire scalp, came away in his paws.

He dropped to the ground where, phoenix-like, he recovered strength and balance and in one tremendous leap hurled himself skyward, regaining the top of the crossroads sign with his trophy.

His previous outcry was nothing to the yell of rage and anguish now torn from poor Ramirez as he stood in the glare of the late setting sun, his head as nude and white as a peeled onion, his secret bared to all his neighbours. Treugang Ramirez was as bald as an ostrich egg and this revelation really put the seal upon his repulsiveness.

Simultaneously a roar of laughter went up from the crowd in the street compounded of both amusement and gratification and one that increased to a pitch of hysteria as little girls and boys pointed to the fearfully nude head and others to the hairpiece, or toupee more vulgarly known as a "rug," in the grasp of the ape.

Mothers raised their babies to get a better look and men slapped their sides and stomachs in derisive laughter. All the pent-up dislike of the neighbourhood for Ramirez now exploded in wave after wave of laughter and hardened in the unhappy core of the victim such a knot of hatred as only a total and violent vengeance could ever dissolve. But of all this he was to be aware only later. Now he was just a thoroughly ridiculous little man with an obscenely nude head, thick eyeglasses, and stubby arms and legs, leaping up and down in the street shouting, "Give me back my hair, give me back my hair!"

Through all this hullabaloo Scruffy was in such an ecstasy of delight as can come to a Barbary ape, or any kind of monkey, but once in a lifetime. For in some mysterious manner, he had secured a treasure beyond his wildest dreams—a soft thing of fur all his own, to have and to hold. No Red Indian ever was more thrilled at having lifted a rare and desirable scalp, though of course he didn't consider it as a scalp, or for that matter even as a trophy. In fact he no longer connected it even with the blob of white beneath him, leaping up and down and making noises. He had lost interest in him and the rest of the people in his enrapturement with his very own and private "thing."

It is known, though not exactly why, that macaques and other monkeys as well will cherish something like a small bit of fur and carry it around with them. Zoologists have attested that they are not particular or too delicate in the origin of this bit of fur. Sometimes it will be a baby monkey which has died and which the mother refuses to relinquish. Or it can be a corpse of a rat or some other field rodent which has had the misfortune to encounter the monkey in an irritable mood and which, dried out by the sun, makes a most attractive combined mascot and toy.

Ignoring the turmoil beneath him, Scruffy now gave his undivided attention to his prize and noticed with increasing satisfaction that it had every qualification calculated to give pleasure. It was large. It appeared to be resilient and strong when tested and it was equipped with long and agreeably bristling hair, hair of the texture almost of Scruffy's own. He clutched it to his bosom, he held it to his face, he cuddled it tenderly in his arms.

It has been recorded that Scruffy hated mankind; he hated his own species and when he encountered himself in a mirror he hated himself as well. Yet there is no kind of cerebral creature that walks, crawls, or flies that is not at some time imbued with some kind of affection for something, some object or living creature it encounters on its travels from the egg to the midden.

Scruffy had met his grand passion in Alfonso T. Ramirez's wig.

"Give me back my hair! Give me back my hair," shouted Ramirez and began to clamber up the cornice of the building to retrieve his toupee.

Scruffy waited until the white disc of Treugang's face, which might have looked to him like the full moon rising from the sea, was level with him. He then spat with unerring accuracy into his eye, or rather onto his spectacle lens, and took off from there.

Using the one hand, and with the other clutching to his breast his new love, Scruffy abandoned his traffic sign, got himself some bounce off the top of a clothesline, swung up to the second-story window, thence on to a gutter pipe of the roof and away, a figure diminishing in the distance until he was lost to sight.

Treugang Ramirez was now left clinging to the cornice stones, halfway up to the crossroad sign, minus every last shred of whatever dignity he had ever possessed, while from below him arose renewed jeers, shouts of laughter, and hoots of joy. This was a day which would never be forgotten in the Calle Mendoza.

It was also a moment that was never to be forgotten by the lineal descendants of the von Waltzes of Ost Waltz, Koenigsberg, Ost Preussen.

One immediate thought, however, did penetrate his fury as he climbed down from the building, and this was that he had only a short while before been in contact with the keeper of the beast who had stolen his wig, and he realised that he must act quickly. Therefore, ignoring his neighbours, as well as the state of his head, he pushed through the crowd and as fast as his stumpy legs could carry him waddled back to the Admiral Nelson.

Gunner Lovejoy was still there, on his fifth Guinness and lime, a soldier pal having come in with still a few bob on him and willing to treat; and now the Gunner's tongue was sufficiently oiled to operate independently of the Gunner himself, and as Ramirez came bursting through the door, his pasty cheeks now streaked with sweat, the soldier shuddered as though he had seen something unreal and said, "Ugh, shoo, go on get back under yer flat stone."

Treugang Ramirez came to a halt in front of Lovejoy, his knees shaking, his little eyes blinking nervously, his small mouth working. He introduced himself formally first, trying to cast aside the civilian skin which appeared offensive to the soldier before by getting some kind of military curtness and rasp into his voice. "Sergeant Lovejoy," he said, "Alfonso T. Ramirez here——"

Gunner Lovejoy said amiably enough, "Well cock, now that I've got your name I still don't know you from a bar of soap, and come to think of it you could do with a bit of scrubbing. What's eating yer?"

"I want you to come at once! One of your blooding monkeys stole my——" and here Ramirez found himself at a complete loss for the proper word to use as his hands went halfway to his shining scalp. Finally, realising that in a moment he would again appear ridiculous, he compromised upon, "My hair."

The Gunner and his mate, a fellow artilleryman, now found themselves genuinely interested and Lovejoy, abandoning his position of leaning against the polished mahogany bar, now made a full tour, circumnavigating the figure of Ramirez and examining him, and in particular his naked head, with great care from all sides.

"Gord luv a duck," said the Gunner at the completion of his tour of inspection. "'Ad your 'airpiece did 'e; well I can't say it's any improvement. I believe now I seen you here a minute ago. You looked better with it on. Who was it, old Scruff?"

Ramirez, who had a fluent supply of unprintable Spanish epithets, used them before he replied, "I don't know the name of your stinking animal—he jumped on me from behind and——"

"That sounds like old Scruff," Lovejoy interrupted cheerfully. "What had you been up to with him? Teasing him I'll wager. That will be a matter for the police to look into then. Against the law to feed or annoy the Rock apes. There's signs up all over."

"You'll go to the police!" Ramirez reiterated, fury and frustration rendering him again almost speechless. "It is I who will go! I will go to your Commanding Officer, I will go to the Colonial Secretary, I will go to the Governor if you do not return my hair to me at once."

The second artilleryman, sucking on his pint of bitter, looked seriously over the rim of his glass at the Gunner and said, "Go on, John, why don't you give him his 'air? If ever I seed a man as what needed it. . . ."

"You joke, you laugh. You think that I am no one, to be made a fool of because I am nobody. You wait what will happen when Captain Russell hears of this. I work in his department."

Even in Gunner Lovejoy's brain undergoing its late-afternoon shock at the hands of his favourite tipple, the name of Captain Russell rang a bell. In charge of naval ordnance he was one of the most capable and efficient officers on the Rock, well liked and one whose reputation extended beyond his own service.

The bell having rung, Gunner Lovejoy shook his head to it a little and said, "Oh, you work for Captain Russell, do you? You don't look like one of his boffins to me. . . . Still, one never knows, does one? Come along then, cock, I've got me van outside. We'll go up the 'ill and see what's to be done about getting yer wig back. It'll be a public service for which I'll be expecting a suitable reward."

He led the way outside, climbed into his van with Ramirez beside him, set it into gear, and made off in the direction of the Queen's Road and the Battery where he hoped to find Scruffy or at least get an idea of how the land lay. If he were able to retrieve the article without a fuss, so much the better. There had been enough trouble that day already with Captain Bailey called on the carpet, and he didn't think the Captain would be in the way of appreciating another row, particularly one involving such a wet and unappetising specimen.

They rode in silence up the steep hill past the skeleton of the Moorish castle, Ramirez taking some satisfaction from the fact that he had at last moved the British Army into taking notice of him. Gunner Lovejoy was driving carefully until the hot sirocco-type breeze, created by the passage of the utility car, should blow some of the fumes from his head.

The road inclined more sharply, and the Gunner began to cast his expert eye through the branches of thorn and olive for nestling apes and the thick, squat figure of old Scruff.

He was not there though, nor further on at Prince Ferdinand's Battery where the rest of the Queen's Gate pack were foregathered for the night.

However, the Gunner knew yet another favourite place of Scruffy when he wished to be alone, and, abandoning the van and gesturing to Ramirez to proceed noiselessly, he climbed up the side of the rock to a small indentation where once there had been a large boulder, probably dislodged by the rains.

The Gunner stopped and placed a finger to his lips. They heard an extraordinary series of sounds coming from above them, a kind of combination of chittering, chattering, cooing, and gurgling. They raised themselves somewhat further and there saw Scruffy in the little hollow, wooing Ramirez's hairpiece. He held it cuddled in his arms close to his chest, stroking it, caressing it, and occasionally bestowing a lingering kiss upon it. The expression upon his ugly countenance, which prior to this had never been anything but malignant, could only be described as tender and loving.

"Ha!" exploded Ramirez, forgetting that he had been admonished to silence. "There it is, get it!"

In a flash the love light faded from the hazel eyes of the beast, his lips retracted from his fangs in a savage snarl, and coughs of rage burst from his throat. With a single motion whipping the hairpiece behind him with one hand, he let fly with a rock from the other.

Possibly it was the movement of concealing the toupee which disturbed his aim. As it was, the stone whistled past Treugang's skull. A few inches to the left and it would have brained him.

Since Ramirez could not turn whiter than he already was, he went a delicate shade of green and slid back down the hill on his stomach. The Gunner, who had ducked the moment he saw the flash of Scruffy's arm, clambered down with more leisure and dignity.

"Told you to keep quiet," he said.

"You go up and get it," Ramirez demanded.

"Not on your life," the Gunner replied. "Not with 'im in that mood. There's no use going after 'im now. 'E'd just skin up to the top. You've 'ad it for today. I'll have another go tomorrow." He started back to the car with Ramirez following, so that he was unable to see the expression of pure cunning which had arrived on the Gunner's face.

For during the brief moment of revelation before Scruffy shied the rock at their heads, Lovejoy had seen something which had caused him wholly to change his plans.

It must be remembered that Gunner Lovejoy had twenty years of experience with the Rock apes behind him, nine of them in close contact with Scruffy himself. He had raised him from an apelet, and there was not a single thing about this monkey that he didn't know and understand. No father was ever closer to his child.

Lovejoy had recognised that Scruffy was so enamoured of his acquisition that, if allowed to retain it, the Rock, or at least that portion of it which had suffered in the past from the ape's depredations, was in for a long period of peace. The wig was probably strongly constructed and, consisting of inorganic matter, would not be subject to decomposition. It could be counted on to last for a long time, keeping Scruffy in a felicitous state for perhaps as much as half a year.

This was the dilemma with which the Gunner found himself face to face. On the one hand he could have a go at retrieving this object and get this ugly-looking bespectacled specimen, and his eventual connections with the Navy, off his neck. On the other hand he was in a position to assure himself and all connected with him a long period of armistice as far as Scruffy was concerned. If he could guarantee that there would be no further trouble from that source, would it not be worth risking whatever difficulties might arise to impale them on the other horn of the dilemma?

The Gunner was intelligent enough to recognise that this problem was too great a one for him to cope with. That was why they had officers in the Army. And so, having stalled off Ramirez for the night, he took it at once to Captain Bailey.

"You're sure," Tim said, captivated by the prospect the Gunner held out to him. Even gaining a few months would be worth it, for by that time Scruffy's day would have been long forgotten and the authorities might again be in a mood to consider some of his projects.

"I'd bet me 'ead on it, sir," the Gunner replied. "You should have seen 'im, sir, lovin' away at it like it was his fancy on a Saturday night. I know the signs; 'e'll be as good as gold as long as it lasts!" He reflected for a moment and then continued. "On the other 'and, sir, there's no gainsaying that this Ramirez chap's a narsty bit o' work, I know the type. He'll go on and on keeping the place in an uproar, and besides he works in Captain Russell's department. I've checked on that, sir. He really seems to be one of their best men."

Tim nodded and thought hard. He said, "You've done well, Lovejoy." A solution struck him. "Look here," he said, "how much do you think one of those things would cost?"

"I wouldn't know, sir. Matter of fifteen quid maybe."

"Let me have that list we're putting through for damages today," Tim said.

The Gunner handed it to him. A gleam came into his cunning little eyes. "Oh I say, sir," he said, "that's a brain wave. Tell 'em it's impossible for us to recover his bleeding 'airpiece and let the Crown pay for a new one."

"They'll thank me for it in the long run," Tim said. "And after all he did pinch it. There'll be such a yell when they see this list they probably won't even notice the item for the wig. You find out for me what it will cost for another and we'll bung it through and hope for the best."

The Gunner nodded, murmuring, "Old Scruff won't be 'alf pleased. You should see him carrying on with that thing."

"Well then, that settles it," Tim said. "Get on with it." He took a ten-shilling note from his pocket and slid it across the desk to the Gunner. "That's for using your loaf," he said. "Have a couple on me and Scruffy. To peace and quiet."

And so it was done. The toupee, it seemed, was the work of a gifted wigmaker in Algeciras who was not only a speedy worker but reasonable, and the replacement came to no more than £13. 18. 6. and was delivered within a week. Tim had proved right, and so appalled were the Government accountants at the damages they had to O.K. for Scruffy's rampage that the item of the wig was never even questioned.

Ramirez declared himself as satisfied with the arrangements since no better could be arrived at and Lovejoy had convinced him it was impossible to retrieve the original article. In a sense he had scored off the British. He had got himself noticed and his property replaced. Still the incident left its scar.

Chapter 6

LADY FRENCH PASSES THE FISH

Some ten days later the telephone rang in the Mount. Felicity, who was near by, picked it up, always with hope, yet quite prepared for continuing disappointment. Tim had not called her since their first meeting. Evidently she had failed to make an impression on him.

But this time it was he. "Hello, hello—Miss French? I say, you probably won't remember me, but this is Captain Bailey. Tim Bailey."

"You may call me Felicity," said Felicity firmly. Now that she had him on the other end of the wire there was going to be no further nonsense. "Where have you been the last ten days?"

"Nursing. It didn't help though; poor old Helen died."

"Helen?"

"Monty's wife."

"Oh, I'm so sorry. Friends of yours?"

"Two of my apes. Helen got pneumonia and I've had to nurse her. Lovejoy and I gave her warm milk, arrowroot, and brandy every morning. And just when I thought I had her over it she suddenly turned around and died. But that isn't actually what I called you about—Miss—I mean Felicity."

"No?" queried Felicity. "Was there something else?" And even as she waited at the instrument she marvelled at the flush mounting to her cheeks and the sudden butterfly flapping about in her stomach to reconfirm her early diagnosis that this odd bod who lived apparently only for his unattractive apes might mean something to her. What strange chemistries decided these affinities?

"Do you remember that perfectly smashing idea you had that day up there by the apes' den?"

Felicity did, but she wasn't going to let on. "Idea——?"

"About naming one of my apelets after Princess Elizabeth. Well, it's come off. I promised I'd let you know."

"Oh Tim, I'm thrilled. Have you heard——?"

"The works," said Tim. "Letter on Palace stationery. Stories in the press. I'd like to show it to you if I may. You wouldn't by any chance be free say in half an hour for a bit? I could get off. Of course I'm sure you're awfully busy, but——"

Felicity decided to abandon coquetry and feminine wiles. She replied, "I'm not busy. I'm free. Where shall we meet?"

"What about the Moorish castle?"

"Done," said Felicity. "Half an hour."

She replaced the receiver and talked to herself. *"Now I must be calm. I must move slowly. I must put on fresh lipstick, run a comb through my hair, and I must get in my car and drive slowly and carefully, trying not to knock people over. Oh dear, what is it about that silly man that has done this to me?"*

The ruined tower of the Moorish castle looks out over the bay and the white houses of Algeciras. From the shore the moulded brown hills of Spain swept backwards to the northwest. Beyond them a red sun was preparing to set. Gazing down from the stone terrace, Tim could see the Casemates with their drill ground, a part of the racecourse, and the narrow neck of the border zone between Gibraltar and La Línea.

"Look here," Tim was saying and handed Felicity the letter on the heavy stationery headed Buckingham Palace, in which the King's Private Secretary advised Captain T. Bailey, OIC Apes, Gibraltar, that His Majesty would be pleased to have him name one of the apes Elizabeth, that the Princess had been delighted with the photographs and would enjoy having reports on the progress of her namesake.

"But," Tim continued with growing excitement, "that's not all. Here's another from the Press Officer at the Palace saying His Majesty has sanctioned a release of this story to the press. It's been given to the wire associations. It's gone off all over the world. Just think of it, they are reading about our apes in Timbuktu, in

Mandalay, in Moscow, in Angola, in Buenos Aires, Brisbane, and New York. And if it hadn't been for you——"

"You wrote the letter," Felicity said.

"It was your idea," countered Tim, "and that makes you merely marvellous. I don't suppose you really know what you've done for me and for them. It takes the heat right off old Scruff for a bit. Makes everybody ape-conscious—now when I go along and ask——"

"Was the Brigadier pleased?" Felicity asked.

The question sounded innocent, but when Timothy looked at her he caught a glimpse of the mischief behind her eyes and suddenly felt the warmth of her particular kind of enchantment. She was such a solidly good kid. That's how you would think of her back home. A good kid. Someone you could rely on, who wouldn't drip and dither if you were in trouble, but would come up with an idea. "Oh, he had me over the coals, of course. Wanted to know what I meant by going over his head."

"I didn't know he'd got one," Felicity commented. "What did you say?"

"I threw paragraph eight, clause A of Standing Part One Orders at him which says, 'It shall be the duty of the Officer in Charge Apes to provide names for all newborn surviving apes bred and born on the Rock and such names shall be duly registered and inscribed upon the rolls, and thereafter the apes shall be referred to by that name. . . .'"

"That must have shaken him," Felicity said. "I suppose he wrote that himself."

"One of his predecessors," Tim explained. "But that's nothing to the next broadside. Listen to this: 'Should the Officer in Charge Apes wish to confer the name of any living person upon an ape he must first secure permission of said person in writing.'"

"Check! Mate in one move," said Felicity. "What did the Brigadier say to that?"

"Poor old boy, he grew rather plaintive and asked why I didn't let him know."

"And——?"

"I had been waiting for that one for days," Tim said. He drew himself to attention and snapped Felicity an exaggeration of the salute he had thrown at the Brigadier. "Sir! You said I was not to pass any more bumph over your desk."

"Mate!" cried Felicity. "Oh Tim, I could love you for that," and she threw back her head and began to roar with laughter.

It set Tim off, too, and the next moment they found that they had laughed themselves into one another's arms, for the joke was so good and the merriment so infectious that they found it easier, in fact almost necessary, to cleave to one another for support. Thus they clung to one another for an instant in a kind of personal ecstasy of enjoyment of the jest and the plot they had hatched out together before separating in quite the most natural manner, except that Tim found that he was tingling strangely.

And far, far below a bugle call arose faintly through the heavy summer air from the Casemates, and then there was a thud as an artillery piece was fired. It was the sunset gun.

Felicity looked out over the Spanish hills. She no longer laughed. A small frown appeared on her brow. "Do you think there is going to be a war, Tim?" she asked.

The young officer was silent for some time while he reflected upon what he knew was concealed there before he replied, "I hope not," and with a little thrill that rippled over her heart Felicity understood the connection between that reply and his next query, which he made after regarding her curiously. "How long do you expect to be here, Felicity?"

"As long as Mother and Dad are," Felicity replied, and for a moment she reflected moodily. "I'm supposed to find a husband. Mother's worried about my becoming a spinster. Are you terrified?" It was a comic question but this time there was a gravity behind her eyes.

"Abou Ben Baileys' name will not be heading Mum's list," Tim replied.

"Why did you ask if I would be staying long?"

"Because if there is a war I hope you will leave the Rock very quickly."

"Why?"

"Your father knows, the Brigadier knows, everybody really

knows excepting the natives." He pointed out towards the rolling brown hills of Spain. "So friendly and innocent-looking," he said, "and loaded. Back in those folds. German 32-centimetre guns. Zeroed in on us."

Felicity looked at him questioningly, "And ours?"

"Pointing the wrong way, most of them," Timothy replied. "Up into the sky or out to sea. And wrong trajectory for firing inland. Typical, isn't it?" He pointed once more to the hills. "All high trajectory guns. It's going to be a mess. They'll have to get the women and children out. The Spaniards have never given up wanting this back, you know." He fell silent for a moment and Felicity didn't speak either; then Tim added, "My apes won't like it at all."

"No?"

"They hate noises of any kind. Must hurt their ears or something. Whenever we have a shoot on, Lovejoy goes up and tells them. They seem to understand him and buzz off to the other side of the Rock where they have a jolly good fight with the Middle Hill pack and come back when it's over."

The sun bowed out below the rim of the hills. Wisps of mist collected on the surface of the sea. Tim said, "Well," and then, "It was good of you to come here and let me chatter at you. I suppose we'd better be getting on back."

"Yes," Felicity replied, "I think so. Will it be another ten days before I shall be hearing from you?"

"No," said Tim, "it won't. May I call you tomorrow?"

"Yes, please."

They walked over to where their respective cars were parked and stood there silently for a moment. Then quietly and simultaneously, as though the idea had generated in both at the same moment, they leaned close and kissed one another gently. Thereafter not even touching hands or murmuring good-bye, they got into their cars and drove off.

Lady French was dressing when Felicity went clattering by the open door of her bedroom. "Felicity dear," she called, "is that you?"

"Yes, Mummy."

"I was beginning to worry you'd be late, and you know how nervous your father gets if he's kept waiting. We've been asked back to dine at the Brigadier's tonight. And darling, don't use water on your hair this time—after half an hour it begins to look like a fright wig. I've bought you some brilliantine—it's up in your room—I think you ought to wear your——"

What Felicity ought to wear was smothered owing to the fact that she had come into the room, gone over to her mother as she sat at her dressing table, put her arms about her neck and her mouth close to her ear, hugged her, and whispered, "Oh Mummy, Mummy, Mummy. He kissed me!"

All the alarm bells went off inside Lady French. "Felicity! Who kissed you?"

Felicity raised her lovely head, her eyes gazed inward at the delectable thing that had happened, and she whispered, "Captain Bailey!"

"Felicity! You're not really serious about this?"

"I don't know, Mummy!"

"You realise, of course, what a blow this would be to your father. His family have always been Navy since before Nelson's time."

Felicity reflected and said, "But he's such a nice boy, even if he seems to dote on monkeys. He's sorry for them."

"But the Army, Felicity," Lady French said. "It's the one branch of service with which—I mean today, darling, one simply doesn't. I suppose there was a time once when it was respectable, but it hasn't been for ever so long. Some of us were discussing—I mean I happened to mention the young man's name—I'm afraid he's nobody."

Something that came into Felicity's face, an expression, a flash of fire in the otherwise gentle eyes suddenly threw Lady French into confusion and she said, "I don't mean really nobody, my dear. Of course I'm sure they're quite nice people; it's just that they've always been only Army and never anything better than a Colonel, I gather. Your father was only a lieutenant when I married him, but it was one of the best naval families. He was bound to succeed. The Baileys don't seem to have been very ambitious. Commander Whitcombe's wife knew a story about one of them who resigned his commission, went into business, and made money. Can you imagine such a thing?"

Felicity reflected carefully before she replied, "Well, oddly enough I think I can. They seem to be able to concentrate."

Lady French took a deep breath, as one does before plunging into a cold bath, and then plunged. "Felicity, my dear," she said, "I don't like to say this, but are you aware that this Captain Bailey is rather loathed on the Rock—in the Army, I mean, amongst his own creatures? He's supposed to have some kind of obsession with apes. People simply can't stand him. He doesn't appear to have a single, solitary friend."

Felicity considered this revelation, too, without rancour, and murmured, "Perhaps that's why he appeals to me. Mother instinct! And I wouldn't be surprised if he turned out to be a very famous man some day." She turned off the prophecy and discussion with, "I shall wear my pink tonight. Don't worry, Mummy, I shan't keep you waiting." She got up, went over, took her mother's face between her hands and kissed one cheek with extraordinary tenderness, and then went out.

Dinner that night at the Brigadier's was identical with the evening the Brigadier and his wife had dined at the Mount with the Admiral, except for the difference in quarters, the Brigadier occupying a villa on the heights on the way to Europa Point. The same people were there, the same food was served, and Lady French was in the process of dissecting an identical slice of fish enveloped in gluey white sauce, when she heard her husband say, "What's all this about one of your apes to be named after Princess Elizabeth, Brigadier? Read about it in the papers. One of your chaps supposed to have written to the King about it. Bit cheeky, what?"

"Eh?" said the Brigadier. "What's that? You mean Captain Bailey? Not at all. Only carrying out my instructions. Thought it was about time we had a bit of favourable publicity and attention here on the Rock. Clever chap, that Bailey. Just the right touch. 'Put it in your own words,' I said to him. By jove, the story's gone out all over the world. Impressive."

Lady French felt her head drawn up as though by a magnet. She did not wish at this moment to look at her daughter, but she was unable to control the turn of her head upon her neck. Felicity was again sitting next to Staff Captain Quennel, to whom she was still paying no attention. At that moment she was glowing like a hundred-watt incandescent bulb and, in addition, managing to look like a cat who has swallowed a whole pet-shop supply of canaries.

Lady French once more desisted from the fish course.

"Hmm—yes, I see," said the Admiral, somewhat disappointed that his dig at the Brigadier had not turned out as well as expected. He had thought to set him off again. He then asked the question which was on all lips, and which was bound to come up during the evening. "Do you think there's going to be a war, Brigadier?"

And in this he was also disappointed, for the Commander of the Artillery Brigade this time did not fuff and huff and pontificate, but suddenly looked a little grey, worried, and tired as he replied with the earnestness of a man who has been thinking about little else, "Yes, I am afraid there will be. And very soon, too soon for us."

Chapter 7

WHEREFORE ART THOU JULIETTE

And then the war was no longer a matter of conjecture, but one of fact.

It was a strange one at the beginning, particularly for Gibraltar. It was far off. It was phony. And outside of a few minor restrictions it appeared to have little effect upon the lives of those dwelling on the Rock. Horse racing went on, the theatre, concerts, and cinema and the Saturday-night dances at the Rock Hotel; the Garden Club continued to exhibit and make plans, as did the amateur theatrical group. After a preliminary black-out trial, lights blazed; transatlantic liners came and went and ten thousand Spanish workmen continued daily to cross the line from La Línea and enter the fortress to go to their jobs in and about the dockyards and military installations, turning any idea of security into a vast joke.

This was the surface of Gibraltar. Beneath this surface there was an anxiety and a ceaseless coming and going of men in command growing haggard over the essential dangers of a position which rested upon a number of ifs. In London office lights were burning late at night as boffins considered these same potentialities, which included the possible entry of Mussolini into the war as an Axis partner and the even more appalling prospect that Franco would sell out to Hitler and the Germans and the Spaniards would attack Gibraltar from the land side.

For the declaration of war simply crystallized what the Army and Navy had known for several years, but in view of the general complacency at Whitehall had not been able to do much about— namely, that the lock of the door of the Mediterranean, which was Gibraltar, the door which if opened would lead to Malta,

Egypt, India, and possibly the total collapse of the British Empire, was rusty, and one firm concerted blow might shatter it.

The fact of the war had turned Gibraltar, taken for granted for years as an impregnable key fortress, into a liability as the planners and strategists recognized that in terms of modern warfare it had become almost obsolete and practically unusuable as a naval base if the Spaniards entered the war against Great Britain.

Overnight more subtle abstractions such as diplomacy, psychology, and morale became paramount and took on greater importance than guns.

One of those most deeply concerned with such problems and charged with responsibility for them far above his rank was a certain Major William S. Clyde, one of those queer characters thrown up by the war who inhabited the warrens of M.I. 5, was not much seen and not much heard, but had a wide acquaintance in high places and wielded an astonishing amount of influence.

If the military-intelligence boffins prided themselves upon selecting officers for their service who didn't look like agents, spies, investigators, or undercover men, they had outdone themselves in the case of Major William (S for Slinker, to his friends) Clyde. Or rather nature had aided them by supplying them with a man and a character who not only didn't look like an agent but also managed not to look like an officer. What he did resemble was a kind of fearfully busy, abstracted stork flapping about on long, stiltlike legs. He was further handicapped by refusing to take himself or the Secret Service seriously, and affecting a conspiratorial air which irritated his superiors of the Regular Army, but amused those more highly placed.

He was six foot four and a half inches tall and excessively thin, and hence shambled about with a slight stoop in order to communicate with medium-sized mortals without seeming constantly to be bending down to them. His hair was darkly Celtic but he had a reddish moustache of which he was very proud and wore droopingly. For the rest, his features were aquiline and his eyes quite wild.

The Master of Christchurch at Oxford University, who was becoming somewhat annoyed at the manner in which the Army, the

Navy, and the Air Force were raiding his staff, had recommended Clyde to Intelligence almost in a vengeful mood when he had been asked for another bright young don, this time one with a background of psychological training. He would hate to lose Clyde, but it would serve the Army right and, the Master reflected, might even do the country some good. His conscience did dictate, however, when he spoke on the telephone to the departmental head who had made the request, that he say, "Look here, I think you ought to know. This is a bright boy, but he is also quite mad. All of those chaps who go in seriously for that subject are a little dotty."

The departmental head had laughed bitterly and said, "He ought to fit beautifully into my squirrel cage then," and thanked the Master.

It soon developed that Clyde was not only bright and as mad as the Master of the House had warned but quite extraordinary as well, and Army Intelligence found itself embarrassed by having on its hands—an intelligence. It was coupled however with charm, persuasiveness, and limitless cheek.

By request he remained a Major. In fact he had acquired a phantom rank of much higher grade, and around his branch one heard such phrases as, "What does Clyde think about this——? Why don't you have a word with Clyde——? Has Clyde agreed to this——?" His job was not even exactly defined. In America he would have been known as a trouble-shooter, and he was moved about where his type of sardonic intelligence and above all his apparent grasp of what went on in the mind of the other fellow appeared most needed.

And since the world over it is the custom to hand the new boy the impossible job that no one else has been able to solve, Major Clyde had found himself with Gibraltar dumped into his lap. A preliminary visit to that bastion and a briefing by Major McPherson, the local security officer, had made it quite plain as to why he had been passed this hot potato.

The naval base was not only indefensible physically without the moving thither of a vast number of guns and men which were not available, but from the security point of view was nothing but a goldfish bowl. Here was one of the most important key fortresses of the Empire with its built in fifth column of Spanish workmen without whose labour the dockyard and installations could not exist.

This made the task of keeping out spies practically insuperable. Sensitive departments might button themselves up against agents and saboteurs, but the community of Gibraltar as a whole was exposed to every kind of infiltration.

Clyde had flown back to London with the suggestion which at first had raised the hair upon the heads of his superiors, but later had been adopted not only because it was the only thing to do but because it appeared that the new boy had actually come up with a solution. Since Gibraltar was not only a goldfish bowl but an open book, it was the Major's idea that its pages should at all times reflect the best of all possible British worlds. As there was no way to stop visits from German and Spanish spies, let them see and hear that the British were unworried, unruffled, and unhampered.

Hence Gibraltar all during the war would be brightly illuminated and all luxury items such as white flour for bread, silks, tobacco, sugar, etc., which the Spanish workmen in peacetime were accustomed to smuggle across the line beneath their shirts, should be available, fulfilling the dual purpose of diddling the enemy and bolstering up the inhabitants.

It was Clyde who had recognized from the very beginning and maintained through the darkest days that the problem of Gibraltar was purely one of morale. If the Spaniards were to be kept out of the war, the window of Gibraltar through which they looked must show them constantly that it would be unprofitable. Should Franco once reach the conclusion that the native Gibraltarians as well as the British had got the wind up, the fat might well be in the fire. Major Clyde concerned himself with the window dressing. Thus, in the early days of the war, Gibraltar was a kind of paradisical oasis.

But if life on the Rock had remained basically unchanged, the war had radically altered the plans of Miss Felicity French and turned them from immediate wedding bells, chintzes, and cushions at Harrods to serious reflections as to how best to arrange the future intelligently and satisfactorily. Felicity was not the daughter of an Admiral for nothing. She was likewise far-sighted.

In the ordinary way of affairs, had there not been a war, propinquity and Felicity would have continued to soften up Captain Bailey as well as the opposition of her parents; there would have been a service wedding with all the trimmings, after which she would have settled down happily enough with Tim in married-officers' quarters and followed him about through station after station of his military career. Now other considerations intruded, such as for instance serving her country.

At the same time being a woman and having thus properly put first things first she saw no reason why they could not be combined with her other designs. She remembered what Tim had told her about the existence of an evacuation plan of women and children from Gibraltar. If such a plan were put into effect, the only women who could remain upon the Rock would be those in service. There was no reason why with her intelligence and connections she should not be one of these. At the same time if she were already married she would never be accepted by the W.R.N.S. In the meantime Tim had not yet mentioned the subject. The apes and his emergency plans for them were taking up a good deal of his time.

Christmas had come and gone. The year 1940 had been ushered in and the war was still static, with the French manning the Maginot Line and a British expeditionary force sitting on the northern flank near Luxemburg. It was time, Felicity thought, to put her plan into action.

They were working upon a young female ape at the small ape clinic set up in St. Michael's Hut. Her name was Juliette, she was nine months old and had suffered a deep gash from a bite on her buttocks inflicted, of course, by Scruffy.

Felicity subscribed to the theory that a man is more likely to succumb to a female who makes herself a partner in his games and hobbies. If Tim's concern and passion was apes, then so was hers. She had made herself almost indispensable to him, accompanying him on his rounds of the apes' village and helping him during the minor emergencies and surgeries that arose, and soon had found herself happily accepted as his second pair of hands.

The apelet was on her stomach and was being held down by Tim while Felicity cleansed the wound and prepared to apply an antiseptic. The monkey had managed to twist its head about and was regarding Felicity with some anxiety, but also with trust and love.

"It's going to sting for just a minute," Felicity said to the apelet as though she were addressing a child, "but after that it's going to be all better." With firm, practised fingers she washed away the dried, coagulated blood. Juliette squirmed.

"Hold still, you little devil, will you," said Tim. "Stop making things more difficult. We're only doing this for your own good." He bent over and peered into the wound now exposed. "Hm, nasty!"

Felicity swabbed it dry once more and poured the antiseptic on a bit of gauze. "If they'd only listen to you about the cages," she said, "these things wouldn't happen. Poor little darling."

"Or at least supply us with a proper vet. That cut could do with a stitch or two."

"One isn't supposed to mind having a scar *there*," Felicity observed. "She'll have one, too. Now then." She applied the gauze. Juliette screamed like a child, then squirmed and whimpered.

Tim said soothingly, "Come on, old girl, it isn't all that bad," and then to Felicity, "Isn't it awful to have to hurt them?"

They smiled at one another across the table and Felicity said, "What a good, kind man you are, Tim."

The Captain flew into a perfect panic of embarrassment. "Nonsense," he replied, "absolute rotter."

"Tim!"

"Yes."

"I've been thinking," Felicity began. Juliette took up her attention for another instant, "Oh, do hold her still for another second, can you?" and then, "I've been thinking we could get married after I come back. Mother will fuss dreadfully of course."

"Will she?" said Tim in a voice of a man whose mind is elsewhere, but who nevertheless has heard the question. "I don't suppose there's any use trying to keep a bandage on her, particularly on her rear. She'd have it off in a second. We'll just have to keep catching her and cleaning it until it's healed. Oh Lord! Your mother, you mean!" He shouted suddenly as the full import of Felicity's last remark penetrated, and then— "What do you mean when you come back?"

"I'm going to volunteer for the WRENS. I'm going to learn coding and signalling and be made an officer with privileges and use Daddy's name and be sent back here. Then I thought——"

Tim was suddenly looking at her with a curious fierceness. "You are not to come back, Felicity. I don't want you to."

"Are you being unkind, Tim?"

"Huh! Unkind! After what I told you about those German guns. They've sprouted a new lot, a regular plantation. I don't want you dismembered." His gaze was now direct and revealing. "I want you membered."

"And you?" queried Felicity.

"I'm in the business," Tim replied briefly. "I shall get under a table."

"Oh Tim," Felicity wailed, "why couldn't you have been a Swiss clockmaker?" She took a tube of soothing antibiotic salve and squeezed some into the wound. Juliette squeaked and they began to laugh. They both suddenly felt themselves singularly happy. Felicity murmured, "Juliette, Juliette, wherefore art thou Juliette. Oh dear, that isn't right, is it?"

Tim asked, "Would she really kick up a row?"

"Oh yes. And Daddy will, too."

Tim reflected, "I imagine he will. I would. All done? I can't hold her much longer."

Felicity replied, "Sissy!" and wiped the edges of the wound clear. Then she said, "Tim, would you rather not marry me?"

Captain Bailey cried, "Oh my God, Felicity!" and in the exclamation managed to express such an abysmal horror at the thought of not marrying her that he conveyed all that she needed to know.

"I oughtn't to be gone more than six months," Felicity said, "seven at the most, but as soon as I have my commission——"

Tim said, "Look here, Felicity, I haven't got a bean, you know."

"Neither have I. No expectations either. Not a single rich relative. And I shall enjoy being a burden to you."

"Life on a Captain's pay——"

"Bliss!" Then Felicity blinked her eyes clear of two large tears which had formed there and added, "You don't mind that I'm too fat? And not very pretty? I can cook. I mean really, not play cooking."

"Felicity!" Tim cried once more in a perfect agony of frustration. And once more he packed into her name whole pages of unspoken emotional literature, and then somehow found some words, "How the devil can a man hang on to a confounded wounded she-ape and at the same time tell someone what he feels —the magnitude of it—the awesomeness of it all—I mean how it makes you think you don't know whether you're going to burst into tears or laugh or fall down in a dead faint. It sort of tears you to pieces inside and makes you all giddy and sick and at the same time you want to yell at the top of your lungs."

"Oh Tim," Felicity said, "you make love so beautifully. You can let her go now."

Tim did so and reached for Felicity, but Juliette was quicker than he. In a flash the little apelet was up from the table, had leaped on to Felicity's bosom and wrapped both her arms about her neck. She turned her wizened face towards Tim, bared her small fangs, and scolded and chittered at him angrily.

Felicity held her close and murmured, "Hush little one, you mustn't be jealous. He loves me." She put her chin down upon the little head and looked across the table at Tim, and on her face was an expression of tenderness which pierced the man and left him shaking with the love that he was experiencing for this odd, kind, and rather wonderful girl. "There's all the rest of the time for us," she said, and then added, "Dear Tim."

Ten days later Felicity sailed for England to volunteer for the WRENS. Because of the war there was no formal announcement of engagement. She and Tim parted with the understanding that when she returned with her commission they would be married.

It was not six months, however, but a whole year and five

months before Felicity was able to return to the Rock wearing the stripes of a WREN Second Officer. The delay in her return had been occasioned by her being just that much too good and too intelligent. She had made Third Officer so easily and so far at the top of her class that she had been retained to train the new cadres joining up, and it was not until she had been promoted to the more exalted position of Second Officer and applied almost unbearable pressure on her already harassed father that she was assigned to Gibraltar in charge of all naval signals and coding there.

And when she did finally return, it was to find Tim in disgrace, dismissed from his job as OIC Apes, his morale practically non-existent, and the morale of all on the Rock not much better. Her own, too, was singularly low.

Chapter 8

BACKGROUND TO A SACKING

The unpleasant consequences of war fall variously upon different communities as well as individuals in accordance with the situations and problems of those communities and individuals. Wars are always seen as through the wrong end of a telescope so that they diminish to what each person can see affecting his life and himself.

For Captain Bailey the conflict had narrowed down to his apes, his guns, and an occasional letter from Felicity. These last were cheerful, straightforward efforts containing a wealth of detail concerning life in the W.R.N.S. at the beginning of the war, and a paucity of sentimentality. Felicity had a theory that men didn't like soppy stuff.

In this she might have been wrong. In Tim's case absence was making the heart grow not only fonder but increasingly nervous. A girl like Felicity loose amongst the Navy in Great Britain could be cutting a swath. Sooner or later she would encounter a naval type who would attract her and who would not be carrying an anchor chain of parental disapproval about his neck. He thought her letters progressively cooler and since he had the shyness of the British and didn't wish to press, he tempered his to hers.

Therefore he concentrated on his guns and his monkeys. The former as far as Captain Bailey was concerned were money for jam. He was a dedicated artilleryman who up to that time had never fired at anything but a target, but who had been passionately devoted to seeing that whatever he threw at that target, and from whatever distance, landed smack in the centre of it. This kind of keenness soon communicated itself to his teams of gun crews; perfection became a game and success a habit. The same attitude,

however, was less successful when it came to carrying on in wartime his job as OIC Apes.

To begin with, there had always been something faintly ludicrous
in not only the official title but also in the job itself. With the
declaration of war, when soldiers' jaws were supposed to set in
hard, grim lines, it became absurd and not even the fact that when
the souls on the Rock were counted and numbered, the apes
were treated as humans and furnished with both identity and
ration cards, made it any less so. In fact if anything it was even
more comic. Lovejoy kept the cards in a small file box up in St.
Michael's Hut close to the apes' village. The Gunner was rather
proud of them, and pleased. There had been moments when both
he and Tim feared that with the onset of the war the apes
might have been ordered destroyed.

There was also a paradox involved; with the war the necessity
of drilling crews for the anti-aircraft guns and the long-range
batteries pointing out to sea became paramount; the infantry had
to be rehearsed and the engineers began blowing, blasting, drilling,
and exploding so that between all of the Services, from morning
until night, something was banging, cracking, booming, chaffering,
rattling, and crashing on the Rock. The apes, who hated noises of
any kind, were in a constant state of nervousness often bordering
upon panic.

Tim soon discovered when he went into long-range planning
for his apes that while they had been rationed and identified as
humans it was merely to avoid double bookkeeping and if his
attempts for his charges had met with little sympathy before the
war, they now encountered downright hostility.

This came to a head one morning after the fall of France when
the Brigadier looked over to his Brigade Major, newly promoted
from Captain, Quennel, who had the schedule, and asked, "Who's
next?"

"Captain Bailey, sir," Quennel replied.

"Bailey?"

"He's been bothering me to give him some time for weeks, sir.
I knew that you didn't—— Well, I put him down for five minutes.

The alarm bell within the Brigadier rang. "Bailey," he said, "you mean that damn monkey fellow? Look here, Quennel, I haven't——"

"He also has the best gun crews on the Rock, sir. They are at the top again."

"Oh! Very well. I'll see him."

When Tim came in, looking smart and respectful as an officer should, the Brigadier was inclined to let him have the benefit of the doubt and gave him a civil good morning. But he also glanced at the clock on his desk and said: "Captain Quennel has allotted you five minutes which we will say begins as of now. I suggest you state what you wish to see me about."

"The apes, sir," said Tim without hesitation.

Brigadier Gaskell sat quietly and made no reply.

"There have been no provisions at all made for them," Tim continued, encouraged by the silence. "Everything and everyone else has been covered either by regulation, plan, or executive order for all contingencies and emergencies, except them, sir."

The Brigadier maintained his silence, but he picked up a paper knife and played with it.

"I know they've been given identity cards and ration books," Tim went on, "but I'll get to that in a moment. It isn't that the ration is insufficient, only that it is the wrong kind. They haven't been getting what they need and what they're used to. Lovejoy says you can see their condition is going off already. You can tell by their coats, sir, and they get coughs and things more quickly."

The Brigadier continued to say nothing, but his eyes strayed to the clock.

"But it is really about the concrete shelters that I have come, and the steel for the cages. I have drawn up the plans, but I won't bother you with them now. There's the target practice, which they can't stand—their eardrums, sir, they're not like ours—and of course there will be bombs sooner or later and if the Germans— I mean the Spanish—well, we all know, sir, it could get very sticky, and where would they go? If they were driven away from their usual haunts by bombardment, they'd starve to death in a week. They might even desert the Rock altogether and get over to the mainland."

The Brigadier now withdrew his eyes from the clock and fastened them upon Captain Bailey and allowed the unspoken thought, "Would that be bad?" to be plainly registered upon his countenance.

"Well, sir," Tim resumed, "if the apes *did* leave the Rock or were all killed off and it got around amongst the men—well, you know how they are, sir, about legends and superstitions and things, and just at the time when you'd most want them to stand fast they'd be thinking about the apes deserting or dying out. . . ."

The look of interest that had settled upon the Brigadier's face at the thought that the apes might be wiped out or disappear for good was now replaced by one of distaste and cold annoyance.

"The way I have worked it out," Tim explained, suddenly anxious that time was running out, "is that with a couple of hundred cubic feet of concrete and a half a ton of steel wire I could manage shelters that would not only be bombproof but practically soundproof as well; I have got the place picked out off Ferdinand's Battery. We'd go into the hill a way; the cages would be to protect the females and their young after breeding——"

Time *was* running out and he rattled on with his plan and his needs somewhat in a panic for fear he would not get it all said or his point sufficiently emphasized.

Gaskell finally did hold up his hand. "Your time is up, Captain Bailey," he said.

To his surprise the Brigadier found himself remarkably controlled, possibly because of the fact that in view of his own needs and problems, the demands of this young idiot were so utterly improbable and ridiculous, not to mention impossible.

"Your time is up, Captain Bailey," the Brigadier repeated, "but I am going to allow myself the pleasure of extending it for the privilege of a little chat with you. Major Quennel tells me that your crew has topped the list again in firing practice, and I am pleased to hear this. The time may come when all our lives may depend upon such accuracy, and if you continue to be a conscientious officer and keep your men up to this mark you have set, you will go far in this service. On the other hand, if you persist in wasting one minute more of my time upon those apes you will, I'm afraid, find this desirable trend severely reversed."

Gaskell sat up in his chair, leaned his elbows on the desk, folded his hands, and said with amazing calmness, "You asked me for concrete, Captain Bailey," and here his calmness suddenly abandoned him as the word triggered his own despair. "Concrete!" And he slammed a fist down upon his desk. "Concrete which I have begged for, pleaded for, humiliated myself for! I need concrete for shelters for my soldiers, Captain Bailey, for bomb-proofs for civilians, for dumps, magazines, shops, first-aid dressing stations and hospitals! Can you picture how sorely I need concrete, Captain Bailey? Aircraft, guns, food, and ammunition, and steel and everything needed to make this vulnerable sitting duck that we are defensible? And I am getting none."

For an instant Tim experienced a pang of culpability. Engrossed with his own problem and responsibility he had for one instant been let into a glimpse of greater responsibilities by a man who was desperately trying to live up to them. Yet at the same time something within Tim maintained that each man has his job according to his rank and experience and was required to get on with it. He had not asked to be made OIC Apes. The beasts were there; they had a part in the life and times of the Rock and had to be coped with.

"And as for superstition, Captain Bailey, may I point out that we are no longer living in the Dark Ages. We are commanding men of modern times who have been at least to elementary school, and if they are not aware that this waffle about a legend is childish and idiotic it is time they found out. I gather that you will hardly wish to sit there and tell me that our position here is dependent upon the behaviour of these monkeys or what happens to them."

There was no room left for reply, for the Brigadier returned once more to that ominous calm which Tim felt was far more difficult than if he had blown his top. "Let me put it this way, Captain Bailey: where in peacetime I might be inclined to condone the zeal of an officer I had appointed OIC Apes and have put up with the fact that for what reason I cannot fathom the best and proudest branch of the service is saddled with a pack of filthy, thieving, defecating apes, in wartime such an attitude becomes a bloody nuisance and, if I may say so, slightly absurd as well. Or don't you reckon human lives as more valuable than monkeys?"

Tim stifled the quite ridiculous cry that arose in him. "But, sir, they didn't ask to be made monkeys, or to be domesticated." Instead he said nothing.

"So let me suggest," concluded the Brigadier, "that you continue to carry out your duties in connection with these brutes as best you may under the circumstances, and if you ever again refer to them in my presence, or if you should be so unfortunate as to have them called to my attention again in any way, shape, manner, or form, you will bitterly regret it. That is all, Captain Bailey."

Chapter 9

THE GREAT GUNPOWDER PLOT

The final stain on Captain Bailey's copybook, which brought to a
swift close his side-line avocation as little father to the anthropoids
and came close to unseating him as an officer as well, was provided
by none other than Alfonso T. Ramirez. Ramirez's object had
not been to get Captain Bailey sacked but to destroy Scruffy. His
motive was not yet the sabotaging of the British position on
Gibraltar but revenge pure and simple for unbearable humiliation. The effects, however, of the Great Gunpowder Plot of A. T.
Ramirez were far-reaching.

The episode of the purloined hairpiece had been quite
the most shaming and mortifying experience that Mr. Ramirez
had ever been called upon to endure, but it was nothing to what
was to follow and stemmed from that same catastrophe as well as
the tolerated friendship which had grown up between him and
the Gunner.

The replacement of the toupee had gone off very well and to
Mr. Ramirez's satisfaction. The wigmaker in Algeciras had outdone himself in speed and reproduction; the new one looked
even better than the original, and payment by the British Government quickly forthcoming.

In fact so pleased was the little Gibraltarian at having got his
own back from the British that on the day his scalp had been
delivered to him he felt once more himself and had again risked
a snub in the Admiral Nelson by offering to buy Gunner Lovejoy
a drink. Only this time, and to do justice to the occasion, Lovejoy
unbent and accepted and permitted Ramirez to set up a couple
of monkey juices for him. As the Gunner downed these, he made
the astonishing and not unpleasant discovery that there was no
change in the flavour of this drink, or in the effects it had upon

his innards, though they had been paid for by a civilian. And thus the ice was broken and the two men became bar neighbours, on speaking and drinking terms.

But there was more to it than that. Lovejoy had detested Ramirez so thoroughly and for so little genuine cause that in the end guilt-feeling led him to lean over backwards to conceal this dislike, and to his horror after a period of practising this conceal-ment he found his feeling had actually turned into a kind of grudging affection. He had insulted the little man, reviled him, turned his back on him, practically spat in his eye, and still found him inclined to be friendly and trying to buy him drinks. In a sense, Ramirez, like the apes, was an outcast, too.

And finally there was the guilty knowledge, shared with Captain Bailey, that they had diddled the little man in the matter of Scruffy and his treasure.

However, alcohol, which encourages toleration and companion-ship, also loosens tongues, and one day the Gunner, standing at the bar which at the close of the working day was filled with Gibraltarians, service men, and Government clerks, was well oiled. Feeling magnanimous towards the ugly little man with the thick-lensed spectacles, he elected to tell the tale of the wig, not cruelly but rather as an achievement scored by one who had managed to get a new hairpiece out of the British Government. He told the story of the theft, the chase, the failure to recover, and the restitution in which His Majesty's Government had forked out £13. 10. 8. and there boys it was, right before their very eyes.

This was bad enough even though well meant, for it brought it all back to Mr. Ramirez, and his small and mean little eyes filled with rage as he suddenly found himself and his toupee the centre of attraction in the bar, for after three or four monkey juices the Gunner's voice was enlarged by a great many decibels.

But the Gunner was not content to let bad enough alone. He was well away now and continued, "Still got it he 'as, 'as old Scruff. Wouldn't part with it for anything. He loves that hairpiece 'e does, like it was his popsy. Likes to bring it down to town around noon and sit a-top the Southport Gate lovin' it up. A sight to melt the 'ardest heart, that's what it is. Romero on 'is balcony got nothing on old Scruff. You take a look next time you go by and you'll see him like as not 'ugging and kissing of it. That's monkey for you!"

This was quite true. It was now four months after the episode and the hairpiece had worn extraordinarily well, in spite of being dragged around night and day through all weather by the big ape and being subjected to wear and tear not ordinarily built into a toupee. And it was also true that Scruffy used to select some public place such as the Southport Gates, the Trafalgar Cemetery, or the schoolyard to sit and croon over and cuddle this article, but the people used to the ways of the apes and their appearances had never much bothered about what it was the big macaque had been fondling.

Twenty-four hours, however, after the Gunner's story in the Admiral Nelson and the tale was all over Gibraltar, in and out of shops and barracks and homes and offices. And now whenever Scruffy appeared with his treasure a small crowd would gather for rude remarks and raucous laughter.

Alfonso T. Ramirez was plunged into such an abyss of humiliation, rage, frustration, and shame that it was a wonder his mind was no more turned than it was. It was bad enough to be an unpopular little man, but now added to this he had become the standing joke of the Rock, with Scruffy furnishing fresh reminders practically daily.

The Great Gunpowder Plot and the opportunity to blow the instigator of his troubles into smithereens was born out of an accident of passage. But when it occurred, and Mr. Ramirez was suddenly brought face to face with the means for securing his revenge, he became aware of the depth of his emotions and the fact that nothing short of total and violent destruction of Scruffy would satisfy him for what he had suffered.

The wherewithal to accomplish this faced him one late afternoon in the grimy window of a small shop in Algeciras fronting some corrugated iron sheds devoted to the manufacture and sale of fireworks. The Spaniards were always involved in fiestas, holy days, political and historical celebrations that called for cannon fire, jubilant explosions, and rockets in the sky.

It was the custom of Mr. Ramirez, who was the possessor of a small car, to journey to Algeciras once a week for the purpose of visiting a lady with whom he had come to an arrangement which enabled him to spend an afternoon in her company. Because of the kind of person he was or even perhaps due to the Teutonic genes in his blood stream, Ramirez was furtive about this business, cautious in his approach, and somewhat guilt-stricken in his departure.

In order that no one should be able to deduce a pattern, he always parked his car several streets away from the lady's lodgings and approached on foot and then returned by other back streets. And it was during one such devious journey to his vehicle that Ramirez came across the obscure little fireworks factory and was brought to a halt by the sight of the object displayed in the window.

It was a firework, or what the Americans would call a giant salute or cannon cracker of truly Gargantuan and formidable proportions, and consisted of a shiny blue cardboard cylinder some fifteen centimetres in diameter, Ramirez estimated, and probably sixty centimetres more or less in height, from the top of which protruded a piece of saltpetre fuse.

In an instant there leaped into the mind of Mr. Ramirez a picture of Scruffy hugging this object to his breast; there would follow an appalling explosion and when the smoke cleared away one might perhaps find small shreds of hair where the brute had been. There were always reports in the press about small boys blowing off their thumbs or landing in the hospital from clinging too long to celebration fireworks of far smaller calibre than this. Here was a bomb calculated to pulverize his enemy, and yet if by some mischance it were found in Mr. Ramirez's possession before he had the opportunity to plant it, it was just a cracker piously hoarded to wake up some saint at the next holy day.

Mr. Ramirez went inside the shop. A bell jangled and the proprietor appeared through a curtained-off partition at the rear. He was a rather untidy-looking Spaniard with a too large head on a too thin neck, and he had a tick or tremor which caused his head constantly to nod "yes" upon his neck. Mr. Ramirez had never before encountered a person with such an affliction and fell into the trap of interpreting the nods as affirmations in accordance with his own thoughts and questions.

"That one in the window. . . ." began Mr. Ramirez.

"Ho, ho," nodded the proprietor, "that one!"

"It is expensive?"

"It is not cheap," agreed the proprietor. "Five hundred pesetas. On the other hand, if you are looking for something——"

"Special?" Mr. Ramirez filled in.

The proprietor's head bobbed in acquiescence. "Something of grandeur and nobility."

Mr. Ramirez found his own head now nodding likewise almost in the same tempo as that of the proprietor. "Yes, yes."

"Something of stunning and memorable impact——"

"That's it," nodded Ramirez.

"A veritable volcano when activated! If it is your intention both to surprise as well as entertain, to create a stupefying and unforgettable effect——"

They were both nodding away at one another now like two mechanical toys. "Exactly," said Mr. Ramirez, for he could not have heard a better description of what he had in store for Scruffy.

"Then this is our finest piece! Four hundred and fifty pesetas to you."

"And throw in a longer fuse?" Ramirez's plan for the delivery of this bomb was already formulating. He wanted to be sure that when it went off he wouldn't be there.

The proprietor's head and intentions were still in agreement. "But of course. As long as you like. With a piece of this magnitude the longer the fuse the greater the suspense. The greater the suspense the more powerful the effect. It will take but a moment to make the change. Shall we say a fuse of twenty minutes? If you desire a shorter period you may cut it yourself."

It was exactly what Mr. Ramirez had in mind. His own nodding head put the seal on the deal as he reached for his wallet. The proprietor took the huge firework out of the window and retired with it through the curtains. He reappeared within five minutes with a new fuse neatly coiled. He wrapped the firework in brown paper and said, "I congratulate you. You will create a sensation."

Ramirez tucked the bundle under his arm, looked carefully right and left up and down the street before emerging from the doorway, but there was no one about to witness his exit. He hurried off to his car where he dumped the package innocently enough onto the back seat where it would rest with other purchases he would make in Algeciras.

Nervous though he was he anticipated no difficulties at the British control point on the border. He was well known to the police, army, and customs guards; working in a sensitive part of the Navy Yard his pass and security were A-1. The customs man gave a perfunctory glance at the paper bags in the rear of the car from which protruded the usual fresh fruits such as bananas, oranges, apples, etc., and waved him through. Mr. Ramirez drove swiftly to his home, mounted the stairs, entered and locked the door, closed the shutters and unpacked the dangerous-looking object which would be the means of regaining his lost self-respect. There only remained the question of the how and the when of the delivery.

As to the method by which he would persuade the big monkey to hug his own annihilation to his bosom, Ramirez didn't envision any grave problem. The Rock apes were known to be inveterate thieves, appropriating for themselves any article that was not nailed or tied down. Since Scruffy was the leader of the Queen's Gate pack, he would most surely pre-empt this beautiful shiny blue and mysterious object for himself and defy all attempts to remove it from his possession. When the fuse reached the appalling amount of powder that must be stored in the cylinder—Mr. Ramirez's precise and methodical mind had already worked out the number of cubic centimetres of explosive that would go up— that would be that. No more Scruffy! No more snide, sly, side glances at him. No more laughter. There only remained the when, since Ramirez must be able to plant his bomb unseen and be far away when it went off.

The time, the place, and the occasion were supplied by none other than the Governor, though behind him, or rather behind the event, was a psychological-warfare boffin, that certain Major Clyde, former Christchurch don, on loan to the Army.

The Major's name didn't even appear in the orders that came from London for the Governor to show the flag on the Rock at a kind of Army Day parade and review, but the letter suggesting this was composed in conciliatory terms, having been written by Major Clyde himself.

Shortly there would occur the opportunity to celebrate the defence of Gibraltar during the great siege against the French and Spanish in 1779 by General Sir George Eliott.

The Governor fixed the day of celebration by decree. Ceremonies were devised to take place in the square before General Eliott's monument, an hour-long parade scheduled, flags ordered out, review stands set up, and all in all a rousing show organized that would bring every man, woman, and child either into the reviewing square or along the route of procession.

And this, of course, provided exactly the opportunity sought for by Mr. Ramirez. On that occasion and during that time there would be not a soul anywhere in the vicinity of Prince Ferdinand's Battery or Queen's Gate Road where the apes hung out.

The day could not have dawned more beautifully for the event. The sky presented its most enticing southern blue. The sun outdid itself glowing from the firmament. Gibraltar was a mass of red, white, and blue bunting, Union Jacks and the colours and flags of regiments and services. The streets and the square were black with people, for the factories had closed down at three that afternoon to give the Spanish workmen, for whom after all the show was being staged, the opportunity to witness the celebrations and see the fun. Although the ceremony was for a General who had defeated them, a fiesta was a fiesta and they all joined in with a will. Gibraltar was never gayer or more feverish with crowds and music and colour.

Tucked away in side streets preparing to lead the procession as per their schedule the various regimental bands tootled away. Street vendors hawked colours. Pretty girls wore their best dresses. Shopkeepers did a rousing business. Everybody was happy and if the enemy were looking, as the Governor, the Colonial Secretary, and Major Clyde were sure he was, he would be most disconcerted at this display of Empire insouciance and high morale.

The high officials augmented by Admiral French, the General, the Brigadier, and Group Captain Howard Cranch of the Royal Air Force, attended by their staffs and aides decked out in all their finery of uniform, medals, gold lace, and cords, were ensconced in the reviewing stand. In the distance with a crashing of cymbals and the glitter of sunlight upon the yellow brass of instruments a band burst into "The British Grenadiers." At the same time a far-off cheer arose from the throats of the spectators. The dignitaries in the reviewing stand stopped their neighbourly chatting and stiffened into proper attitudes; the parade had begun and soon its first elements would be winding into the square. And on the upper Rock, unhurried, unmolested, Alfonso T. Ramirez was going about the business of getting even.

He was unhurried because again at the behest of his German blood he had been quietly efficient and had gone through several dry runs of his scheme.

Parking his car at the side of Queen's Road, Ramirez looked down into town where he could see the populace collected like black ants along the route of procession. The apes were gathered a slight distance farther up the road, some still nibbling at scraps of the lunch Lovejoy had brought them at midday, some fighting, some scratching or skin picking, some torpid.

In their midst Ramirez saw Scruffy, his old wig still clutched in his paw. Rage filled the heart of Ramirez as he saw the object held by the monkey, but it was replaced almost immediately by his little o of a mouth forming itself into rather a horrid smile of joy. According to the schedule, Scruffy had little more than twenty-one minutes left to live.

Mr. Ramirez produced his blue-lacquered bomb from the back of his car and uncoiling the length of the twenty-minute fuse laid its end carefully in the grass behind his vehicle and walked up the road, concealing it in the shrubbery at the side.

As he approached the apes they became alerted to his presence and sat up regarding him or moving restlessly, all except Scruffy who squatted like an old pasha eyeing the newcomer and what he carried, calculating no doubt, as always, what was in it for him.

From far below, wafted on a bit of warm breeze from the continent of Africa, came a snatch of band music. Ramirez reflected happily that his old enemy would expire to the strains of an Empire march.

He had now, as he had calculated, reached the end of the piece of fuse and he set the giant salute down on the ground a few yards from the big ape, who was watching him out of his golden eyes. Ramirez sat down himself beside the big cannon cracker and held it to his side as though it was something precious and valuable. He was convinced that Scruffy had all of the human faculties. Hence he had a scenario carefully worked out.

For five minutes Ramirez sat there cuddling and nursing the blue firecracker, while from below arose the thump, thump, thump of beaten drums and the crash and blare of martial music. Scruffy watched him.

When Ramirez judged that five minutes had passed he looked at his watch as though remembering an appointment somewhere, arose and went off, leaving the firecracker poised on the ground behind him.

As he walked away he saw out of the corner of his eye a lightning-like movement as Scruffy bounced forward, collected the blue cylinder, and held it clutched to him. The coughings, barkings, and scoldings he heard from behind him confirmed the fact that other apes were disputing Scruffy's ownership of this new prize, and that Scruffy was determined to hang on to it whatever the odds.

Filled with admiration for the mind beneath the toupee which had conceived this revenge, Ramirez reached his car, knelt for a moment, ignited the end of the fuse, and then leaping into the driver's seat set off down the hill as fast as safety would permit. Through his brain there sang an unctuous and self-congratulatory German phrase. *"Alles geht wie geschmiert"—everything goes as though greased*. And it did indeed.

Encountering not a single car or lorry on the roads, he fairly whizzed down the mountain side and arrived at his destination in eleven minutes flat. The parking space he had selected for his car

was still vacant. He cut through a back lot down a side alley and
around by Trafalgar Cemetery and in three minutes more found
himself mingling with the crowd in the square in front of the
grandstand where, to his delight, he spotted Gunner Lovejoy, who
had never held with parading and had got out of this one on the
score of his duties with the apes. However, he was there to take
in the sights. Pleased with this piece of luck in encountering
someone who could identify him, and if need be furnish him with
an alibi, Ramirez joined up with him at once and began to make
conversational time. When the explosion rang out from the upper
Rock, Ramirez's presence in the Main Square would have been
already established.

The parade and ceremony had been thoroughly organized and
prepared and by now the last of the procession led by the band
was entering the plaza, already jammed with the crowd, regiments of artillery, infantry, engineers, naval forces, all of the
power that the British could muster on their isolated bastion, a
brave, glittering, and imposing sight.

Ramirez hugged himself. In exactly two hundred and forty
more seconds the dastardly monkey who had stolen his toupee
and caused him to be held up to ridicule would be dead, dead,
dead.

On the upper Rock the drama was drawing to its conclusion,
though no longer quite in the manner that had been planned.

Two thirds of the Queen's Gate pack were now gathered in a
circle about Scruffy and the gleaming blue object he was hugging
to himself, and from their ranks now moved another dog ape by
the name of Arthur, Scruffy's only formidable rival for domination
of the pack.

Arthur wanted the cracker. His whole covetous monkey being
was convulsed with jealousy. He craved it not only because of its
lovely colour and the fun it would be to tear it to pieces to see
what was inside it but also because Scruffy had it. Barking his
challenge and intention to contest, he moved warily closer while
the rest of the apes spread out and occupied grandstand seats for
what was obviously going to line up as the battle of the century.

There was no yellow in Scruffy. He was never one to decline a

good brawl, particularly with Arthur, who he felt he could lick
with one hand tied behind him. But now his possessions, the old
and the new, the wig and the pretty blue thing, posed him a
problem. If he put them down or dropped them to take on Arthur,
he might lose one or the other or both.

There was a sudden and startling flash of brown fur and glazed
blue cardboard as Scruffy solved his dilemma. Pinning back Arthur's ears could wait. What he wanted now was to be alone
with his new toy. He headed down the road at top speed.

With a scream of rage, bilked not only of his battle but the
desired object, Arthur set off behind him, and after Arthur the rest
of the Queen's Gate pack.

Under ordinary circumstances, with Scruffy burdened and
Arthur unhindered, even with Scruffy's surprise headstart, Arthur
would have caught up with him after a few dozen yards and had
things out. But now another and wholly unexpected element
manifested itself. Scruffy found himself pursued not only by his
angry rival and all his friends but also by a long, fire-from-the-
wrong-end-spitting snake. This snake, an elongated, white ropy
thing with sparks and smoke cracking and hissing from its tail,
was coming after him, and the faster he ran, the faster it came.

Panic engendered by this startling development lent him speed
beyond anything he had ever revved up before. He went pelting
down the side of the Queen's Road, skirting the iron fence at the
edge of the cliff, whizzing past trees and bushes and when he
slackened for an instant to look over his shoulder the snake was
still there, and if anything even a little closer. With but one
thought, to shake it off, he now veered sharply to the left and
plunged down King Charles V Wall in the direction of town. If
Scruffy knew anything about snakes, Mr. Snake wouldn't like
that. On his heels, hard put to keep up with the acceleration
brought on by Scruffy's terror, followed Arthur and the gang.

The macaque, when he wants to, can move with incredible
speed. Scruffy wanted to and so did his pursuers. They fairly
poured down the wall and into town, over rooftops and the
continuation of the wall, which led directly to the twin arches of
the Old Cannon Gate overlooking the square, where at that very

moment the military hierarchy, to the strains of the massed bands, was preparing to pay its respects to its illustrious predecessor, General Sir George Eliott.

With a leap and a bound Scruffy was perched atop the arch and with similar graceful leaps and bounds the pack joined him there. However, the sound of the music and the glitter and colour of the close-packed military, as well as the crowds in the square below, drained all thoughts of battle from Arthur, while Scruffy made the agreeable discovery that the thing which had been pursuing him was not a snake at all; in fact it had practically disappeared. There was still something fizzing, crackling, and smelling from the end of his toy, but it appeared not to be bent upon harming him. For the moment he had it, his wig, and all nine points of the law.

It was the combined murmur and laughter of the crowd and the cry of Gunner Lovejoy, "Gord bless me, it's old Scruff. What's that imp of Satan got 'old of now?" that drew the attention of Mr. Ramirez to the event that was about to take place, not only in his presence but that of the Governor of Gibraltar, his colonial and military staff, the clergy, the laity, and most of the inhabitants.

Lovejoy was not the only one to be appalled at the tableau. Young Captain Bailey stared aghast, not only at the apparition of Scruffy which in the Captain's lexicon could only spell trouble but at the object that Scruffy was nursing. For his trained artillery-man's eye saw at once that it was either a dangerous firework or an even more dangerous dynamite bomb from which depended now no more than a short length of burning fuse which was growing shorter every second.

So horrified was he at what he could only diagnose as the imminent dissolution of the brute upon whom he had expended so much energy and affection that he committed the military crime of stepping out of ranks, leaving his appointed place at the head of his battery and striding forward into the square over which a stunned and shocked silence had fallen as all became aware of what was about to happen. He called up in anguished tones, "Drop it Scruffy! I say drop it, old boy!"

But Scruffy had not the slightest intention of doing so, and besides it was too late. There was only a matter of five seconds

of countdown left for the burning fuse to traverse the last inch
and ignite the thing.

The sputtering flame reached the top of the giant cannon
cracker, hesitated there for a moment, and then dived down into
its innards. For one fraction of a second while Alfonso T. Ramirez
awaited his moment of glory, time seemed to stand still. Thou-
sands of eardrums and nerves quivered in anticipation of the
terrible explosion to come. What then took place, when time
consented once more to move, was in a sense far, far worse than
what had been awaited.

For instead of the gigantic ear-splitting thunderclap expected
by one and all, there was only a kind of soft "thup" as the top of
the blue cardboard cylinder was wafted off, barely missing the
nose of old Scruffy who chittered nervously, but showed no other
signs of relinquishing his prize.

If there was any black powder in the firework which Ramirez
had purchased, it had been limited to an amount just sufficient
to displace the lid of the thing and activate a series of powerful
springs concealed in the interior.

But when the proprietor of the factory had predicted something
of grandeur and nobility, a veritable volcano which would leave
none witnessing its eruption the same as they had been before, he
had not lied. For, following the soft preliminary pop, the thing
began to erupt the most diverse and splendid party favours at an
heroic rate and in more than generous quantities. To the utter
enthrallment of the apes and the equally hysterical joy of the
crowd below, bonbons, paper hats, whistles, hooters, horns, small
toys, coloured handkerchiefs, and everything conceivable in the
line of party delights rained down.

The thing spewed forth clouds of confetti, uncoiled endless
ribbons of coloured paper streamers, and unloaded miniature
parachutes, rubber balloons, gifts in the form of sets of crayons,
celluloid dolls, and small musical instruments.

As far as the people in the street below were concerned, it was
Christmas, and the spectators forthwith broke up in a mad scramble for the seemingly unending shower of goodies that fortune,

personified by the ugly magot perched atop the arch, was pouring forth from his blue cornucopia.

In a moment the square was filled with the braying of party horns, thumping of tin drums, shrilling of whistles, and clamour of toy trumpets. Sweets, biscuits, and further favours were being battled for. The distinguished guests in the reviewing stand were powdered with confetti, their shoulders festooned with coloured streamers.

Atop the gate it was Yule for the Queen's Gate pack as well. A good third of the loot erupting from the cylinder fell into their hands. Paper hats were donned, false noses and moustaches applied, whistles were shrilled, horns were blown or banged, packages of sweets, chocs, and cakes unwrapped and gorged. Arthur, all thought of vengeance or battle driven from his mind, was wearing the paper shako of a Spanish grenadier and clutching two hooters, a doll, a small box of plasticine, and an assortment of stale goodies. He had never been happier.

But the best had been reserved for the last. The slow match which had been releasing all this bounty finally reached the bottom of the case where it ignited a last half teaspoonful of black powder and, with a "plop" hardly louder than the first introductory "thup," propelled into the air a large flag attached to a parachute. The parachute opened, the flag unfurled and showed itself to be the red and yellow ensign of Franco Spain with the rousing slogan "*Viva España*" stencilled across one side and "*Arriba Franco*" on the other. There being no wind the 'chute descended in exactly the same line of the ascent, permitting the flag to drape the shoulders of Scruffy upon whom it lay like the mantle of a Cardinal.

Again faced with a dilemma and not at all liking the thing which had fallen upon his shoulders, Scruffy proceeded to solve it in the manner of no ordinary monkey. In one hand he still clutched the blue cylinder which he had no intention of relinquishing and in the other he still had what everyone in the square below recognized as the famous stolen toupee.

He therefore set the remains of the wig upon his head where it gave him the aspect of an infernal golliwog, and with his free hand he now seized the flag from about his shoulders and waved it, though actually he was shaking it at the crowd in the square, from whom roars of delighted laughter were now ascending. The two slogans, "*Viva España*" on one side and "*Arriba Franco*" on the other, glittered in the afternoon sunlight.

Down in the reviewers' stand the Governor turned icily to his aide and said loudly enough for all to hear, "I don't consider that at all funny."

The atmosphere in the office of Brigadier Gaskell was at one and the same time white-heated fury and cold, glaring, icy anger, and Tim knew that he was for it. Whereas before when the Brigadier had chewed him out over the apes it had been part routine bluster and part the Brigadier enjoying himself letting off steam, this time he was genuinely outraged and angry and therefore spoke in curt, controlled tones that were all the more biting for their restraint.

"Captain Bailey."

"Yes, sir."

"You realise that full responsibility for this disgraceful affair rests upon your shoulders as OIC Apes?"

"Yes, sir."

"Have you any explanation?"

"No, sir. Someone must have been playing a practical joke."

"Brilliant, Captain Bailey. I was able to deduce that myself. Have you any idea who?"

"No, sir."

"There will be an investigation. In the meantime you are no longer Officer in Charge of Apes and if I had my way you would not be officer in charge of anything. You would no longer be an officer at all. I intend to confer with the Judge Advocate to see what charges, if any, can be preferred against you for this humiliating incident. In the meantime you will return to your duties. That is all, Captain Bailey. Dismissed."

"Yes, sir," said Tim numbly and almost by now from habit.

Chapter 10

FELICITY'S RETURN

It didn't take Tim long to find out in army terms what it meant to displease the boss, though in fact the Brigadier was not a vindictive man and had no time to spend hounding a Captain of Artillery. There actually had been no charge which could be brought against Captain Bailey which would stand up in a court-martial, nor had anyone really wanted to investigate what had seemed like a very bad practical joke, for fear of whom it might turn up. Likewise since Scruffy had made off with the container of the firework and it was never seen again there wasn't even an adequate clue upon which to base a probe.

But the fact that the General was furious communicated itself down the ranks and his subordinates took it upon themselves to make things as uncomfortable as possible for young Bailey.

To begin with, Tim found himself ousted from his comfortable quarters and banished to Outer Siberia, which were the stark, unfinished bungalows out near Europa Point where the unmarried Second Lieutenants were housed. Every unpleasant chore and duty that could be visited upon one who was still an officer was handed to him, in addition to his guns, so that he was kept working from seven in the morning until eleven o'clock at night in order to keep up.

Worst of all, it had been made plain to him that he was not welcome anywhere on the upper Rock near the apes' village. A new OIC Apes had been appointed, a young subaltern by the name of Barton, who had come to the Army from civilian life and arrived on the Rock with a recent draft, a pink-cheeked, rabbity young man whom Tim was not even allowed to meet or contact to act as the link in the chain of handing on an office, instructions, and bumph connected therewith.

Apparently the General himself had supplied these instructions and from what Lovejoy had been able to tell Tim in a brief encounter on the library steps they had been short and to the point.

"'E seemed very put out, the young subaltern did," Lovejoy confided to Tim, "and said I was to carry on and look after them as before and not to worry if I didn't see much of him. Ha, ha," Lovejoy laughed, "see much of him! That's a good one. Not 'ide nor 'air nor so much as a shadow you might say, sir. I gather the Brigadier told him if he ever 'eard of him going near the apes he'd 'ave his scalp off. He wasn't even to be seen talking to me beyond getting a monthly report, and as for talking to you, sir——" Lovejoy suddenly looked around to see if anyone was near by.

"I know, I know," Tim had said hastily. "Unclean! I'm contagious."

"I'm sorry, sir," Lovejoy said, "but you know how it is. They'll miss you terribly. I'll do me best for 'em, but it's best to lay low while the 'eat is on, don't you think so?"

"That's it, Lovejoy," Tim had said. "If they take you off as well, I don't know what will happen to the poor creatures. We'd best not be seen speaking together any more. Good luck and look after them, Gunner." The Gunner watched the Captain hurrying off and felt curiously choked, even though life was to be happily unsupervised from there on. It had been a pleasure to work with a man like Bailey.

If one lives for a long time in a doghouse one becomes eventually doghouse-minded. One tends to see all life as through the small, low-down archway of the kennel, and by the time he had news of Felicity's imminent arrival Tim had all but managed to convince himself that he had lost out on this front as well.

The wall of the grey transport helped by the tugs pushing against her port side loomed massively over the dock, closing the gap of open water. Her rails were lined with troops of every kind, and topside in their dark blue uniform and circular or tricorn hats was a group of some twenty WRENS. Standing on the pier below in the crowd, Tim Bailey gazed upward, looking for Felicity amongst them, and failed to find her.

He felt a momentary stab of panic. Had he then so completely forgotten what she looked like? He brought into the focus of his mind the framed photograph of her he had on his desk, the rather plain-looking, stoutish girl with the round chubby face, merry quizzical eyes, and gentle, kind expression. It had never been her looks so to speak, but the entity, the wholeness of her, the girl within, who blended with her exterior, that had penetrated and reached to his heart.

Without realising it, Tim had fallen victim to that mischief inevitably worked by a long separation where affection and desire have not yet changed into the love and familiarity of mind and body that come with intimacy.

Felicity was a framed picture, a mop of unruly hair surmounting the black and white contrast by which a photograph defines a face. She was a particular kind of bubbling laugh, a manner of walking, ways and tricks of speaking, and the memory of a soft, yielding mouth and kisses in the shadow of the wisteria-covered trellis of the Mount. And all this had begun increasingly to fade, had become more and more difficult to recall, until sometimes Tim would spend a morning trying to recapture a sound, an image, a look, and pinion once more who and what it was he loved.

Thus it was with all kinds of doubts, anxieties, and trepidations that Tim found himself on the dock that morning, fearful of not seeing Felicity, equally fearful of seeing her.

What would she be like? Would she still remember him? Would she want to see him? Or would her brief romance with an unknown and penniless artillery officer be a burden and an embarrassment to her? She was almost two years older now and in that time must have encountered dozens of men more attractive, important, and eligible than he.

True she had written him that she had succeeded in being posted to Gibraltar in command of the detachment of WRENS being sent out to lighten some of the load in the Navy Yard, but under the restrictions of censorship she had not been able to write exactly when she would be arriving on the Rock, or by what means, but only that it would be soon. It had been rather an impersonal and diffident letter, Tim felt, and never guessed that she was suffering from the same doubts and qualms resulting from the erosions of time.

She didn't wish to tie him to the memory of an instant. She was aware that he was a bachelor officer in wartime and that although the women had been evacuated from the Rock there was no dearth of them crossing the line each day and returning at night. Tim well could have found someone far more attractive than she.

The grapevine had it that when next the Transport "Dart" docked she would have a contingent of WRENS aboard. Hence Tim's presence to meet it. Yet he didn't make himself conspicuous upon the pier, but hung back on the fringe at the far side.

No Felicity it seemed. Tim raised his field glasses again and swept the row of girls lining the rail at the centre of the boat deck. Faces under tricorn hats, faces under little funny round sailor caps. There were two stunners amongst them, a small girl with dark, glossy hair and sombre, smouldering kind of looks, and a slender blonde with beautifully chiselled features and exquisite complexion. Her hair was lemon-gold in colour, burnished and gleaming from beneath her hat. They were both rare types and Tim thought with a half smile of the chaos they would create on the Rock. Each had a naval officer on one side and an army officer on the other. The naval officer attending the blonde had the gold leaf of a Commander on his cap and was being solicitous and attentive. Tim half smiled to himself; the chap looked like a man in love. That kind of beauty frightened Tim. He had never pursued it. It made him feel inadequate. Once more he swept the ranks of the twenty or so WRENS, looking for Felicity.

There then occurred one of those strange and dramatic silences which are so often encountered during a docking, when for no known reason all sound and cries suddenly die away. One can hear the rushing of water from one of the bilge holes in the side, the chuffing of the pushing tugs, and the ring of the engine-room telegraph from the bridge. This silence was shattered by Felicity's laugh.

Unmistakably the bubbling, pealing laughter came from Felicity, and it at once evoked her living, vibrant, desirable, as she always had been in Tim's mind.

Once more with eagerness he turned his glasses topside. He heard the laugh again; he was focused upon the slender, petite, exquisite blonde next to the tall, handsome Commander. Felicity's laugh was coming from her throat. And then Tim saw that it *was* Felicity.

Felicity! But how changed! And not *his* Felicity, this ravishing beauty. It was a Felicity thinned down by hard work and discipline, her hair groomed and shining. But the greatest change had taken place in her features, which had been marred, or rather disguised by the baby fat about which she had never bothered. It had melted away to leave a classic loveliness, finely sculptured nose and lips, and a movingly enchanting line of jaw sweeping from ear to chin.

And now that Tim stared and stared he saw what had always been most surely there, buried beneath the chubbiness, and it terrified him. It set his heart to beating and filled him with a thousand fears and sadnesses and the certainty that this glorious creature was no longer for him. Already she belonged to the tall Commander at her side with whom she was in laughing unison. Something within Tim told him that such a beauty occurred only once or twice in a generation, and by its very uniqueness made the wearer a child of destiny.

He held her in the round field of his glasses and for a moment found himself looking directly into her eyes, those same frank, sweet eyes, but now seemingly enhanced a thousand times, and for an instant he was panic-stricken that she might see and recognise him, not realising that the glasses were hiding his face. Yes, Felicity had returned, but no longer his Felicity. She was lost to him forever. He turned and fled into the shadows of the shed and thence out into the street where he climbed into his car and raced off blindly to nowhere as though the furies were after him.

Felicity's immediate disappointment at Tim's failure to meet

her was mitigated by her thought that in the first place she had
not been able to let him know the date and time of her arrival,
and in the second, he had probably drawn duty at that hour and
had no way of letting her know.

Too, she realised that she had steeled herself to expect it. It
was the simplest way for a man to say, "I hope you didn't take
our little instant of several years ago seriously."

Immediately upon her arrival she found herself overwhelmed
with details and problems connected with the department in her
charge. Nothing, of course, was as it should be. The quarters
provided were inhospitable and unsanitary, kitchen arrangements
inadequate, orders confused, and there was plenty to do to occupy
the time and patience of WREN Second Officer Commanding,
Felicity French. It was a week before her head was above water
sufficiently to realise that that amount of time had passed and
she had neither seen nor heard from Tim. She herself had received
permission to quarter at the Mount, even though it had mostly
been turned into sets of offices, and she had her old room.

What saddened Felicity almost as much as the loss of the man
she had thought she loved was his neglect of his manners. For
surely by that time Tim would have heard of her arrival. There
wasn't a man in Gibraltar who didn't know by then that twenty
females, to be permanently stationed amongst them, had arrived
on the Rock. It would have been more kind and less cowardly
and rude if he had sent around a note or telephoned an amicable
coup de grâce to say, "Heard you were back. Frightfully busy. We
must have lunch some time."

Once Felicity had queried her father as to whether he had
ever seen or heard from Captain Bailey—she had thought perhaps
a message or a letter from him had gone astray—causing the
Admiral to go back so far in his memory for a reply that he was
forced to query, "Eh? Who?" and then as he remembered finally,
"Haven't laid eyes on the fellow." Then he asked his daughter
anxiously, "That's not still on, is it? I thought your mother
wrote me——"

"It was a long time ago, wasn't it?" was all that Felicity had
replied, to which the Admiral had given vent to a great and

audible exhalation of relief while mumbling audibly: "Whew, I'm glad that's over and done with," then adding, "you'll have enough to keep you busy here."

Once in a moment of weakness, loneliness, and longing she had picked up the receiver of the telephone and dialled the number of Tim's quarters one evening. A strange voice had replied, "Captain Ducrow speaking," and Felicity had hung up. He was no longer in his old quarters. Perhaps he was not even on the Rock any more. She laid hold of the service telephone directory with a gesture that was almost savage and thumbed through it. Well he *was* on the Rock still. There it was, "Captain Timothy Bailey, R.A. office. First Battalion H.Q., Tel: 134, Home Catchment Road, Europa Point Barracks, Tel. 84–972." But she didn't pick up the telephone again; she only sat looking at the name and thinking. What she knew she had dreaded was that she might have found him in the married barracks. But what was strange was that he should have been moved out to Catchment Road. This was the Sahara as far as quarters were concerned, where young Lieutenants were parked until they had gained some seniority, experience, and rank.

She thought she was over it; she put Tim out of her mind; she no longer raised her head and listened when the telephone in the Mount rang. The arrival of the WRENS had resparked a fraction of social life on the Rock, at least amongst the Navy. Yet quite unaccountably one afternoon Felicity found herself in her car, headed out of town and up the road past the ruins of the Moorish castle, then sharply around the bend, climbing along the face of the cliff on the familiar road that led to St. Michael's Hut and the place known as the village of the apes.

She didn't know why she was going; she didn't care. She simply drove. Perhaps Gunner Lovejoy would be there. She had not seen him either since her return. This, however, was not surprising, for even in such a minute area as Gibraltar, intermingling of the services occurred only at top levels when the brass met to see how they could do one another down. The lower echelons of the Navy, the Army, and the Air Force circulated in their own orbits without ever making contact.

What Felicity found where the apes' village had been just before
the ruins of the emplacement of Prince Ferdinand's Battery surprised and shocked her. Lovejoy was not there. Nor was anyone
else. And furthermore the place was filthy with scraps of foul and
rotting carrots and lettuce, ordure, dirty bits of dried-up orange
skins, pieces of sodden and mouldy bread, and remnants of other
food that had become unrecognizable to the sight and offensive
to the nostrils. Heretofore the place where the apes fed was kept
scrupulously clean by Lovejoy, nor had Tim been above taking a
hand. All left-overs remaining after the apes had had their fill were
swept up and disposed of in a dustbin and carted away.

Felicity heard a sound between a cough, a squeak and a wheeze.
It came from a dog ape, a young male macaque curled up in a
tree. She parked her car, got out, and went to the thorn tree and
looked to see if it was someone she knew. The ape regarded her
with apathy, pulling back its lips to bare its canines. It wheezed
and coughed again. Felicity knew enough about apes to know a
sick one when she saw it. Someone ought to be looking after it.
No one was.

A loose pebble rolled and she heard a scuffling sound and
turned in time to see a full-grown female gliding along at the
side of the road. She was carrying an apelet in her arms, but it
was dead. When she had got past Felicity, the girl saw the dark
stain of clotted blood behind the left ear of the female or rather
where the left ear should have been. She felt suddenly as though
she wanted to weep.

Uncertain of herself, thoroughly put out, miserable, Felicity
walked somewhat further up the road to the place where she had
first come upon Captain Timothy Bailey of His Majesty's Royal
Artillery and Officer in Charge of Apes. This was the small, curved
and railed-in concreted enclosure which jutted out slightly over the
cliff, looking out over the port and the sea, and there she saw a
familiar figure which made her heart leap.

"Scruffy," cried Felicity. "Oh dear, dear, Scruffy."

The old boy had been sitting there scratching himself and
reflecting. He was bored; he was hungry, and he was out of sorts.
He was permanently out of sorts these days and resenting the

changed world in which there were no longer tourists who brought him goodies to eat and cameras and field glasses to throw over the cliff; where cars no longer parked, enabling one to remove the windscreen wipers and chew the rubber off them; where visits to town no longer paid off in either entertainment or illicit nourishment, and where his eardrums were in permanent pain from bangs and explosions of one kind or another.

Scruffy recognised Felicity at once, whether from voice or smell or because he was a bit sharper than Captain Bailey was beside the point. His amber eyes lit up, his black lips were drawn back from his yellow teeth, and he leaped up and down and coughed and barked and scolded her.

The tears were now so close to Felicity's eyes that the big macaque looked almost beautiful.

"Oh Scruffy, dear," she cried, "how good it is to see *someone*." And from force of habit she put her hand into her pocket to see what was there, and found a chocolate bonbon wrapped in silver paper.

She unwrapped it slowly and as she did so Scruffy came forward. The memory tubes and transistors of his own computer system had this situation taped and Felicity labelled as The Girl Who Always Had Something.

"Come, my darling," crooned Felicity and held out the bonbon.

Scruffy sidled over mostly on his behind and reached with his firm, black leathery hands. With one he clutched Felicity's wrist and the other took the praline. He smelled the sweet and, for a second, a look of blissful anticipation crossed his otherwise grumpy features. This was more like it. On the other hand there was no reason to exclude the amenities. He therefore pulled Felicity's wrist toward him and bit her severely in the thumb, then skipped away eight paces, clutching his comfit and leaping up and down, coughing and railing at her. Felicity let out a scream of pain followed by four orthodox naval curses and one that she made up herself on the spur of the moment.

And at that instant she found herself possessed of a savage and unreasoning rage against Captain Timothy A. Bailey. It was as though Tim had bitten her. The blood spurted from two deep gashes, one on top, the other on the bottom of the fleshy part of her thumb, but no more freely than the hot tears of anger that came welling from her eyes. Everything that had happened, or had not happened, since her return combined to fuse into one petrol-soaked knot of fury. Scruffy's bite had now set it alight and flaming.

Unmindful of the gore dripping from her wound on to her uniform she ran to her car, climbed in, crashed the gears into place, and went rocketing down the mountain, half crying, half muttering phrases to herself in which things and allusions uncomplimentary were coupled with the name of Timothy Bailey.

She careered through the town taking corners on two wheels, frightening dogs and civilians, zoomed down Main Street, charged through the Southport Gates and up past the Rock Hotel, breaking all speed laws in her haste to reach her destination before the heat of the fire which had been kindled should diminish by so much as a single calorie. She wrenched the car off Engineer Road into Europa Road towards the point so that the tyres squealed, hurtled onwards into the bare, tatty area of the barracks, and caught the sign indicating Catchment Road. Her glance peeled off the names over the doors outside the barracks until she glimpsed that of Captain Bailey. She stopped the car which gave vent to an agonized cry of tortured brakes and metal, coupled with the growl and crunch of displaced gravel.

The screen door was closed but the inner door to Captain Bailey's quarters was open. There was a small lamp burning inside and the Captain was seated at his desk in his shirt sleeves. Before he had time to do more than look up from the papers on which he had been working, there were two loud, practically simultaneous bangs as Felicity slammed first her car door and then the screen door behind her.

She roared up to the desk and the astonished Captain, thrust her thumb, still leaking her life's blood, in front of his nose and cried, "Your damn bloody monkey bit me."

Tim arose, knocking over his chair. "Oh my God," he said, "Felicity!" Then he said, "But he's not mine any more," and with a note of despair and pathos that reached right to Felicity's heart, "Felicity, I'm no longer OIC Apes. I'm nothing at all."

"Tim, oh my dear, darling Tim," Felicity wailed. "What have they done to you?" For she recognised something of a broken man. Also she was no longer angry with him, for over his shoulder, on his desk, was the framed photograph of herself, or at least of the person she seemed once to have been.

A large bright red drop of blood fell with an audible splash on to the company report on which Tim had been working and spread out blot-shaped.

"Felicity!"

"Tim, dear Tim!"

They were so close now in one another's arms that they no longer needed to shout, or even to speak, but could whisper their names and terms of endearment into one another's ears.

"Tim, why didn't you meet me?"

"I did."

"What happened?"

"I was frightened, I ran away."

"Why?"

"You were too beautiful! I couldn't bear it. I was afraid! I'm afraid now."

They separated for a moment and looked at one another.

"Don't you know what has happened to you?" Tim asked. "Look." He pointed to a mirror. "Can't you see, it's almost blinding?"

It was enough to make any woman exult, but strangely Felicity felt more like crying at the moment. "Do you mean to say," she said indicating the photograph, "that you like her more than me? I did it all for you."

Young Captain Bailey looked from the fat girl in the picture to the goddess by his side and at that moment had no answer for her, so storm tossed were his emotions.

"I'll cross my eyes," Felicity wailed and proceeded to do so, "I'll cut my hair and stuff pillows in my bosom until I can fatten up for you again. I'll do anything you ask, Tim, if it will make you happier."

Afterwards Tim said that it was as though a light shining down from heaven had pierced him with the joyous and everlasting revelation that his adored and chubby girl was still there. She had changed her outer appearance and he supposed eventually he would get used to it and be able to regard her without the aid of dark glasses, but within she was still Felicity, funny, droll, dear, kindly, tender Felicity.

He went to pieces then again over his love for her, the hurt she had suffered which he had inflicted, the wound that was bleeding, and the resolving of the pain that he himself had experienced.

They were both covered with her blood by this time and when he had bandaged her and they had tidied themselves and she had announced that having compromised him by practically assaulting him in his quarters they would have to be married at once, he told her of what had happened to him since she had left and of the events leading to his disgrace and sacking.

"Darling," he said, "I can't let you. I've been dropped so many numbers I'll be a Captain until I'm forty. I've been banished to these quarters. If the C.O. could have knocked a pip off my shoulder he would have done so. I can't drag you down."

Felicity sat on the edge of the table. Her now long, fine-spun hair was gathered in a bun at the back of her head. Trojan Helen had never looked more beautiful. She said, "You love me, don't you, Tim?"

Tim replied, "Oh my God."

"Well," said Felicity firmly, "that's where we start from."

The wartime marriage of Tim and Felicity was a quiet affair conducted in the chapel in the presence of the Admiral, Tim's best man, and a few friends, and Gunner Lovejoy slipping into the rear of the church at the last moment.

Denied the support of his wife who was back in England and faced with a determined Felicity, the Admiral had not had sufficient stamina to continue his objections, even though he was aware that in the interim his son-in-law had not made himself any more desirable. However, the young people had survived a long separation and since Felicity was insistent the Admiral put

the best face he could upon the matter, and the modest celebration of the union took place.

There was no leave granted for a honeymoon. When Tim
applied for it, his application was turned down. The doghouse
was still operating as far as the Army was concerned, except now
they were to occupy a kennel built for two, for the married
quarters assigned to them were the shabbiest and most run-down
located in Outer Siberia. This, it should be added, was not at all
the doing of the Brigadier who was no longer even aware of the
fact of Captain Bailey's existence beyond his satisfactory performance of his duties with his guns. The General had other
worries as had been noted. The vindictiveness was simply that
continuation of the status quo. Captain Bailey had been declared
beyond the pale and would be maintained there until someone
higher up ordered him out of limbo.

None of this affected Felicity whatsoever. She simply moved in
with her husband. The honeymoon, a doubtful blessing, was
not missed, for they discovered very quickly how genuinely lucky
they had been to choose one another, as they now proceeded to
fall violently and passionately in love in quite a different way than
they had ever dreamed possible.

At first Timothy was harrowed by the depressing bungalow in
the tatty and unimproved neighbourhood down near Europa
Point, but Felicity soon cured him of that. She was a comfortable
girl, sensible and agreeable with no false notions about being
owed anything by life. As far as that went, she felt overpaid, for
she had acquired all for herself the one man who had touched
her deeply and permanently.

In her spare time she set about making their home as cheerful
as possible, with plaster walls peeling and cracking from the damp-
ness, bed sheets that were never quite dry, Government furniture
that was ugly and insufficient, and the garden patch where nothing
would grow because they were allowed no water for such purposes. Undaunted, Felicity bought artificial flowers and set them
out in the garden patch, where their colour cheered the entire
neighbourhood, at least until the first rainstorm undid them.

When Tim saw Felicity giggling at the wreckage, he loved her more than ever and no longer worried about her.

There too was enjoyed their first and practically last quarrel, the issue of which was unimportant, the main point being that they had no more than really warmed up to a tempestuous exchange of amenities and personalities when suddenly and simultaneously they recognised the absurdity of the proceedings, called it a draw, and began to shout with laughter.

Thus they were off to a more than auspicious start to a slightly less than humdrum life of a married service couple when Gunner Lovejoy decided to change the formula of his usual drink at the Admiral Nelson and thereby altered the lives of a great number of people.

Chapter 11

MR. RAMIREZ WRITES A LETTER

"'Alf me apes dead or dying from malnutrition and diseases resulting from privations due to same and no one to turn to. That's what's got me down. It's enough to drive a man to drink!" And so saying Gunner John Lovejoy, to emphasise the last point, took a large swallow of the drink he had been driven to. In this instance a variation of his usual tipple was in some ways a fatal one. He was accustomed and conditioned to his own invented combination, Guinness laced with a dash of lime juice, but upon this occasion and due no doubt to the anguish collected in his soul, he was substituting Málaga wine for the lime juice.

The Gunner was holding forth in the Admiral Nelson before a mixed audience consisting of several of his artillery pals, two sailors from a destroyer undergoing repairs at the Navy Yard, some civilians from the town, and Alfonso T. Ramirez.

Ramirez was always eager and willing to stand treat, and if the Gunner had given any thought to the matter he would have felt certain that the incident of the stolen wig had been forgotten. In this, however, he would have been wrong. Ramirez was merely biding his time.

"If they want apes let them have apes," the Gunner said, "and if they don't want them let them shoot the beggars and have done with it. But don't let the creatures starve to death and die off piecemeal before me very eyes, that's looked after them the past twenty years. It's more'n flesh and blood can stand."

All the listeners made sympathetic noises and shuffled their feet and hoped for more, for this was fine talk to be listening to while drinking, containing as it did elements of news, story, sentiment, and emotion.

The Gunner himself lifted up his dark glass and drank deeply.

The acids of the Málaga joined hands with the esters of Lord Iveagh's Guinness and mounting airily to his head they further unloosed his tongue to permit him to pour forth details of the tragedy that was being enacted before his eyes.

"'Ow would you like to see your personal friends carried off one after the other? Seems like every time I go up there these days I'm trippin' over the corpse of one of me pals. You've all 'eard tell, 'aven't you, how them apes are supposed to disappear when they die and not a flippin' sign of 'em? Well, that's a lot of malarky, too. Last week it was Tess rolled up in a ball with her stummick all swole out like she's swallered a balloon. This morning it was Mona. I showed 'em to a medic friend of mine. 'Colic,' he says, 'from eating unripe fruit. I've seen babies like that only babies can get rid of it; monkeys can't.' Like me own daughters they were, Mona and Tess. Brought 'em up practically by hand as you might say, when their mothers was killed. Fed 'em with a medicine dropper and then out of a bottle. Cried like a baby I did when I met Captain Tim in town today and told him. That's Captain Bailey who used to be OIC Apes, and a proper one, too. I thought 'e was about to bawl same as me. He was there when they was born. Very fond 'e was of their mothers and them, too. It was a black day for the hapes when Captain Bailey was sacked and that's a fact, and they put in that yellow belly as doesn't dare show the flag or stick up for the poor brutes for fear of blotting 'is copybook."

"I buy another drink," said Alfonso T. Ramirez. "Another drink all round." All of the men at the bar stirred approvingly.

"That's big-hearted of you, chum," conceded the Gunner, "I could do with another." The barman set them up. Ramirez paid.

The Gunner took a long, deep draught. "And Scruffy on the rampage and doing in old Arthur. He was bound to kill him sooner or later, they two never getting on. But it seemed like he knowed we couldn't afford to lose no hapes and done it a-purpose. And me not able to use the balloons on him to stop it."

One of the sailors asked the question that Ramirez was popping to put in. "Balloons? Did I 'ear yer say balloons?"

"You did that," replied the Gunner, and fishing into his

pocket brought out a small red rubber toy balloon, the stem
of which he set to his lips. Taking a deep breath he began to blow.
The balloon filling with the mixed fumes of Málaga and Guinness
swelled out to enormous size, distending beyond its capacity,
and blew up with an appalling bang.

"There you are," the Gunner said, "that's 'ow it's done. It's the
only way to control old Scruff. Terrifies him. Like a lamb 'e is
when the balloon goes up. But what good is it now, I ask? When
I come upon Scruff and Arthur he'd got his tusks in Arthur's
throat and his 'ead nearly tore off——"

Ramirez asked, "Why you not blow?"

The Gunner regarded him with contempt. "Asked like a
hamateur," he said. "What, and kill 'em both? Ain't I just told
you the hapes are nervous wrecks from all the shooting? That's
what got into old Scruff there, all the banging and blasting. He
couldn't stand no noise. If I gave 'im a balloon like as not he
could have died on me 'ands, and then where would we have
been?" He looked around for an answer but collected no more
than some sympathetic shakes of the head until Ramirez said,
"You have a difficult job, Gunner. I buy another drink."

The Gunner regarded Ramirez now with benevolence. "Man-
nie," he said, "you've hit upon me needs. So with Arthur dying
of 'aving no 'ead, that puts the Queen's Gate pack down below
'arf."

Ramirez in the act of paying for his investment turned and
asked, "Did you say half, Gunner?"

"You count 'em," replied the Gunner. "There used to be twenty-
six in the Queen's Gate pack. Who's left now? There's old Scruff,
Pat and Tony, Ronnie and Millie, Kathleen, Sally, Judy, and
three hapelets that don't look like they'd last more'n a couple of
days. And it's the same with the Middle Hill bunch. They get
the worst of it when there's shooting; they can't stand noise and
they just quietly gets a nervous breakdown and dies." The
Gunner now looked around at his once more enthralled audience
and queried, "And what am I to do? Knock on the brass's door
and say, 'Brigadier, your bleeding hapes are dying off and unless
you call off that babu you've put in as OIC Apes there won't be

none left?' Not me, chums, I got seven days and another seven from that half-wit Lieutenant for laying me hands on a bit of extra rations for me friends, a couple of lettuces and some mouldy carrots and bread. And who put 'im in there with hinstructions to do same? The Brigadier."

And the Gunner now well lubricated had a further question to ask of his audience. "What's to happen if the whole blooming lot dies out? What's the Rock going to be like without apes? What 'appens to me job? And what about where it tells what's to become of us British when there's no more apes here? Kicked off the Rock, that's what the Spanish say. Who am I to say that it can't happen? Or you, or you?"

Those singled out by this direct question shook their heads in lugubrious assent.

"If the brass ain't thinking about it, I am," asserted the Gunner. "A legend they calls it, but what's the use of having a legend if yer don't live by it? I've given me life to raising and looking after their ruddy apes and there they all are sending it down the drain."

The Gunner's mind suddenly took them back to the morning's tragedy. "Like a daughter she was to me, was Mona. There she was curled up in a thorn tree, her belly blown up like someone took a bicycle pump to her. Her little face looked that natural, I cried like a baby." The tears once more rolled down the seams and furrows of the Gunner's leathery face.

One of the artillerymen put his arm around the Gunner's shoulder and said, "Don't take it so 'ard, pal, there must be plenty more where they came from."

One of the sailors said, "That's tough, chum," and the other one agreed, "Yeah, that's tough."

Alfonso T. Ramirez drained his glass of beer and set it back upon the bar soundlessly. He stood there regarding it for a moment and then as quietly left. No one saw him go, or would have cared if they had, which was an error. For Mr. Ramirez had been struck with an idea and he was hastening home as quickly as he could to seek the privacy of his four walls and have it out to look at.

The fact that he wished to be in his room with the door securely locked before entertaining the thought which had invaded his mind in the Admiral Nelson was the measure of the courage of Mr. Ramirez, or rather total lack of it. He was a physical and moral coward, fearing death, pain, disgrace, punishment, all of the deterrents against wrongdoing, yet at the same time he enjoyed the greatest fantasies and illusions of grandeur and derring-do.

In his secret soul he was a dedicated Nazi and potential traitor by virtue of his hatred of the British, fanned by such unfortunate incidents as have been noted. In his mind's eye he saw the Knight's Cross being pinned on his breast by Hitler himself for some glorious and definitive exploit such as blowing up the ammunition dump at Gibraltar; sabotaging the water supply; discovering and giving away the secret pathway up which, should war be declared, the Germans could enter and overwhelm the Rock.

That same imagination, however, was equally capable of projecting another film upon the same screen, showing Alfonso T. Ramirez poised on the trap door with a rope around his neck, or with his back to a wall facing a British firing squad for espionage or treason during wartime. So terrifying were these rushes that Ramirez didn't so much as dare to fiddle with a prism in the optical shop of the Navy Yard where he worked. But ever since the declaration of war, burning with resentment against the British, he had been nursing the ambition to have some small share in the eventual triumph of the master race, to perform some deed or exploit which would aid in the downfall of the English.

There was a German Consulate in Algeciras, overstaffed to the point of absurdity, and everyone in Gibraltar knew that this was the operating base of the German Gestapo and Intelligence Service, and it was known as well that there must unquestionably be spies amongst the workmen who crossed the line every day. At one time Ramirez had entertained the idea of nipping across the border to that same German Consulate and offering his services, his value being that he had access to at least one sensitive spot in the scheme of British operations and defence, namely the Navy Yard.

His cowardice and his shrewdness had combined to prevent

him from carrying out any project so rash. For he was clever enough to know that if a spy can be rewarded, he can also be blackmailed by his masters, and once committed can be ordered or compelled to undertake all kinds of hazardous operations. He saw himself being required to steal plans, plant bombs, even collaborate perhaps in assassinations. He had no stomach for any of this. He was terrified of weapons and even more fearful of being caught.

And now the idea which had presented itself to him appeared to be foolproof on all counts, and effective as well. Nevertheless he examined it first carefully from all angles.

It was that he would nominate himself as a secret spy and saboteur for the Third Reich. No one would ever know it but himself. He would inflict serious damage upon the British position in Gibraltar by dealing a heavy blow to their morale, and one which might well lead, or certainly contribute in the end, to the loss of the position.

Gunner Lovejoy had said that the reason for the careful maintenance of the ape packs on the Rock by the Army was because of their being coupled with the legend and superstition that if ever the apes should leave Gibraltar the British would be driven from the Rock. If the Germans could be appraised that attrition had begun in the ape pack and that it had been reduced by half, they could use it for propaganda purposes and stir up unrest and discontent amongst both the civilian and military population of this key bastion, an unrest which might lead to fear, panic, and eventually defeat. History was full of instances where battles had been won or lost, or the tide of events turned by omens, superstition, or unreasoning fear induced by religious beliefs.

How to transmit this information without endangering his own watertight security as a loyal Gibraltarian permitted access to naval secrets or destroying his own incognito? The answer was simple. An anonymous letter. There wasn't even any danger of such a document being found upon his person since he would not write it until he was safely on Spanish soil. There were no restrictions confining the civilian population of Gibraltar to the Rock. Equipped with proper passes and identification, they could cross over into Spain as they wished, provided they returned before the border was closed at night. He had only then, some Sunday when it was customary for Gibraltarians to wish to leave the confines of their narrow community for a bit of leg-stretching in the country, to cross over, write his letter either in La Línea or Algeciras, post it, and return. There was no possible way it could be traced to him.

Ramirez hugged to himself the perfection of his scheme. He determined to put it into effect at once.

Had Dr. Hans Hott, the German Consul at Algeciras, been the genuine article he might have dropped the anonymous letter he had just read into the wastepaper basket as another example of the crank mail that passes over every diplomat's desk. He was, however, not a Consul at all, but a highly educated and intelligent member of the German espionage system. He therefore perused the letter a second time, more carefully. It read as follows in printed letters:

DR. HANS HOTT, GERMAN CONSULATE, ALGECIRAS.
HEIL HITLER:
SOMETHING YOU SHOULD KNOW. THE APES ON THE ROCK ARE DYING. ONLY HALF ARE LEFT. YOU SHOULD MAKE THIS PUBLIC. THE BRITISH BELIEVE IF THE APES DIE OFF FROM THE ROCK THEY WILL BE DEFEATED AND HAVE TO GO. THERE ARE ONLY THIRTEEN LEFT OF THE QUEEN'S GATE PACK AND TWELVE OF THE MIDDLE HILL. IF I HAVE ANY FURTHER NEWS I WILL WRITE AGAIN. YOU MAY TRUST ME. I AM OF THE BLOOD. HEIL HITLER.

The German smiled to himself. Obviously the contents of the letter were to be trusted, and likewise could be easily checked. He wondered why no one had made use of this before, and it struck him quite simply that probably no one had thought of it. It was small, seemingly unimportant items such as these that sometimes could be pyramided into great results. He reached for the telephone to put the machinery in motion.

Gloomy Gustave came on from the German broadcasting station somewhere in Spain immediately after the six o'clock news.

Most of Gibraltar listened to him, the British for laughs or the cathartic effect of his irritating voice upon their livers and systems, and the Gibraltarians from their not too ill-founded suspicions that they might not be getting all the news from the British side. Gloomy Gustave spoke in English in a voice that was oiled and buttered with self-satisfaction, righteousness, and doom. His accent was that of the German who has learned English but never mastered it, and its perfection was a further irritant to which the listeners on the Rock looked forward each evening with some enjoyment.

However, the broadcast of Gloomy Gustave made a few days after the anonymous letter had arrived at the desk of Consul Hott brought neither pleasure nor entertainment to the auditors as the greasy voice emerged from their wireless sets.

"Are the days of the British on Gibraltar numbered? Are all you Gibraltarians now groaning under the lash of the perfidious English soon to be free of the imperialist tyrant? If the deaths that have recently occurred amongst the Barbary apes of Gibraltar may be taken as a sign, that day is not far off."

In their quarters where Felicity was clattering in the kitchen and Tim sipping the thimbleful of gin and Italian that was his nightly ration, the Captain, who had been only half listening, brought his head up with a snap and called, "Hoy love! Hold it for a sec! You'd better come out and hear this."

In his office Major McPherson, who listened nightly with ears of an Intelligence officer, got up from his desk and went over and stood in front of his wireless set to be sure to miss nothing.

In the Admiral Nelson, Alfonso Treugang Ramirez was conscious for a moment of a million butterflies struggling within his stomach and a feeling of sudden panic that the next moment the police or security forces would come bursting in through the door and lay violent hands upon him. Lovejoy, who had pricked up his ears at the word apes, had not yet connected it with the wireless box and was looking about him as though someone there in the bar had mentioned it.

And in far-off London Major Clyde, the Intelligence officer charged with over-all responsibility for Gibraltar and Malta and who listened nightly to the German broadcasts from the monitoring room of the BBC, frowned and settled the earphones of his head set more securely.

Gustave continued: "As is well known on Gibraltar, a legend that when the last of the Barbary apes leaves the Rock the British will be driven from Gibraltar is based upon more than mere superstition, and the British have maintained these monkeys at considerable expense to avoid the fulfillment of this prophecy, even going so far as to appoint an officer of the Royal Artillery to look after their welfare. The British will, of course, deny this, but it can now be revealed that in recent weeks the number of both the ape packs has been reduced by half. There are only thirteen left in the famous Queen's Gate pack and the Middle Hill group is down to twelve. The German and Italian air and naval blockade of Gibraltar has been successful and many of the apes have succumbed to malnutrition and exposure to diseases resulting from the fact that there is insufficient food.

"At this rate it will not be long before there will be no more apes remaining and freedom-loving Gibraltarians will rejoice with their Spanish brothers that the oppression of British rule is drawing to an end."

Captain Timothy Bailey swore helplessly in front of his wireless set. "That's exactly what I was working to prevent! Oh damn their stupidity."

Felicity looked anxiously from the set to her husband as Gustave turned to his nightly crowing about German successes. "But do you suppose it's true, Tim?" she asked.

"I'm afraid so. I met Lovejoy in town the other day. He was blubbering. He'd just lost Mona and Tess. Damn near had me going, too. Do you remember them?"

"The sweet ones that we used to cuddle?" Felicity asked. She looked at her husband with sudden sympathy and cried, "Oh dear Tim, is this awful for you? You had tried so hard."

He looked down at her, as always with fresh enchantment at her warmth and understanding. "It will be damned awkward if it goes on," he replied. "I wonder what McPherson is thinking?"

What Major McPherson was thinking standing in front of his

set in his office was not printable. Out of the blue a new and serious Intelligence burden had been landed upon his shoulders. In the first place swamped by security problems, most of them unsolvable, he had given no thought to the apes for months, had not yet known of their situation. And in the second even had he known, it would not have dawned upon him that the Germans could so quickly turn this information into a damaging and dangerous bit of propaganda. In so confined a community as the Rock, spirit and morale, although intangible, were nevertheless as vulnerable and perilous as the high explosives in the magazines.

In the pub Gunner Lovejoy stared at the old, battered wireless box over the bar with an expression of mingled surprise and distaste upon his leathery countenance. "Gord!" he exclaimed, "the Barstids. How ever did that blighter find that out?"

Ramirez, his momentary panic dispelled and secure that no one would ever penetrate his dark secret, said, "That's terrible for you, Gunner. Can I buy another beer?"

In London Major Clyde had returned to his office and was re-reading a transcript of the broadcast and pulling at his lower lip. Like Captain Bailey's, his mind was projecting itself to the future, except more quickly and subtly, with more corners cut. He also travelled further along the paths of imagination by which some men are able to chart catastrophe and breakdown, starting with no more than a single grain of sand introduced into the machinery.

He, in his turn, picked up the telephone. The number he called was a very private one and the person who answered most highly placed. The Major spoke to him using his first name, which was surprising for a mere Major, but less so considering the weight he pulled and the respect in which he was held.

"So I think I'd better get out there, John, don't you?" Major Clyde concluded.

"Yes I do, I quite agree with you."

"Will you authorise what is necessary?"

"Yes. See Peter about the flight out. Do you want the P.M. alerted?"

"Not yet, until after I've had a dekko. I'll be off in the morning."

Chapter 12

MAJOR CLYDE PAYS SOME VISITS

Major McPherson, the senior security officer on the Rock, looked up as the door to his office opened and closed with lightning rapidity and recognised the tall, stooped figure of Major William Clyde.

A look of enormous relief spread across McPherson's broad Scots countenance. A thick, florid, capable man, he was a conscientious Intelligence officer, staggered by but not panicked at the enormity of the security job with which they had to cope. He always welcomed the visits of Major Clyde, who was helping to bring about some order out of the security tangle by facing up to what could not be helped or improved and concentrating on areas where matters could be mended.

For one thing Clyde had succeeded in ending the nightmare of a Trojan Horse invasion of the Rock. There was nothing to be done about the ten thousand Spanish workmen who crossed over into Gibraltar each morning. Without them not a wheel or a lathe on the Rock would have turned. The Fortress would have run down like an unwound clock. But he had put a stop to their crossing the line seated in the buses coming from La Línea and Algeciras. Now they arrived at the narrow neck of land at the entrance to Gibraltar where the customs police and military control posts were set up, disembarked, marched over the line holding their passes under the scrutiny of the Army, climbed into a fleet of empty charabancs waiting on the other side, and were carried to their work, thus effectively countering any scheme to rush half a division of troops disguised as workmen into the fortress.

Now McPherson said, "By God, Slinker, I'm glad to see you. I thought this would bring you back, but not quite that quickly. What did you do, dematerialise?"

"Apes," said Major Clyde, "seeping apes! And at my age! I thought I was all through with them the last time Nanny took me to the zoo. Here we are losing the war in a nice, quiet, gentlemanly manner and then this has to happen. Who's the clot in charge of those brutes? Aren't you supposed to have something called an OIC Apes? There's hell to pay at Whitehall over this. The Spaniards are teetering on the brink while our chaps in Madrid are working their heads off to hold them back. It just wants one good push for Franco to take the plunge. Something as silly as this could give it to him." He went over to a chair and collapsed his frame into it and repeated, "Seeping apes!"

"Where do you want me to begin?" McPherson asked.

Clyde said morosely, "The usual place."

McPherson reflected and said, "I'd say it began when they sacked Tim Bailey."

"Bailey, who's he?"

"He was the OIC Apes here when the war started, and a damned good one. Conscientious bloke. Made a sort of a hobby of it, he and Lovejoy."

"Lovejoy?"

"Keeper fellow. Gunner in charge. Half an ape himself. They love him. Tim got on the Brig's nerves."

"How?"

"Worrying him about the apes. Wanting shelters and cages built. More food. Took the job seriously. Became the Rock bore on the subject."

"Sounds as though he might have some sense."

"Who?"

"This Bailey fellow. Saw this coming, didn't he?"

Major McPherson nodded. "Actually he did. He used to deafen my ears with it when nobody else would listen. Well, then there was this incident at the General Sir George Eliott celebration, your do. Someone picked the occasion to play a practical joke."

Major Clyde said, "I remember something, what was it——?"

Major McPherson gave him the details, concluding, "The C.R.A. made Bailey responsible, sacked him, and put in this dim bulb, Barton, with instructions for him to keep away from the apes. So nobody's bothered." He added, "We have had other things on our mind."

"I suppose you had," concurred Clyde. "Did you ever turn up the joker?"

"No. The firework could have come from anywhere. We were working on it when the Brigadier called off the hunt. Anyway, he'd had Bailey's head which he'd been wanting, and that was that."

Clyde reflected, tugging at his lower lip. He said, "It wasn't a joke, but it seems nevertheless to have been damn practical. Get me the files on everyone concerned and then I think I might have a word with Captain Bailey."

"You'll find him occupying a doghouse down near Europa Point, he and his wife."

Major Clyde raised an eyebrow. "Oh, married, too?"

"Wife's a WREN officer, Admiral French's daughter."

The eyebrows went even higher. "Oh," he said, "the man must have something. I hear she's a nice girl."

The entrance of Major William Clyde into the family circle of the Bailey's, Captain R.A., and ex-OIC Apes, and Second Officer W.R.N.S. Felicity could not have been more dramatic had it been staged by a director of Wagnerian opera at Bayreuth.

It was night and the Rock was having one of its occasional tropic-like thunderstorms, in themselves stagey affairs with fork lightning, torrents of rain, high wind, and utterly appalling explosions of thunder. It was the kind of night which made Tim groan in his heart for his lost apes, the kind of night when they should have been shut away, dry and safe in proper shelters. Sometimes these storms were followed by a cold Levanter. Thinking of the effect upon the drenched monkeys made him shudder.

With the shades pulled down, Timothy and Felicity had been each working upon their company administration papers by the uncertain and flickering lights that threatened to go at any moment, and they had flash lamps to hand for the emergency.

There came a really fearful glare of lightning that penetrated into their living room, accompanied by an ear-splitting crack-of-doom thunderclap, immediately followed by Stygian darkness as all the lights went out. Into their rather stunned silence that followed when the thunder had rolled away there came a knocking at the door of the bungalow. Tim took a torch and opened it. Felicity shone a second torch upon the figure standing in the doorway, the collar of his raincoat turned up, water cascading from it. The light travelled over a figure as tall and gangling as Don Quixote, with a droopy red moustache which was now parted by a finger put there in an attitude of secrets and silence.

Thus he stood there for a moment, the torches shining upon him like spotlights. "Good, what?" he said. "Always hoped for an entrance like that some time. Clyde of the Secret Service." He crossed the threshold as though he were wearing a cloak. The wind blew the door shut behind him with a satisfying bang. Tim and Felicity dissolved into roars of laughter.

"Come in," Tim cried, "and get dry outside and wet inside if we can find something."

At that moment the lights came on again, revealing the figure of the Major, and Tim saw that for all the mockery of his entrance his eyes were very shrewd. So this was the famous Major Clyde of M.I. 5, already something of a legend in the service.

"Good timing what?" said the Major. "Carry my own lighting effects around with me." He reintroduced himself, "William Clyde of the Cloak and Dagger. My friends call me Slinker."

Felicity went to him and took the dripping raincoat and disposed of it, and for a moment the newcomer stood, his eyes roving about the room, and Tim had the feeling that he was missing nothing, and that in all probability knew all there was to know about him, including the reason for the poor quarters. He said apologetically, "Sorry about the hovel."

Major Clyde nodded and said evenly, "Yes, I know. You've got the special Army Mark VII, doghouse. Reserved for chums of our little wild friends. I hope no one saw me come here in case it's catching." He went over to the small wireless set on the sideboard, switched it on, and at the first note that squawked from it flipped it off again. "Did you hear that broadcast earlier this evening?"

"Did I!" exclaimed Tim.

"What did you think?" the Major asked.

Felicity suddenly had had enough of clowning and said, "I'll tell you what I think, and you can tell them, too. It couldn't have happened if Tim had been there."

The Major turned away from the wireless and regarded her with quiet interest. "No?" he said. "Why?"

"Because he cared." Felicity cried passionately. "We both did. We couldn't help it."

"There," said Major Clyde. "You see, I knew it was catching."

"Oh do be serious," Felicity said, "can't you? It's nearly broken Tim's heart."

The Major smiled at her in a most friendly fashion. "My cover," he said. "Best tradition of the English detective novel. Sleuth pretends he's a blithering idiot and all the while the great brain is working. Well, what would have happened if Captain Bailey hadn't got the sack?"

"They'd have been looked after properly," Felicity replied. She wasn't yet quite sure whether or not she liked the Major or on whose side she might expect to find him. "They'd have had enough to eat. What Lovejoy couldn't steal or scrounge they used to pay for out of their own pockets. And if they had listened to him there would have been proper cages and shelters built. He's been at them to have those done ever since he took the job. That's one reason they got rid of him."

Major Clyde raised an eyebrow. "Shelters," he said. "I thought the blighters were supposed to be able to look after themselves and live out in the open."

Another thunder peal as of a thousand guns shook the windows and rattled the dishes in the kitchen. A violent burst of wind slapped a bucketful of rain against the windowpanes.

"Would *you* like to be out with no clothes on on a night like this?" Felicity said furiously. "They're not all that different from us, you know. Except that they get diseases and die more quickly and wretchedly. What we've done is half domesticated and then abandoned them. If there is sun tomorrow they will probably dry out all right——"

"And if there isn't?" queried the Major.

"More of them will catch cold and probably die," Felicity said with finality. "This is the dangerous time of year for them when the temperature can drop fifteen degrees. Tim has always told them that, and that they ought to have concrete caves built where they can keep warm and dry in the winter, and cages to segregate nursing mothers, and—and," she trailed off, suddenly feeling ashamed and embarrassed for her outburst, but Tim, who had been watching her with grave affection, merely said, "Go on Counsellor, you're doing fine. It's all gospel, only it wouldn't be becoming for me to be saying it." He nodded with his head towards the wireless. "The dead ones were mostly females. It wants about eight females to one male for proper breeding in the season. The pack is not only halved, but the chances of its coming back to strength are practically nullified."

"Oh," said the Major and wrinkled his nose in an expression of distaste. "That's one I wasn't aware of; they didn't tell me. I wonder why the Jerries haven't latched on to that?" Then he asked, "What about that dreg who's supposed to be looking after them?"

Tim started to say, "You mean Lovejoy? The Gunner's a hundred per——"

"No, I don't mean Lovejoy," Clyde interrupted, "I mean that clot they've put in as OIC Apes."

Felicity looked at the Major with a new interest. Perhaps he was going to turn out to be on the side of the angels. She was about to say something when she caught a signal from Tim to be quiet.

"Oh, you mean Lieutenant Barton," Tim said. "He's all right."

The Major regarded Tim quizzically. "Judgment of men: nought Captain Bailey," he said, "if you're serious, which I don't believe you are. I've had a chat with him. Utter dim bulb. Furthermore I detected a look of beagles in his eye. When the old Brig put him in there he told him that if he ever heard a single word about apes or a line of bumph passed his desk he'd stay Lieutenant for the rest of his life. He hasn't dared open his mouth since. And as for the apes, he hasn't been near them. He caught Lovejoy scrounging some food for them and ran him in. Lovejoy got seven days' field punishment and his source of supply was shut off. What's all right about a midden like that?"

Felicity's eyes were suddenly filled with tenderness. "Oh Major Clyde," she said, "I do apologise."

"Eh?" said Clyde. "For what?"

"Things I've been thinking," Felicity said simply. The two smiled cheerfully at one another.

Tim said tentatively, "We've got a bit of gin."

The Major made a deprecating gesture, "As long as it's fire water."

The doors rattled again as the thunder banged. Felicity went and got the gin bottle and some glasses and they sat round the table and sipped. The Major asked, "What about this Lovejoy?"

"Right arm in the fire," said Tim. "Bet anything you like on Lovejoy. First-rate chap, the Gunner."

"Hangs out at the Admiral Nelson, doesn't he? Talkative bloke."

Tim dipped his head again in the direction of the wireless and said, "You mean——"

"Not to worry," the Major said. "There are some ten thousand other possible sources, security being what it is around here." Then he added, "What about food? What do they take?"

"About two pounds a day," Tim replied. "They're supposed to get sweet potatoes, ground nuts, carrots, lettuces, oranges or pomegranates and bananas, of course. They're potty about bananas."

"Are they getting it?"

Tim shrugged. "You've looked through my record, haven't you?" Major Clyde nodded. "And saw the bit about the row I had with the Government of Sierra Leone over the blackguards raising the price of ground nuts due to the war."

Major Clyde nodded again and said, "And ever since then?"

Tim shrugged again.

Major Clyde grunted and then asked, "Where do the blighters come from?"

"North Africa," Tim replied. "The Moors consider them a

nuisance. They gang up and raid their farms. Why, would you like one?"

"How would I go about acquiring one if I did?"

Tim grinned, "As of a year ago when I was sacked, the price for one around Ceuta, Tangier, and Rabat was half a case of whisky per specimen. It's probably a case by now."

"That's an interesting piece of information. What else do you know?"

Tim got up, went over to a cupboard from whence he produced a black loose-leaf notebook, two inches thick with pages. "Care for a dekko at this?" he asked. "It's all here. My life and times with *macaca silvanus*. Some day I thought I'd make a book of it."

The Major's eyes glittered. "With a special chapter devoted no doubt to an old bastard by the name of Scruffy." To Tim's surprise he didn't turn the book down, but said, "May I have this for a time? I'll let you have it back when I'm finished." He bundled it under his arm as though it was the secret plans of a new weapon, climbed into his raincoat, said, "Cheerio! Who knows, better days may lie ahead," waited for an appropriate flash of lightning and clap of thunder and spirited himself out of the door.

"The violent thunderstorm which took place between nine and ten o'clock in the Gibraltar—La Línea—Algeciras area last Tuesday night," said the smarmy voice of Gloomy Gustave from the radios on the Rock and to which Gibraltarians tuned, "caused considerable damage to installations at Gibraltar. Lightning struck the main powerhouse, plunging the Rock into darkness, and several churches were hit. Mrs. Antonio Morales, returning with her husband from a visit to her sister, was injured by stones and flying debris when lightning struck the steeple of the Church of the Ascension. High winds blew down cables and power lines and work in the naval machine shops had to be suspended. Some workers were sent home. This is expected to delay completion of repairs to the destroyer *Proteus* now at the Mole, which had been due to sail on Thursday."

"Clever boy," said Major Clyde moodily and pulled at his

lower lip. He and Major McPherson were listening to the wireless in McPherson's office. A male stenographer was taking down the broadcast in shorthand. "That's stuff anyone could sweep up off the floor."

"Still——" McPherson began with doubt in his voice, "it's a nasty feeling having them looking over your shoulder to see whether you had eggs for breakfast."

The announcer continued his listing of further minor damage by the thunderstorm. "I wish I had his job," Major Clyde said.

"Whose? Gloomy Gustave's?"

"No. The bloke who's getting paid for collecting this intelligence. He probably works all of ten minutes a day."

Gloomy Gustave returned to a now not unfamiliar topic in his broadcasts.

"More damaging to the morale of citizens of Gibraltar and their British masters was the death of four more of the rapidly diminishing number of the Barbary apes, three of them females, due to the storm which did great harm to the already demoralised apes. The three females were sheltering in an acacia tree near the apes' village, which was apparently struck by lightning. Their burned bodies were found in the morning. The fourth, a young male, succumbed to galloping pneumonia. Gibraltarians who have long complained of the depredations practised by these unruly beasts kept as mascots by the British to show their contempt for the natives, as well as to insure themselves against the prophecy of the legend connected with them, will rejoice that with the elimination of a further quartette of these nuisances the day of their total liberation would seem to be moving closer."

Major Clyde looked at McPherson over the head of the stenographer and said, "I don't care much for that."

McPherson nodded. "There's been talk."

Major Clyde lifted an interrogatory eyebrow.

"In bars and shops and my wife says at her hairdresser's. It's a joke now, of course——"

"If I had my way every Intelligence officer would have to take a course in hairdressing. Best listening post in the world." He pulled at his lower lip again. "But it might not be a joke tomorrow. We've got to put a stop to this pattern. What are the chances of getting Captain Bailey restored as OIC Apes?"

The reply of Major McPherson was succinct. "None! And I shouldn't even try. You might consult Tim on the Q.T., but the Brigadier is fed up. Furthermore the old man never could stand the apes and he'd be tickled to death to be rid of them. He doesn't dare order them shot or exterminated because he's a stickler for tradition, but if nature would just take its course and eliminate them he'd be delighted."

Major Clyde nodded, but there was an expression almost of sympathy on his face. He said, "It's not his fault. It's his up-bringing. They've taught him that war is what comes out of the mouth of a cannon. He hasn't learned that the boffins have taken over and that war can likewise be——" he nodded his head in the direction of the wireless set from which issued the nightly sign-off of Gloomy Gustave.

"And now, dear friends, we wish you goodnight and good sleep in the knowledge that you are twenty-four hours nearer to your liberation. Tomorrow night at the same time we will be back on the air with more interesting news and comment about happenings in Gibraltar and the world at large which your British rulers have kept from you."

Music replaced the smarmy voice; Major Clyde stood regarding the wireless set, his lower lip characteristically between his fingers, his red moustache drooping, he said, "Thank goodness."

Major McPherson stared at him, "Thank goodness for what?"

"The P.M. believes in us. I think I'd better have a word with John."

Major William Clyde's second visit to the quarters of Captain Bailey was less dramatic than his first. He had telephoned and asked if he could come by for a moment around seven, had been invited to come for dinner, and had accepted.

He turned up this time unenveloped in any clouds of fire and brimstone, but with a file under one arm and a package shaped suspiciously like a bottle under the other. This suspicion was confirmed when he unveiled the parcel and revealed it as a bottle of King William Scotch whisky.

"In the words of Gunner Lovejoy," Tim said, "Gord luv you."
Felicity was more simple. "Our benefactor," she beamed.

"Currency," said Major Clyde. They both looked at him not
catching the allusion. "One twelfth of a Barbary ape, C.O.D.,
Tangier, Rabat, or Ceuta. Your quotation," the Major explained.
"Plenty more where that came from." Then he added, "It's a more
reliable conversational drink. Gin always makes me think I'm
more clever than I am."

Tim and Felicity exchanged a glance. Apes in the wind. They
sat down to dinner. Felicity had made a stew to which she had
added a number of exotic but available vegetables and spices, as
the best way of expanding their ration. It was savoury and deli-
cious, leading the Major to comment, "They didn't teach you
that in the WRENS, did they?"

"Oh no," said Felicity, "my father taught me that."

It was Major Clyde who was caught by surprise. "Good God,"
he said, "the Admiral? Oh I say, I do beg your pardon. I didn't
mean——"

"Daddy is a wonderful cook," Felicity said. "He loves it. It's his
hobby. When he commanded H.M.S. *Unconquerable* he had
his own galley built next to his quarters. All the Captains used to
like to be asked to his little dinners."

Major Clyde said, "I suppose God *will* permit us to survive as
long as we continue to amuse Him." But there were more words
and phrases than amused in his mind, thinking of the British,
words he would never dream of using, such as staunch and gallant
and true to themselves, and not giving a damn for what anybody
thought. For here was the daughter of a Vice Admiral married to
a penniless Captain because she loved him, sharing the doghouse
into which her husband had got himself through zeal which was
likewise unique and British. He found himself pleased with their
company.

After dinner was over and the Major had produced two cigars
which Felicity had eyed with suspicion, they being such a rarity
on the Rock, Clyde got down to business.

From his folder he produced the thick loose-leaf notebook he
had borrowed from Tim, along with a batch of material, notes,

and statistics apparently filched from the files. "I've been through
your stuff," the Major began, leafing through the notebook, "and
the odd thing, you know, which will probably surprise your native
modesty is that it *will* make a book some day which can be read
with considerable profit by the high domes who have to hook
everything up to a machine before they believe it. I'll be dining
out on it when I get back to London. 'Would you believe it, my
dear Duchess, that the gestation period of *macaca silvanus* is one
hundred and eighty days, or just three months less than ours?
That the male reaches his adult stage at the age of five? That
the females have their heats only between December 15 and
January 15 of each year, and consequently the offspring are born
in June and July? That young apes are breast fed for six months
and have their milk teeth at about five months? Gospel, ma'am.
Personal observation of a friend of mine.' I have also," the Major
continued, "been through the files, which are instructive, if not
horrifying. If I were the German High Command I would simply
concentrate upon capturing these documents and publishing
them."

The Major fingered through some of the bumph from out of
his case and continued, "I have here indisputable and documen-
tary evidence that the Secretary of State for the Colonies and the
Governor of Gibraltar once exchanged official telegrams regarding the subsistence allowance of the ape population; that the
Crown Surveyor and Engineer has complained to the Honourable
Colonial Secretary that the apes have been dribbling into the
fresh-water supplies; that a Senior Medical Officer performed a
post-mortem operation on the body of a young ape, found a total
collapse of the left lung and so reported to the Brigadier; that
another Brigadier was politely turned down when he proposed to
wish some of his apes on to the Regent's Park Zoo; that one of
your harassed predecessors had the honour to request of the
authorities that he might dispose of two recalcitrant male apes
known as Abraham and Wilfred; that after a brawl amongst the
apes the Brigadier Commander of the Royal Artillery paid a visit
to the scene of battle, possibly to count the pieces of fur that had
flown, and interview the OIC Rock Apes, thereafter correspond-

ing on the subject with the Colonial Secretary; that the Revenue Inspector from the Revenue Department used up good Government stationery to advise the Financial Secretary that the peanuts in the two bins at Queen's Gate on the upper Rock were of a very inferior quality; that the demise of a Rock ape named Judy was reported with all the clinical detail accorded to the passing of a film star or a demi-mondaine, and that further bumph shows graduates from Sandhurst who have reached Brigade rank corresponding with their Excellencies the Governors, Colonial Secretaries, Foreign Office chaps, and members of Parliament on subjects concerning the apes, from the proper age for copulation to the vendetta staged between two males named Antonio and Patrick for exclusive rights to a harem of ten females amongst whom appeared the attractive names of Beatrice, Mona, Maureen, Mary, and Kathleen."

Major Clyde took a deep breath and expelled it with a "Phew! Would anyone believe it?"

"And finally," concluded the Major, producing a very grubby bit of paper, scrawled upon almost illegibly in pencil, "I have got out of Lovejoy the gen on the present number and status of apes on the Rock. I might report that the Gunner's morale is low. He still loves the apes, but he doesn't love your Lieutenant Barton or anybody else and is drowning his sorrows. He tells me that the Queen's Gate pack is down to nine, of which no females are of breedable age and four are young apes not yet in adult stage. This is the outfit your friend Scruffy runs. There had been ten, but this morning Scruffy killed one of his rivals. The Middle Hill pack is down to eleven, of which only two are of any value in breeding. The Gunner says that when the packs get down that low with less females available the fights to own them are more frequent and savage. He expects there will be pieces of apes scattered all over the top."

"That's right," Tim said. "That's in my notes"

"So how would you like to be OIC Apes again?" Clyde asked with no change in the inflection of his voice, letting the question carry its own impact.

Tim's snap-back was almost immediate. "Fine," he said.

"He wouldn't," remarked Felicity.

"Oh," said Tim, looking over at her in surprise. "Sorry, I thought I would."

"You wouldn't," Felicity reiterated, and the two men saw that her eyes were shining and her face rosy. They also noticed that the level of the liquid attributed to King William had fallen considerably. The bottle which had been passing around between them clockwise had been halted close beside her for some time.

"You've been treated ablominably," she said. Or at least that is what it sounded like to Tim. "They've got themselves into a mess or Major Clyde wouldn't be here and now they want you to pull their horseshoes out of the fire for them." She reflected, "It is horseshoes, isn't it, Tim?"

"Horse chestnuts," said Tim. "You were halfway home."

"And that's a fact," added Major Clyde, though he didn't state what.

"They humiliated you because you were doing the best job ever on your—on their filthy apes. They gave you a slum to live in, all the Brigade dirty work they could find to pile on to you, and now because old Smarmy-In-The-Box over there has got under their skins and people on the Rock are beginning to get the jitters, they think they can——"

Major Clyde interrupted sharply, "See here, young lady, how do you know people on the Rock have got the jitters?"

"I heard it at my hairdresser's," Felicity replied, "where all of you M.I. boys would go if you had any——"

"I know, I know," Major Clyde said hastily, "I was only saying the same to McPherson earlier today. Well, never mind."

"Ablominably," Felicity said again, and now Tim squinted at her and was sure that that was what she had said, and also that she was a little tight. She continued, "You're scared that your nasty old apes will all die, the Germans will find out and egg the Spaniards into the war and the legend will come true. And you want Tim to pull——"

Tim said, "I thought you loved the apes, Felicity."

"I do, but I love you more. It's true, isn't it?" This last was addressed to Major Clyde, who was considering the powers of accurate analysis which could descend upon a woman when some decent, uncut Scotch mixed with long-seething indignation.

The Major said, "May I have the bottle, please?" Felicity giggled and said, "Oh dear, I'm so sorry, I've been pigging it."

The Major poured a good dollop and topped Tim's drink as well. "Well then," he said, "supposing we get down to business and discuss price."

Tim started to speak, but was too slow and Felicity was in the breach with lightning speed. "Some rank," she said, "not temporary. Permanent. Just you try to get anything done around here as a Captain. A Sergeant has more rank than a Captain."

"I see," said Major Clyde smoothly. "Anything in mind, ma'am?"

"Well," replied Felicity, "he ought to be able to look you in the eye."

Tim gawked at his wife in utter amazement and his glance went from her to the bottle to his own glass from which he proceeded to take a long draught. If this was tiger juice he'd better have some, too.

Major Clyde had got out a pencil and was scribbling on the back of one of the documents. "Major Bailey," he murmured half to himself. "Anything else, young lady?"

"Decent living quarters. They've treated him ab——"

"Blominably," Major Clyde found himself completing for Felicity. "I know. Lieutenant Colonel Hoskins's house is going. He's posted out to Aden."

Felicity instantly turned all woman. "You mean that ducky cottage in Battery Street? Would I be allowed to do it over?"

"I suggest you wait until the Colonel has departed before you start pulling down curtains. He's house proud. Well, is it a deal?"

The tigress returned once more. "Anything Tim says goes," announced Felicity. "And anything he wants—cages, caves, bananas, and no interference from anybody. And Lovejoy is to have his scrounging privileges restored."

"Darling," Tim said, "one can't have everything."

Major Clyde said to Tim, "Look here, Bailey, if one got you what you needed and you had, say, unlimited—currency, how long would it take you to build up the ape packs back to prewar strength and keep them there?"

Tim did some quick figuring based on his experience and devotion to the apes, as well as his African contacts. "Nine months," he said, "nine months to a year at most, but in the meantime the existing pack would be kept up to strength and we ought to have nothing to worry about. We could get cracking at once on——" he stopped and suddenly looked bleakly at both Felicity and Clyde. "But what's the use?" he said half angrily. "We're out and they're in. The Brigadier wouldn't hear of it and, begging your pardon, sir, you're only a Major. What the hell are we all sitting here gassing about?"

Major Clyde gathered up his papers and files, restoring them to his case, arose and, considering the amount of King William he himself had consumed, reached the door with commendable steadiness. There he turned for a moment before going out and spoke but one sentence. "Just you wait, Major Blaily," and then he was gone.

Chapter 13

THE PRIME MINISTER
EXPRESSES CONCERN

Brigadier J. W. Gaskell, D.S.O., M.C., O.B.E., sat at the desk which at that moment occupied the centre of a shattered world and contemplated the most appalling and disturbing signal that had come to his attention in his entire military career. It was from the Secretary of State to the Governor of Gibraltar. It had been transmitted in top-secret cipher and decoded privately by the chief of the Decoding Bureau, Wren Second Officer F. Bailey. On the margin had been scrawled and signed with the Governor's initials, "J.W.G., this came this morning. Your toddler I think. Keep me posted. F.L."

It read as follows:

"The Prime Minister has expressed some concern as to welfare of Barbary apes on Gibraltar about which he has heard disquieting rumours. He is most anxious that they should NOT be allowed to die out. I have received direction from the Prime Minister that the establishment of apes should be no less than twenty-four and that every effort should be made to achieve this number as soon as possible and maintaining it as a minimum thereafter. Grateful if you would take steps accordingly and inform me as to the result."

There it lay upon his desk, a single sheet of white bumph, and he sat looking at it as though it were a snake, transfixed and fascinated. Words from the message leaped up from the page and burned through the bone of his skull into the unhappy grey matter beneath. "Prime Minister," "expresses concern," "disquieting rumors," "NOT be allowed to die out," "every effort should be made." If he had read the communication once, he had been through it some dozens of times. He knew it by heart and yet what refused to filter through to his brain was the connection between the Prime Minister—THE PRIME MINISTER OF GREAT BRITAIN, Winston Churchill, the director and guiding genius of the Empire and of the war—and a pack of monkeys.

The Brigadier was a soldier and not a psychologist. He had been growing greyer for months with the problems of defending an indefensible position should Spain become involved. He was part of a command under which absolute prodigies were being performed by British engineers hollowing out the Rock so as to provide bombproof shelters, shops, and ammunition depots. An air strip was taking form in a frenzy of round-the-clock labour, all under the noses of the Germans, of course, but time was desperately wanted, and men and money. All this was going reasonably well, discounting frustrations and exasperations to be expected when a work of this nature is being rushed through in the face of possible enemy action at any moment. And here was the leader of the greatest nation on the face of the earth expressing concern over a pack of apes—monkeys. Filthy beasts that prowled the street, urinating, defecating, and spoiling peoples' gardens.

It is axiomatic that no commander except the genius at the very top is able to see a war as more than a piece with which he is intimately concerned. That anyone's concern over the welfare of a pack of ugly and useless macaques could have anything to do with gaining some of the time so desperately needed to complete the works in progress was a connection too tenuous and farfetched to be appreciated by a military man responsible for the lives of the civilian as well as military population under his command.

The apes had not been called to his attention for almost a year, ever since he had dismissed Captain Bailey and installed a new OIC Apes. He had successfully got rid of a recurring irritation and if ever a thought of them had intruded upon him he had congratulated himself upon the successful way in which he had coped.

And now out of the blue the whole subject of apes was suddenly revived, alive, vibrating, worrying, and at the hands of none other than the Prime Minister of Great Britain. The Prime Minister! And here as he said the potent and magic name to himself the thoughts of the Brigadier whirled and tumbled and panicked as to what he was to do. For old and experienced and full of rank as he was, the chain of command was still a part of his life, and if he was a potentate before whom Captains and subalterns trembled, yes and Majors and Lieutenant Colonels, too, so he himself was but a callow youth quaking before the august presence of the P.M. and even more the power that he represented. All the lives, the fears, and the hopes of the British people and of himself as well were bound up in the person of this one great man. And there he was demanding to know about a lot of monkeys.

The Brigadier touched a button and when his secretary appeared ordered, "Get me Lieutenant Barton and tell Major Quennel I want to see him when he comes in." Staff Captain Quennel had been promoted to Brigade Major.

Ten minutes later Lieutenant Barton, OIC Apes, was ushered in. He was a fresh-faced boy with rosy cheeks and curly hair, with the still innocent eyes of one who had not yet discovered that most men will lie, cheat, or steal to gain their ends. He went through the ritual of the greeting salutes and attention as though he meant it, which indeed he did.

"Sit down, Barton," commanded the Brigadier. "Now what's all this about those rotten apes?"

"What's all what, sir?"

Momentarily disarmed by the innocence of the young man's eyes, the Brigadier realised that he had started off wrong. The boy could have no knowledge of the contents of the message on the desk before him, and at that moment the Brigadier was not altogether wishful that he should. What he wanted was information. Right information, proper information, *happy* information. Something he could bung into an answering telegram to the Secretary of State who would convey it to the ear of the great man and close off this little matter forever. He tried a new and more affable tack. "How are you and the monkeys getting along, Barton?"

The young man looked surprised but not yet distressed. "Why—why I don't know, sir."

Brigadier Gaskell glared. "You don't know? What do you mean you don't know? You're OIC Apes, aren't you?"

"That's right, sir, but you said I wasn't to go near them. You said I was to make out my report on a single sheet of paper twice a year and if you ever caught me mucking about the apes' village or sticking my nose into any kind of monkey business you'd have the pips off my shoulders quicker than I could sing 'Who is Sylvia?' Those were your words, sir."

They were, too, as the Brigadier remembered. He said, "Oh come now, Barton, I may have joked a bit but when you accepted the OIC Apes you assumed certain responsibilities which I expected you to carry out."

The innocent eyes widened somewhat and some of the innocence began to fade. Lieutenant Barton was encountering some of man's inhumanity to man and what seemed to be the beginning of a military double cross in the higher echelons. "But, sir, you said——"

"Never mind what I said, you're supposed to use your head in this service; that's why we make you officers."

"You said," Lieutenant Barton went on doggedly, continuing to bat on the only wicket available, "you said I was to leave everything to that slob Lovejoy and if you ever caught me——"

Gaskell cut him short. "Yes, yes, I've heard that. Now then, how many apes are there at present in the Queen's Gate pack?"

"I don't know, sir."

"Why not?"

"I haven't counted them, sir. My report isn't due for another two months, sir."

Major Quennel came in.

"Oh there you are Quennel," the Brigadier said. "Have you seen this yet?" He passed him the signal. The aide read it and as an old and trusted assistant permitted himself a whistle.

"Damnable, what?" the Brigadier said. He turned to young Barton again. "Well, what about their health? Are they in good health or bad?"

"I don't know, sir. I haven't been near——"

Gaskell suddenly looking cunning. "Well," he said, "have you heard any rumours that they weren't feeling too fit perhaps?"

"Only the Nazi broadcast, sir."

The Brigadier was genuinely startled. "The what?" he cried.

"The broadcasts in Spanish from that German station in Algeciras saying the apes were dying out. I didn't pay any attention to it. Anyway I thought you'd be pleased."

A sinking feeling differing from his initial bewilderment played with the pit of the Brigadier's stomach. For the first time it began to dawn upon him that there was more behind the message on the desk before him than he had imagined. He turned angrily upon Quennel. "Had you heard those broadcasts, Quennel?"

"Yes, sir."

"Then why wasn't I informed?"

"I thought you'd have heard them yourself, sir, and anyway it was a matter for OIC Apes."

That frightened officer leaped into that breach with all his youth and agility. "You said I wasn't to mention apes to you, sir, not under any circum——"

The Brigadier felt the trap closing in about him and struggled to break the strands. "My God," he said, "I am surrounded by imbeciles. What's the good of my relying on you, Quennel? And this forty-watter here," indicating the hurt and unhappy Barton. "Doesn't know how many apes there are, where they are, whether they are sick or well, alive or dead."

Major Quennel said soothingly, "Why don't you have a word with Gunner Lovejoy, sir; he knows all about them."

"Get him then," the Brigadier ordered, "and quickly."

The Brigade Major said some harsh things into the black mouthpiece of his telephone and the Gunner was produced with miraculous rapidity almost resembling a pantomime entrance. He stood at rigid attention. All his buttons were buttoned and his mind was galloping at a thousand r.p.m.s in an endeavour to deliver an estimate of the offence he was about to be charged with, and how long it would be before he would once more emerge into the sunshine from durance vile. He had never before been called before such high brass.

Brigadier Gaskell, however, said, "Stand easy, Lovejoy. I want you to answer some questions. How many apes are there in the Queen's Gate pack?"

"Nine, sir. There's old Scruff, Pat, Tony, Helen, Pansy——"

"Never mind the names. Is that all?"

"Yes, sir."

"How many were there originally?"

For one instant the eyes of Gunner Lovejoy shifted to OIC Apes Barton and back again, and now the young Lieutenant knew that he was really in for it. He was to be squeezed between top and bottom for doing what he had been told was his duty and carrying out his orders.

"Originally, sir? Originally when?"

"Well, whenever you like, or say when Lieutenant Barton took over."

"Twenty-six, sir."

The sinking feeling returned to the Brigadier's centre. "And the Middle Hill pack?"

"Eleven, sir—no, ten. I found Martha dead this morning."

"Martha?" queried the Brigadier.

"She was Bill's wife, sir, or rather he had his eye on her, when she moved over to Alf. Bill took it 'ard. There was a blood row. Martha got herself in the middle of it."

The Brigadier was nearing the boiling point once more. "Who the devil are you talking about, Lovejoy?"

"The apes, sir."

The Brigadier exhaled a long breath. "Ten down from what?"

"Twenty-four, sir."

"Why? What's been happening?"

"Lot of sickness, sir. We've had some bad storms. Not getting enough to eat, sir. Malnurtition! Weakens 'em. Along comes a big wet and down they go."

"Look here," said Gaskell, "that won't do. Aren't you supposed to be looking after them?"

"Yes, sir."

"Why don't you feed them properly?"

The Gunner's eyes went to Lieutenant Barton again. The subaltern, although he was learning fast, was both a gentleman as well as an officer. He said, "Not enough food for them on rations, sir. Lovejoy there used to scrounge the rest. I caught him at it and put a stop to it. Seven days' punishment. You said——"

Brigadier Gaskell thought that if he heard the phrase 'you said' once more the top of his head would blow off.

"It would break your 'eart, sir," Lovejoy said, "to see them like that. It's the wrong time of the year for them to forage for themselves after the dry spell, and the prickly pears, locust beans, and American fruit being off."

The Brigadier did not think it would break his heart, and then very quickly as his eye caught the fatal signal on his desk he thought it probably would. The answer to it was going to be very dusty indeed unless a miracle of some kind were to take place. There were half a dozen questions which sprang to his lips and he was at pains to stifle all of them and think again since there was every likelihood that they would lead to that extraordinary dim bulb of a Barton saying: "But you said, sir——" He supposed one might maintain the status quo by increasing the rations, but if the Gunner's information and calculations were correct he was six filthy beasts off what the Prime Minister had laid down as minimum. He said to Lovejoy, "Don't they, ah—breed? I thought monkeys were always——"

"No, sir," replied the Gunner. "It's just exploration, sir, in a way of speaking. The females don't come on until the winter, about a month from the middle of December through January."

"What's the gestation period?"

"About six months, sir."

The Brigadier did some rapid calculations in his head. Three months to fertility, after which if every male did his duty and was on target, one might reasonably expect the Prime Minister's quota to be reached by the following June or July.

The Gunner, who had seen the Brigadier's lips moving as he did his mental mathematics, dashed these hopes very quickly. "There's not enough females, sir," he said. "It wants about eight to ten females to one male for proper breeding. You lose a lot of them young hapelets anyway. I've had 'em stillborn or killed in fights."

"Well," said Gaskell, "get some more females then. The Prime Minister wants the apes kept up to strength."

"Get them from where, sir?"

The net was closing in indeed. The Brigadier threw what almost might have been interpreted as a despairing glance at his OIC Apes, but young Barton, who had been badly bruised, was not having any. "I don't know, sir," he put in. "I just thought they sort of were here all the time, or came through a tunnel."

The Brigadier was too beaten even to permit himself the luxury of a fury. "Very well," he said. "Double ration for the time being. I'll speak to the Quartermaster. That will be all."

Outside the office, Lovejoy pinched himself, unbelieving. He had been in the very lair of the tiger and emerged not only unscathed but with double rations for the apes. But it had been a most shattering experience. He felt badly in need of a Guinness and lime.

Lieutenant Barton and the Gunner departed, leaving the Brigadier and his Brigade Major alone. They had been together long enough for Gaskell to be able to relax when by himself with Quennel. "What the devil do we do now, Roger?"

The compelling bit of paper with its ineradicable message lay on the desk before them. A name, an unspoken name hovered in the air between them. The Brigadier did not wish to speak it, in fact was quite incapable of bringing it forth, and his adjutant did not dare and in fact had actually been warned against it during a briefing he had had several days ago from a mysterious Major who had arrived on the Rock from London not long before, one of the hush-hush boys who had joined Major McPherson, the security officer. The briefing had in a way been prophetic, and Major Quennel was marvelling at the manner in which the present had followed the line of the future that the mystery Major had predicted. He now proceeded as instructed to carry out the final part of the briefing. He picked up the message, read it again, put it down, and said, "There's a Major Clyde here, sir, I wonder if perhaps——"

"What? Who?" snapped the Brigadier, ready to grasp at any straw.

"Major Clyde, sir. Posted to Major McPherson in Intelligence."

"Does he know anything about apes?"

"I don't know, sir, but he's just out here from home." He indicated the cable with his head. "He might know something more about that—I mean those Intelligence chaps manage to get their fingers into all sorts of pies. They seem to pull a lot of weight, sir, if you know what I mean."

"Humph," snorted the Brigadier, and then said, "I don't suppose it would do any harm to have a word with him."

Major Quennel reached for the telephone.

When it rang in Major McPherson's office, the Scot picked up the receiver and then handed it to Major Clyde with an expression of amazement on his face. "My God," he said. "Right on schedule. You said he'd be calling before ten."

Major Clyde spoke into the instrument, saying, "Yes, Major. Certainly, Major. Not at all, Major. I'll be right over." He hung up, picked up his cap and swagger stick, and went to the door.

McPherson looked after him admiringly and said, "How the devil do you do it, Slinker?"

Clyde merely grinned. "You might give old Bailey a buzz," he said, "and tell him to get ready to move."

"I was wondering," Brigadier Gaskell said to the tall, gangling odd-looking Major who sat at his desk, "whether you might have heard anything connected with this." He slid the signal across.

They were alone, Major Quennel having been excused upon the arrival of Major Clyde and was having to content himself with straining his ears to the murmur of voices which came through the thin partition dividing the Brigadier's office from his own. The Brigadier was being cagey and tentative. For the interview Major Clyde had suppressed his natural flamboyance and was playing the respectful officer in the presence of a powerful superior.

The Major took the telegram and gave a creditable performance of interest and surprise at reading it, since he had been familiar with the contents for some time, indeed had been responsible for some of the wording in which the wishes of the P.M. had finally been couched.

"A great man," the Major murmured when he had finished.

"Eh?" said the Brigadier.

"Nothing gets past him."

"Then you think it is serious?"

"Very."

And in just such a simple and subtle manner, without even having really said anything, the Major established his ascendancy and himself as someone in the know on the subject. By means of silence and respectful attention and all the things he didn't say, Major Clyde had succeeded almost in evoking an image of himself as the personal representative of the Prime Minister in the mind of the Brigadier.

"Quite frankly," Gaskell said, "I'm worried. It's got to be answered; something's got to be done. I have had the clots in who are supposed to be looking after the beasts. Completely clueless. All they kept saying was that it wasn't their can."

Major Clyde nodded and merely remarked, "Not very helpful, sir," and waited.

"Look here," said the Brigadier suddenly, "there's a chap here on the Rock who knows a lot about these stinkers—I mean he seems to have made himself fairly knowledgeable on the subject."

The Major waited, his eyes downcast as though restudying the message.

"Fellow named Bailey. Captain Bailey. Used to be OIC Apes before the war."

Major Clyde raised his eyes from the paper and the Brigadier searched them for any hint of reaction or knowledge of whom he was speaking, but they appeared to be blank and at the same time filling up with soothing sympathy for the Brigadier and his dilemma. The Major continued to say nothing.

"The thing is," the Brigadier burst out, "I've treated the man damnably!"

There, it was out. For some time now he had been aching to purge himself of his guilt, to speak the name of Captain Timothy Bailey, and to confess that his dealing with him had been somewhat less than fair, for the Brigadier was a gentleman.

And who better to confess to than this stranger whose existence he had not been aware of until five minutes before, this quiet, intelligent officer who did not go shooting off advice to him or try to tell him what to do in the manner of the young soldiers of the day. "He irritated me with his seeping monkeys and his demands for them. Got on my nerves. What was I sent out here to command? Guns or a pack of monkeys? Still, I oughtn't to have done it. The man was doing the job I'd set him to and doing it well. Better zeal in an officer than slackness, what?"

The Major nodded gently, "Still, too *much* zeal——"

The Brigadier now knew that he liked this Major, liked him very much indeed. "Exactly," he said. "You've hit the nail on the head. Always coming in here laying bumph on my desk. Wanting cages built! Concrete shelters! Concrete flooring! Cooling systems! Germ-proof maternity wards! Special kinds of food! Own veterinary! Bananas out of season! Pampering and coddling! Gave him the sack for it." And then as his eyes were once more offended by the mandatory signal, he muttered a deflated sigh and said, "I wish I'd listened to him."

"And you'd like him to help you now," the Major murmured quite impersonally and half to himself.

"Impossible," said the Brigadier. "Couldn't look the fellow in the eye. Humiliated him. Had him bunged into Siberia."

The Major elevated a gently questioning eyebrow to draw the C.R.A. further.

"The Europa Point end of the Rock," the Brigadier elucidated. "You don't know Gibraltar yet. Worst quarters on the peninsula. Damned vindictive of me, but there it is. But if you'd heard him carry on about these haemorrhaging chimpanzees, you'd have——"

"I know," agreed the Major. "Those one-track Johnnies can drive you right up the wall."

"There you have it," said Gaskell eagerly, "yet——"

"And yet I suppose," Major Clyde suggested, "if he were an all-right chap and we made amends——"

The Brigadier was looking at the Major with a faint light of hope in his eyes. The "we" used by Major Clyde had struck a particularly responsive chord. At last there seemed to be somebody prepared to stand by and help.

"Offer him promotion, say," the Major went on, "set him up in better quarters—he's married, I take it?"

The Brigadier made a grimace. "Admiral's daughter. Rotten for her," he confessed, "but then she oughtn't to have married the fellow. Parents dead set against it. Nobody in the garrison could stand him. Him and his eternal monkeys. He even got on the Chaplain's nerves."

"Still," suggested the Major.

Hope faded from the Brigadier's expression. "It won't do, Major. Not a chance. Too young. He's not due for three years. Might create ill feeling. Yet——" He looked to Major Clyde to see whether any help might be forthcoming, so quickly had he been conditioned to lean upon him.

The Major continued to act smoothly and without precipitation. Instead of replying immediately he picked up the message from the Secretary of State and pretended to read it again. "Sir," he said, "I don't know how much aware you are of it, but this is a very powerful signal. One would not like to see it entrusted to someone less scrupulous than yourself."

Gaskell was regarding him warily. "Eh?" he said. "I don't quite understand."

"The dynamite," said the Major, "is contained in the phrase 'every effort should be made.' For instance," he continued, "what is it you are most in need of at the moment?"

All of the Brigadier's troubles, the difficulties that beset every commanding officer in a war when there is never enough of anything and everything to meet his needs, came flooding back upon the Brigadier and he replied savagely, "Cement! A bloody great shipload of it for concrete. The engineers are hollowing out this Rock and they need concrete, concrete, concrete. We need it for the shops; we need it for the bombproofs, for ammunition dumps. We're getting it in driblets, confounded parsimonious spoonfuls——"

Major Clyde flicked the cable with a fingernail, "There you are, sir," he said quietly. "All you require."

Gaskell was still groping for the penny; he looked his query in the direction of the Major.

"Major Bailey will be requesting concrete for the shelters he'd be building for the apes——" Clyde said.

The penny made a fine brazen clangour within the Brigadier's skull as it finally dropped. "By God," he exclaimed. "You mean——?"

"Oh yes," replied the Major simply. "Quite! We'll see that there's enough for everyone."

It was the turn of the Brigadier to pick up the signal and regard it, and the look he bestowed upon it was now a fond one. By some alchemy it had been transformed from his enemy to his friend. And the five words, "every effort should be made," now stood out from the pages as though they had been written in raised and burnished gold. "You mean promote young Bailey and no trouble?"

"Exactly, sir. When the P.M. says he wants every effort made— no one's going to stop to ask questions."

"Gad," said Gaskell again, glancing once more at the treasure between his fingers; then, "I say, look here, Major."

"Yes, sir."

"You chaps know a lot more about this kind of thing than I do."

"If I can be of any help, sir."

"Well I thought perhaps if I turned the whole business over to you to look after——"

"If you wanted me to, sir."

"Well, I do want it. I'd appreciate it."

"I'd be glad to, sir—— If you'd just initial that perhaps and let me have it. You might add that I have your instructions and they are to be carried out."

The Brigadier almost upset the ink in his eagerness to reach the pen. "Exactly. And you'd send a signal to——"

"Of course," said Major Clyde, "saying that all steps to comply with the wishes of the P.M. were being undertaken and in hand."

"Splendid," said the Brigadier, and he scribbled upon the sheet and handed it to the Major, arising. "Very good of you. Wish they'd send out a few more officers like yourself." He arose and proffered his hand, which the Major shook warmly and departed. Gaskell felt as though the entire weight of the Rock had been lifted from his shoulders.

Chapter 14

GROUP CAPTAIN CRANCH IS BRIEFED

The first council of war following the reinstatement of Captain, now Major, Bailey as Officer in Charge Apes took place in the office of Major McPherson. Present were the Majors Bailey, Clyde, and McPherson and Gunner Lovejoy. For the first time Tim was loaded with bumph, plans, maps, and statistics, none of which was going to be thrown back at him. Also he had a bandaged thumb.

Major McPherson raised an eyebrow and queried, "Hit it with a hammer moving in?"

Tim shook his head. "Welcome home from Scruffy," he replied happily. "Got me in the same place. Nothing like an occasional bit of human blood for old Scruff."

McPherson took the chair. "Okay, Tim, let's hear."

"It really breaks down into two parts," Tim began. "Surviving Apes, Care and Protection Of, and New Apes, Purchase Of and Transporting To."

"That's right, boy," Major Clyde said with a straight face, "keep it all official."

"You don't belong to the same Army I do," Tim said. "Eventually all this is going to wind up in some Colonel's in-basket, maybe even the Brigadier's."

"Not the Brigadier's," Clyde remarked. "He's been short-circuited. Own request. Anyway he's as happy as a sand boy. We are getting him enough cement to duplicate the pyramids. Also he's asked for steel to armour plate his bunkers. You know what getting steel is like. We've bunged it under additional fencing for apes' cages. The old boy is purring like a kitten. He goes around muttering to himself the new password to Brigadier's heaven—'The P.M. wants it.'"

"War *can* be beautiful," observed Major McPherson.

Tim said, "Give us the gen on your end of it, Lovejoy."

"Yes, sir," replied the Gunner and arose in the manner of the Company Chairman about to reply to the toast at the twenty-fifth anniversary banquet. "And I may say, sir, that no one is 'appier to 'ave you back on the job than John C. Lovejoy, though it would 'ave been better for everyone if they could 'ave got around to it sooner." He produced his usual grubby bit of paper and read, "Queen's Gate pack, there's old Scruff; Tony, though he ain't much use since Scruffy got to him last night—almost tore 'im in 'alf; Pat and Bill, Judy and Muriel, and a young female hapelet as yet unnamed; I'd say she wasn't looking too fit right now since she lost her mother."

Major Clyde let out a whistle. "Seven!"

"The Middle Hill pack is worse off than that," the Gunner said gloomily. "They're around on the weather side of the Rock. There's Frank—he's the leader, he's in pretty good shape—Sammy, Jim, and Ike, though I wouldn't give you much for them; they've all had a mauling at one time or another, and there's two male hapelets."

"No females," said Major Clyde.

"Thirteen altogether. That's a jolly number. Wait 'til the Jerry catches on to that happy notion."

"And speaking of that," Major Clyde suggested, "what about your security, McPherson?"

"The apes' village will be out of bounds," McPherson replied, "and the area will be road-blocked. The Middle Hill pack is somewhat more of a problem. Tim tells me the two can't be kept together or they'd destroy one another. We'll keep a guard posted at the entrance to the old gun galleries and another at the top twenty-four hours. Gloomy Gustave may be able to guess, but they won't be able to verify."

Major Clyde nodded. "That's good. Oh, and incidentally, Lovejoy, keep out of the Admiral Nelson for a while, will you, there's a good chap, and any other bar as well."

The Gunner looked hurt. "Who me, sir?"

"Yes, you."

The Gunner looked woeful and wistful. "For how long, sir?"

"Duration of the emergency." Major Clyde took some of the sting out of his last remark by adding, "I suggest that all of us keep out of public bars and places for the time being and do our drinking in private. What's that foul tipple you swill, Gunner— Guinness and lime juice? I'll see that you get a supply."

"Thank you, sir," said the Gunner gratefully. "Ah, it's wonderful stuff. Gets into your blood and puts your nerves right."

"I wouldn't doubt it," the Major agreed. He said to Tim, "How is the new work going?"

"Capital," Tim replied. "We're waiting on a shipment of cement and wire for the big cages and shelters, but I've got two small cages up and some fair enough shelters at both Middle Hill and Queen's Gate from what the Gunner and I could liberate."

"Splendid," said the Major. "That leaves, then, only——"

"The new stuff," Tim concluded, and got out his maps.

There were different-coloured marks and notations on his map of North Africa, checks, circles, crosses, triangles, marking such cities as Tangier, Rabat, Ceuta, and Casablanca and even such more remote towns as Fez and Ouida. "You see, sir," he explained to Major Clyde, to whom although he was the same rank as Tim now and not much older he accorded the same respect that he would have a headmaster or a genuine operating wizard, "the trouble is that these are all now more than eighteen months old and we don't actually know the real situation with regard to available beasts in more than one or two of them. When the Gunner and I [the Gunner looked pleased and flattered at being included] were on the job, what we tried to do was get some reserve in depth. You never know with apes. They're tough brutes who can survive the worst kind of mauling, or they can keel over quick as a wink from some silly bug in the chest or a pain in the tummy. It takes a year or two usually to get a new beast acclimated to the Rock and we wanted to know at all times where we could lay our hands on some if it looked as though we might be going to need them."

Major Clyde murmured, "Son, you'll wind up at Staff College if you're not careful."

"But, as I say, that was almost two years ago and the picture may all be changed now. The only one I'm at all reasonably certain about because of a chap I know who is a pal of this Spanish fellow is over in Ceuta."

They all bent their heads over the map to see the town and its location which Tim had marked not only with a cross but with the female symbol.

"What's the gen?" Major Clyde asked.

"Spaniard," Tim replied, "fellow by the name of Blasco Irun. Bachelor, top-heavy with ducats. Has a female, and he's short of whisky. Chap I know was over there not more than a month ago. And this Blasco fellow was feeling him out on what the chances were of getting his hands on some real Scotch. He sounded thirsty enough to make a deal."

McPherson said, "Why don't we start with the Señor then?"

"That's what I was thinking," Tim said. "It's females we need. He's got one. We've got the kind of currency he wants, and in the meantime if we can buy up enough apes to make up the twenty-four the P.M. wants, we can send him a signal and keep him happy, and if the majority of them are females, with the new cages we might get them breeding this Christmas. By next spring——"

"You make it all sound so simple," commented Major Clyde, "and how do we get the lady over here?"

"I thought perhaps you might be able to use your influence with Group Captain Cranch. He's here now supervising the building of the air strip."

"Howard Cranch," Major Clyde said meditatively. "It's an idea," but he didn't add that something inside him whispered faintly, "*But not a very good one.*" It was not that Group Captain Cranch was not a fine flyer; it was merely that Major Clyde had a certain distrust of all air-force types. They were not stable people. Stable people didn't depart from the earth in contraptions made, of all things, of steel. Still, even though he disliked and distrusted it as a means of transport, the Major had to concede that the airplane had come to stay and that if Cranch was willing it was a cheap and expeditious way to get their first ape in a hurry. "I'll have a word with Howard," he said. "O.K., lads, let's get cracking."

Group Captain Howard Cranch, in command of the collection of dodos passing for aircraft and assigned to the defence of Gibraltar, was a burly man almost as broad as he was long. His head was planted on his shoulders, the neck having been practically omitted. The ends of his R.A.F. moustache stuck out from either side of a small but full mouth, which any physiognomist would have told you indicated a love of pleasure, unrestricted and unconfined, and he had the small, twinkling, merry eyes of the confirmed party-thrower and life of same.

Group Captain Howard Cranch's parties and his routines at them were well known on the Rock. They took place in his house down near the apology for an air strip, usually every Saturday night. There was liquor, there was food, and there were Group Captain Cranch's routines, unfailing and unvarying.

The Group Captain kept a small supply of costumes in a side bedroom, and from time to time he would vanish from the general merriment, to reappear as an Arab, a toreador, an African hunter, a sailor, or Lady Maude opening a garden fête.

He put his heart and soul into these impersonations, and therefore managed to be screamingly funny, even after he had been seen many times by guests who were practically the same week in and week out. The Group Captain could sing—he had a fine, robust baritone voice; he could dance—for all of his bulk of one hundred and ninety pounds, he could move about as gracefully and lightly as a gazelle; he could mimic—his impersonations of certain high personages on the Rock were famous; he could recite bawdy poetry by the hour; he could play the piano, the drums, and the cornet; and he could hold his liquor like a gentleman.

Like so many of his kind, however, in the air Group Captain Cranch was quite a different specimen. The other half of definitely a dual personality was a born flyer, and one who could keep a faltering aircraft aloft by sheer will power and strength of stomach muscles.

In command of a covey of Stirlings, Albatrosses, and a pair of lumbering Blackwell Bothas left over from World War I, he flew them all as though they were gliders and managed to imbue his command with something of the grace and elegance of his flying.

It was to this extraordinary person that the mission was entrusted of flying to Ceuta, contacting the mysterious Señor Blasco Irun, delivering to him a case of illicitly procured Black and White Scotch whisky, and returning in exchange with one female Barbary ape. On this all-important operation Group Captain Cranch was briefed by Major Tim Bailey and Major McPherson.

The briefing took place as usual in Major McPherson's musty office behind the Colonial Secretariat. Present were Majors Clyde, McPherson, and Bailey, the latter looking preoccupied and guarding a large box-shaped, mysterious something beneath a cloth.

A shadow shaped somewhat like a bull elephant or a rhino showed up on the opaque glass panelling of the door which now flew open and in exactly the manner of one or the other of those beasts on a charge, Group Captain Howard Cranch burst into the office. It was curious that although the flyer was senior in rank to all those present he seemed the youngest and the most exuberant of the lot. He came in shouting, "Ho Cads! What's the gen? I hear I'm supposed to jockey some flipping monkey across the Straits."

Himself flapping like a giant crane, Major Clyde leaped to the door, locked it, flapped to the window, and pulled down a shade, shouting, "Security! Hear no evil, see no evil, speak no evil."

"Oh-oh-oh," said the Group Captain, "sorry," and went tiptoeing about the room, his hands over his ears and his eyes and his mouth pantomiming; then he said, "Oh hello, Slinker. This your show? I thought you were back in London with the bulging brains. I've a feeling I'm not going to like this."

"Piece of cake," Clyde said. "How'd you like to save the Empire and win a medal?"

Group Captain Cranch wrinkled his nose and said, "I've got a medal. Got it for falling out of an aircraft. There I was at ten thousand feet minding my own business when this Hun who up to that time had taken no part in the conversation——"

"Yes, yes," said Major Clyde hastily. "You know all these chaps, I gather? There's really nothing to it, Howard, there's a Spaniard lives in a villa five miles out of Ceuta on the road to Casablanca. He's got a female ape by the name of Ramona which he's going to sell to us. There'll be a car and escort waiting for you at the airport. Everything's laid on. All you do is pick up the ape, fly it back here, and earn the undying gratitude of the nation."

"What, with it in my lap?" asked Cranch.

"Show him, Tim," Clyde said.

With a gesture filled with the import and drama of a magician climaxing his trick, Tim whipped a cloth off what it was concealing and revealed a small wooden case containing a most marvellous network of straps, webbing, and strips of live rubber.

The Group Captain regarded it with fascination. "What the devil is that? And what am I supposed to do with it?"

"It's for the female, sir," Tim explained, "so that she won't get tossed about. You see, her head goes in here, and her body here, and this rubber takes up the strain. She'll be really almost weightless. I've worked it out. The harness will hold her tummy here, and you fit this over her bottom part, and that takes the stress off, should you happen to hit any air pockets."

The Group Captain marched around this contraption three times with one finger pressed against the side of his nose, and muttering under his breath some kind of unintelligible air-force jargon. At the end of his tour he said fondly to Tim, "That's absolutely wizard, my boy. But would you mind telling me who puts the flipping ape inside that thing?"

Tim threw an I-told-you-so look at Major Clyde and said, "There, you see? That's just what I was saying. I really ought to be going along on this mission."

Clyde said sternly, "No you don't, laddie. What's the good of the Grouper bringing the bitch over if in the meantime someone does old Scruffy in?"

Tim sighed and said, "I know. I was afraid of that." Then turning to the flyer, he said, "But I've provided for it." He produced an envelope which he handed to the Group Captain, who regarded it suspiciously and then looked inside at what appeared to be some white powder.

He said, "What do I do—put some of that on its tail?"

Tim said, "It's to be administered internally an hour before take-off. Got it from the Medical Officer. He's worked out the proportions. Once you get her off to sleep you'll have no trouble putting her into her harness in the box."

The Group Captain said, "I'm going to love this. And how am I supposed to get this stuff inside her?"

Tim had an answer to that, too. "If I might suggest," he said, "I should wear gloves." He reached into his pocket and produced a pair of heavy leather ones. "The teeth rarely go through these," he promised.

The Group Captain regarded him admiringly. "You think of everything, don't you, Junior?"

"We try," Major Clyde said modestly.

Major McPherson now spoke and said, "Look here, Howard, I know it's all pretty silly, but this one really is hush-hush and we want all the security we can get. Someone's been tipping the Hun about what's been going on in Tim's department. You've heard the broadcasts, haven't you? People are getting windy. We haven't been able to locate it yet. It's an inside job, that's all we know."

"Probably the clot who looks after them. What's his name—Lovejoy?" said the Group Captain, and knew not how close he had come to hitting the nail on the head.

Tim flared in hot protest, forgetting that Group Captain Cranch was equal to a Colonel in rank.

"Dammit, that's not true. Gunner Lovejoy would die before he'd leak anything."

Cranch suddenly went stepping about the room on tiptoes as though walking on eggs and saying, "Oh-oh-oh. Sorry, sorry, sorry. No offence intended. Probably old Scruff himself got on the blower to the Germans. I hear he's a prime stinker."

Major McPherson said, "We can fill you in later on this. The point is the Brigadier wants the apes kept up to strength. Tim here has located this Spanish chap with a female of the right age. We've got the price the fellow wants, but by tomorrow the Hun might get on to him and double it. We are depending on you."

Cranch looked wise. "I get it," he said. "What do I pay?"

Major Clyde and Tim exchanged glances, after which the Major opened the door of a cupboard, revealing a nailed-down case of Black and White Scotch whisky.

A look of sheer horror settled upon the countenance of the Group Captain as the implications of the situation became clear. "What?" he shouted, forgetting security. "You're asking me to ferry a case of Scotch whisky *off* the Rock and bring back a seeping chimp in return? Ho now, come on, you trio of middens, there's a limit to what you can ask a man to do even in a war!"

McPherson, being a Scot, had no difficulty looking properly sympathetic. "I know," he said, "it's a shocking waste, but there it is. That's what he wants."

Cranch growled, "Where the devil did you get it? I didn't know there was any more of this stuff about. We've been drinking anti-freeze the last six weeks."

"It was the Governor's," Major Clyde explained, his long face sad and grave. "Tim stole it. The police are looking for him now. The sooner you get this hot cargo out of here——"

For a moment Cranch had the air of a man who was out of his depth and ready to admit it. He said, "And they say the Air Force is crackers. O.K. What's this dog stealer's name I'm supposed to contact?"

Tim consulted some papers from his file. "His name is Blasco Irun. Supposed to be loaded with pesetas. But what he hasn't got is whisky. He knows you're coming."

The Group Captain was regarding the case of Scotch with a finger pressed to the side of his nose, and he again suddenly went into his little walking-on-eggs dance about the room. "Whish," he said, "whish, whish. Maybe the blighter mightn't be so bad if he knows a good drink of Scotch whisky, O.K., lads I'm your man."

Chapter 15

RAMONA

The Group Captain took off in an old Albatross on this mission, since there was not room in the cockpit of his personal Hawker Fury for the case of Scotch or the contraption in which his prize was to be returned.

However, he flew without a co-pilot for the sake of security, and the case of Scotch rested upon the seat next to him.

Before his departure he had been additionally briefed by the Major and Tim on the importance of the operation upon which he was engaged, but truth to tell it had not entirely sunk in, due in part to his overwhelming aversion to exporting so precious a fluid and handing it over to a foreigner in exchange for some filthy kind of ape. That sort of thing simply went against the grain. And because of the seriousness of the situation the Major was actually prevented from letting the Group Captain in on exactly *how* important the matter was, and that the P.M. himself had sent a signal—Top Secret—and was keeping an eye on the affair.

As far as the Group Captain was concerned, this project appeared to be one of those wet shows cooked up by psychological-warfare boffins. Still, the orders for the mission had come from the proper authority and Cranch was not in favour of irritating the Higher Ups.

However, the case of whisky at his side, which would have provided an absolutely smashing party, was very much on his mind, and all during the flight across to Africa the Group Captain, by association, was bellowing, "The Spaniard who blighted my life," above the roar of his single engine, meaning, of course, Señor Blasco Irun, and a song which he made up himself, which

went: "Blast old Blasco—bung him on his arsco," and could get
no further with than the first couplet.

In deference to his cargo, Cranch made an eggshell landing on
the Ceuta air strip and, in accordance with his instructions, remained at the far end of the runway. The Consul had done his
work well in the matter of bribes. Eight Guardias Civil in their
patent-leather hats, and armed with carbines, formed a cordon
around the aircraft; the car appeared with a Moroccan driver who
exhibited a mouthful of gold teeth, quickly removed the case of
Scotch and the transportation box to the rear of his vehicle, and
motioned the Group Captain into the front seat. They set off in
the direction of the darkling and sombre hills back of the coast
line. The time was six o'clock.

By this time some of the gloom cast over him by his mission
had begun to evaporate from Cranch, who was too cheerful an
individual to remain depressed over long periods. He reflected
that he was off the Rock; it obviously was going to be an overnight
job; Ceuta was a place not exactly noted for its restrictions; he'd
bung the powder into the old monkey, sew her up into her box,
and go off on the town. Things could be a lot worse. He might
even be able to import a few bottles of Spanish brandy, though
this was known on the Rock as The Fate Worse Than Death and
indicated why the Spaniards put such a high value on honest
Scotch whisky.

The Group Captain's spirits lifted further as the road on which
his driver took him, instead of leading to some slum or scruffy
bit of farmland, began to pass through exquisitely cultivated fruit
orchards and private estates featuring splendid villas with red roofs
and walls almost hidden beneath wistaria and bougainvillaea. In
his mind he had pictured the monkey-keeping Señor Irun as
being a ragged fellow with a stubble beard and broken teeth
who stank of garlic.

Now they were obviously heading for the residential section—
the Señor might even be the type who would offer a chap a
snort.

The villas grew larger and more luxurious, and finally they
turned up a broad avenue of palms, passed through a pair of

large wrought-iron gates, and drew up before a hacienda of truly magnificent style and proportions. An African in snow-white trousers, red jacket, and tarboosh opened the door; another took the Group Captain's cap. Cranch revised his opinion of Señor Irun upwards again and imagined the owner of so much magnificence as a stately don, when a small, rotund man with somewhat baggy cheeks and ten long hairs laid in parallel lines across his otherwise bald head appeared and said, "You are the Captain Cranch? I am Blasco Irun. You are most welcome here." And then he added with just a trace of anxiety. "You have eet weeth you?"

"It's just out in the car, Señor," Cranch reported, "all ticketyboo. Dropped it in light as a feather. I'll bet there wasn't even a ripple."

The Señor brightened perceptibly and clapped his hands; four more Africans appeared and he went into a torrent of instructions in Spanish, with elegant and expressive pantomime from which the Group Captain gathered they had been advised to transport the case as gently as though it were the corpse of their late grandmother.

Cranch, who had been in Spain long enough to appreciate the décor, noted that the huge room in which he found himself was a treasure chamber luxuriously furnished in examples of Spanish, Moorish, and African art and handicraft. "Blimey," he said to himself, "there's lolly 'ere."

The four Africans entered bearing the case with the reverence called for and brought it to another feather landing on the floor. Two more approached with hammer and chisel and applied themselves to the task of prying open the case with the same care used by an archaeologist approaching some priceless find embedded in the earth. The Señor, clad in immaculate white trousers and white shirt, bound with a broad red sash draped about his protuberant stomach, hovered over them, his hands fluttering, lips pursed, and eyes filled with anxiety. Cranch made another quick revision, but this time downwards. "Oh no, no, no," he said to himself, "this drain isn't buying a drink. He'll want it all for himself."

With a gentle creaking the lid came off, revealing the bottles secured in straw, and each one sealed and intact.

As the Group Captain had reported, not even a ripple had disturbed their contents. The round, anxious face of the Señor now relaxed into an enchanting and childlike smile. *"Muy bien,"* and he went over and shook Cranch solemnly by the hand. "Well," he said, "well, well," and Cranch suddenly realised he was translating from *bien* and meant "good." "Now come weeth me, please."

He led the Group Captain through a succession of rooms of bewildering beauty and luxury until they came to a conservatory at one end of which was a large cage in which sat a full-grown African macaque, or Barbary ape, squatting on her haunches and eating a banana. Upon their entrance she ceased for a moment, looked and regarded them with disinterest out of her golden-brown eyes, and then returned to her fruit.

The Señor flung out an arm proudly. "There she ees! Ees she not beautiful? She make you ver' fine babies, I theenk. Her name ees Ramona."

Something in the name stirred a memory in Group Captain Cranch, a memory of other times and other places, of girls and parties, wailing saxophones and dancing. He suddenly filled his lungs and in his resonant baritone gave forth with——

"Ramona, I hear the mission bells above.
Ramona, they're ringing out our song of love.
I press you, caress you,
And bless the day you taught me to care. . . ."

The song filled the patio, causing Ramona to drop her banana in amazement, and the Señor to regard the Group Captain with a kind of astonished and excited interest.

Señor Irun cried, "You seeng?"

The Group Captain was now seized with the exaltation that sometimes filled him when he heard the sound of his own voice. "Do I sing?" he repeated. "Do I sing?" And then, filling the vast box of his chest with air, he let fly with *"Ridi Pagliacci,"* causing some Moorish lamps hanging from the ceiling to stir uneasily, and Ramona to leap up the side of her cage and chatter at him, though whether it was with love or anger was impossible to say.

At the conclusion of the rendition, Cranch swept the rotund little man a bow. Irun clapped two small, pudgy hands together and cried, "Well! *Magnífico! Maravilloso!* You are very versatile, no?"

The Group Captain swept the Señor another bow. "Howard Arthur Cranch, at your service," he said. "Songs, dances, impersonations and recitations, sleight of hand, and tricks with string."

Señor Irun did not react to this note of pleasantry as one might have expected him to, either as a wealthy Spanish gentleman or a fellow who could take a joke. Instead the look that he turned upon the Group Captain was full of a curious kind of eagerness mingled with wistfulness. "Thees is true?" he asked. "You can do all theese theengs?"

"Bookings available now until Christmas," Cranch replied. "Performances guaranteed, or money refunded."

"Maybe," the Señor said, "maybe perhaps then you could stay and we could have a little party?"

The word "party" acted upon Cranch like an electric shock and drove all banter out of his system. "Eh—what's that?" he said. "A party? Do you mean it?"

"Oh yes, pleese," the Señor said. A certain amount of becoming shyness suddenly suffused him as he asked, "Do you like girls?"

The Group Captain turned his eyes heavenward and repeated the question twice, "Do I like girls? He asks me do I like girls?"

"I like girls," the Señor confided.

The Group Captain extended one of his large hands and said, "Señor, that makes us brothers."

"Oh well, well!" cried the Señor, confusing Cranch momentarily until he translated it back into, "Good, good!" "I know many girls who like the party. They live in the town. I will invite them and they will come because I am the black ship."

"Are you, old boy?" said Cranch. "Sort of a piratey chap, what? Skull and crossbones, eh?"

"No, no," the Señor said. "The black ship of the family. The other ships have white wool—mine, she is black, because I am the playboy. Always I have been the playboy. No nice girl of a good family will marry with me, even though I am ver' wealthy. But of thees I am glad, because I am different from other Spaniards. I love the party. I will invite the girls. You have brought the liquor, and you will seeng and do for us all your tricks. Then they will love you ver' much."

For a moment Cranch felt a dreamlike quality as though he had suddenly been trapped into acting out a major role in a story which had just gone the rounds of the services on the Rock and which began: "It seems that this commercial traveller suddenly found himself in the Sultan's harem with all these beautiful girls around him, when——" He shook himself mentally like a terrier to snap himself out of it. For all he knew the Señor might produce a lot of old bags with buck teeth. However, the chance was well worth taking, the Scotch was real, and so was the Señor's eagerness. He placed his finger alongside his nose and said, "Whish," took a few tiptoe steps up and down the room, and said, "Lead on, son. Let's get cracking."

"Oh well, well!" cried Señor Irun and clapped his hands. The slaves of his particular lamp appeared from all doorways.

The party was a huge and outstanding success. The measure of its attainment can be judged by the fact that the Group Captain was not compelled to exaggerate when upon his return he narrated the story for the benefit of his fellow officers. The girls resembled either Rita Hayworth or Betty Grable, or a blending of both. They were gay and untrammelled. The young men called upon to fill in the interstices were handsome and docile, immediately relinquishing any young lady with whom either the Señor or the Group Captain wished to dance.

There were two orchestras imported from Ceuta so that the music was continuous, except when Cranch was rendering his specialty numbers that did not call for orchestral accompaniment. There were carloads of sherry, lorryloads of champagne, caviar, and foie gras, but the basis of it all was really the case of Black and White Scotch whisky, which provided in a way the theme of the party. The war had shut down the supply and the communi-

cants approached this gift of the gods with veneration and gratitude. It even, black ship or not, brought out some of the nice
people, who applauded Howard Cranch's performance with enthusiasm. None of them had ever seen anyone like Group
Captain Cranch before; Cranch had never had such an audience,
or such a good time, in his life, and toward the middle of the
evening he rewrote his couplet into: "Blessing on old Blasco—
the Señor's the Tabasco," and after a while they all sang it like a
hymn.

The Señor himself waddled from room to room to make sure
that everybody was having a good time, thus enjoying the best of
good times himself.

The high point of the affair was reached about 1 A.M., when
Group Captain Cranch, who had retired to a bedroom for a
change of costume (it seems that the Señor, who also had a
predilection for fancy-dress balls, kept a supply on hand), appeared as a Chinaman with a long queue and, aided by the
Señor, the orchestra, and the ape of that name, sang "Ramona"
as it probably never had been rendered before.

It was fortunate that the monkey actually liked noise and people, and when freed from her cage leaped about and screeched
and screamed as enthusiastically as any of them. She had taken a
shine to Cranch apparently and offered no difficulties when
called upon to assist him in the execution of the famous song.

"Lamona," sang the Chinese Cranch, "I hear the mission bells
above."

Over his head Señor Irun rang a large dinner bell.

"Lamona, they're ringee out our song of love. I press-ee you,
caress-ee you. . . ."

Ramona loved that part and pressed and caressed right back,
howling with excitement.

"Lamona, when day is done I'll hear you call. . . ." (Aside:
you can hear this one clear down to Tangier.) "Lamona, I'll meet
you by the waterfall."

This performance taking place in the patio where there was a
fountain, the Group Captain suited action to the words and got
into it.

"I dread the dawn when I awake-ee to find you gawn. . . ."

Ramona here supplied the action, not caring for water, and went up onto the balcony.

"Lamona," sang the Group Captain, raising his arms to her, "I need you—my own."

It was agreed that there had never before in the history of Spanish Africa, or any other place, been a party the like of this, and Señor Irun was as happy as a child.

But afterward, when he had got out of his Chinese costume and reappeared to mingle with the guests in uniform, Cranch for the first time was preoccupied. His recent act had reminded him of something which had quite slipped his mind; he had a mission to perform which was only half completed. He had delivered the case of whisky all right, but there was still this chimp, or rather, Ramona, to be handed over to some dim bulbs by the names of Bailey, McPherson, and Clyde.

Vaguely through his somewhat fume-invaded mind there passed recollections of instructions, warnings, a contraption of strings, straps, and slings and rubber bands, and white powder in an envelope, leather gloves, Top Secret, hush-hush, and "For God's sake, old man, don't fail us."

The gloves, he suddenly remembered, were back in the aeroplane, some ten miles off, but the envelope with the knock-out powder which would enable him to place Ramona in her box was in the inside breast pocket of his tunic, and he could feel it crackling there.

Señor Irun came up and said, "Here, what's this, Howard? You are looking serious? This is not the time for serious! Gay-gay-gay! Always gay! You have make me the best party. Come, we weel have a dreenk of Black and Whites together and then you will laugh again."

But now that memory had returned, Cranch was not to be put off. He said, "No, no, old boy, it isn't that easy. We've got a problem on our hands. You remember that little box I brought? We've got to get Ramona into it so she won't get hurt." He produced the envelope with the powder and said, "They gave me this to quiet her down—but how the devil do we get it inside her?"

The Señor, who, like Cranch, gave no outward sign of the amount of liquor he had consumed, found himself equally baffled by the problem, but knew one ready step to solution. He said, "We weel go have a drink, and perhaps these will give us idea." He put his fingers to his mouth and emitted a shrill whistle, whereupon Ramona came running and hopping from wherever she had been and leaped onto his shoulder.

They went up to the Señor's bedroom, where the case of Scotch had been stashed, since it would have been fatal to have let the thirsty mob at it in one fell swoop, and they had been doling it out a bottle at a time. They poured themselves each a dollop and toasted one another.

Somehow a whiff of the spirit was wafted to Ramona, and she reached up a long, thin arm and begged for a sip. The Group Captain and the Spaniard exchanged glances as the penny dropped simultaneously for both of them. Not a word was spoken. Cranch produced the envelope with the powder, Señor Irun filled a fifth of a tumbler with Scotch whisky, the powder dissolved without a trace, leaving the liquid clear and amber-coloured. The Señor handed the potion to Ramona, who tossed it off like a debutante, sneezed, coughed, and then applauded violently, smacking her lips at the same time.

"There you are, my pretty," said the Señor, "you will sleep now. Come, you shall sleep on my bed, for it is your last night here before you journey to Gibraltar to be a bride."

He picked up the monkey and laid her on the silken coverlet of his bed, where she curled up with her hands over her face, as though to shield herself from the light.

"Come," said Señor Irun, "she will be asleep in the morning when we will return and put her in the box, and you will fly away. But now there are still more hours left to be gay. When will you show us your tricks with streeng?"

As they left the room, Cranch looked back over his shoulder. He had the impression that the fingers of the ape's hands had opened, and that her golden-brown eyes looking through them were watching them depart. He could not quite catch the expression in them.

There was only one incident to mar the best of all parties: someone stole a bottle of the Scotch whisky, a breach of hospitality that Señor Irun would not have believed possible even from some of the town characters. But there was no doubt about it; when they returned to the bedroom for a fresh bottle, one was missing. Someone had found their cache. On the silken counterpane Ramona was sleeping like an angel, the potion having evidently knocked her for six in jig time, as Captain Bailey had predicted. A search of the room yielded no clues. Señor Irun then decided to put the little unpleasantness out of his mind entirely, and to prevent a repetition of it he and Cranch gathered up the remaining bottles and took them below. The pace and tempo of the party stepped up.

Eventually came the party's end and the dawn. Unlike the song, Ramona was not "gawn" but still reposed on the silk coverlet, out like the well-known light. She was not only out, she was limp, and tight as they were themselves, the two men had no difficulty in inserting her into the intricate network of webbing that Major Bailey had devised for her security.

Now that he saw how it worked, the Group Captain was quite stiff with admiration for the ingenuity of his colleague. "Clever chap," he kept muttering. "Damned clever chap! She'll ride like a baby." While Señor Irun kept repeating, "Well," over and over.

He insisted upon driving the Group Captain to the air strip himself in his special-bodied Fleetwood Cadillac, the back of which he first loaded with a parting gift of the last remaining bottle of Scotch, a case of champagne, a case of sherry, and half a dozen bottles of Fundador brandy of a superior type which was almost drinkable, for at some time during the morning he and Cranch had sworn blood brotherhood and eternal friendship, and the promise of another party when the war was concluded.

At the air strip the Guardia Civil formed ranks; Ramona, slumbering still peacefully in her shock-proof crate, was placed next the pilot, where the whisky had been, after which the potables were stowed in a way that wouldn't interfere with the balance of the Albatross or meet the eye of casual inspection.

The Group Captain and his host expended five minutes of embrazios, after which the flyer climbed into his seat, pushed the self-starter button, revved up his engine, and took off.

Since flying was a gift as well as a profession with him, he aviated quite as well with his blood stream full of alcohol, if not better. His landing an hour later on the Gibraltar air strip before the anxious eyes of Tim Bailey, Major McPherson, and Gunner Lovejoy was an absolute masterpiece—a fairy kiss of lightness. When he rolled to a stop, the three men were at his side in a utility car. They shouted up to him: "Have you got her? Is she all right, sir? Was there any trouble? It's O.K., isn't it?"

Cranch was at first tempted to launch into a description of how O.K. everything had been, but then something warned him that considering the amount he had imbibed it might be just as well not to engender jealousy in the hearts of his inferiors in rank. Looking down from the officer of the bomber, he merely said, "Tickety-boo, lads. Tickety-boo." And then without realising it added, "Well!"

They invaded his aircraft and tenderly lifted the crate containing Ramona and brought it to earth. Major Bailey raised the lid and peered at the ape safely suspended by his brilliant contraption. McPherson also glanced inside with a sigh of relief.

"Oh good, sir," Tim said to the Group Captain, who by this time had climbed down out of the aircraft and stood leaning against it in what seemed to be a nonchalant pose but actually expressed a need for support. "Splendid! It all worked out just as I said. She's still asleep."

Into this tender scene of mission accomplished and congratulations cut the harsh voice of Gunner Lovejoy, who was feeling about the same as the Group Captain, having had to stay up all night with the two officers waiting for the aircraft, without recourse to Guinness and lime juice. "Asleep!—my eye and Betty Martin," he rasped, "she's dead. She's deader than Kelcy's you-know-whats," a phrase he had learned from some American. "I'd say she's been dead for a couple of hours."

The cries of anguish and dismay that rose from the throats of the four men were sincere: "What?—Oh no!—Oh I say, not dead?"

His heart sinking and his conscience already saddened by the necessity for some thumping lies, the Group Captain came over and looked into the box. "Why, the little rascal was alive and kicking when I put her in this morning," he said. "We had the devil's own time. Here—you can see the print of her teeth in my thumb. Oh well—it's worn off by now." Then, and he hated to do this to a junior officer who was probably not a bad chap, he said, looking at Tim Bailey, "It's that confounded contraption of yours strangled her to death, I'll wager. She was just as gentle—I could have brought her over sitting on my shoulder. That's what did it, that blasted net of yours. Well, sorry, boys. I'm for some shuteye." He hoisted his parachute over his shoulder and marched off, leaving young Captain Bailey staring aghast into the box at the death trap he had set for this much needed female.

It was to Cranch's credit that he felt like a thorough rotter— but, after all, what else had there been to do? If there was any comfort in the situation, the monkey was dead and couldn't talk, and nobody would ever find out about the party. The liquor he had brought with him could bide in the aircraft until nightfall, when he could safely remove it.

This complacent frame of mind lasted just thirty-six hours, when he returned to his office from an observation flight to find an official envelope from the Medical Officer on his desk addressed to himself. It was a carbon copy of an autopsy report on the body of the ape Ramona, conducted by Major Llewellyn Jones, R.A.M.C., and read in part:

"As a result of an autopsy conducted by me upon the body of a female of the species of African macaque, or Barbary ape, delivered to me at 0900 hours on the 5th November by Major McPherson, Captain Bailey, OIC Apes, and Gunner Lovejoy, it is my conclusion that this specimen died of acute alcoholic poisoning.

"An analysis of the blood showed the presence of 13 per cent per c.c. of alcohol in the brain and circulatory system, of which 6 per cent may be considered a fatal dose.

"Analysis of some of the contents of the stomach indicated that this alcohol was Scotch-type whisky.

"Off the findings, I would deduce unofficially that this ape had consumed from three fourths to four fifths of a bottle of Scotch whisky before being embarked.

"All other indications of death negative."

(Signed) LLEWELLYN JONES,
M.D., R.A.M.C., etc.

The Group Captain sat staring down at the document. He rested one finger on the side of his nose and said, "Whish," but this time with no tiptoeing about the room, only with infinite sadness, to which he added an "oh dear, oh dear." He knew now what had become of the missing bottle of Scotch.

The final disaster took place a month after the return of Group Captain Cranch to the Rock with the remains of the female macaque and sent the Majors Bailey, McPherson, and Clyde and Gunner Lovejoy into an anxious and worried huddle in McPherson's office which Clyde was using as a base.

Towards the end of August there had been another violent thunderstorm of shattering intensity, accompanied by torrential rain, high winds, and destructive lightning which had worked considerable damage to installations on the Rock. On its heels, instead of a warm, dry period, had followed a Levanter, the first and fatal harbinger of summer's end, a cold damp cloud that clamped itself upon the upjutting Rock and had maintained its grip for seventy-two hours, at the end of which time half of the inhabitants of the Rock were down with influenza, colds, bronchitis, or Gibraltar fever, and most of the ape pack were dead. It was all the more tragic because construction of the shelters had begun. If they had been ready for use, practically all of the beasts would have survived.

"All right, Lovejoy," Clyde said, "let's have it."

"There ain't too much to 'ave," Lovejoy replied. "It's like Major Bailey said, there's old Scruffy and four hapelets. Three of them sick. We might pull one through——"

"So to all intents and purposes," suggested Major Clyde.

"There's only old Scruff," concluded the Gunner, "and if he wasn't so tough we'd be at rock bottom and on the way to being cleaned out."

"If we can keep the Germans from finding out——"

"We can keep them from knowing," Major Clyde said, "but not from guessing. I could write the next German broadcast for you: 'as a result of the severe electrical storm followed by a dangerous Levanter further deaths have occurred in the ranks of the Barbary apes located on Gibraltar, diminishing the pack to the point where panic is about to set in amongst the British stationed there,' and so on and so on."

"I suppose we ought to keep Scruffy under lock and key. But how can we when we haven't even——"

"That's just what we don't do," Clyde contradicted. "We are going to have to rely on Scruffy to show the flag for us—or rather show the monkey."

It was Lovejoy who twigged first. "Spread him around town, eh sir?" he said.

"That's it. We will have to take a chance. He's tough and that's a fact. The more places he's seen——"

"He can do enough mischief by hisself for a whole pack of monkeys," the Gunner observed.

"That's the purpose of the exercise. We need a breather. Tim, what have you got to report?"

Tim produced a folder of correspondence. His expression was glum.

"I've cabled some and written others," he said. "We've drawn nothing but blanks. Some moved away, some no have apes, several no reply at all, but most of them had ape but sold recently. It's almost like a pattern developing."

Major Clyde had his lank form wrapped around an office chair and was regarding Tim quizzically. "Well, what did you expect?"

"Why I—good Lord, Will, you don't mean——"

"Oh yes," Clyde said. "They've been buying them up like stink. We have had chaps out. They've been scouring North Africa. The Germans are always ahead of us. Thorough bastards when they think they're on to something. We've got lines out to trap some wild ones, but so far no go. They may even have some men up in the hills scaring them off. And anyway they wouldn't do us much good for rebuilding the pack. You've said they want to be at least half domesticated before they'll breed."

"Particularly with old Scruff," Tim said, "he'd be apt to kill a wild one."

"In that case," Major Clyde said, "I think I had better be off to London." They all looked at him. Clyde said, "Whatever in the world anyone might want, the chances are that at least one of it can be found in London."

Tim shook his head. "I doubt if you will turn one up in the zoo. Not according to our records. We haven't sent a female to England since 1924. Look here, Will, maybe if I went over to Africa——"

Major Clyde shook his head, "Nothing doing. The place for an OIC Apes is with his apes, whether he's got any or not. Look here, lads! Here's the plot." Major Clyde unwound himself from his chair and reached for a pencil and pad on which to doodle while he talked. "We're in a damned bad spot and there's no use our not admitting it. The Germans know we've lost the bulk of our apes and that it's the kind of thing likely to put the wind up, but fortunately they don't know how near the bottom of the barrel we are. And it's up to us to keep them from finding out. That's where you and Lovejoy come in, Tim. Everything normal on the Rock, food supplies go out to Prince Ferdinand's Battery as usual, even if you have to eat it yourselves. Apes seen around town. Scruffy tears up the Chaplain's garden. We'll get the local rag to print another editorial about the apes fouling the water catchments, and Something Must Be Done About It. If the Jerries put a real red-hot spy in here, a chap who knows his onions as well as his apes, Mac will turn him up and land him in the cooler, so they'll have to rely upon information which will be both inexpert and inaccurate. In the meantime I'll beetle off to London——"

"You would," commented McPherson.

"We have the organization there," Clyde said. "If there's a lady Barbarian in the British Isles we'll turn her up. We'll fly

her over here. She and old Scruff get matey. Apelet is born on the
Rock. An heir to the throne! All hail the crown prince! The line
of succession is preserved."

"One ruddy ape," Bailey said, unconvinced, "and say we still
have three; three and one makes four. The P.M. said twenty-
four——"

"The thing you don't appreciate, my boy, and what is going to
get us out of the bloody mess all of us are in, and I mean the
Empire as well as just the four of us, is that while the Jerry is
highly efficient and capable and a nasty fellow in a war, he is
also a supreme fathead, which is something you can give odds on.
He's also a great front runner, but if you look him in the eye in the
stretch he's likely to curl and head for the outside."

McPherson said, "I don't get the point, Will."

"The point, my dear fellow, is that if we can produce an ape on
the Rock and the chaps in Berlin get the idea that their bloke in
Algeciras has been feeding them a lot of duff gen they're quite
likely to drop it, call off their ape buyers, and forget the whole
business."

"And if it doesn't work?" Tim asked. "If we don't get the
crown prince?"

Major Clyde stopped his doodling and looked up at them, and
they saw that he had gone quite serious, the usual lighthearted
gaiety missing from his expression. "Why we just must, mates," he
replied, "if for no other reason than that people are so damn silly
you never know what they're going to do. They're supposed to
have brains and judgment, but it takes no more than a feather to
tip the scales one way or another. A lot of Greeks lost a battle
because some birds flew in the wrong direction. The Romans were
smart enough to use omens and entrails for political purposes, but
the point is the foot soldiers believed in them. And if a sheep or a
lamb happened to be liverish when cut open, it could turn a
brave man into a coward, eh? Right now we don't know which
way the Spaniard is going to jump. Maybe he's looking for an
omen. Maybe he isn't. The point is either way we don't give him
one, and if we do, it is one he doesn't like. One can't win a war

like that, but you can damn well keep from losing one. I wouldn't tell this to anyone but you blokes or the P.M." He arose. "You handle this end, Tim. When I've found a prospective bride I'll let you know."

Chapter 16

LOVEJOY TO HOPE COVE
VIA LONDON. . . .

"Lovejoy," Timothy said, "you're to go to London."

"Yes, sir," the Gunner replied automatically and then did what his opposite number in the American Army would have described as a triple take plus one. He stared at Tim simply pop-eyed. His mouth flew wide open. He shut it, and opened it again quickly and came close to losing his balance. "What? What did you say, sir?"

"I said you were to go to London," Timothy repeated. "Special orders. You're to be flown out tomorrow morning at six; they've even detached a Wellington for you. Simmonds is writing your orders now."

Gunner Lovejoy was breathless with delight and could only try to stiffen his spine to attention repeatedly, in the manner of a puppy compelled to wag his entire rear end because of a too stumpy tail and he murmured as he did so, "Oh I say, sir." At the moment far-off London seemed like the Persian poet's dream of paradise.

For he was remembering, of course, the London of his youth, left behind some twenty-five years ago—Wanstead with its rows of old, ugly, comfortable houses one exactly like the other, its corner pubs fragrant with spilled bitters and the reek of pipe and cigarettes, and the delectable girls who dressed themselves up and went out a-walking on Saturday nights.

In that moment of revelation the Gunner was hard put to decide which of the visions conjured up was the most attractive, the beer flowing unlimited or the Saturday-night girls. And then with a thrill the Gunner realised that there was nothing to stop him from having both—all the girls he could walk with, all the beer he could drink, and once more all the old sights, sounds, smells, and haunts.

London, London, London! Tubes and buses and flicks that weren't three years old, busy shops and proper tobacconists, Piccadilly, Trafalgar Square, and the good honest thick yellow London fog that a man could draw into his lungs with all the gratifying agony of cheap shag.

Poor Lovejoy! Had he only known it, the London to which he was bound was only a delusion of his own fantasy. The city was under siege, the lights were out, the beer diluted, food, what there was of it, practically inedible, and all the pretty Saturday-night girls hustled away into the land army or women's auxiliaries, factories, or monopolised by openhanded American soldiers with large pay packets and no inhibitions.

Still the name London rang in the Gunner's ears like a trumpet call. He asked, "What's the gen, sir?"

Tim said, "Major Clyde has come across an ape, a female. You are to fly back there, collect it, and bring it here. I won't even impress upon you the importance of the mission or what it means if it fails."

For the first time the Gunner, with his marvellous instinct for trouble a-cooking somewhere, felt some of the shine rubbed off from his beautiful fantasy. "But why me, sir?" he asked. "Why not you? After all, the responsibility——"

Tim sailed the half sheet of the message which Felicity herself had decoded less than an hour ago across his desk to the Gunner, saying, "You see what it says across the top."

Lovejoy did indeed for it was stamped "Top Secret" and read:

"SUITABLE FEMALE APE SIX YEARS OLD VIRGIN GUARANTEED MACAQUE SYLVANA AFRICANA IN PRIVATE HANDS PET OWNER PROVING TROUBLESOME EXPERT APE HANDLER OF CHARM AND PERSUASIVENESS WANTED CANNOT SPARE YOU FROM ROCK SUGGEST SEND LOVEJOY BUT CLEAN HIM UP STOP ALSO PHOTOGRAPHS WANTED REMEMBER ANNE OF CLEVES IF NO LOCAL HOLBEIN AVAILABLE SUGGEST GOOD RETOUCH-

ING JOB OR BETTER STILL SUBSTITUTE PICTURE OF MORE AMIABLE
SPECIMEN EVERYTHING DEPENDS ON MAKING GOOD IMPRESSION P.M.'S
PRIVATE WELLINGTON ON AIR STRIP 6 A.M. TOMORROW"

Lovejoy read it through twice, pushing back his cap and scratching his head. Alarm bells were going off again. He didn't like
obscurantism, obfuscation, mystery, or hanky-panky; he liked everything straightforward. Who was this owner who was proving
difficult, and why? What was the meaning of the nasty crack in the
signal about cleaning him up?

"I don't like it, sir," he said.

"Don't like what?"

"About cleaning me up, sir. What——"

"Oh," said Tim, "That's just Major Clyde's way of putting the
situation without using a lot of words. You know we're pretty
relaxed here on the Rock in the matter of dress. Probably a lot of
spit and polish around H.Q. in London. Get your hair cut and I've
arranged to have a new uniform issued to you which I'll thank
you to keep buttoned."

"And what's all that about charm and persuasiveness, sir——?"

Undoubtedly, Tim thought, Major Clyde had his reasons for
being mysterious but he wished he had been a little more explicit
if he expected him to cope. He said, "I shouldn't let that worry
you, Lovejoy. I've known you to charm a whole pack of apes down
from the trees, and as for powers of persuasion if there is a better
man on the Rock for talking a supply man out of Government
property——"

But the Gunner was still regarding the dispatch with an un-
resolved frown. "I don't quite get the picture, sir."

"Oh, come on, man," Tim said, tapping the signal, "it's not all
that difficult. Major Clyde has located an ape, but the owner is
proving sticky. You go back there and win the confidence of the
beast, which you will be able to do at the drop of a hat, the owner
withdraws objections and Bob's your uncle. And besides it's a
trip back home to London, isn't it?"

The Gunner brightened again. "That's right, sir," he said, "I'll
do me best."

Major "Slinker" Clyde didn't exactly cause the welkin to re-
sound with whoops of joy when Gunner John Lovejoy was ushered
into his presence in the cubbyhole that served him as his office
in the M.I. 5 section near Whitehall.

"Oh, it's you," he said, looking at the Gunner with a most
misanthropic expression. "Is that the best those middens back
there could do with you?"

Gunner Lovejoy felt deeply hurt. He was drawn up to attention;
all his buttons were buttoned; the new uniform was uncomfortable,
the collar was tight and not at all like the soft denims he was able
to wear around the Rock; and furthermore London, wartime
London—at least that portion of it which he had been able to
sample before being hurried on to keep his rendezvous with the
Major—had proved a bitter disappointment. "What's the matter
with me, sir?" he asked and, in an attempt to improve whatever it
was that appeared to have found disfavour with the Major, stiffened still more into military rigidity.

"Everything," Major Clyde announced flatly. He had the feeling
that in a moment Gunner Lovejoy might begin to revolve like a
model at a dress show in an attempt to register his good points.
"Relax, man, relax. For God's sake, sit down."

Insulted beyond words, the Gunner, having taken a chair by
the edge of the Major's desk as commanded, reached into his tunic
and produced a large envelope containing photographs and a
letter which read as follows:

"Dear Slinker,
Don't know what you're up to but herewith the new Lovejoy.
There wasn't time for plastic surgery but we have tidied him up
as best we could. There is no better hand with an ape living and
I know he'll fill the job. . . . Furthermore, as you know, he has
the reputation of being the foremost scrounger on the Rock, which
ought to take care of the persuasiveness department. I enclose
herewith several photographs purporting to be old Scruff. If these
don't entice your virgin, I give up.
    Good luck.
                                        Yours,
                                          Tim."

The Major regarded the photographs which he extracted from the envelope and jumped as though he had sat upon a scorpion. "Holy Methuselah on a bicycle," he exclaimed.

There was no doubt but that the photographs which had brought forth this outburst were masterpieces. If Herr Holbein had managed to make of Anne of Cleves a sixteenth-century forerunner of Greta Garbo, Tim had dug up a photographer and local retouching artist who had caused the magot supposed to represent Scruffy, nee Harold, look like a combination of Cary Grant, Billy Graham, and a Raphael Madonna. By some magic of the etcher's tool he had changed the usual expression of suspicion, meanness, and general malevolence to be found in the piggy hazel eyes of the Barbary ape into one of love for, and faith in, all humanity and the wish, if possible, to redeem it.

The Major's spirits rose somewhat as he fingered these two speaking un-likenesses, one profile and one full face, and he said, "Damned good job. Full marks to Bailey," then, "Look here, Lovejoy, no offence intended. I may have been a little harsh, but then you don't know what we're up against. As Major Bailey says, you're first class with the apes. You may be just the man for this job. I apologise for remarks conceived and spoken too hastily."

While speaking the Major had been opening the bottom drawer of his desk and produced a bottle of Scotch and two tumblers. He poured a generous portion into each and pushed one over to the Gunner whose figure relaxed and eyes sparkled as he was at once shriven of all hurt and resentment by this generous gesture. He leaned forward and his fingers curled firmly around the base of the glass.

"Yes, yes," said the Major. "Drink up and enjoy it, for it's the last drop you're going to have until this mission is completed." His countenance suddenly assumed the darkest hues of villainy. "If I hear of you so much as smelling the cork of a bottle or even walking past a pub on the same side of the street, you're for the Tower. Now bring your chair around to this side of the desk and listen carefully to what I have to say."

The Gunner did as he had been bade, moved his chair around to the side of the Major's desk, and waited.

Clyde arose, locked the door of his office, and pulled down the window blinds. "There are spies everywhere," he said, which sounded to Lovejoy like a joke, he having tabbed the Major as one of those odd officer types inclined to exaggeration and jape. The trouble was, there was a good deal of truth in it. He went to a wall safe, opened it, and, removing a file stamped "Top Top Secret," returned with it to his desk. He regarded the first pages moodily for a moment, leafing through the material, and then began:

"The owner of this ape is a Miss Constance Boddy, spinster, of 12, Wilton Gardens, Streatham, though at present she is residing at Cooks Hotel, Hope Cove, South Devonshire. She was born in Tilbury where her mother kept a kind of seafarers' boardinghouse. Her father was a sea captain, about whom more later, and her mother it seems died when Miss Boddy was very young, and hence she never knew her very well. Since her father, who never rose above the captaincy of small, insignificant tramp steamers, was always on voyages of long duration, she was brought up by an aunt and uncle, her father's brother, who had a greengrocer's shop in Streatham. This aunt and uncle raised their niece inculcated with all the virtues and stern morality of the British, and when Miss Boddy had reached the age of twenty-five, they abruptly departed this world within a few weeks of one another. They left her not only the greengrocer's business but, since she was the only relation and they were childless, the tidy fortune they had amassed during their lifetime, a matter of some £15,000."

Major Clyde looked up for a moment from the file which had been feeding him this information and said, "And so you see, that made her completely independent."

Lovejoy said, "And very nice for her, too."

"The young Miss Constance Boddy," the Major went on, "was no fool with her money. She sold the greengrocer's business, thus adding to her capital, invested the money wisely, and settled down in the small house in Streatham to make a home for her father, Captain Boddy, during the periods he spent ashore, which were few and far between."

Major Clyde looked up from the file again and said, "I make

the point, Lovejoy, that this is one way a man can maintain a reputation as a kind of little tin god, if you know what I mean. He is away enough of the time to build up the image of perfection and doesn't stick around long enough to break it down. That's why there are so few divorces in the families of sea captains."

Lovejoy said, "Yes, sir," and waited for more.

Major Clyde continued: "Although Miss Boddy was fond of her aunt and uncle, who, incidentally, were pacifists, a philosophy with which she herself is strongly imbued, it was her absent father whom she really worshipped, and as frequently happens in these intense father and daughter relationships, when she was left alone and well off, having reached maturity, she devoted her life to him and never married. There was just one weakness afflicting Captain Boddy during these periods spent ashore in the loving care of his daughter and which he was unable to conceal from her. Can you guess what this was, Lovejoy?"

"Women," Lovejoy suggested.

"Drink," corrected Major Clyde. "No, it seemed that stops in foreign ports were sufficient to take care of the natural urges of the Captain and there was no scandal in his life while ashore at home, but he did like the bottle, and who," continued the Major in an aside during which he took a pull at his glass of Scotch and water, and in which Lovejoy joined him, "shall blame him? Yet it doesn't do to over-indulge and it was, I suspect, this addiction which kept Captain Boddy from rising in his profession."

The Major leafed through the notes looking for something in another section and when he found it said, "As reported by some of the neighbours in the vicinity of 12, Wilton Gardens, the Captain would often come rolling home, roaring drunk, to be taken in and put to bed like a child by his daughter. Outwardly Constance Boddy ignored this failing as though it did not exist. Inwardly she formed an abiding hatred for intoxicating liquors and their effects upon human beings."

"Shocking, sir, ain't they?" commented Lovejoy.

Major Clyde looked at him sharply for an instant but there was only innocence on the Gunner's countenance, and the Major saw that he meant it. "Well," he said, "there you have a picture of

Miss Boddy's life over a period of more than fifteen years; an active delver in the fields of temperance, peace, anti-vivisection, R.S.P.C.A., and other good works during her father's absence, and total dedication to his person and comfort when he came ashore."

The Major again leafed through another portion of the notes and then continued: "On one of his trips shortly before the Captain succumbed suddenly to a heart attack, he brought his daughter as a gift a small female macaque acquired during a stop in Morocco. Apparently the mother of this apelet had strayed into the seaport with her young one clinging to her and had been set upon by Arab children who stoned and killed her and were tormenting the infant when Captain Boddy happened to come along and rescued it. He took the little creature aboard his vessel, fed it with a medicine dropper, nursed it into health and vigour, and upon his return to the Pool of London presented it to his daughter for a pet."

"Most fortuitous, the Captain's happening by just then," remarked the Gunner, stirred to sentiment by the whisky.

"That remains to be seen," replied the Major somewhat snappishly, as his problem settled upon his shoulders again. "The point is that a strong bond was immediately welded between the woman who had been a motherless girl and the motherless ape, who was named Amelia. This bond," continued the Major, upon whom the whisky had the effect of drastically augmenting the imagery of his speech, "was forged later into a link of unbreakable steel when the Captain regrettably passed on during a voyage through the Straits of Malacca and was buried at sea, leaving Miss Boddy alone in the world except for Amelia. Does the strength of this attachment begin to dawn upon you, Gunner?"

"Gord, yes," replied Lovejoy, "mother and daughter bound together inseparably by the slings and arrows of adversity."

The Major again looked up at the Gunner sharply to see whether his leg was being pulled, but there was no guile in the soldier's seamed countenance and Clyde felt a momentary flash of encouragement. If there was that much poetry in the Gunner's soul, his mission might stand a chance of success. "That's it," he said. "Got it in one. Amelia was the only living reminder of the man to whom she had devoted the whole of her adult life. The situation only confirmed Miss Boddy in her spinsterhood all the more determinedly, since no mere man could substitute for the image she had created of her father, and at the same time, by psychological processes I'll not go into at the moment, Amelia became as her child, born of her spiritual union with her father. Do you twig some facets of the problem, Gunner?"

The odd thing was that some of it had penetrated to the Gunner, in spite of the Major's complicated rhetoric. "Narsty it could be, sir, couldn't it?"

"Just you wait," the Major concluded, "for see here: her house is her own, her investments have prospered so that she is provided for and very well for the rest of her life"—the Major paused here and then, some of the waspishness returning to his voice, he said —"so there is no question of bribery. Absolutely impossible! She's a simple soul who wants nothing. She's naturally shy of men and has high moral principles."

"Gord," said Lovejoy.

"We were hoping," the Major suggested, speaking softly now, "that through your work with the apes you might manage to make some impression on her."

"How old is she?" asked Lovejoy.

"Forty-three," replied the Major.

The Gunner looked glum.

"And teetotal," added the Major sternly. "Got it, Lovejoy? A dedicated enemy of the demon rum; a woman addicted to good works."

"Gord," said the Gunner again.

"Yes, I know," said the Major, "a bloodless, kill-joy spinster, you'll say, going about poking her nose into other people's business. It all adds up to a rather repulsive picture, doesn't it, but the point is, Miss Boddy isn't like that at all. Here she is." And the Major uncovered the photograph.

The Major was pleased with his effect; the Gunner was indeed surprised for in his mind he had been forming a picture of a bony, acidulous woman, hook-nosed, dried-out, and resentful of having

become a feminine derelict. At forty-three Miss Constance Boddy
was buxom and well padded, her body apparently still harbouring
the juices of life. She had soft hair, light in colour, which she wore
cut short and which curled naturally and attractively. There was
nothing stern or severe about the mouth or the chin; the eyes
that looked up at Gunner Lovejoy from the picture seemed to be
most kind and the whole expression of the face was one of
friendliness and gentleness.

"Yes, yes," said the Major, reading the thoughts mirrored on
the Gunner's open countenance, "surprising, isn't it?" He knew
that what was baffling the Gunner was the unmistakable air of
gentility revealed by the photograph, in view of what he had told
him of Miss Boddy's origins. "And when you speak with her," he
added, "it is even more astonishing." The Major had not had too
much whisky to neglect to be tactful. "It isn't too difficult to
better yourself when you have a bit of money," he commented.

Lovejoy got the point, appreciated the Major's finesse, and
wished now to put him at his ease in return and said, "It's money
makes the 'orse go, sir."

"Exactly," agreed the Major, "but there is still another facet to
the character of this rather remarkable woman which makes our
problem just that much more difficult."

Here Major Clyde reached for the bottle and repeated the potion in his and the Gunner's glass. The Gunner looked at him
diffidently and forebore to reach for it, remembering the Major's
threats, but the latter nodded in a friendly enough fashion and
said, "It's all right, Lovejoy, go ahead. Your enforced monasticism
doesn't begin officially until you leave this room." He himself
quaffed deeply and then set his glass down with a sigh. "Every
so often, Lovejoy," he began, "one encounters on this earth
women possessed of a deep and abiding innocence. They can be
of any age beginning with six months, or in any guise, and the
thing to remember is that experience of life, buffets, difficulties,
or disasters encountered have nothing whatsoever to do with it.
They ride the storms; they emerge from the eye of the cyclone
unhurt, the fundamental innocence with which they were born
unaltered. One of the most innocent women I have ever en-

countered was a case-hardened Matto Grosso prostitute who
ended up in a brothel in Singapore."

"Ain't it the truth, sir," the Gunner began confidentially, "I
remember once when we were out in Madras and went to a place
we——"

"Yes, yes," interrupted the Major, who had merely been trying
to be graphically illustrative and had not meant to embark upon
an exchange of army reminiscences. "I'm sure you have. The point
I have been trying to make is that such a one is Miss Constance
Boddy."

The Gunner was startled. "Good Lord, sir," he said, "you don't
mean that she——"

"Heavens no," the Major exclaimed, "certainly not. I'm merely
stating that she has that kind of innocence which renders her
immune to men, to money, to hate, to love, wars, earthquakes,
catastrophes, man-made and natural cataclysms."

"Hasn't she any weaknesses?" asked the Gunner.

"She has none, at least none that we have been able to ascertain.
We were hoping that whoever approached her on the project
might be able to find some, or at least one hitherto unsuspected,
and work the vein."

The Gunner remained silent at this implication that obviously
he wouldn't do for this job, and the Major continued, "As you
can well imagine, Miss Boddy is against war, cruelty, and killing
and is not in sympathy with our avowed intentions of slaughtering
the Germans until they cry quits. I should add here that neither
is she in agreement with the German practice of dropping bombs
upon the British. She believes that both sides are wrong and for
all I know she may have something there. After you have been
with her for a little while you find yourself inclined to think somewhat along the lines that she does. Also you can't be angry with
her, for there is a certain childlike quality to her innocence. She
has almost some of that enchanting feyness I would not hesitate to
describe as loony if she weren't so eminently sensible in a great
many other areas."

Lovejoy, who was becoming increasingly depressed by the Major's recital, took a powerful swallow of his medicine, so large a

one in fact that arriving at the first stop in his system it caused him to shudder violently from head to foot. He then asked, "Sir, have you—ah—presented the matter to the lady as yet?"

The Major also took a large gulp, almost as though wishing perhaps to drown the memories of the encounter. "In a round-about way," he replied. "It's a subject that one simply doesn't plunge into with a lady without a great deal of preliminary and adequate preparation, as you will discover for yourself. I have mentioned her innocence, I think."

"And did she——"

"No. I'm afraid not." The Major shook his head sadly. "I'm afraid not at all, not any of it. Not even the beginning of a suggestion that to lend us the services of Amelia might appreciably shorten the war. She was quite horrified that we should even be thinking of such a thing. Wars were the concern of those who started them and she certainly was not going to involve either Amelia or herself in any manner. She must be persuaded to change her mind. We need Amelia." He flipped a page in the file, picked up a photograph, and spun it across the desk to Lovejoy. "This is Amelia," he said.

Lovejoy glanced at the photograph, then did a second take and an expression of horror came over his open countenance. "Crikey!" he said. He reached for the rest of his whisky and emptied the glass. Major Clyde did the same with his and then poured two more stiff ones.

"Oh, Crikey," Lovejoy repeated and studied the photograph of the second most misbegotten Barbary ape ever to come to his notice. To begin with, she was cross-eyed. She was also deformed in some manner, with one shoulder higher than the other, no doubt the result of the mishandling she had received at the time her mother was killed. Her coat was in good condition, testifying to the loving care lavished upon her by Miss Boddy, but for the rest she was as repulsive a monkey as one could expect to find in a month of monkeys. She caricatured not only the human race but her own species as well.

"Gord!" The Gunner gave vent to his favourite expletive again. "Scruffy won't like 'er."

"He has got to like her," the Major said fiercely. "That is provided we can ever get her hatched—what I mean to say is if we can get her across that bridge—dammit all, man, you know what I am trying to say."

"Yes, yes," said the Gunner soothingly, "of course, sir, something to do about not counting your chickens before you come to them."

"That's it," said the Major. "Got it in one. You're a smart fellow, Lovejoy."

The Gunner took a drink on this statement, which tended to make him morose. Whenever officers flattered him, it usually was the beginning of an assignment leading to trouble.

"Yes, sir," reiterated the Major. "I'm beginning to like you, Lovejoy. Right! At the present moment Miss Boddy and Amelia are located in rooms comprising the entire second floor of Cooks Hotel at Hope Cove, near Kingsbridge-by-the-Sea in South Devon. Miss Boddy retired thither last year when the bombing began, not because of any question of her own safety since I might also add she is a person of indomitable courage as well as principle, but because Amelia could not stand the noise of the explosions. Hope Cove," the Major continued, "is a tiny fishing hamlet around the corner from Bolt Tail, consisting of a group of thatched cottages, Cooks Hotel, a few boardinghouses for taking summer visitors, two rowing boats, and half a dozen lobster pots. You will proceed thither tomorrow, leaving Paddington at 10.30 hours, and will register at the hotel where a room has been reserved for you and——"

"I don't like it, sir," Lovejoy interrupted suddenly with a definite shake of his head. "No, sir, I don't like anything about it. I'm not the man for the job. Cozening innocent women, that's not John C. Lovejoy. Never 'as been, sir. I've 'ad me share of hard knocks and ups and downs and women ain't played much of a part in them and such as 'as 'as known what they've been about. There it is, sir, straightforward like out of the horse's mouth and no beating about the moss, if you'll excuse me, sir, for speaking so frankly."

The Major didn't reply immediately to this outburst, but sat there regarding the Gunner silently, his thin dark brows drawn into a straight line. Hunched up in his office chair with one knee drawn up, his eyes glittering, he looked like a dark fiend, a purposeful and malevolent Mephistopheles. And yet when he spoke again there was another surprise in store for Gunner Lovejoy. His voice was soft, caressing, and barely audible at first. "Lovejoy," he asked, "do you love your country?"

The Gunner was as startled as though he had been asked whether he believed in motherhood, the Lord, and the Virgin birth. He could hardly credit his ears. That an Englishman, an officer and a gentleman, should put such a direct and wholly embarrassing question to him was quite beyond the scope of his experience.

"Wha—what's that, sir?" he stammered.

"I asked," reiterated the Major still softly with slightly more emphasis, "whether you really loved your country—not only here," and the Major touched his skull with his forefinger, "but deep down in here," and the Major placed the same forefinger on his chest, indicating the general location of his heart.

Astonished and baffled, Lovejoy could do no more than reply, "Why yes, sir, I suppose so!"

"Oh it's more than guess," said the Major, "it's something you know, something you feel, eh, Lovejoy?" He had lifted his gaze from his glass now and turned it full upon the Gunner, his eyes full of earnestness and quite darkly moist. "They teach us to respect the flag, Lovejoy, don't they? Salute the colours! Bare the head! Eh? It's a symbol, that's all, a symbol. What it stands for is up to you!"

"If you say so, sir," said Lovejoy, still bewildered, but beginning to feel most queer.

"I do say so," replied Major Clyde. "We all carry self-preservation around in our nut, but in here is where England lives"— the location still being just at the left of his wishbone. "The England that to me is a wooded hill in Westmorland, the small farm by a lake side, and mountains in the twilight with the wild geese flying homeward overhead; the grinding of old cart wheels over dirt roads and old men holding the reins and looking out over

the rumps of their horses with faraway eyes; children walking
hand in hand to school; grey mists of rain blotting out the light
like curtains closing; the distant whistle of a train and the glow of
yellow light in the night from a farm house on a hillside. That's
my England."

The Gunner suddenly found himself strangely moved. He
didn't know how drunk the Major was but he knew how drunk
he himself was on almost half a bottle of the best Scotch whisky.
What moved him was not the Major's England which was as
foreign to him as Timbuktu, but his own. Beer and the Saturday-
night girls were back again, or rather it was the London of his
youth, the crowded pavements; the people shuffling home from
work at night; the glare of torchlight over the carts of the barrow
boys lined up along the curb; the smell of frying fish, cheap
tobacco, old clothes, and tired bodies; housewives with their
sleeves rolled back, gossiping on the threshold of their houses,
and, rolling over all, the beautiful and interminable roar and
rattle of London.

"Bonny England," said the Major, who was well away under
the influence of his half of the bottle, though no one would have
guessed from either his or Lovejoy's outward appearance that they
had had a drink.

"Bonny England," the Major repeated, "but what are we going
to do about it, Lovejoy? She's under fire! Back to the wall! Things
aren't going too well. Question is do we lie down and quit? Is
she worth fighting for?"

"No, sir! Yes, sir!" It was both the alcohol and the inner person
that was John C. Lovejoy which was responding to this extraordinary sentimental attack.

"That's the stuff," said the Major and looked as though Lovejoy's
reaction had put new life into him, too. "That's the stuff," he
repeated. "England needs that bloody ape and she's going to have
her and blast the filthy Hun."

"Yes, sir," Lovejoy said again, and for the first time in his life
was hearing trumpets call in his soul. "Blast the filthy Hun."

"And you're the one who can do it, Lovejoy," cried the Major,
his voice no longer soft but full of steel and fire. "You are going

down to Hope Cove and persuade Miss Constance Boddy to let us have her flipping chimpanzee—you'll take her back to Gibraltar and you'll boot old Scruff in the behind until he comes through like a man. If it turns out a boy we'll name it John C. Lovejoy after the man who saved the whole bloody Empire."

He was on his feet now and so was the Gunner. "Right, Gunner?"

"Right, sir—if you say so!"

"I do say so," and the Major touched his heart again. "Here is where you feel it."

Overflowing with emotion, Lovejoy could only say, "Sir!" and delivered himself of a prodigious salute.

"That's all then, Gunner, carry on!" and then added the only slightly sour note to the beautiful and emotion-packed scene, "and remember, Lovejoy, if you take another drink until this job is done, I'll have you flayed and your hide nailed to that door."

Somehow the Gunner found himself on the street below, looking up at the Union Jack which floated over the building. The feeling in his heart still lingered, but the nut was beginning to take over somewhat. Depression began to set in.

Chapter 17

... WHERE HE ENCOUNTERS
INNOCENCE

With pubs interdicted, the girls at war, and London a pool of darkness illuminated only by the fingers of the searchlights groping the sky for German aircraft, Gunner Lovejoy was almost pleased to find himself on a train for the West Country, although once he had settled into his compartment all his old fears and worries over his mission returned.

His interview with the Major, which had been diluted with strong drink, had left him with addled thoughts and confused memory. Somewhere in a fishing hamlet he must contact a virginal spinster, the proprietor of an equally virginal magot, an ape of most repulsive appearance, and persuade the former to surrender the person of the latter to an equally revolting ape by the name of Scruffy situated on the Rock and the last of its clan. Upon his success or failure the course of the war might turn. Besides which the Gunner found his mind befuddled by what now in hazy retrospect seemed to have been a fuzzy plea by the Major to him, John C. Lovejoy, to save Westmorland from the Hun.

He was also sweating out the fact that he did not have the faintest notion where to begin. Major Clyde had deemed it better that he should not be supplied with an introduction to Miss Boddy since preliminary contact with the lady had not gone too well and had judged it best to let Lovejoy spend a day scouting the situation and decide upon the best method of attack.

The war not only had failed to touch Hope Cove, it had not even noticed it. Except for blackouts and ration cards it was as though no international strife existed. The tiny village was snuggled up inside the sheltering arm of the promontory of Bolt Tail thrusting out into the Atlantic. To the right lay the pierced rock of Thurlestone and the golf links high on the cliff now dotted with sheep, and as the Gunner, carrying his bag past the enchanting little square of thatched cottages, trudged on to the little harbour he saw two fishing boats drawn up on the sandy beach and above on the bluff the Victorian pile of Cooks Hotel with its towers and scrollwork and dormer windows. He wondered how long it would be before he would see Miss Boddy, where she kept the ape, how he would get to know her.

Entering the hotel, Gunner Lovejoy presented himself at the desk and gave his name to an angular but pleasant-faced woman, a Miss Neville, who said at once in a most agreeable and sympathetic fashion, "Oh yes, how do you do, Mr. Lovejoy, your reservation has been made. We have been expecting you. You have been wounded, haven't you? We do hope you will be fit again soon. The air is wonderful down here and it's very quiet. May I show you to your room?"

Silently the Gunner cursed the machinations of Major Clyde, who obviously had pinned the false heroism of a non-existent wound upon him which he would have to live up to. On the other hand, Lovejoy reflected, as he mounted the stairs to the first floor, perhaps the Major was not as crazy as he seemed. To provide him with a fictitious war wound would earn him the sympathy of females and since Miss Boddy was anti-war it was perhaps best to present himself as a victim of the holocaust.

The Gunner found his room clean and pleasant. The window looked out upon the bit of beach protected by a stone jetty. Two small children were paddling in the shallows and on the horizon was a curl of smoke.

Overhead Lovejoy heard footsteps moving back and forth and since he knew that Miss Boddy had taken the entire second floor of the hotel, that would be she.

He listened to the footsteps. Then there came a scraping, shuffling sound. That would be Amelia. Here he was, the hunter, and above him, separated by one thin floor, his quarry.

He hoped to have a glimpse of Miss Boddy at dinner, one which would perhaps provide him with some clue as to how to begin, but in this he was disappointed. There was only one other couple in this small dining room. However, he did manage to glean some useful and preliminary intelligence.

Miss Neville also waited on table since servants were unobtainable and brought him a chop in a covered dish, whispering, "It isn't chop night, but we must do something for our wounded men to make them well and strong, mustn't we?"

Gunner Lovejoy felt like a dog, but he also liked the look of the chop and to cover his embarrassment he said, "Not many people here, are there?"

"Oh no," the woman said. "It's the war, of course. That's Mr. and Mrs. Carwood over there and then of course there's Miss Boddy, but she doesn't come down to dinner ever. She has it in her room. Because of the monkey, you know. Oh, but I suppose you don't know about that; she has a pet monkey. We don't mind it coming into the dining room for lunch—it's really good as gold, but some of the other guests might object in the evening, so she has her tray in her room. But I expect you will be meeting her at lunch. She always takes her monkey for a walk on the beach in the morning. If you want to lie in bed in the morning and rest we can send you up a tray. I don't doubt but what we can manage an egg for you."

Not flippin' likely, the Gunner thought to himself. Not when she finds out what I'm after and the only wound I ever had was skinning my knuckle on a ruddy breechblock. Still he was grateful for the intelligence. He now had a line on the enemy's movements. He, too, would be walking on the beach in the morning.

The Gunner slept well, enjoyed his egg, bathed and shaved and made himself presentable and went out on to the beach ostensibly examining it for seashells and other flotsam and jetsam and strolling about with a casual air until he saw the door of Cooks Hotel open and the buxom figure of Miss Constance Boddy appear. On her shoulder perched a large and mature female macaque. The two of them came down the pathway across the motor road and descended onto the beach where the magot leaped from her shoulder to the sand. Gunner Lovejoy saw that the monkey wore a collar and was attached to Miss Boddy by a long thin chain which, however, gave them both leeway to walk.

If Miss Boddy was even more prepossessing in countenance than her photograph, round-faced, dimpled, and sunny with light blue and friendly eyes which had not registered in the picture, Amelia was uglier than her likeness conveyed. Her eyes were more severely crossed than he had thought possible and her expression miserable.

Miss Boddy and her monkey now approached from one direction and the Gunner was rapidly closing the distance from the other. He was in a sweat again wondering what he should do and how, whether it was too soon to say "Good day," whether the sight of his uniform would frighten or anger her, whether he should await a formal introduction by the woman of the hotel, or what.

He found himself within a few yards of the two and in an absolute panic when the solution to his difficulties was supplied in miraculous fashion by none other than Amelia. As the Gunner was about to pass, the ape, who had been loping along at the end of her chain, halted, looked up at him, gave the most extraordinary screech of joy, denoting what could only have been love at sight and leaped for him.

Quite naturally, the Gunner halted and opened his arms wide to receive the ugliest of all magots, who threw her arms about his neck in an ecstasy of adoration and kissed him full upon the lips.

"Hello there, old girl," the Gunner said when the loving greeting had somewhat subsided. "Ain't you the one."

There was no explanation for what Amelia had done—was doing, except that she had looked upon the Gunner and loved him. The result was that all of the preliminary obstacles the Gunner had feared were cleared away and he was provided with the best possible introduction to Miss Constance Boddy.

That lady approached the loving pair with a most beatific smile upon her round countenance. Amelia tightened the grip of her arms around his neck, leaned her cheek against his, and kissed him again.

"My good man," said Miss Boddy, "I don't know who you are but you must have a very beautiful soul!"

Almost overcome, Lovejoy replied, "I don't know, I tries me best, ma'am."

"Oh yes you have," Miss Boddy reiterated. "Otherwise Amelia would not love you!"

"Maybe they know," the Gunner said, "I've been around them kind of apes for the last twenty years." He fondled Amelia, who went into an ecstasy of chittering and cooing and then, as if to show her mistress that although someone new had come into her life she was not prepared to abandon everything for him, she leaped from Lovejoy's arms back to Miss Boddy's shoulder, gave her a peck, and grinned at the Gunner, who decided that while Amelia might be most unprepossessing physically she appeared to have a most amiable disposition.

"Why, how wonderful," exclaimed Miss Boddy. "You must tell me all about it some time." Then she took him in with her gaze, his features, his uniform, his presence, and said, "Oh of course, you must be the wounded soldier Miss Neville has been expecting. Oh you poor man. Is it very bad? How you must be suffering!"

In a flash Gunner Lovejoy saw how very clever Major Clyde had been to supply him with this automatic entrée into sympathetic feminine hearts. And in an equal flash he tumbled the Major's carefully built edifice to the ground. For he looked into the gentle eyes of Miss Boddy, now filled with genuine pity for him, and for the first time in any female encountered that innocence of which the Major had spoken to him at such length.

"It isn't true," he said, "I never have been wounded. It's all— it's a mistake. I'm as healthy as you are."

This confession elicited neither shock nor surprise from Miss Boddy, who merely gave him a sunny and dimpled smile, saying, "Oh how glad I am for your sake. It must be dreadful to be wounded. It must be even more dreadful, I suppose, to have to kill someone. Have you ever killed anyone?"

Amelia leaped onto the sandy beach and came over to the Gunner, stood up on her hindlegs, took his hand and tugged at it, and looked up at him beseechingly. With a gesture that was almost automatic, the Gunner reached into his pockets for the odd bit of sugar, carrot, or peanuts, but found nothing. "Sorry, luv," he said, "the next time," and then he replied to Miss Boddy's question. "No, ma'am, I don't think so, leastways not that I know of. I have spent the last twenty years of me life on Gibraltar looking after a lot of bleedin'—I mean taking care of the apes there for the Government. That's my job!"

With a sinking feeling at the pit of his stomach, the Gunner realised that he had given himself away first crack out of the box. Since Miss Boddy had already been approached on behalf of the Crown to donate or lend her pet ape to the Rock, and had refused, the presence of the self-confessed keeper of those animals must surely add up to two and two. But he had reckoned without the trust and innocence of the chubby and cheerful little person who appeared prepared to accept him for what he was, or said he was, without any thought to ulterior motives for his presence.

"How very wonderful for you," she said, "to be able to live with them. Are they not the dearest creatures in the world? How you must miss them. What brings you to this part of the world?"

And then a most astonishing and even more horrifying thing happened to Gunner John Lovejoy, for while with one part of his cerebral system he realised that his error had gone unnoticed and he had been granted a reprieve which would enable him to answer with an adequate lie, the emotional hemisphere of his brain, hitherto a total stranger to him, rejected this subterfuge.

"I've been sent 'ere to bring your ape back to Gibraltar with me," the Gunner found himself blurting. "We've got to have a mate for old Scruff—'arold, that is. That's his Christian name. 'E's the last ape left on the Rock and the 'uns caught on to it and 'as bought up all the apes around Africa and the P.M. sent a message we've got to start breeding the hapes on the Rock again or we'll be druved off like it says in the history books and there goes your flippin' war—at least that's what Major Clyde says. There," concluded the Gunner, "now you know."

The Gunner then stood like a small boy feeling aghast at what he had done, knowing that his idiot declaration had knocked the props out from under the carefully built structure of his superior officers, and, in all probability, hastened the collapse of the British Empire. The anguish in his soul communicated itself to Amelia, who climbed gently up his leg, then up his waist thence to his shoulder where she clung, putting her cheek against his and making small noises in her throat.

Miss Boddy rose from the rock on which she had been sitting and contemplated the soldier and her pet, looking with her clear eyes, now troubled, upon the lines and leathery countenance of the Gunner close to the little animal she had loved so long. And suddenly she was powerfully reminded of her father. But this was not all. With this memory somehow the Gunner had evoked a kind of nostalgia which swept through her of old times and places and people and ways of life. Had she closed her eyes she would have heard the mournful hooting of river craft on a foggy night, or the rumble of drays through the streets, or the cries and bustles of the barrow boys and street vendors. And then it was gone.

She took a second look at the Gunner. The new clean uniform, the shave, plus the anguish of soul, had eradicated a good deal of the dissoluteness and cynicism from his general appearance. His cap sat at a rakish angle, giving him rather a youthful aspect and not disagreeable. Nevertheless she was shocked and somewhat hurt at this continued invasion of her privacy when she had already told the young man who had come upon a similar mission that she would have nothing whatever to do with the scheme of surrendering her innocent and virginal pet to the embraces of an unknown monster, in order that a lot of ridiculous and wicked-minded humans should be able to go on fighting and killing one another.

Yet even though she found the revelation distasteful she was able to experience commiseration with the one who had confessed. She said with some severity, "Well at least you are honest," and then more gently, "and a good person at heart, I am sure, for Amelia loves you. Come, Amelia, we must be going."

It was to the credit of the ape that new love or no she didn't hesitate a moment upon the command of her mistress but leaped to the shoulders of Miss Boddy, who marched off with her.

The Gunner collapsed onto the rock vacated by the spinster and let his shamed head sink between his hands. He felt like an utter fool. The first time he had ever been entrusted with a mission more important than clearing out the barracks, scrounging ground-nuts for his charges, or polishing an anti-aircraft piece, he had let everyone down. Also for the first time during his rather rough and lonely life as a soldier during which his prime concern had been the welfare of John C. Lovejoy, the Gunner felt he had hurt someone he didn't wish to hurt.

He sat there a shrunken little figure of a man who seemed to have sunk inside his uniform. The hair emerging from his military cap was salted with grey and the hands that hid his unhappy countenance were knotted and veined. He silently cursed himself, Tim Bailey, Major Clyde, the Brigadier, and even somewhat more timidly the Prime Minister, but mostly and with the greatest fervour the Army, which could uproot a man and order him into situations and actions which he would otherwise never even contemplate. Lovejoy's shoulder heaved in a prodigious sigh, for he was feeling very sorry for himself.

"There, there," said a gentle voice which came from somewhere above him, "don't take on so. Of course I should not dream of letting you have Amelia for such a horrid purpose, but if you like, some time later, you can tell me about Harold and his friends."

It was indeed Miss Boddy who had returned. Grief-stricken at the misery of her new-found love, Amelia had tugged at her mistress until she, too, had turned around and observed the woebe-gone scene and her kindly heart had sped her back.

The Gunner felt his heart give a strange and unaccustomed leap within its cage. Again it seemed he had suffered a reprieve at the hands of this extraordinary woman.

He stood up, "Yes, ma'am," he said. "Thank you, ma'am. Tell you about 'arold? That'd take time. 'E's the best, 'e is. None other like 'im."

Amelia clapped her hands with pleasure. She could not of course understand what they had said, but she was sensitive to the fact that her mistress as well as her new-found friend were no longer unhappy.

Gunner Lovejoy was no hagiographer; it's even doubtful whether in his elementary education he had encountered the life of a single saint or was familiar with the method employed by both professionals and amateurs of this form of literature in building up a narrative, history, tradition, saga, and personal characteristics of their holy men. But it would seem that every man, not completely insensitive, has within himself the ability to weave legends about his fellow man and elevate him to a superior position.

Major Clyde had also found evidence of a vein of poetry imbedded in the Gunner. This now came to light as over the period of the next few days the Gunner proceeded to canonise old Scruff into St. Harold the Blessed, Patron Saint of Gibraltar.

"Right from the beginning I could tell 'e was different from the others," the Gunner was saying in the cool of the evening after supper. They were occupying a corner of the porch where Miss Boddy was enjoying a postprandial cigarette, her feud with the various manifestations of wickedness on earth oddly enough not extending to nicotine, while Lovejoy with Amelia entwined about his neck tried to stomach a lime and water. Heaven could have testified his need to have Guinness replace the water, but mindful of Major Clyde's awful threats the Gunner was still playing it straight and getting on with it as best he could, unsupported and unfortified.

"Y-a-a-s," the Gunner went on, "like I was saying, 'e wasn't like the rest, even when he was a little tiny baby. Why I remember the day I gave him 'is first groundnut. As you know, ma'am, they'd rather have groundnuts than anything."

"Oh yes," sighed Miss Boddy, luxuriating in the pleasure of being told stories, "Amelia loves them; I always try to have some on me. But of course the war, you know——"

"Oh, we've lashings of them on the Rock, ma'am," said the Gunner, getting in a quick bit of propaganda, and then continued, "Well, as you can imagine, there was a scramble for them, half a dozen little hapclets squealing and jumping about, fighting to get their peanuts. Well when it come to Harold's turn—and I can see him now like it was yesterday, he was only a year old— he comes up nice and quiet and stands there waiting. If 'e'd have 'ad a hat on 'e'd have taken it off he was that polite. I gave him 'is hand full of nuts and what do you think he did, ma'am?"

Miss Boddy's friendly blue eyes were shining with delight and somewhat breathlessly she guessed, "Shared them with his fellows?"

"Oh better than that, ma'am," said Lovejoy. "Off in one corner there was an apelet that had 'urt himself a bit and was afraid to get into the scuffle. He was just sitting over there, mournful, wishing he had some groundnuts when Harold went over to 'im and handed 'im *all* of 'is."

"Oh, how beautiful," said Miss Boddy. "How happy you must have been."

For an instant Lovejoy experienced the ineffable joy of the appreciated author. He, of course, had no idea that he was already, and by sheer instinct, abiding by the first rule adhered to by biographers of saints down through the ages, which was to endow the youth of the subject with suitable miracles and Sunday-school deeds.

Success led the Gunner on to further flights.

"There was never any mischief or 'arm in 'im. The cars of the tourists used to park up by the apes, you know, and the little beggars would jump up on the bonnets and steal the windscreen wipers off. They used to like to eat the rubber and then throw what was left over the cliff. Harold, 'e never took part in such doings, not 'im. Instead he would sit off by 'imself on a rock, keeping an eye open for when people would come back to their cars; then he'd shout monkey for 'Cave!' and warn 'is mates!"

Miss Boddy was silent for a moment at the conclusion of this anecdote and then said gently, "Would not it have been better for Harold to have reproved his little friends and taught them that it was wrong to steal, instead of aiding and abetting their mischief by acting as—ah—lookout?"

"Oh yes, ma'am, he did, he did!" the Gunner said, hastily realising quickly that he and Miss Boddy apparently didn't see eye to eye on questions of morality and that like so many authors who adorn their fiction with their own philosophy he had trodden upon dangerous ground.

"Oh he did that, ma'am, after he found out. He was so very young, you see, but after I had told him it was wrong and he had seen me scold the other apes he'd wait until he'd see one of his pals pinch one and then go and take it from 'im gently and put it back. 'E got so good at hanging them windscreen wipers back on the 'ooks we thought for a while of training him for a garage 'elper."

"Adorable," said Miss Boddy, her scruples satisfied, and fascinated with the tale, "and did you?"

"Oh no," said the Gunner, " 'e was destined for better things; he became me assistant, me own right-'and man in charge, me first leftenant, so to speak. There would not be a hape left on the Rock today but for 'im," the Gunner concluded, finding to his surprise that fiction could sometimes be laced with truth.

The trouble was, or developed, that Miss Boddy was insatiable for Harold stories, and she came to look forward more and more to those evenings on the verandah when their two cigarette ends glowed like fireflies and there was no sound but the lapping of the waves upon the beach, the soft, contented chittering of Amelia, and the voice of the soldier picturesquely embroidering the saga of Harold.

Her childlike eagerness and delight in his stories pleased Lovejoy, at the same time taxing his imagination to the utmost. In fact the Gunner found that he was plumbing depths in himself hitherto totally unsuspected, leaving him often staggered with surprise at his own inventiveness which seemed to flower even without the dew of strong waters. He was also more keenly aware of the hazards and pitfalls of inspirational narrative, realising that no man who composes for an audience can ever wholly ignore or forget the presence of same.

"Why one day," narrated the Gunner, "I was downtown walking parst Trafalgar Cemetery with Harold on me shoulder when one of those German bast—tourists, I mean, drives by a mile a minute in one of them blarsted Mercedes cars, 'onking like he owned the ruddy road, when to me 'orror right in the path of the oncoming vehicle I sees——" Lovejoy here found himself faced with deciding in the twinkling of an eye what it was in the path of the speeding motor car—a kitten, a child, a dog. Maybe Miss Boddy didn't like children. Would she prefer cats or dogs? All this had to be debated and solved in the lightning-like flash of an instant passing. "An 'elpless little kitten." Distress showing on Miss Boddy's chubby countenance told the Gunner that he had chosen correctly.

"Oh," gasped Miss Boddy, "the poor thing!"

"I was turned to stone," continued Lovejoy, "but not Harold. Quicker than you could say, 'I'll 'ave a beer,' he was off my shoulder and onto the bonnet of the car. He reaches down and scoops up the kitten, does a back flip, and lands twenty yards away with the little thing safe and sound as though it was with its own mother."

"How wonderfully thrilling," Miss Boddy breathed, "what a splendid thing to do. What happened to the kitten afterward?"

"Harold and me brung 'im up. 'E's 'ad 'is home with me ever since. Finest cat you ever seed."

Miss Boddy's cigarette end glowed in the darkness; then she sighed with contentment. "What a dear, good, kind man you must be, Mr. Lovejoy, to love animals so. And to think you don't drink either like so many of the rough soldiery."

The Gunner felt like a dog, having made a point of his tee-totalism with Miss Boddy and his agreement with her that the most frequent early guise of the devil was in the shape of demon rum. However, he felt in one of his more distant bones, down around the ankles, that he might at some time or other be needing a hedge and so he said, "Y-a-a-s, ma'am, but it ain't been all that easy. It's not that I haven't had me battle with strong drink before I saw the light, or that there ain't days when the tempteyshun comes over me to backslide, a tempteyshun which up to now I have resisted."

In the darkness of the blacked-out village Miss Boddy's voice vibrated with emotion. "Oh Mr. Lovejoy," she quavered, "how very brave of you. If ever the feeling should come over you when I am with you—if you told me about it, I should be proud to help you."

Something tickled the back of Gunner Lovejoy's mind, a scrap of his conversation with Major Clyde in his office, something to do with the fact that Miss Boddy so far had evinced no weakness and that the Army was expecing him to discover one, if any, and make use of it.

Was this then one, this passion for prohibition, and could it be put to account? The Gunner filed this away in his mind for future reference and continued enlarging the epic of Harold, in the hopes that Miss Boddy eventually could be led to consent to the idea of giving Amelia in marriage to this paragon.

Lovejoy had his own built-in set of ethics and morals which served him very well in his profession, and, though he had found it impossible to conceal his mission from Miss Boddy, he was not at all bothered by the false and smarmy picture of Harold he was setting up in the mind of Miss Boddy, or by scruples over what would occur should she yield and allow her pet to make the trip to Gibraltar. His job was to persuade her to let this happen, collect the ape, accompany it to the Rock, and thereafter his responsibility would end. What took place then would be up to Captain Bailey and the rest.

But what made his task even attractive now and left his conscience free was that like so many writers he was falling a victim to his own creation and was beginning to believe wholeheartedly in its reality.

Thus Harold-Scruffy became a kind of split or dual personality. Scruffy was bad, but Harold was good. Scruffy was Scruffy and no remedy for that, but Harold became endowed with a life and character of his own, speeding toward canonization.

Nor was the legend thus created in any way diminished by the cunning photographs of Harold with which Lovejoy had been supplied by Tim Bailey and one of which now resided on the dressing table in Miss Boddy's room, so that in privacy she could continue to contemplate the hero to whose saga she was listening nightly.

Aside from compulsory teetotalism, Gunner Lovejoy found himself enjoying his holiday in Devon. The hotel spoiled him with extra eggs and titbits and other things off-ration for his meals, having remained convinced that while his wound remained invisible he was bleeding internally. It was peaceful and quiet away from the racketing guns on the Rock and the onerous duties visited inevitably upon the ranker, and finally the pleasant personality of the plump spinster coupled with the love of Amelia combined to make the time pass quickly and delightfully.

This idyll was shattered by a telephone call which turned out to have Major Clyde sharply at the other end of the line.

"What the devil is going on down there, Lovejoy, and why haven't you reported? The Governor is giving me hell, the Colonial Secretary is cluttering up the cables, the Brigadier is getting hot under the collar, Major Bailey is close to a nervous breakdown, and the P.M. has asked what's been done about his directive to bring and keep the Rock apes up to strength. What are you trying to do, send us all down the drain?"

"No, sir," said the Gunner, genuinely startled to find that there was another world outside of Hope Cove, South Devon, and an irritable and angry one which apparently was still at war. "I was just thinking of writing you a letter, sir."

"Charming of you, Lovejoy," came the acid voice of the Major. "Send it on by pigeon post, eh? Or maybe by dog sled via the Great Circle! What's happening, man, what's happening? That's what I want to know. Have you got anywhere?"

"Y-yes, sir, at least I think so. She loves me!"

There was a moment of silence from the other end of the line after which the voice of Major Clyde filled it again, so freezingly that icicles must have formed on the wires between London and Devonshire. "May I be the first to congratulate you, Gunner, and at the same time might I also remind you that this is an army at war and not a matrimonial bureau. In this instance your private life——"

"Oh for Gord's sake, sir," the Gunner rushed to explain as the penny clanked, "not 'er! Amelia, sir."

Major Clyde said, "Well, what's going to come of it, or do you want me to ask for an armistice until you can make up your mind?"

"No, sir," said the unhappy Gunner, "I've been getting the old girl warmed up. I was going to ask 'er pretty soon to let me take Amelia——"

"When?" asked the Major.

"S-Saturday night," replied the Gunner with a sinking feeling at the pit of his stomach as he realised that he had irrevocably committed himself, it being Friday morning.

"O.K.," said the Major. "Ring me as soon as she gives her answer," and hung up.

The Gunner made all of the preparations consistent with the behaviour of an anxious swain who had brought himself to the point of popping the question. He walked three miles to Thurlstone to the barber to have his hair cut, took a bath, changed his linen, shaved twice over, removed some spots from his tunic, and polished his shoes until his seamed and anxious face was reflected in them. The only thing he lacked was the solitaire in its box concealed about his person. Instead, he had such titbits as sugar, some fresh carrots, and a package of shelled hazelnuts of which Amelia was inordinately fond.

The wording of his proposal, too, was worrying. He had never proposed to an ape before. Actually, he realised it was not to Amelia he would be making overtures, but to Miss Boddy, but on the other hand he was not proposing to Miss Boddy for Miss Boddy, but for Amelia. The situation was enough to try a professional poet, and Lovejoy, whose inventiveness in describing the prospective groom had not flagged, now found himself bogged down.

The scene was familiar, the darkened verandah, the glowing cigarette ends, the contented chittering and caresses of Amelia.

"Miss Boddy—may I call you Constance?" Ridiculous sentences like that which he had seen in joke books flashed through the Gunner's mind. And absurd scenes, too, such as himself on his knees before Miss Boddy—also from joke books. Except that this was no joke.

And then, quite suddenly, out of the blue, almost as though she had guessed that this idyll was drawing to a close, Miss Boddy relieved him by giving him the opening for which he was desperately seeking. She said, "It has been so pleasant having you here, Mr. Lovejoy, with your wonderful stories about Harold. I feel as though I know him almost as well as I do Amelia. I suppose you will have to be getting back to him soon; he must miss you dreadfully!"

"Yes, ma'am, that's it!" the Gunner said, rushing the words forth lest the opportunity pass. "I 'ad a letter from 'im only the other day, I mean from the chap who's looking after 'im. Lonely 'e is. And pining that's wot. A mate is what 'e needs, a mate and a family like everyone else. Look 'ere, Miss Boddy, what about letting me take Amelia back to old Harold? They're made for each other, that's wot they are. Think how 'appy they'd be up there on the old Rock together by Prince Ferdinand's Battery. Coo, the view from there would knock your eye out, the 'arbour stretching out below and Mount Atlas across the Strytes. All the peanuts they could eat and a lot of little hapelets running around. You could trust her with me. I've had the care of hapes for twenty years. I'd see her all right, ma'am. Why the number of little hapes I've helped to deliver——"

Miss Boddy stirred uneasily in the darkness and the interruption had the effect of stemming the Gunner's flow. Then she said softly, "Oh no, Mr. Lovejoy, I'm afraid I would not want Amelia ever to do anything like that."

"But ma'am," said the Gunner impassionedly, "it's nature, ain't it? Amelia here has got a heart brimming over with love, look at 'er (indeed Amelia was nibbling dreamily at the Gunner's ear). Every creature has got to 'ave a mate, like!"

"We don't," said Miss Boddy, speaking even more softly. "Not Amelia and I."

"But, ma'am," said Lovejoy, beginning to flounder as he realised he had put his foot in it, "this is different, don't you understand, it's on account of the war."

"But surely you will remember," replied Miss Boddy, "that I don't approve of the war."

"But Harold there all by himself on the Rock there pining for Amelia."

"How does he know about her?"

"I wrote," said the Gunner.

Miss Boddy was very gentle but very firm. "It's no use, Mr. Lovejoy," she said, "I should never permit Amelia to leave my side to go so far away even with someone as—as kindhearted and trustworthy as you. I told the young man who came down here to speak to me about this a month or so ago and I'm very sorry to have to tell you the same. The answer is no."

And from that position there was no budging her.

"I think I'll go for a walk," the Gunner said and arose.

"Poor Mr. Lovejoy," Miss Boddy said, "I know you are disappointed. I'm so sorry."

It was still early, before nine o'clock in fact, and the Gunner proceeded down the path that led along the cliff to the village, which consisted of no more than a post office, an artycrafty shoppe, a general store, and The Crown and Anchor, an attractive pub done in frigate style in black and white timber with tarred rope and ship's bells and other nautical paraphernalia enticingly displayed. Up to that moment the Gunner had passed this edifice resolutely, or had carefully planned his walks in the other direction. Now with his mission a bust, himself a failure, the Rock snatched from the Empire, and the war lost, Lovejoy came to a halt in front of the pub.

What did anything matter? What even could Major Clyde do to him, there being no rank lower than the one he occupied, and what of his own personal pride? It was also a fact that he had been more than a week without spending a penny and his pockets were bursting with money. Also it was Saturday night. Farewell, Gibraltar, Major Bailey, Scruffy–Harold, and all his friends! Adieu Miss Constance Boddy, adieu Amelia! Good-bye then to tee-totalism.

With purposeful step, Gunner John C. Lovejoy entered the oak-beamed lounge of The Crown and Anchor.

When he emerged at closing time the Gunner was loaded. He had not been tossed out, nor did he have to be helped across the threshold, his reaction to strong drink being mainly internal, and he had the ability to stand up to a bar for hours without any visible change in his appearance. However, for years Lovejoy had been doing his drinking in an even temperature which enabled him to give at least the outward appearance of holding his liquor. At Hope Cove in The Crown and Anchor, however, he experienced new conditions, to which he was unaccustomed.

Since the pub was blacked out and every crack that might show a light to sea was stuffed, the atmosphere within can be imagined. Without, the Devon nights were cool verging on the chill, so when Lovejoy passed from the steamy fog of the pub into the teeth of a wind that had decided to come visiting from Iceland, he suddenly found his metabolism affected with results damaging to his sense of equilibrium.

It was now dark. The last green of the northern-latitude sunset had faded from the West. The path back to the hotel seemed higher, wobblier, narrower, windier, and unfamiliar. As no light was showing anywhere he had to guide himself by the faint glimmer of a not very prosperous moon seen through scudding clouds and the phosphorescence of the sea.

Since he was a monumental flop he had no wish to encounter either Miss Boddy, Amelia, or Major Clyde again and the sea suddenly appeared to him the most direct route home to the simpler life where he need no longer be teetotal and could shuck all responsibility.

Thus he made his way onto the beach, lurching and staggering, but in his own opinion quite competent, reversing in his mind the flight plan of his journey thither and with what he remembered of school geography. He would turn left around Bolt Tail, strike out on a diagonal line for the Bay of Biscay, past France and Portugal, turn the corner after Cádiz, and there he would be. Major Bailey would be glad to see him if no one else.

So fiery was the Gunner's internal combustion that he didn't even notice the temperature of the water that filled his shoes and sloshed around his calves as he waded in.

Fortunately, at this moment Miss Constance Boddy appeared with Amelia, it being her custom to take her pet for a final duty airing on the beach before retiring for the night. The clouds at this moment obligingly parted, permitting the moon to reveal the silhouette of Gunner Lovejoy, his military uniform now comfortably dishevelled, his cap askew over one eye, hip deep in the ocean, departing for Gibraltar.

The sight filled the spinster with alarm and caused Amelia at the end of her leash to leap up and down, shrieking. "Mr. Lovejoy!" cried Miss Boddy. "What has happened? Are you ill? Where are you going?"

Lovejoy stopped in his tracks, creamy foam swirling about his thighs, to turn around and contemplate one of the two people he specifically didn't wish to see. Alcohol, sea water, Arctic winds, metabolism, hurt pride, and frustration all came to a boil. "'Ome," he replied. "Good-bye forever, ma'am."

The sight of the Gunner standing in the sea was so bizarre that Miss Boddy, in a fearful flutter and not yet realising that he was drunk, panicked and quite naturally misunderstood, believing that it was the Gunner's intention to take farewell not only from her but from life. "Mr. Lovejoy—dear Mr. Lovejoy," she cried, "you mustn't. Come back at once. Oh please do." Reaching new heights at the end of her chain, Amelia added her cries to those of her mistress.

"Come back!" repeated the Gunner scornfully, making no move to do so. "What for I'd like to know? You and your ruddy hape! Not good enough for my Harold. What's there for me to come back for? I'm a failure. Let the side down, that's what I 'ave. They'll be pointing the finger at me, 'See that bloke there? That's Gunner Lovejoy what lost the bloomin' war for us!' I'm going 'ome and bury meself."

The word bury set up new alarms inside the poor confused woman and she could only beg him, "Oh Mr. Lovejoy, please dear, good, kind Mr. Lovejoy come back, I want to talk to you."

"Ho ho! Talk to me!" echoed the Gunner, but at least he didn't go any farther out to sea. "What's there to talk about? You've made your decision, ain't you?" His voice went into that falsetto used by a drunk or a husband trying to imitate his wife's voice, "Oh no Mr. Lovejoy I could not let Amelia do anything like that! Gord love us, look at 'er jumping up and down there. You want to ruin 'er life and keep 'er from 'aving a fambly like yourself?"

The mixtures which Lovejoy had been imbibing at The Crown and Anchor now all took hold with a will and made him angry so that he came sloshing out of the sea to be greeted with hysterical joy as one returned from the dead by Amelia, who leaped into his arms, covering his face with kisses and caresses.

"And what about you?" shouted the Gunner at Miss Boddy when he had managed to get his face disentangled from Amelia. "Where's your patriotism? You're British, ain't you? What about that there flag up there?" and then pointed to the roof of the hotel where there was no flag, but it didn't matter to Gunner Lovejoy, who now somehow had become Major Clyde. "Bonny England! It's a symbol, old girl, it's not 'ere you find it," Lovejoy continued, looking to touch his skull and marked Amelia's instead, "but down 'ere," and this time he hit the general region of his stomach. "You don't approve of war, says you, but we're in it and the bloody 'uns on our tails. What do you care about the Major's farm up there wherever it is? And the geese and the kiddies walking 'and in 'and to school, and the bloomin' train whistles! Cor, you're the one to talk, sitting out the war 'ere living off the fat of the land while others is dodging bombs and working themselves to the bone."

Miss Boddy suddenly put her hand to her face and cried, "Oh Mr. Lovejoy, you're hurting me!"

"'Urting you," repeated the Gunner, dripping and swaying. "Look at what you've done to me."

He took a half a dozen steps forward and came closer. Miss Boddy not only looked but sniffed. "Why Mr. Lovejoy," she cried, horrified, "you're drunk."

Lovejoy pulled himself erect proudly and said, "That's it! Got it in one. I'm drunk! Good and bloody drunk. I've lost me battle with the demon rum. The tragedy of having to go back and tell Harold there's nothing doing 'as proved too much for me. Look upon me, ma'am, I've fallen by the wayside."

And at this point the Gunner discovered that though many ingredients can be mingled with alcohol without disaster, emotion is not one of them. . . . "And blimey," he added, "if I don't think I'm going to be sick, too." He then knelt upon the moonlit sands and proceeded to be so.

Miss Boddy made sympathetic clucking sounds, held his head,

wiped his clammy brow, and said, "Oh poor, poor Mr. Lovejoy, come let me help put you to bed."

Lightened and unresisting, the Gunner permitted her to guide him up to the hotel and to his room, after which he remembered no more until he awoke eleven hours later with a thundering hangover and enough of memory returning to let him know that if he hadn't ruined everything before he most certainly had now, by getting blind, staggering drunk and cursing a teetotal lady he had been sent to blandish and charm.

He arose and began throwing things into his suitcase. An hour later he paid his bill with funds provided by Major Clyde, made his farewells to Miss Neville, and slipped out the back door so as not to encounter Miss Boddy, intending to trudge the three miles to the bus route and get the hell out of there and back to London to his punishment, whatever it should be.

But he failed to reckon with Miss Constance Boddy and the processes of mind which had kept her awake half the night. When he reached the end of the lane from the hotel leading to the high-hedged road, there she was with Amelia on her shoulders, straddling the path, and on her face a most curious expression, which in his own surprise and anguish of mind he failed to recognise as the zealous lovelight in the eyes of the reformer who contemplates a brand to be snatched from the burning. To her, Lovejoy had been teetotal, had struggled to fight the good fight for the white flag of purity; he had proved not strong enough, he needed help.

"Mr. Lovejoy," she said, "I have been thinking over last night. I have decided to let Amelia go to Gibraltar. But, of course, I could not possibly be separated from her. I am sure you will be able to arrange for me to accompany her—and you."

The Gunner set down his suitcase and sat on it because he felt his legs would no longer support him. He passed a handkerchief over his brow while Amelia came over and hugged him.

"Gord, ma'am," he said, "do you really mean it? I can hardly believe it. It's mighty good of you." He could hardly credit that victory should thus have been snatched from total catastrophe.

"It was last night that decided me," said Miss Boddy. "It was all my fault. And after you had told me of your struggle against strong drink and the necessity from time to time of a helping hand. Yet in the hour when you needed me most I failed you."

Some of the shine went off the Gunner's triumph. The presence of Miss Boddy in Gibraltar monitoring his visits to the Admiral Nelson, or even picketing the place, would be disturbing. Still, the Gunner had lived long enough to accept and be grateful for half victories and if that was the only way Amelia could be got to Gibraltar, chaperoned by her mistress, then that was how it had to be, provided he could get by Major Clyde.

But to Lovejoy's surprise the Major found Miss Boddy's decision no obstacle. On the contrary when the Gunner got through to him on the telephone he was both pleased and congratulatory. "Good man," he cried, "well done! Splendid show! You've saved the situation! I knew you could do it! Bravo! I'll set up the flight back at once. Group Captain Cranch happens to be in London."

The Gunner hung up in a daze. Never had such an all-embracing bender, which by rights should have ended in the most appalling disaster, brought such immediate and staggering rewards.

It has been recorded that only once in his entire brave and gallant career did Group Captain Howard Cranch ever conduct a flight in total silence. Noted for his entertaining songs, chatter, and imitation over the W.T. and during combat as well, there was one trip he made without ever opening his mouth.

In this instance the phrase "He was struck dumb" applied, and this was exactly what occurred in the case of Captain Cranch, who waited by his ship on the tarmac of a little-used airport to begin a most secret journey on which he had been given no briefing except that there would be four passengers.

At precisely the time appointed a limousine with the blinds pulled down drove out upon the concrete and up to the aircraft. Out from it spilled a stout, cheerful-looking woman. She was followed by a man Cranch had no idea was in London, Gunner Lovejoy of Gibraltar. On the Gunner's shoulder perched quite the most repulsive ape he had ever laid eyes on, and to close the procession there came the tall, gangling figure of Major Clyde.

The Group Captain spoke only once and that was to take in

vain the name of his Lord. And after that he said not a single, solitary word, except that his head never did stop shaking from side to side.

However, as always, he flew his bizarre passenger list with care and meticulousness and after the requisite number of hours landed them feather light and rolled up to the Headquarters Building to be met by Major Bailey and his attractive wife, the Brigadier's Brigade Major, and a man from the office of the Colonial Secretary. Only then did he once more give tongue, regrettably for a second time to take the name in vain.

Chapter 18

SCRUFFY DECLINES

It certainly had not been anyone's intention, but somehow the expedition from the Rock Hotel to Tim's new cages by the apes' village close to Ferdinand's Battery took on the aspect of a bride's wedding party proceeding to the church.

That morning there was actually nothing more afoot than the introduction of Amelia to Scruffy and vice versa. It had been planned to place Amelia in the cage adjoining Scruffy's with, however, the door between them securely locked until it appeared that an exchange of visits might be agreeable to both.

Yet the party took on a most festive air. To begin with, the men had put on their best uniforms and Lovejoy turned up tubbed, scrubbed, brushed, and spruced almost beyond endurance. Felicity chose to wear a pair of black silk stockings for the occasion instead of the regulation cotton ones. Major McPherson carried his swagger stick. The security guard which preceded and followed the caravan fairly glittered with spit and polish. But what really set the tone was, of course, Miss Boddy, and it was as though all of them had guessed that she would be dressed for the event.

All that was missing was a cluster of roses or a spray of lilies of the valley at the shoulder of her smart blue costume. She wore a freshly starched white blouse with a white lace jabot at her neck and a half hat, a semi-circle with a bit of veiling in front. Her white gloves were immaculate, her pumps silver-buckled. There was high colour in her cheeks and a sparkle to her eyes. In a sense it was she rather than Amelia who was faring forth to meet her intended.

There was something both sweet and touching in the way that she had got herself up for the occasion, and the ones who were moved most by it were Felicity and Lovejoy, Felicity, who understood the woman's heart that beat beneath the white blouse, the heart that never ceases to hope even long after the mind has surrendered, and Lovejoy, who was full of guilt for the part he had played in building up the picture of St. Harold of the Rock.

Because Lovejoy was himself a simple and uncomplicated soul he was able to detect and be oddly stirred by the simplicity of Miss Boddy. They had learned to know one another during the days in Devon and on the flight to Gibraltar and the care with which the chubby little spinster had dressed was, he knew, a manifestation of her love for her own pet as well as a tribute to the Gunner's imagination and powers of prevarication. Miss Boddy was preparing to meet a paragon of a macaque, a hero, one of the heavenly elect among beasts, a veritable seraph who would confer upon her Amelia those blessings of holy matrimony which she herself had been denied. And as she came down the steps of the Rock Hotel with Amelia perched upon her shoulder there was a great charm about her, and Major Clyde again reflected how right he had been in assessing her innocence as her most powerful weapon against the world.

The caravan consisted of four soldiers in the leading vehicle, a second car containing Major Clyde, Major McPherson, and Gunner Lovejoy, and then a limousine in which rode Miss Boddy with Amelia, Timothy, and Felicity, the latter clutching a large spray of bougainvillaea. She had been waiting outside the car and when Miss Boddy had descended the steps, drawing on her white gloves, Felicity had moved to the terrace of the hotel and annexed some branches of the flowers growing there. She felt like a bridesmaid.

With Tim on the jump seat and Felicity, Miss Boddy, and Amelia comfortably settled in the back, the journey up the face of the great bastion Rock began.

Miss Boddy tittered, "I'm so nervous. I feel just like a girl going to meet her first celebrity. I can hardly wait."

Felicity and Tim exchanged looks. Felicity's look could have been interpreted. "Oh dear!" and Tim's, "Crikey!"

"You see," Miss Boddy said almost in reply to Tim's look, "I feel that I know Harold almost as well as I do my own Amelia."

Felicity elevated an eyebrow. The elevation meant, "Harold? Since when?"

Tim imperceptibly lowered his, meaning, "Well, you wouldn't want her to know he was called Scruffy, would you?"

"Mr. Lovejoy has told me the most wonderful stories about Harold and what a help he has been to everyone, how he protects the motor cars from the wicked ones who would like to steal the windscreen wipers, shares his goodies with his less fortunate brothers, and retrieves lost property for the visitors."

Felicity's looks now became loaded with more words than she could successfully transfer via that route and meant, "In heaven's name, Tim, what have you done to this poor woman, filling her up on lies like that? What is going to happen when she sets eyes on that utterly revolting specimen? It's not fair."

If the gist didn't reach Tim, the import did, but he had no success whatsoever in broadcasting back to Felicity his anguished excuses. "It weren't me, Mum. This was Major Clyde's idea. I just loaned him Lovejoy."

"Of course," said Felicity tentatively, having in mind somehow trying to soften the blow, "you might not find him *exactly* like that."

Miss Boddy smiled sweetly and trustingly, "Oh but I'm sure I shall," she said. "Lovejoy has told me everything about his sweetness, his gentleness, his generosity, and besides," concluded Miss Boddy, "he's so beautiful."

"Beautiful!" The exclamation fraught with sheer horror burst from Felicity's lips before she could control it. But Miss Boddy was not even aware.

"Oh yes. We think he's lovely, Amelia and I. Don't we, dear?" and she opened her purse and withdrew a glossy print of the re-touched photograph that had been sent to Lovejoy to pass on to Miss Boddy as a reproduction of Amelia's prospective spouse. The ape gazed at the picture and chittered softly. There was a melting look in her eyes. "I have carried it about with me ever since Mr. Lovejoy gave it to me—that is, ever since Amelia and I decided to come out here. And to think that in a few minutes we will be seeing him face to face."

Felicity glanced briefly at the angelic countenance depicted, and choked. She then didn't even bother to transfer her thoughts to her husband with a look; instead her lips directed at him the silently formed words, "You bastard!" It threw Tim into a panic, for he knew no way of lip forming, wigwagging, or telepathing back to her, "What about that bloke Holbein who gimmicked that portrait of Anne of Cleves? It's all in a good cause, isn't it?"

They had already climbed high past the Moorish castle and were bowling along the Queen's Road. To their right and below them Gibraltar lay spread out like a relief map. Tim felt a slight sense of injury. There was the key to the East which they were all struggling to preserve. On the other hand as a fair man, although a husband, he had to admit that a girl would naturally side with another woman, particularly one who had been led up the garden path. As the caravan slowed down approaching Ferdinand's Battery and the ape cages, he breathed a silent prayer to St. Whoever-It-Was in charge of *macaca sylvana* to let it be one of old Scruff's better days.

The same thing was weighing on the mind of Gunner Lovejoy, for when the command car in which he had been riding came to a halt he walked back to the vehicle from which Tim and his party were alighting and said, "Old Scruff—I mean Harold might be just a wee bit nervous at first." He held out his arms to Amelia. "Perhaps I had better take her." Amelia went to him as obediently and lovingly as a child to a father, wrapping her arms about the Gunner's leathery neck and placing her jowl next to his seamed cheeks.

Miss Boddy looked fondly upon the scene and said, "She loves you, Mr. Lovejoy. It makes me so happy." They then walked in silent file to the cages. One of these stood empty and in the adjoining one, at the far end, sat huddled with his back turned the brown figure of the full-grown macaque.

Scruffy was brooding and nursing a large grievance made up of an accumulation of changes and things gone wrong. Life on the Rock had been charging to hell in a hand barrow. All the other apes he used to fight, bully, beat up, bite, and make love to had vanished, and in recent weeks, instead of being free to go to town where he could break windows, tear up people's gardens, and foul the catchments, he had been locked up in a cage surrounded by soldiers carrying loaded guns. He did not understand this solitary confinement, and what was more he didn't like it and thus, had they but known it, had managed to accumulate the father of all grouches.

Although crouched in his corner he looked to be calm and even contemplative, he was loaded. Never a sterling character to begin with, anti-human, anti-social, and an unmitigated tyrant, all he needed was the sight of one strange monkey or one strange human to pull the trigger. These the British Government had now provided in the shape of Amelia and Miss Boddy.

What was wanted at that moment was one of the early nineteenth-century French painters who used to perpetrate those vast canvases showing Napoleon with his generals just before the battle of Something-or-Other. It had all arranged itself into that kind of tableau, Lovejoy inside the empty cage with Amelia on his shoulders, Miss Boddy a few paces from Lovejoy, and beyond at the door the anxious group consisting of the Majors Clyde, McPherson, and Bailey, and 2nd Officer Felicity Bailey. To complete the picture there were the two groups of soldiery, the security troops already on guard at the Battery to protect the lone surviving Barbary ape, and the other squads that had come up from the troop carrier, and for the instant they were all frozen in tense silence, waiting to see what would happen.

They didn't have long to wait. It was all over in what might be characterised as a jiffy. Hearing the noise, Scruffy turned around and an expression crossed his ugly features more vicious and cantankerous than Tim had ever seen there before.

Whether it was the sight of a strange female perched on the shoulders of Lovejoy, or the not too attractive countenance of that female, Scruffy was across the intervening space in a blinding flash of speed, gathered up a handful of dung on the way, flung it through the bars at Amelia, squirted Lovejoy, and finished off with a record-breaking display of magot temper, inexhaustible cursing and bad behaviour, during which time he pelted everyone within reach with all and any garbage in the form of carrots, cabbages, and banana skins plucked from the floor of his cage. Only Felicity, who had expected this and therefore remained calm and observant throughout, caught the final tragedy which was that after one look at this repellent brute Amelia fell violently and head over heels in love with him and, in spite of the reception she had received and what had been thrown at her, stretched out yearning arms and chittered lovingly.

"Oh dear," said Miss Boddy, and then repeated again almost pathetically as though she could not believe what her ears and eyes told her, "Oh dear, dear."

"Scruff!" bawled Gunner Lovejoy, enraged by this performance to the point where he completely forgot himself and his surroundings. "Cut that out or I'll come in there and kick your bloody arse for you."

The shock waves of what appeared to be a thoroughly disintegrating society rolled over all of them. Miss Boddy murmured, "My poor Amelia," and held out her arms, and when her ape came to her moved out of range. Amelia, perched on her shoulder, continued to look beseechingly at the fiend in the cage. Major McPherson had his head buried in his hands as one who could no longer look, while Major Clyde had both arms upraised in the gesture reminiscent of the wicket keeper appealing to the umpire, only in this case the umpire was God and he was asking how He, if He indeed loved the British Empire and was on its side as the clergy kept insisting, could permit its plans to be brought to nought by one foul beast.

Timothy and Felicity, impelled by the magnitude of the disaster, had drawn close together, for Felicity was aware of how stricken her husband must be at that moment and in need of comfort. She was torn between loyalty to him and sympathy for Miss Boddy.

But if anyone needed commiseration it was Gunner Lovejoy. Deep in his heart he had known all along that it would happen, that Scruffy would topple the edifice of the tales he had told.

Yet somehow he had hoped for the miracle, banking on the theory that Scruffy incarcerated and alone, removed from his own species, would somehow take kindly to a female when presented.

All this was now up in smoke and not only that, he had so far forgotten himself as to use barrack-room language in the presence of one he had grown both to like and respect. Besides, he saw an end to his own cushy tenure as Keeper of the Apes. The brass would have its revenge for this calamity.

All of this human anguish arising from the afflicted collected somewhat like electricity in a wet cell and communicated itself to Scruffy, showing him that he was definitely on the right track. By now he had had a good look at Amelia perched on the shoulders of a strange female, holding out her arms to him, making kissing movements with her mouth, her eyes still further crossed with love, and his sense of injury was deepened that such a specimen should have been offered to him—to him, Scruffy, King of the Rock, who could have any girl he wanted.

He barked and coughed with rage. He spat. He bounced up and down on all fours. He combed his area for ammunition to hurl. He leaped onto the side of the cage, bared his yellow canines, and shook the wire netting so that the entire structure rattled and clattered.

Felicity could see the hurt look growing in the eyes of Miss Boddy and the appearance of tears at the corners.

It was quite true. Miss Boddy was not only appalled by the behaviour of one who had been held out to her as a paragon and a saint but disappointed as well in the human species. She had grown truly fond of Mr. Lovejoy and his stories and to have him thus exposed as a shameless prevaricator was almost more than she could bear. And what was really so awful for all of them was that her gentleness was never for an instant diminished.

"Oh no," she murmured, "no, no. I am afraid I could never permit Amelia to associate with such a creature. Quite impossible." She turned reproachful eyes upon the Gunner. "I am afraid that you have told me a number of falsehoods for your own ends, Mr. Lovejoy. That was unkind. I trusted you."

The essential truth that lay behind this accusation was more than flesh and blood and Gunner Lovejoy could stand. He would not have cared to have been made the mug in private by his superiors for their own shortcomings—this was after all the accepted lot of every ranker—but not before Miss Boddy. For the second time that day the Gunner forgot himself.

"It was 'im," he cried, pointing an accusing finger at Major Clyde. "He made me. I never wanted to do it, but 'e's got the crowns on his shoulders and what's a man to do? Who gave me the photo to give to you? Who filled me up with a bellyful of psychology or whatever he called it? 'Stand up and salute the colours,' 'e says, and a lot of balls about the wild geese flying homewards and children walking 'and in 'and, bonny England and backs to the wall and blast the filthy Hun. It was 'IM put me up to it."

All eyes were now focussed upon Major Clyde, who under the accusing finger of the indignant Gunner suddenly looked exactly as he had thirty years before when hauled up on the carpet before the headmaster. And for the first time in his military career as a clever and competent organizer and administrator of an Intelligence branch, the Major felt himself thoroughly discombobulated. This was one of the effects of Miss Boddy's innocence against which all normal human standards of behaviour seemed to shatter. It was utterly ridiculous that a grown man should feel himself so confused, ill at ease, out of countenance, and unable to think clearly, but there it was.

Under the reproachful gaze that Miss Boddy turned upon him, Major Clyde went completely to pieces and said quite the last thing which would ever have passed the lips of an English officer in his right mind and in front of people, "All I said to him was about England and what it was like, and did he love it or didn't he, and what would happen if the filty Hun took over and it was up to him to prevent it."

The tears that had been so close to Miss Boddy's eyes now did spill over, for she was frightened, lonely, and homesick among these alien people who spoke and behaved in such a queer manner. In an instant Felicity was at her side with her arms about her, crying, "Oh poor, dear Miss Boddy, you mustn't mind. Men are always like children when they make war; they grow quite soft in the head." She looked around at the others. "Perhaps we had better go back to the hotel."

In his cage, and now out of things to throw, Scruffy bounced up and down on all fours in a gleeful rage and continued to do so until his visitors had departed and the riflemen once more took up their sentry positions around his cage. From his point of view it had been the first thoroughly satisfactory morning in a long, long time.

There appeared to be no hope of budging Miss Boddy from her position. With the revelation that not only was Harold unsanctified, but a fiend ascended unquestionably directly from the nethermost pits of hell, her objections were crystallized more firm than steel, more hard than diamonds. To this was added the sense of loss and disappointment. Two figures with whom she had lived for a time with affection and admiration, one the phantom Harold and the other flesh and blood Lovejoy, had been shattered. She longed to return to the peace and quiet and the simple routine of living she had evolved in Hope Cove in South Devon. This great, huge Rock, this weird community populated half with Britons in uniform and half with a strange, swarthy people who spoke a foreign language, was not for her. All the paraphernalia of war which she detested was too close here, the armed men, the warships, and the great cannons staring with their single eyes into the sky and out to sea.

The committee, minus Felicity and Gunner Lovejoy, met in Tim's office late that evening and be it said to their credit that there were no recriminations or attempts to lay blame for the fiasco, though McPherson did ask blandly of Major Clyde, "I say, Slinker, did you really fill up old Lovejoy with that St. George for England stuff?" To which the Major replied gloomily, "Well, it worked, didn't it? Up to a point? He got her here. In my business you get to learn to try everything including even an appeal to patriotism."

"The point," Timothy said, "at the moment seems rather to be—what do we do now?"

"She wants to go home," Major Clyde said cheerlessly. "She asked for transportation back to England. I said there were no ships available at the moment, but there was no sale. We can't keep her here against her will. I suppose we can get old Howard to flip her home again."

"And in the meantime?" put in Tim.

"I have something lined up in Oran," Major McPherson said, "but I have to wait and see how it develops. It may be another six months before we can be certain and in the meantime if the Germans get on to it——"

"It won't do," Tim burst out. "It's a birth we need, as Slinker says. We've got to have a new apelet born on the Rock with photographs and all that sort of thing. It will be a year before we can breed any of the apelets that survived. If the Jerries manage to get to them in the meantime—but if we can announce a normal birth, that would knock them all right back on to their heels."

"You're telling me." Major Clyde picked up the thread morosely. "Our morale is being shot to hell."

"I might have Felicity try to have another go at the old girl," Tim said. "She's sort of taken to her."

Major Clyde said, "Yes do." Nobody could think of anything better.

But that didn't work either, even though Felicity was working for her harassed and worried husband. She tried to explain the necessity of the situation to Miss Boddy, only to be met with irreducible resistance. Harold was no saint but a fiend. She and Amelia had been lied to. She wanted to go home immediately. The R.A.F. had a transport plane scheduled to fly out the day after next. Yes, there was room on it for Miss Boddy and her ape, and that was that.

Chapter 19

MISS BODDY ACCEPTS

The lounge of the Rock Hotel at Gibraltar is what you would expect of the best British hotel in a foreign port, though rather more cheerfully arrayed in chintzes, with the setting further enhanced by large bowls of sub-tropical flowers. There were some bright paintings by local artists on the walls and, of course, the view from the windows was the irresistibly exciting one of the harbour, the sea, and Algeciras across the bay. Nevertheless it remained the public lounge of a hotel.

And in one corner of it the afternoon before her projected departure from Gibraltar sat Miss Constance Boddy and recently promoted to Bombardier Lovejoy in earnest conversation. The interview was at the request of Lovejoy. No one was more surprised than Miss Boddy, engaged in the last rites of assembling her possessions when the telephone rang in her room and the receptionist announced, "There's a soldier—I beg your pardon, a Bombardier Lovejoy downstairs to see you."

The name brought a most strange pang of pain to the heart of Miss Boddy and for a moment she had contemplated an excuse to avoid seeing him. But then her innate kindness rejected this and she had agreed to go down.

In the lobby had waited an embarrassed Lovejoy, even more brushed and spruced than he had been on the fateful expedition to the apes' village the day before. His cap was tucked under one arm, a fixative applied to his hair so that every grain and wisp was in place, his boots were twin mirrors, and in one sweating hand was clutched a wrapped bouquet, open at one end, of red roses.

When Miss Boddy had emerged from the lift, he had moved

towards her with the uncertain tread of one proceeding to his execution, gulped and declared, "I came to say good-bye."

He had then stood there quite petrified and apparently incapable of further speech, nor did he make any move to present her with the flowers. It became evident to Miss Boddy that he had something more to say than just good-bye; that it was proving extraordinarily difficult for him; that he would never get it said standing there in the lobby, and she took pity on him. Hence the conference in the lounge.

When they were seated, the Bombardier still clinging desperately to his cap in one hand and the flowers in the other, Miss Boddy asked, "Would you like something to drink?"

"Gord," said Lovejoy from the very bottom of his being, "would I?"

"Then I'll order tea," Miss Boddy said and did so forthwith.

It had not been what the Bombardier had in mind, but it was strong when it arrived and its tannin content did supply the minimum of stimulant needed to settle Lovejoy's nerves.

"I have come to apologise," he said, "that was a rotten dirty thing I done."

The heart within Miss Boddy was as soft and cushiony as her exterior. "That's quite all right, Mr. Lovejoy," she said. "You were only carrying out the orders of your superiors."

The first step in self-purging and condemnation having been taken, the second was easier. "That's not exactly true," said the Bombardier. "There ain't nothing in the regulations that compels a man to turn himself into a liar for no one. You know the orful thing was I enjoyed making up them tales. I didn't know I 'ad it in me."

Miss Boddy sighed, for her memory had swiftly taken her back to the strand at Hope Cove and the happy days she had spent there in the company of Lovejoy. "I'm afraid I enjoyed listening to them, too," she admitted.

"Makes me feel a proper swine," confessed Lovejoy. "It was all a pack of lies from beginning to end. Gord! And me who had lived with old Scruff for the last ten years and knew every crochet and wickedness of his black heart. He 'adn't got one redeeming feature." Then almost as an afterthought he added, "I suppose that's what made me love 'im."

Miss Boddy made no reply to this astonishing admission, but the thought that anyone could love such a specimen was startling to her. And yet there was no questioning the sincerity of the soldier.

"I wanted you and Amelia to come along back with me to Gib," said the Bombardier.

"Yes, I'm sure you did," remarked Miss Boddy, but her manner of saying it fired something in Lovejoy and he suddenly cried with a vehemence that amazed him: "No, not *them* with their plots and schemes for the bloody Empire, but me! Oh Lord, me and my mouth, I've said the word again I oughtn't! Please excuse me, ma'am."

Now that he reminded her, Miss Boddy was surprised to find that she had not even heard "the word." She had still been back in Devon immersed in the memory of those days and the particular charm that Bombardier Lovejoy had exercised upon her.

"Me," repeated Lovejoy. "There was old Scruff back on the Rock needing a mate, there was the war, and there was——" he trailed off.

"Yes," prompted Miss Boddy, curious as to where these confessions were leading.

"Well me and everybody like," the Bombardier concluded somewhat lamely.

There was a silence while she poured a second cup of tea.

"You'll be off in the morning, I expect," Lovejoy opened.

"Yes."

"That's a good aircraft, the Handley, you're flying in. You'll be safe as a rock," the Bombardier assured her, using perhaps not the happiest metaphor. Then he added, "I wish you wasn't going."

"Really? That's kind of you to say so." Miss Boddy was regarding the soldier curiously through the lenses of her gold-rimmed spectacles as she sat, a teacup poised in one hand, her little finger elegantly crooked, and a chocolate cream biscuit in the other. Yet something other than curiosity impelled her to ask, "Why?"

The Bombardier had got himself forward to the edge of his

chair. He, too, had his teacup in one hand; the other was still clutching the undelivered bouquet of roses. "Oh I don't know," he replied. "I just wish as how you weren't."

Miss Boddy thought she had read him. Men after all were all alike and particularly men in war. For whatever the reason or cause they wanted their way.

"Everyone has been at me to make me stay," Miss Boddy said with some sadness. "All those officers and even that sweet child married to one of them. All they care about is to get what they want. And I suppose you, too, Mr. Lovejoy."

"No," Lovejoy heard himself say to his utter horror, "I'd miss you after you were gone and that's a fact."

Something in his tone disarmed Miss Boddy for a moment. "Would you really, Mr. Lovejoy? No one has ever said that to me before."

"Ma'am, I would, so help me, and I never thought that John C. Lovejoy would be saying that to any woman. Couldn't you perhaps stay, ma'am?"

Miss Boddy shook her head. "Our home is in England," she said.

"But couldn't you make your home here with me?" Lovejoy pleaded. "Look how Amelia gets on with me," and again the Bombardier felt both thrill and shock at the sound of his own words. For he was wholly unfamiliar with those processes that take over in a man vis-à-vis a woman in which the head has every intention of remaining in control only to be treacherously sold out by the heart.

Miss Boddy couldn't keep the astonishment out of her voice even while she felt her heart suddenly accelerating. "Did you say make our home with you, Mr. Lovejoy?" she asked.

He had not wanted to say it, but he had, and now his head was nodding in silent assent to the question.

A new and cold suspicion suddenly chilled the sweet warmth that for a moment had flooded Miss Boddy. "Mr. Lovejoy," she asked, "are you by any chance asking me to marry you?"

Bombardier Lovejoy's mind silently dictated the reply. "*Me marry? Never in a million years."* His heart, however, translated it into a simply spoken, "Yes, ma'am, please, if you would."

"Mr. Lovejoy," said Miss Boddy, and only a woman would have been able to detect the quiet misery and pain in her voice, "did they send you here to do this to me? To ask me to marry you to keep me and Amelia here?"

It was now the turn of Lovejoy to be filled with dismay at this evidence of how misunderstanding, suspicion, and exigency can distort and twist an honest emotion. "What?" he cried. "The likes of them, a lot of bleeding orficers force me to put my head in the noose? Not——" he caught the naughty word just in time and swallowed it "—likely."

"Then why, why?" asked Miss Boddy, and now her own internal anguish lent vehemence to her query. "I am a weak and perhaps silly woman, Mr. Lovejoy, and unused to the ways of the world, but don't take me for a fool. So many lies have been told to me already. It is because of Amelia——"

Lovejoy looked stunned at this outburst and repeated, "Take you for a fool, ma'am? No one would ever do that."

"Then why have you tried to make me one by asking me to marry you?"

And now there settled upon John C. Lovejoy an alarming and protracted silence as the most fearful struggle went on inside him, words and thoughts and feelings that couldn't get themselves said. He was like a cocoon from which something was endeavouring to free itself. "Ma'am," he finally articulated miserably, "I just 'aven't the words! Can't you *see?"*

Miss Boddy peered at him and did see. She saw his red, seamed, leathery face, wet with perspiration, a pair of blue eyes shining with sincerity, and many other things that she had never seen before in the eyes of any man, and for a moment her own grew misty.

She was still holding her teacup and the unbitten chocolate cream biscuit and was suddenly and oddly aware of the angle at which her little finger was poised. Lovejoy, opposite, was also clinging to his teacup and his roses. The hotel lounge was deserted and those passing through the lobby to the lift who might have glanced over towards the corner where they sat saw only a chubby spinster and a middle-aged artilleryman chatting over their tea and would never have imagined the love and the yearning that was overflowing in those two hearts, struggling to be expressed between them.

"I am a lonely man, ma'am. We'd get on well together. For instance, there's you liking stories. I could be telling you some that would curl your——" he stopped, realising that he had slipped on to dangerous ground, but Miss Boddy seemed unaware of the gaff.

She was in a turmoil. Her heart thumping in her bosom, her head reeling, she heard herself saying, "You are kind, Mr. Lovejoy, it is kind of you to ask me. I can never marry! You see, Amelia and I—— It is too late now, I couldn't——"

"Ma'am," pleaded Bombardier Lovejoy, "do you want to send me back to my old ways? Drink and Lord knows what? You've had me straightened out. I haven't had a monkey juice since I've been back. It's hard for me to do it alone."

There was never a stranger love declaration, or in this instance one more calculated to affect the one to whom it was addressed. For in the excitement of the journey and the subsequent disappointment brought on by the collapse of St. Harold, Constance Boddy had quite forgotten that what had really moved her to make the voyage with her pet to Gibraltar and acquiesce to the plans to mate Amelia with Scruffy had been her desire to snatch the brand of John Lovejoy from the burning of the Demon Rum.

And, of course, never admitted to herself but likewise never far from the surface was the memory of how very like the father she had so loved was the same John C. Lovejoy. In a reeling world that was spinning about her like a teetotum, she was suddenly aware of the absurdity of her tilted little finger and consciously, unobserved by Lovejoy, curved it around the handle of her tea-cup. It was a gesture of abdication. Constance Boddy had had enough of all those airs and graces she had laboriously acquired and with a tremendous and joyful yearning she felt that she was on the threshold of becoming herself again.

But the force of Lovejoy's argument, the lightning-like revelation that had come to her, plus the affection she felt for this stray of the world, so like herself and who had truly characterised himself as a lonely man, had thrown her into a state of confusion.

"Oh Mr. Lovejoy," she cried, "I just don't know what to say." Then she set down her teacup and biscuit, arose and ran for the lift, which providentially had descended and opened its door just as she arrived. The door closed again and she vanished.

Bombardier Lovejoy sighed and rose, brushing the crumbs from his lap. He called for the bill and paid the 2/6d. with a 6d. tip for the tea and walked through the lounge to the lobby, and only when he reached there was he aware that he was still holding on to the bouquet of roses, so tightly in fact that several of the thorns had come through the paper and pierced his palm. But he didn't feel it.

His feet were carrying him down the steps to the exit when a page caught up with him and said, "Bombardier Lovejoy?"

"Yes."

"You are wanted on the telephone."

He went into the booth and picked up the receiver. He supposed Tim or Major Clyde had somehow traced him to the hotel, and automatically he said, "Bombardier Lovejoy here."

But it was not Tim or the Major; the voice at the other end was that of Miss Constance Boddy. She said, "John?"

"Yes, ma'am."

"If—if you want me to still, I will." Then before he could reply the phone was put down.

Lovejoy in his turn set down the receiver. He left the booth in a daze, still clutching his bouquet. He was aware suddenly that he was inordinately happy.

The telephone rang in the Fortress H.Q. office. Major McPherson picked it up and said, "Oh hello, Tim," when the speaker identified himself. "Yes, just a moment." He passed the instrument over to Major Clyde, saying, "It's for you, Slinker. Tim Bailey."

Major Clyde said with resignation, "Fire away. Things couldn't be any worse."

Tim's voice came through, "They might be better though."

"I can't bear it! Don't tell me that old Scruffy has divided parthenogenetically."

"No," said Tim, "thank God. One is enough. But you can cancel the passengers for tomorrow's flight—the Handley-Page going to London."

"What! You mean the old girl and that cross-eyed she-ape have changed their minds."

"That's it."

"I can't believe it. Who persuaded her?"

"Lovejoy."

"By God," said the Major, "there's a man. I'll see that he gets the George Medal for this. How did he do it?"

"He's going to marry her."

"What!" yelled the Major.

"I said he's going to marry her. They've fixed it up."

"In that case, it's nothing less than a V.C. And talk about a man sacrificing himself for his country over and above the line of duty." His voice took on the imitative quality of a radio announcer, "They laughed when I said I had appealed to patriotism."

The diaphragm of the telephone instrument rattled. "Patriotism my eye! Look here, Slinker. Don't say anything to Lovejoy when you see him."

"Why not?" asked the Major. "I want to embrace him like a brother, pat him on the shoulder, buy him a drink."

"Don't," said Tim. "I understand that's part of the deal, that he's off the stuff. You see, it's love. Lovejoy hasn't got used to the idea yet and it's killing him."

"Good God," said the Major. "Did you say love?"

"Love," the instrument reiterated.

The Major looked at it for a moment and then said to McPherson, "He said it's love."

"O.K.," McPherson replied, "give him mine, too."

"No, no, you don't understand," Major Clyde said. "It's Lovejoy——"

Tim's voice came through again. "I say, Slinker," and when

the Major had grunted, continued, "we'll want some wires pulled."

"What do you want, the P.M. for best man? He'd love it."

"This is serious. We'll have to fix it so that Miss Boddy can stay on the Rock."

"Just say the P.M. said it was O.K.," Clyde advised. "That's what I've been doing all along."

"Lovejoy is asking for a sergeant's married quarters."

"Give it to him," said the Major.

"But he's not a sergeant."

"Tim, my boy, you surprise me," the Major chortled. "You're sitting in the driver's seat. You just don't know your own powers. Wave your little wand and say, 'Hear ye, hear ye, hear ye, I hereby create Bombardier John C. Lovejoy a full sergeant with all the emoluments and appurtenances thereto appertaining."

"Do you really think——"

"Just say the P.M. wants it. By the way, when is the wedding?"

"In two weeks."

"There should be a party," said the Major. "We ought to get Howard Cranch to organize it."

"God forbid," Tim said. "But I haven't told you the best piece of news yet. She's withdrawn her objections to Amelia and Scruffy."

A kind of tremolo came into the Major's voice as he said, "History will remember this."

"What, what?" said Tim. "What's that?"

"Turning point of the war," said Major Clyde and hung up.

The metamorphosis of Miss Constance Boddy was dramatic and complete. Almost overnight she had changed from a spinster, stiffened into one unalterable way of life, to a pliable woman, a bride-to-be, devoted to the wishes of her man. She was not ridiculous in her surrender, only absolute. She had always had dignity, but it was that of the shield she had thrown up between herself and the world, the protective screen of the unfulfilled woman. Now, late in life, a man had not only pleaded with her to share his life but had brought her as a gift abnegation of self. For her he was willing to give up the habits of a lifetime and start afresh, and this she wore like a crown.

Miss Boddy's temperance was not the tight-lipped spoil-sport kill-joy type nor was her hatred of war of the crackpot peace-marcher variety. She hated war because she was a woman of good will and common sense plus courage to speak out against the imbecility of human slaughter. She hated drink because of the damage it had done to her illusions concerning her father.

Her life had been one long pattern of devotion, first to her father, then to the ape which surely represented the child that she had never had. Now this devotion was shifted to the man who had offered her his life and asked for hers. He became paramount to her and thus Amelia swiftly fell into her proper place, no less loved, but downgraded from child to beast, from obsession to household pet. If Lovejoy wanted her mated with the man in the moon, she would not have protested. Thus she no longer objected to the alliance of Amelia and Scruffy since it seemed that such a union would make Lovejoy happy.

Unfortunately, the one that continued to object was Scruffy.

Tim's euphoria brought about by what appeared to be the solution of his problems via the heroism and gallantry of Bombardier, now Sergeant, Lovejoy, was short-lived and the pin that punctured it was, of course, the intransigence of Scruffy. Never had the old adage that you can drive a horse to water but you cannot make him drink had a more thorough illustration. By dint of bribery, threatening, cajoling, and watching, Tim and the Sergeant had brought Scruffy to the point where he would tolerate Amelia in the same cage, but that was as far as he would go. And Amelia was now full in heat and psychologically as well as physically prepared. Scruffy stubbornly refused and resolutely kept his back turned. When she tried to approach him, or made advances, he either cuffed her, spat at her, or bit her.

"It's just damn bad luck," Tim explained to Major Clyde. "He doesn't like her looks."

"I didn't know they cared," said the Major. "I just thought that when——"

"They don't," Tim asserted. "But HE does. That's the trouble.

Old Scruff is such a bastard he's practically human. The more she chucks herself at him the less he seems to be inclined."

The Major nodded morosely. "I know," he agreed. "There was a girl at a cocktail party once. Practically chased me into the bedroom. No go! A fellow likes to feel——"

"The hunter not the hunted," Tim concluded with masculine illogic, having quite forgotten how Felicity had tracked him down.

The point was that Scruffy could, but wouldn't. Somehow, through osmosis or sheer instinct, the urgency of the affair and what was wanted of him had communicated itself. Scruffy would have made the perfect Russian Foreign Minister. Whatever anybody else was for, he was against.

Nevertheless, Tim and the Sergeant kept a twenty-four-hour watch on the cage containing Scruffy and Amelia, divided into alternating eight-hour shifts, for they were the only ones on the Rock sufficiently familiar with the physiology and habits of primates to be able to know and be sure that a union had taken place.

These vigils accomplished a dual purpose. They kept track of any possible goings-on between the unhappy couple and at the same time mounted a thoroughly reliable twenty-four-hour guard upon the last two monkeys that stood between the British Empire and the downhill path. However, one reason for this close observation would come to an end within a week or so when that period of combustion which nature sets alight in all its two-footed and four-footed female victims burned out and Amelia would no longer be a candidate for motherhood. Tim had no doubt but that as soon as this moment was to hand and the lady was no longer pregnable Scruffy would want her for his very own. It was maddening and at the same time admirable. If ever there had been a truly free soul cast up on the shores of the planet who did exactly what he wanted with no consideration for anyone or anything, and got away with it, it was Scruff.

With no one else to be trusted, Tim had put himself and Lovejoy on a consecutive eight-hour-watch schedule, midnight to eight in the morning, eight to four, and four to midnight, which meant that one of them stayed up on alternate nights keeping an eye on the pair from St. Michael's Hut, a small shack close by the cages. This played hell with Timothy's home life since Felicity was herself doing a ten-hour shift, locked up in the Coding Office. Their paths seemed to cross only occasionally and less and less frequently, sometimes for a hastily snatched meal, sometimes as Timothy would be coming home to a bed still warm from Felicity's departure. It was on one of those occasions when turn and schedule enabled Tim and Felicity to spend half an evening together that the OIC Apes confessed to his wife that he, or rather they, faced defeat and at the same time was let in to a piece of intelligence, which, had he not been so busy and occupied with affairs of state, he might have suspected and confirmed a good deal sooner.

That evening when they were together until midnight, when it was Tim's trick to go up to the cages, he had been more than usually downcast, failing to respond to all of Felicity's attempts to lift his spirits. Cries of "Cheer up, chicken" were of no avail; her martinis instead of elevating acted as a depressant; she even tried a few shameless advances of which her husband, unlike him, did not even seem to be aware.

"Oh Tim," Felicity groaned finally, "you mustn't take it so to heart. I'll buy you another Empire if this one goes."

"I feel so helpless," Tim complained. "Here I am, Officer in Charges of Apes for the first time in history when it means something. The Brigadier's depending on me; he said so. For two years I've been telling him I'm the only one who knows all about these blighters and now that it's up to me to prove it I can't get that blasted magot to climb over the bolster."

Felicity said, "Shhh—don't be vulgar, darling. Have you tried forbidding him to have anything to do with her? Maybe if you segregated them now so that he *couldn't* get to——"

"Not with old Scruff. He knows that one. The Sergeant and I tried that the other morning. Scruff hopped up and down and clapped his hands. He was delighted and acted as though we had finally got it through our heads what he had been driving at. We had to put them back together again for our own self-respect. He wins, he always wins."

"I don't suppose there is anything we could do for Amelia," Felicity suggested.

"Short of a month's course at Elizabeth Arden's—no," said Tim. "And that wouldn't get her eyes uncrossed. We have groomed her and brushed her; he doesn't like her looks, he doesn't like her smell; he's not having any."

As though smitten by a sudden idea Felicity arose quietly and left the room. When she returned she held in her fingers a small bottle at the bottom of which was a minute amount of yellowish liquid.

Tim looked at her and the little bottle enquiringly.

"The supreme sacrifice," Felicity said. "It's all I've got left. There won't be any more until after the war. You can have it."

"What is it?" Tim asked, his state being such that he was unable to recognize the bottle.

"Chanel No. 5," said Felicity. "Try it on Amelia. Maybe it's just the touch that will get Scruffy."

For a moment Tim was inclined to be angry. His nerves were badly jangled from continued frustration and it was no time for joking. Then, as suddenly as his anger had been about to flare, it vanished, for he was aware of two things—one that Felicity was serious and in her child-woman way really believed it might be of help, and the other that there was something oddly touching in the offer and behind it something even more touching, some kind of a mystery that he could not fathom. "Felicity," he said, "It—I'm afraid it wouldn't work. I don't want to take it if it is your last."

Felicity was now regarding him with a most curious expression on her features and her voice suddenly sounded like a small far-away and wistful echo. "It worked for us," she declared, and then pushed the little bottle across to him. "Take it, I don't need it any more."

The universe about Tim's eyes and ears began to do strange things, take on queer shapes, pulled out long and thin and then patted down flat and round; it made curious noises, sweet music and the rolling sound of thunder, the floor beneath his chair was swaying gently and he had the feeling that his eyes were suddenly crossed at an angle even greater than those of Amelia. His tongue had gone up somewhere into the roof of his skull where he could no longer use it.

Felicity, who as always knew when he was in difficulties, elected to play out the comedy for him. She came swiftly around to his side of the table, assumed his attitude, and cried, "You mean——?" then nipped around back to her side to answer the question, "Oh, my darling, how clever of you to have guessed. Yes, it is true, you are about to become a father."

All the things pent up inside Major Tim Bailey exploded in one agonized cry. "Oh my God, why couldn't it have been Amelia!"

For the first time Felicity was genuinely shocked and hurt, even though a part of her understood. "I suppose because you are not that kind of ape," she cried in outrage. "If that's all you think of——"

Tim was across the table, his arms about her as the enormity of what he had said penetrated through the chaos into which he had been plunged. "Darling, I didn't mean that, you know it. I want to be a mother—you to be a mother, I mean—are you? Will you? I'm proud! I'm excited! I'm the exultant male! Watch me, I'll stand drinks all round. I'll take space in the *Rock Gazette*."

Felicity was mollified. "You'll do no such thing," she said. "Save the treat until I produce it and as for exulting in the *Gazette* or anywhere else you'll keep your big mouth shut."

"But why, my darling, why? This is the sort of thing one wants to clarion."

Felicity took his face between her hands and kissed it. "Not if Mum-to-be also happens to wear the insignia of Second Officer Bailey of the W.R.N.S."

"Oh Gord," said Major Bailey, unconsciously paraphrasing the Sergeant as the light dawned.

"That's my bright boy," said Felicity. "One whisper that Officer Bailey is that way and out she goes from the Navy; once out of the Navy and off she goes from the Rock. End of paradise enow."

"But—but," stammered Tim, "what happens when—when? Well, you know."

Felicity smiled a grave and satisfied smile. "Oh I've thought of that," she said. "I was known as the fat girl once. I can be again."

Chapter 20

MR. RAMIREZ PLAYS CUPID

John Lovejoy, now promoted to Sergeant, had been considering his forthcoming nuptials with what might be described as mixed emotions. He had plenty of time, alone in the barracks, to reflect upon the meaning of such a step and the effect it would have upon his life. He was aware that something stronger than himself had willed that he should spend the rest of his days with this agreeable, pleasant, and sweet-tempered woman. The Sergeant didn't argue with this. It was only that for a man who had spent twenty-five years of his life as a soldier and a bachelor the price was a little steep. No more monkey juice, no more drinks of any kind; no more standing up against a mahogany bar with the comfortable feeling of a glass in the fingers, a glow in the stomach, and a fluency to the tongue.

The Sergeant was neither a drunk nor even a compulsive drinker. He imbibed only socially or under stress of great sorrow or crisis, which, of course, made the embrace of teetotalism that much more difficult since there was no drama connected with it.

Not that Lovejoy couldn't from time to time drink himself into a state verging upon total inebriation, but it called for, as has been indicated, an occasion, a piece of bad news, a piece of good news, a great joy, a great sorrow. Such a happening was about to be visited upon the Sergeant and one which strangely enough managed to combine the two opposites—and this was his wedding to Miss Constance Boddy. He would be exchanging one kind of companionship for another; happiness and sadness thus would walk hand in hand.

Lovejoy felt no qualms of conscience at the idea he was con-templating of enjoying one final bang-up party. He was entitled to it both as a bachelor about to embark on a matrimonial voyage and as a man bidding farewell to spirits. The calamity that befell him was that he found it incumbent upon him to take leave of each one individually.

And the sad thing was that it happened not on the evening that Sergeant Lovejoy had intended it should, which was before the day when he would present himself with his bride-to-be to the Chaplain, and which he had set aside for just this purpose with three of his best friends and drinking companions in the regiment, but several nights previous, and shamefully alone in the Admiral Nelson with none other than Treugang Ramirez.

Sheer chance, coupled with the dogged persistence with which Treugang Ramirez had clung to Sergeant Lovejoy as a source of information about the apes, paid off in the most unexpected manner and gave the little home-grown saboteur his long-awaited opportunity to deal the death blow to the morale of the British garrison as well as the civilians marooned on the Rock.

For the secret that there were now but two apes left, that all efforts to import them in quantity from Africa had failed, and that the British were pinning their hopes on one obstreperous, cantankerous, and obstructionist monkey mating with a total stranger he had not laid eyes upon up to a fortnight before, had remained a secret indeed.

The two Intelligence officers, Majors McPherson and Clyde, had done a highly creditable job in tightening up security where the apes were concerned and putting forth counter-propaganda. Since the construction of Tim's cages by the apes' village and the closing of the area by troops, no one could get close enough to verify how many apes there were.

Thus, the source of information upon which the German propaganda machine was relying from inside the Rock was dried up. Their broadcasts continued in the same vein, but lacked the venom, bounce, and conviction of the earlier ones. Counter-propaganda put out by Clyde, McPherson, and Company had the ape pack flourishing again and breeding normally, and these fables were generally accepted on the Rock, but the situation was tenuous in the extreme.

Although the troops guarding the cages were a picked lot and

sworn to secrecy, one of them might blab and reveal the true
situation. Or some officious secretary might remind the Prime
Minister of the signal sent to the Rock with regard to keeping
the apes up to strength and suggest that perhaps the P.M. would
wish him to see how these had been carried out. This would loose
an official enquiry. What they needed was a bona fide ape birth on
the Rock with the publication of an equally bona fide photograph
of mother and child. Bluff wouldn't do in this instance, Major
Clyde recognized. It had to be the real thing. Major Clyde was
certain that if he could produce this birth upon the Rock, a
genuine one, genuinely substantiated, the Germans would cease
to credit their own propaganda and would begin to believe *his*.
The campaign would be considered a failure; the agents who
could be better used in other projects would be called in and the
funds cut off. Within three months, thus unhampered, the British
would be able to instigate an ape hunt in Africa and within a
short time begin the importing of macaques in fresh numbers to
avert not only the immediate danger but to satisfy any nosy-parker
questioners in Parliament as well. It was subtle, long-range thinking and planning, all held up and being brought to nought by
probably the only time in the entire life history of the primates
when the biological urge hadn't done so.

Thus while there was still a gleam of hope that it might work
before it was too late, it was wholly unforeseen misfortune that
Sergeant Lovejoy should drop into the Admiral Nelson at a time
when it was usually deserted, ten o'clock in the evening, to find
Treugang Ramirez lurking there nursing a beer. It had been a
continuing ten-day lurk for Ramirez, always waiting, always
hoping, for Lovejoy had not visited his favourite pub, or any other
pub for that matter, ever since he had arrived back at the Rock
with Miss Constance Boddy and Amelia.

Nor was there any backsliding or mischief inherent in the visit
of Lovejoy. He had not come to sneak a drink, but to have a word
with the proprietor as to the bachelor party and farewell to spirits
he intended to stage two nights hence. But with a sense of tact
and fitness newly acquired since his association with Miss Boddy
he had no intention of being caught falling down drunk in the

public bar, and so had come to engage a private room for himself and three of his regular cronies where they could enjoy their evening away from prying eyes.

At the entrance of the Sergeant, Ramirez had to look twice to make sure that it was the same man, for Lovejoy wore not the usual rumpled and stained denims, which was his ape uniform, but clean ones, the trousers creased to knife-sharp edge, his hair properly cut, and his cap set at the smart Rock angle. On his sleeve gleamed the three chevrons newly sewn there by a woman's hand. It was not the old Gunner Lovejoy who had entered but a brand-new Sergeant Lovejoy.

But once he had taken in the apparition it didn't take Treugang long to twig. "Sergeant," he cried, "Sergeant Lovejoy. What a surprise! You have been promoted! Have I not always said you deserved it? Congratulations, oh a thousand congratulations!"

"Oh," grunted Sergeant Lovejoy, "it's you." Ramirez leaning up against the bar grasping a beer was a reminder of the bad old days, or the good old days, whichever way one chose to regard the matter.

The Sergeant now addressed the barman, "Boss in, Joe?"

The barman paused only long enough in his eternal polishing of the bar to reply, "Back in half an hour. Had to see a man."

Sergeant Lovejoy consulted his watch. It had just gone ten. Then ten-thirty or shortly after would see him in plenty of time to discharge an errand or two and drive up to Ferdinand's Battery to take over the midnight-to-eight watch over the non-goings-on between Scruffy and Amelia. He and Major Bailey had a thorough understanding as to the importance of the operation, but didn't fuss over the matter of a few minutes. Tim departed promptly at the stroke of midnight. Lovejoy arrived simultaneously or a minute or so later. Several times their cars had passed on the road, one going up and one going down.

"I'll wait," said Sergeant Lovejoy.

The barman nodded, "What will it be?" He wagged his head in the direction of the new stripes and added, "It's on the house. The boss would want it."

"No, no, no," cried Treugang Ramirez. "Let me, Sergeant, it's my treat! Your promotion! Let me buy."

It wasn't the fact that not one but two free libations were offered that led Lovejoy to succumb, but because it was too complicated to explain. In a pub whose upkeep he had helped to maintain for some ten years, a man with newly sewn Sergeant's stripes on his sleeve was most certainly entitled to one at the expense of the management, and Lovejoy would have had to confess that he was on the verge of taking the pledge, which would have called for humiliating details. Lovejoy was not yet ready to have his impending nuptials broadcast about the Rock nor the fact that it was bound up with total abstention. Hence he would nurse a drink or two, the boss would return, he would make his arrangements, and no palaver would be involved.

Ramirez permitted himself the liberty of fingering the new stripes and said, "I am as proud as if it was myself. We will drink to this. What will you have, Sergeant?"

The barman cut in, "First drink for the Sergeant on the house like I said. You can buy later. What'll it be, Sarge?"

Now it had been on Lovejoy's mind to ask for a monkey juice— Guinness and lime—and nurse it, secure in the knowledge that he would take no harm from it, but there was something, unfortunately, in this offer of a drink on the house which precluded this.

The house would be offended if he called for anything but the best. "I'll have a double whisky," said the Sergeant.

"I'll have the same," called Treugang Ramirez, and when the barman looked at him slipped a ten-shilling note on the bar. "To drink the Sergeant's health," he added. "Mine is the next."

With one more in the offing Lovejoy saw no need to nurse the one the barman had set up for him. For full enjoyment he liked to knock it back, feel the shock of its arrival down below, followed by the spreading glow. He knocked it back. Treugang Ramirez did likewise. The barman took a sip of water, raising his glass towards Lovejoy and saying, "Cheer-ho, Sarge."

"Now my turn," cried Ramirez. "Two more doubles."

"Two more doubles," echoed the barman and set them up.

Lovejoy saw no need to nurse that one either since the afore-
mentioned etiquette and protocol now called for him to invest in
a third round. He knocked back the second as did Ramirez.

Ordinarily two double whiskies would not have turned a single
grey hair of Lovejoy's head, or brought so much as a bead of
perspiration to his lip, and the Sergeant had no reason to fear its
effects. Alas, familiar as he was with the physiology of the Barbary
ape, he was less acquainted with that of Homo sapiens. He had
forgotten that except for the one bender at Hope Cove he had
just come through weeks of total abstinence, and furthermore he
had not the faintest notion of the metabolic changes brought
about by emotional strains, or their unpredictability.

Sergeant Lovejoy thus got drunk quickly and thoroughly and
perilously, and not far behind him followed Treugang Ramirez,
who was paying for it all. For he had had a momentary flash of
cunning or intuition which told him that the Sergeant would not
have received his sergeant's stripes for nothing. Ramirez meant to
find out why and what it was for and had no idea what a sterling
start had been achieved through the two doubles.

Now the Sergeant was on his third double, and was well away.

The immediate result of these drinks was to muddle Lovejoy's
wits so that he became confused as to time, place, and the relationship of past, present, and future. It seemed to him that the final
party he had come to arrange had already begun and that he was
bidding his last farewell to all those flavours and jolts with which
he had so long been familiar. And since there seemed to be no
end to the generosity of his dear and good friend Treugang
Ramirez, whom he now knew that he loved better than a brother,
he began to mix his treats.

Farewell then to gin and its inseparable tonic, good-bye to
monkey juice, adieu cognac, *adios* Bacardi, *auf wiedersehen* to
wines red, white, and pink, and good-bye likewise to Sergeant
Lovejoy.

For the boss, catastrophically, didn't return for over an hour,
and by that time the damage was done. Into the interested and
sympathetic ear of the barman and the thrilled and fascinated one
of Treugang Ramirez, Lovejoy had spilled every last bean con-

cerning himself, the non-existent ape pack, the fact that but two remained and the salvation of the Empire hung upon their immediate copulation.

To Treugang Ramirez, the inspired Nazi patriot, came the knowledge that he held in his hands now or never the opportunity to destroy the last two apes on the Rock, relay the news to the Germans, and thereby break the British.

It was then that Ramirez most desperately deplored his cowardice with regard to firearms. Two well-placed shots from even a small pocket piece, granting that one could pierce the cordon of guards surrounding the area, and for the first time in over a hundred and fifty years the Rock would be without a single one of its good-luck mascots. Panic might well be expected to follow. His dismay would have been even greater had he known how close he was to a penetration of the forbidden zone, for at twenty-five minutes to twelve there came to Sergeant Lovejoy, now nine-tenths sozzled, and practically paralysed from the waist down, one of those awful moments of clarity which have been known to visit a drunken man shortly before a complete pass-out.

It began with an unexpected and short-lived unclouding of his vision which enabled Lovejoy to make out the time on the face of the bar-room clock and for it to penetrate that he was just twenty-five minutes away from having to steer his car up the mountain side, utter the password, let himself into the caged area with his keys, and begin the midnight-to-eight watch over Scruffy and Amelia.

Twelve o'clock midnight would soon be booming from all of the Gibraltar tower clocks; Major Tim Bailey would be sitting himself in his vehicle and departing the area; Sergeant Lovejoy would not be arriving. Neither his hands nor his legs were any longer his own. Any instant the fog of fumes would once more descend and becloud his brain and he would be caught absent from his post, derelict in his duty, drunk on guard, and all the other concurrent crimes they could cook up against him.

But worse, the two apes would be alone and unwatched for eight hours until Major Bailey returned.

If during that time "it" happened, nobody would know. And

if, as seemed much more likely, unobserved and unattended, Scruffy were to choose this period, free from surveillance, to kill Amelia, apeslaughter would be added to the list of crimes charged against the Sergeant. It was indeed a farewell party that somehow he had been inveigled into staging. Good-bye to his stripes, Miss Boddy, and everything.

"Oh Gord," groaned Sergeant Lovejoy. "Got to go! Apes! Midnight! My trick!" and then he repeated, "Oh Gord," and added, "Legs no good."

Nor indeed were they, for when he tried to arise from the table at which he had been sitting they buckled under him.

Treugang Ramirez was drunk, too, but not all *that* drunk, for he had managed surreptitiously to pour some drinks out and leave others half consumed in his determination to probe Lovejoy's secrets. He was far tighter than he had ever been in his life before, but still able vaguely to cerebrate and function.

"What is it?" he said to the Sergeant. "What is the matter?"

The instant of clarity still lingered long enough for Lovejoy to know that he was trapped, and by his own weakness. He could never make the car, much less the Rock, under his own steam. "The hapes," he moaned, "my trick! Midnight. Got to get there. Can't drive."

And here Ramirez showed that he could improvise. "I'll drive you," he said, "I'll take you."

Lovejoy was now fighting against final mists which were closing in upon him and through which he saw Treugang Ramirez not as a nasty-looking little man wearing a Prussian hairpiece and thick-lensed spectacles but as his saviour angel descended from heaven. "Will you?" he muttered. "You're a pal, Ramirez. I always said you were O.K. Password for tonight! 'Silly mid-on.' Get it? Cricket! Keys in m' right-hand pocket. Door sticks when you unlock it. Got to lift it a bit. That's all."

Between them the barman and Ramirez managed to get Lovejoy out of the pub and into the car. It was fourteen minutes to twelve. The barman helped Ramirez into the driver's seat and asked, "Can you make it all right?" Ramirez nodded. "Look after him," the barman said, "he's a good bloke, Lovejoy. None better."

"I'll look after him," Ramirez promised.

"You're a good scout," said the barman. "I didn't think you had it in you."

Fighting off the fumes of alcohol in his own head, Ramirez got the engine going and started off through the sleeping town, past the Moorish castle and on up the hill. Two thirds there he was met by headlights going down the hill and knew from what Lovejoy had spilled in the bar that this must be Major Bailey descending. He didn't dim his own headlights and in the glare Major Bailey saw only that it was Lovejoy's vehicle and not who was at the wheel.

As they approached the zone in which the apes were kept and Ramirez saw a flashlight signalling in the middle of the road, he slowed down sufficiently to pull Lovejoy erect beside him. When he arrived at the military road block and the light momentarily was shone upon them he managed to repeat the password, "Silly mid-on," and was waved through. He had already possessed himself of the keys in Lovejoy's pocket as directed and let himself into the area of the cages and cages within cages.

Inside he found everything as Lovejoy had described it. In one corner of the inner cage sat a full-grown female monkey, a most ugly and ill-favoured specimen whose eyes didn't seem to match and who huddled in the corner moaning and making little chittering noises.

In the other corner, wide awake, his honey-coloured eyes glistening with malevolence, sat Scruffy, the ape who had stolen his wig, and the last surviving member of the Gibraltar pack.

Every so often the ill-favoured female would creep forward timidly and present herself to the male, wrong end first. When she did this he would throw dirt at her until she went away. Oh, everything was indeed as Sergeant Lovejoy had revealed.

For the moment the vista opening before his eyes of success unparalleled conquered the quantities of alcohol he had consumed and made Ramirez temporarily sober and able both to think and to act. Here at hand was the opportunity not only to find himself one day standing before the Fuehrer to receive the Knight's Cross with Oak Leaf Cluster but likewise to have his revenge upon the British swine who had always scorned and derided him even while accepting his drinks, and who had been the chief witness of the humiliating episode of the stolen hairpiece. The plan was already whirling about in his head. Somewhere, somehow, he would come upon the weapon wherewith to exterminate the last two remaining apes and not only that but in the morning Sergeant Lovejoy—Sergeant indeed—would be found in a drunken slumber upon the scene and blamed for it.

It was all so neat and tidy that Ramirez could barely refrain from hugging himself.

The first thing to be done was to get Sergeant Lovejoy out of the car and on to the premises. The second was to secure a weapon.

The former called for a serious effort, during the execution of which Ramirez discovered that he was not as sober as he thought he was, but still he managed. He dragged the now wholly unconscious Lovejoy out from the vehicle, got one of the Sergeant's arms around his shoulder and puffing and groaning worked him through the doors and into the enclosure from which it was his wont to keep a watch upon the apes. During this manoeuvre the female ape presented herself once more, had dirt thrown at her again, and retired. Scruffy sat in his corner watching Ramirez out of his baleful light-brown eyes as though trying to evaluate the newcomer, what was going on, and how the proceedings might be turned to his advantage.

With Lovejoy deposited on a bench conveniently there, Ramirez next set about the problem of the weapon. He knew that if he could lay his hands on a firearm, frightened as he was of them, he would not let this opportunity escape him. The question was where and how. There were armed troops in the vicinity he knew, but the mere thought of attempting to steal a rifle or a submachine gun from one of these was more than he could bear. He then recalled a small shack at the entrance of the cages, identified by Lovejoy as the headquarters of himself and Major Bailey, and it struck him that surely he would find some kind of armament there to be used in case of emergency.

He hurried out and entered the small hut. His first glance

showed him there was no rifle there, not even so much as a pistol in a holster hanging up. There was a cot, a table, a primus stove, a tea kettle, a tin of tea and some unwashed cups, a tobacco tin, and a few odds and ends. He was about to write this off in disgust when a coloured box upon the shelf caught his eye, a box with a curious legend on the side which spelled out the word "Party-loons." He inspected the box further and on the cover saw a picture of a boy blowing up a huge rubber balloon and again the inscription "Partyloons," with the addition, "Finest Rubber Party Balloons—Blow Up to Enormous Size." With trembling fingers he lifted the cover of the box and saw an assortment of more than two dozen coloured balloons. Something he had once heard the Sergeant say flashed back into his memory and he now knew that in his shaking hands he held the means to destroy the last two apes on the Rock of Gibraltar.

His mind went back to the time once in the Admiral Nelson when Lovejoy had produced just such an article from his pocket and blew it up in a demonstration of the method he used to control Scruffy or the other apes when they got out of hand. "Reduces 'im to a jelly," he remembered Lovejoy saying, plus his admonishment that at the most one or two turned the trick. More might overwhelm their nerves and kill them.

Tucking the box of "Partyloons" under his arm, he returned to the cages and set about his work of destruction as best he was able, for he was still quite drunk and his exertions had further de-pleted him. Lovejoy was snoring peacefully on his bench and was sure to remain that way until morning when he would be dis-covered amongst the debris of shredded balloons with two dead apes.

There remained now only to send up what might be most aptly termed a trial balloon for the purpose of verifying its effect. Treugang selected a red one, approached that part of the cage where Scruffy crouched watching him, placed the open end to his lips, and commenced to blow. The effects exceeded his wildest expectations, leaving no doubt in his mind but that it would work.

At the very first swelling of the article from the size of a lemon to that of an orange to that of a grapefruit, a change came over the big monkey. His lips were drawn back from his fangs, his eyes grew large and filled with terror though he continued to stare transfixed and hypnotized; his limbs began to tremble and he took on every aspect of a person on the verge of a nervous breakdown.

As the balloon increased in size with every puff that Ramirez could muster, Scruffy began to moan and shake all over. He covered his eyes with his paws as though unable to look any more and then removed his hands as though no longer able *not* to look. He beat the ground with his feet and his knuckles, tore at tufts of hair on his breast and head, whimpered and cried pitifully and in general began to come apart.

Until science has conquered the speech of apes and made communication possible, no one will ever know exactly what it was about the balloon swelling to bursting point which reduced the world's toughest and most malignant ape to a trembling heap of frightened fur. For all anyone ever would be able to tell he might even have accepted the manifestation as something theological. It hypnotized and fascinated him the way a snake captivates a bird. Suspense unquestionably had something to do with it, the awful period of waiting for it to pop, a period extended almost beyond endurance by the excellent material and craftsmanship of the Partyloon Company.

Larger and larger grew the red balloon, now completely concealing the face and the inflating force behind it, to the point where it attracted Amelia from the far side of the cage. What she saw intrigued her enormously, but didn't frighten her. Whatever the swelling balloon meant to Scruffy, it didn't mean the same to Amelia.

What drew her fascinated attention was her boy friend's dither and disintegration. The erstwhile bully and tyrant had been reduced to a trembling coward. This didn't in any way diminish her love and admiration for him. It merely put a different aspect on the case. It was no longer dangerous or chancy to approach him. For the first time nothing was being thrown at her. She sat a little distance away regarding Scruffy's convulsions with grave and thoughtful contemplation in her eyes. But none of this did Treugang Ramirez see, since he was now completely concealed behind a swelling sphere and himself growing pretty nervous as to what would happen when at last it blew up.

He didn't have long to wait. Two more deep breaths and puffs exceeded even the most optimistic stresses the Partyloon Company had built into their product. There was a sudden sharp and ringing pop, frightening even to one who had been expecting it. A shred of torn red rubber hung from the lips of Ramirez; and his view now unimpeded, he saw Scruffy in what appeared to be mortal anguish, undone, unstrung, nerve-shattered, and crying for mercy. There was no doubt but that one or two more such experiences would, with their accumulative effect, turn the trick.

But now Ramirez was likewise aware of a curious and unexpected by-product of his effort. As every action had a reaction, every gun its recoil, so Ramirez found that the rapid and consecutive gusts of boozy wind he had been exhaling into the balloon, combined with the unaccustomed poison of too much alcohol in his system, had left him feeling weak, a little sick, and very dizzy in the head.

An insidious fear now inserted itself into the mind of the saboteur. If inflating a fatal number of balloons could have the desired accumulative effect upon Scruffy, what would this same accumulation of effort do to him? And who would last longer, Scruffy or himself? He was feeling most queer, but deemed himself committed now beyond the point of no return. He took a second balloon, a yellow one, and began to blow. He found that he was swaying and so unsteady on his feet that he had to drop to his knees. The effort forced him to close his eyes. Either the yellow balloon was tougher or he was growing weaker for it seemed to take many more puffs and twice as long before it exploded.

If the first effort had dizzied him, the second one had him reeling and gasping and feeling most faint; yet in his difficulty a picture marched through his mind to buoy him up and lend him strength, that of a little man wearing a small moustache and an outsize military cap, pinning an Iron Cross on his chest.

Ramirez reached for a blue balloon and strained. Curtains of blood seemed to be descending over his closed eyes; his heart was pounding, his lungs heaving, and there was such a roaring in his ears that he hardly heard the bang when it went off. Blindly he groped for yet another, not even aware of the colour (it turned out to be a white one), and bravely tried to fill it with what he was now convinced were his last breaths and which he therefore dedicated to that side of his family and their Fatherland which had so long obsessed him.

He blew, but more weakly. Each puff became a hell, but he would not desist. This was his moment of gallantry and devotion above the line of duty. The red before his eyes turned to maroon, then purple; the roaring in his ears a cataract of sound to be followed at last and mercifully by silence and darkness, sweet silence, sweet darkness, sweet peace that enshrouded him, as quietly he toppled over dead out, but still breathing, to join the unconscious figure of Sergeant John C. Lovejoy.

Their complicated schedules permitted Tim and Felicity to snatch breakfast together every other day. Felicity was usually out of the house first, leaving Tim with a few more minutes to digest the two- or three-day-old newspapers flown in from Britain, but on this particular morning he was uniformed and capped and ready to leave the house at the same time as his wife. She looked at him with astonishment and said, "What, going up early? I suppose you just can't bear to be away from the lovebirds."

Tim said, "You are kindly requested not to clown, Second Officer Bailey. Procreation is a serious business, as I understand you are about to discover for yourself. I had a rotten dream last night. I dreamt that Scruffy got out his cage, murdered the watch, and then seizing Amelia in his arms committed suicide off Lovers' Leap."

"You should consult Madame Zaza's Dream Book," Felicity told him airily. "It probably means we are going to get a lot of money." She eyed him fondly for a moment. "You're worried, aren't you?" she said. "Is there anything serious—I mean outside of what we know?"

Tim shrugged and said, "Stupid of me, I suppose. I passed Lovejoy going up as I came down last night. Nothing unusual in that. But he didn't dip his lights. He always does. There was such a glare I couldn't see who was driving."

Felicity said, "Well, Lovejoy obviously if he was going up as usual."

Tim frowned. "That's just it. I wasn't sure. Silly of me. Of course it was Lovejoy, but then why didn't he dip? When I got to the bottom of the hill I considered turning around and going back up to check. And then I thought of you here and your grand-mother's four-poster——"

Felicity looked shocked. "Bailey, you must be careful! Don't let it get around or you will have people thinking you love me more than that revolting chimpanzee."

"Macaque," Tim corrected.

"They're all monkeys to me!" She reached up and kissed him. "Go, my white knight, your country calls." She glanced at her watch, "Dammit and so does mine. Do you suppose we'll ever be able to live together like normal people?"

She climbed into her roadster and he into his utility car. They waved farewell to one another and Tim drove up the hill to Ferdinand's Battery fifteen minutes earlier.

Thus Major Bailey was in some measure not wholly unpre-pared for the scene and the shock that awaited him upon his arrival at the apes' village. He let himself into the locked-off area and then proceeded through to the cages where the sight that met his eyes was one which not only defied description but beggared it as well.

"All I could think of," he explained later in trying to put together a coherent picture of what he had seen "was that old Scruff had got loose somehow and scalped this scorp. There he was lying on his back with his haircut down over his eyes and the morning sun shining on his nut." But this was only the beginning. The scorp, of course, was Treugang Ramirez still sleeping it off, and on the bench opposite him was the living corpse of Sergeant John C. Lovejoy, likewise dead to the world.

When he had collapsed the night before, Ramirez's flailing arms had somehow managed to dislodge his hairpiece and push it over his face, giving him the aspect somewhat of a man trying to hide underneath a mat. Open at his side was a box of coloured balloons and strewn about him was the wreckage of four torn bits of red, white, blue, and yellow rubber.

Although the setting for this mystery tableau was in the great outdoors, nevertheless there was a familiar scent or fragrance that hung about the place and which the educated nostrils of Major Bailey had no difficulty in identifying as of secondhand alcohol.

Coming on top of the dream he had recounted to Felicity only a few minutes before, the Major was not to be blamed for the terrors and fears which assailed him. Drunk? Drugged? Sabotaged? Murdered? There was something familiar about the man under the hairpiece. He had seen him before, but could not think where. But if Lovejoy was in a stupor and dead out as he appeared to be, God knows what had happened to the apes, and hardly daring to do so Major Bailey turned to the inner cage and looked and, strong man that he was, he thought he might faint if he didn't grasp hold of the mesh of the cages to support himself.

He stared. He closed his eyes and rubbed them hard, and stared again, and the spectacle remained unaltered. For Scruffy and Amelia were locked in an embrace for which the word close was wholly inadequate.

For a few moments Major Timothy Bailey felt that he must be bereft of his senses because a reproduction of the statue of Cupid and Psyche that he had seen not long before flashed through his mind. Then he thought of a reissue of an old Greta Garbo–John Gilbert film that had recently been shown in the Garrison Cinema and finally of himself and Felicity preparatory to going to sleep.

Major Bailey succeeded in banishing the incongruous pictures from his mind, but not the marvellous, incredible, miraculous, and wonderful vision that remained before his eyes.

So tightly were the two intertwined that it was impossible to tell who was in whose arms, how many hands and feet there were, where which began and who left off. One didn't need to be a physiologist, a veterinarian, or even an OIC Apes who had lived in close association with the macaque and had made a study of their ways and habits to know that bells should be pealed, cannon fired, patriotic songs chanted, and a holiday be declared with dancing in the street in national costume. For the King of the Apes had consented to receive and bless his Queen. And if the Lord were good and the watchdogs of science, medicine, and midwifery were on their toes, she would in due time be delivered of an heir, and the land and the nation would rejoice and flourish.

But what this incomprehensible miracle had to do with the shambles behind him from which arose alcoholic fumes and the unlovely snores of the two unconscious men, Tim could not fathom. And at that moment Sergeant John C. Lovejoy opened first one eye, then the other, sat up and gradually what he saw with each eye blended and focused into one scene, and if there was confusion and wonder in the soul of Major Bailey, it was as a clear and lucid light compared to what went on inside the Sergeant as he looked upon his Major, the still unconscious Treugang Ramirez, the burst balloons, and the oblivious and wholly enamoured couple a few yards away in the cage.

And yet at that very moment when the Sergeant should have been overwhelmed by the grandfather of all hangovers and unable to give the right answer if asked the sum of two and two, his mind was working at a furious and incredibly accelerated speed. What had taken over in Lovejoy, who if nothing else in the first flash had recognized the enormity of the crisis and the depth of the mess he was in, was the instinct of self-preservation. And just as though he had never touched a drop, all the guile, cunning, and accumulated experience of twenty-five years of dealing with the officer class were alert and ready to come to his rescue.

If only he could solve the mystery of the man lying on the floor, who appeared to have the hide of some small fur-bearing animal instead of a face, balloons burst and whole scattered all over the place, the two magots apparently trying to emulate Romeo and Juliet, and Major Bailey looking ecstatically happy and alternately furiously angry. Of the events of the night before, the Sergeant had not so much as a glimmer. All was a blank, but already his razor-sharp wits told him that the Major was both annoyed with him and highly pleased with the development in the cage. It was plain that what was good must be exploited to ameliorate what was bad. But how?

At that moment the mystery object on the floor returned to the world with a deep groan of pain as simultaneously consciousness and the full force of *his* hangover hit him. He sat up, pushed the hairpiece back into position on to the shining egg of his skull, and suddenly became once more Treugang Ramirez, but a Ramirez who was looking not at all well. The eyes behind the thick spectacle lenses were bloodshot, the small polyp mouth framed a sickish expression, and what HE saw further reduced him into a state of absolute quaking terror.

For he, the great patriot spy and saboteur who ought to have been safely in his home or on his way to his workbench in the Optical Department of the Navy Yard, laughing up his sleeve at the stupidity of the British, was now caught red-handed upon the scene of his crime, surrounded by the evidence of the weapons he had used to commit it, nabbed not only by Lovejoy but that fool of a British officer who concerned himself with the apes and who would now unquestionably and summarily hand him over to be shot. And one further guilty glance in the direction of the cage where he expected to see two corpses littering the floor told him that when he was stood up against a wall and riddled with bullets for the Fatherland there would not even be any point in murmuring "Heil Hitler," for he would be expiring ingloriously and in vain. The apes were quite the opposite from dead. Treugang had none of the reserves that Sergeant Lovejoy could bring to bear to help him.

"Lovejoy," Tim demanded. "What the devil is the meaning of all this?"

"Meaning of what, sir?" replied Lovejoy, elbowing for one smidgen, one fraction, one split iota of time. Never had he needed or wanted time so badly. For his spinning wits had already revealed one aspect of the case against him: he had been asleep at his post when Major Bailey had arrived, not an inconsiderable crime in wartime, and the object on the floor having evolved itself into Treugang Ramirez he had likewise obviously admitted an unauthorized person into the most top-secret and closely guarded

area on the Rock. And to know what one is about to be charged
with, if not half the battle, at least permits one to organize one's
defences.

"Don't waffle, Sergeant," Tim said sternly. "You know crashing
well what I mean. Drunk and asleep on duty. Who the devil is
that midden on the floor over there? What's the meaning of the
balloons all over the place? What's been going on here?"

Rule Number One, Lovejoy's quarter of a century in the Army
had taught him, was when charged to sow doubt immediately.
"Oh not drunk, sir," he said sorrowfully. "Not drunk."

The shock of this barefaced denial threw Tim momentarily out
of stride and now that wonder worker, that other Lovejoy, the
trained psychologist, applied the gambit diversion and the well-
tried move of changing the subject to something pleasant. "Coo,"
he said, indicating the two apes with his glance and ignoring the
Major's other questions and accusations as well as the presence of
Ramirez. "Look at 'em there like a pair of lovers canoodling in
'Yde Park, sir. 'Oo would have believed it possible?"

With a rush, joy, excitement, and a sense of fulfilment swept
through Major Bailey, temporarily displacing the choler which
had collected there. "By God, Lovejoy," he cried. "We've done it,
haven't we?"

"Yes, sir," said Lovejoy, swiftly following up his advantage, "by
the looks of them you have, sir, and congratulations. Wait 'til
Major Clyde hears about this. He won't half be pleased."

"That's right," said Tim, "get on the blower from St. Michael's
Hut and tell him to come up here as fast as he can and bring
McPherson. But don't give away what's happened."

"Yes, sir, I will! No, sir, I won't," replied Lovejoy, delighted to
be allowed to retire from the scene for a moment.

He hustled to St. Michael's Hut to carry out his errand, called
Fortress H.Q., and transmitted Major Bailey's message to Major
Clyde. Then, before returning, he took a moment of desperate
endeavour to recapture something of what must have happened
before, and dimly, like that most faint and almost indistinguisha-
ble image one can sometimes catch on a light-struck film, he saw
the Admiral Nelson and remembered a polishing motion that the

barman had been making on the surface of the long bar. Ramirez, too, was vaguely on the film. Then he had been there and he must have got very drunk. Yet somehow he had managed to get to his post, he and Ramirez together.

Back at the cages Tim continued to ignore the groaning man still seated on the floor; it would be up to Lovejoy to explain that one, and once more he turned his attention to the Sergeant, who had returned to report.

"Did you get him?" Tim asked.

"Yes, sir. He and Major McPherson will be right along."

"Did he want to know what it was about?"

"He was very worried, sir. Wanted to know if the worst 'ad 'appened. I said he was to cheer up, that life wasn't all that bad, and he'd see when he got here."

Major Bailey nodded approval and then said, "So you weren't drunk last night?"

"No, sir," said Lovejoy. "Ill. Very ill, I'm afraid, sir."

Tim said, "Humph. What's that stink of booze about the place?"

"My medicine, sir, I expect," Lovejoy replied. "It's got some funny stuff in it. I can taste it for days afterwards."

Tim said, "Humph," again and then indicated with his head in the direction of Ramirez. "And that?"

"My pal, sir. He brought me here. I didn't want to disturb you, sir. I thought if I got here I'd be all right. I didn't think I was going to pass out, sir."

"And him?" Tim questioned. "Was he sick, too?"

"I couldn't say, sir," Lovejoy replied, and then added for truth perforce, "He doesn't look very well, does he?" He tried the subject change again. "The main thing is, sir, you've pulled it off. You've got the pair together. There ought to be a gong in it for you!"

"Come off it; I wasn't here last night," Tim said curtly and turned once more to study the situation in the light of Lovejoy's explanation so far. He was wondering whether it would stand up.

And Lovejoy's alert, lively, and brilliantly functioning mind was speculating upon a characteristic of the Army and the sometimes complicated relationship between officer and man. Some officers were twerps and liked nothing better than to tear a strip off a ranker, but there were others who not only were human but sometimes downright protective when you were in trouble, particularly if you worked well for them and they depended upon you. That kind of officer relied upon you when you were in difficulties to invent a story that somehow he could manage to believe. It made everything that much easier, avoided the complications of disciplinary action, bumph, paper work, and a lot of fuss. Tim was one of these and in their association working for the apes an understanding, if not a kind of affection, had grown up between them. The fact that Tim had not chewed him out for the palpable lie about not being drunk, but ill, told the Sergeant that if he could only cook up a story which would slide down the Major's gullet without choking him he would be home. But what story?

What had happened during the night when he was unconscious, blotto? What was the meaning of the box of balloons, and, above all, the burst ones? Had he himself blown them up? No distant bell rang in answer. Then Ramirez must have. But why? Surely not with malice intent, since Ramirez was his pal who bought him drinks and when he was sozzled had brought him up to his post so that he wouldn't be A.W.O.L. But there he was and there was likewise the evidence of *something*.

Unquestionably some extraordinary hanky-panky had gone on there during the night, but what it was at the moment he could not tell. All that was certain was that it had achieved the effect that they had all been striving for in vain ever since the arrival of Amelia.

Major Bailey looked once more with undiminished amazement at the twin huddle of monkeys and then at Ramirez.

"Who is this bloke?" he asked of Lovejoy.

Lovejoy's reply was one of those pure, heaven-sent inspirational flashes. The occasion called for a whopping, but digestible lie. Lovejoy thought he had it.

"He's an expert, sir. An expert on apes."

"He's a what?" said Tim.

Sick, terrified, bewildered, and baffled as he was, what Lovejoy
had just said penetrated to the ears of Ramirez and stirred the
first faint whisper of hope within his breast. For some reason he
was unable to fathom the Sergeant was not going to give him
away immediately. Perhaps secretly, even, the Sergeant was one
of them. How fortunate that he had not yet revealed himself. But
he must not rejoice too soon; perhaps this was only a trap into
which he was being led to gain a full and easy confession.

"Alfonso Ramirez, sir," replied Lovejoy, rendering a formal
introduction. "Works for Captain Russell in the Navy Yard, sir,
Optical Department. Double-A security. But he's an expert, sir.
Used to 'ave apes when he was a boy. It was his idea, sir."

"What was his idea?"

"To scare 'em into it, sir. It's the only thing we didn't try."

Major Bailey looked from Lovejoy to Ramirez to the loving apes
and back to Lovejoy again.

Lovejoy watched him warily, for if Major Bailey had not twigged
to at least one sequence of events that had taken place that night,
he himself had. "Had a case like it, Mr. Ramirez did. Told me
about it last night. Owned a pair of lemurs once that wouldn't
breed. Scared them into each other's arms and away they went
merry as crickets."

"Is this so, Mr. Ramirez?" Major Bailey enquired.

"*Gott!*" thought Treugang Ramirez, apostrophising the German
rather than the English deity in his gratitude. The stupidity of
these British. Not only was he not going to be placed against a
wall and shot but he was not even going to be found out or
punished, or so much as accused of anything. It was incredible,
but seemingly true. "Oh yes," he said. "Every word. It is true as
my friend Lovejoy here has told."

"'If everything else fails, you scare 'em,' Mr. Ramirez says to
me." Lovejoy picked up the narrative. "'But how can you frighten
such a beast as Scruffy?' he asks. You may remember, sir, that
Mr. Ramirez had an unfortunate experience with the animal."

"Oh yes," said Tim, and involuntarily his glance strayed to the
hairpiece now only slightly askew on the Señor's head, and he
immediately felt embarrassed and sorry for Ramirez.

"'Why,'" continued Sergeant Lovejoy, "'balloons,' I said to him. 'Old Scruff can't abide balloons. Maybe if we blew up a couple of balloons for him it would work.'"

"Was that about the way it was, Mr. Ramirez?"

"Oh yes, sir! Every word of it."

"And where did this conversation take place?" enquired Tim.

"Oh, outside the Admiral Nelson," Lovejoy replied ingenuously. He was also a great devotee of the half-truth. "We happened to encounter there."

"This was before you were taken ill, I gather," Tim said solicitously.

"Ah yes, sir. My attack hadn't come on me yet,"

"I see. Then you both came on up here——"

Sergeant Lovejoy drew a deep breath, the first since his awakening. Could it be that it really had gone down the Major's gullet smoothly and properly and that he was actually asking for more? "That's it, sir," he said. "And there they was like you've always seen 'em. Her loving and eager; him cruel and cold. 'Now then,' says Mr. Ramirez, 'shall we try? You blow one!' 'No,' says I, 'it's your idea and your honour. You blow, I'll observe.' So 'e blows one. 'E blows a second. 'E blows another. You know the effect them balloons has always had on Scruff. Well, this time it's exactly the same. Terror-stricken 'e is, shaking and unnerved, sir. Only this time there's a difference!" Sergeant Lovejoy paused dramatically to prepare for the revelation of that difference. "This time there awaited him the arms of a comforting and loving woman. Haven't you had that experience yourself, sir? When everything seemed to be going against you and you didn't know which way to turn? It's the woman that's the saving grace of us, sir. First it's our mothers, later on it's our—— Well, there's always one that seems to come along when you need her most, isn't there, sir?"

Major Bailey didn't reply. Lovejoy hoped it was because he was too deeply moved for words.

"Well, that's how it was with old Scruff, sir. There 'e was, one moment shivering and shaking, whimpering and crying; there she was, sir, eager to 'elp him, sympathetic, warmhearted. 'Olding out her arms. And the next moment there *they* were!"

"*You bastard*," thought Tim. "*You clever, lying, shrimshranking, convincing bastard!*" But the point was that the story would stand up. It would stand up beautifully if one didn't pry into or refer back to the condition the two men had been in when he arrived, and the obvious but rapidly diminishing fragrance of booze. Facts were facts, and there was no getting around the fact that there were the burst balloons and there were Scruffy and Amelia no longer two but one.

There was a snort and a clatter as a car drew up outside the enclosure and disgorged the Majors McPherson and Clyde.

In the manner of a master showman, Tim stepped aside to clear their view, pointed dramatically, and said, "Behold! The miracle."

They stared unbelieving at first, then gave vent to relieving expletives.

"By Nebuchadnezzar!" said Major Clyde.

"On a bicycle," breathed Major McPherson.

"Tim, you are a wizard," congratulated Major Clyde.

Major Bailey still dramatically pointing now semaphored in the direction of Señor Ramirez. "We owe it all to this gentleman here," he declared.

The Majors McPherson and Clyde looked in the direction indicated and were momentarily stunned into silence. The person pointed to didn't look exactly what might be expected of the saviour of the key bastion of the British Empire. The physical malaise brought about by the debauch of the night before had abated not one whit; abject terror had but recently been replaced by slowly returned confidence; his rug still wasn't on straight and his clothes were a mess.

"He knows more about apes than any of us," Major Bailey elucidated. "Had 'em when he was a boy. Lovejoy will tell you about it. They engineered it together. Frightened the wits out of old Scruff. Reduced him to a jelly. Quivering wreck goes for comfort to loving arms of woman. Once arrived there, nature takes its course. That about the straight of it, Sergeant?"

"Yes, sir," agreed Lovejoy. "But it was Mr. Ramirez's idea." He was thrilled about being off the hook and he wanted no part of the credit, and, besides, Ramirez had come through like a brick the night before. There was still the unexplained matter of the exploded balloons, but he reasoned that quite possibly during the night Scruffy had turned savage and perhaps threatened to kill the female, and Ramirez had resorted to the trick he had heard Lovejoy discourse upon sometime or other in the Admiral Nelson. Anyway, results were results and he had no intention of pressing the matter further if Major Bailey was satisfied. He loved the Major like a brother and would wish nothing better than to spend the rest of his life serving under him. A man who could not only swallow what he had offered but blandly pass on the same serving to his pals was more than just all right. He was bang on.

The pals took another look at the trembling, sweating Ramirez and were not impressed and then turned their gaze to Major Bailey. But there was no hint of guile in Tim's face.

"Look here, Tim, are you sure?" Clyde queried.

Tim passed the buck. "What about it, Lovejoy?"

"I'd lay me 'ead to a stack of Bibles on it," Lovejoy said fervently. "If I may point out, sir, it's the right time, the right place——"

"—the right girl," Major Clyde concluded for him.

They all turned now and gazed fondly upon the temporarily subdued Scruffy enfolded in the arms of his mistress, or vice versa. It was, of course, silly and utterly ridiculous—to reason that the eventual stability of Gibraltar and the subsequent defence of the Mediterranean stemmed from this momentary coupling of a pair of ill-matched and ill-favoured macaques. But certainly the delighted group observing them outside their cage believed this to be the case. They had worked so long and hard upon the project, had taken so to heart the message of the Prime Minister that the apes, for reason of morale, must be kept up to strength, that it seemed as though the burden of the entire war effort had been shifted to their shoulders. Now that for the first time it looked as though that burden was to be lifted and the success of Major Clyde's long-range planning just around the corner, they were filled with relief and joy.

Major Clyde was trying to paraphrase or catch a quotation,

something like, "When the doors of history are thrown open, the right man is always found standing upon the threshold." He then had a vision of great bronze doors swinging open and the shocking little man with his wig all askew, his clothes wrinkled and eyes blinking behind the thick-lensed spectacles, standing there. But he also remembered another saying from his youth that the Lord often worked in a mysterious way His wonders to perform.

His thoughts then turned wholly practical and, looking towards the future, "Oughtn't we have a gyno?"

"My God, yes," chimed in Major McPherson. "The best!"

"Holy smokes!" cried Major Timothy Bailey. "Me, too!"

They all turned and stared at him.

Chapter 21

DR. LOVEJOY'S TECHNIQUE

The nurse thrust her attractive face inside the door and said, "Dr. Rosen on the line, Sir Archibald."

Sir Archibald Cruft raised his massive head from the circular and free sample of a new drug which had come through the mail, something with the imposing name of *Pronovocosylnembucaine,* and which as far as he could make out from its components was not much more useful than aspirin, and said, "Oh good."

Sir Archibald was a gynaecologist. He was *the* gynaecologist. There were rich babies, poor babies, noble babies, common babies, and then there were Cruft babies. And the Cruft babies all turned out to be quite extraordinary. If it was necessary to register one's son at Eton at birth, it was advisable to book Sir Archibald upon the announcement of one's engagement. A Cruft baby was a guarantee. Once one had managed to pass through the portals of 81A, Harley Street and into his consulting room, which was more like the library of a stately home than a doctor's office, with its two Renoirs and a Modigliani on the walls, all one's worries were over. Baby would be produced with the minimum of fuss, in good health, and with all its buttons. He was consultant emeritus at the births of the Royal family was Sir Archibald. He was——

Sir Archibald picked up the telephone and said, "Hello, Saul?"

"Sir Archibald!"

If you couldn't achieve a Cruft baby, you acquired a Rosen baby. Dr. Saul Rosen was as good and great a gynaecologist as Sir Archibald, but he was a Jew and a German refugee, and a number of British fathers objected to having a baby by "that foreign fellow." Yet Rosen babies were likewise brought into the world with less fuss and cackle than the production of an egg. They were also strong, healthy specimens and some said even a trifle more acute and likely to succeed in the diplomatic and political world than the Cruft babies, who tended to staff the universities, the Army, and the world of finance.

"Look here, Saul," said Sir Archibald and turned upon the black instrument of the telephone all the charm that he worked upon his patients, which eased them so swiftly and happily through their labour, for everything about him was compelling—his head, his deep sunken eyes, his hook of a nose, he strong forward-thrust chin, and his great mane of white hair. "I suppose you've more than you can handle as usual."

"Well, in a way. It's those charity cases that take up all one's time. Why the East Enders outproduce the West Enders when they have that much less leisure—except when they're striking—— Is there anything I can do to help you?"

"Yes," said Sir Archibald, seeing no point in beating about the bush. "Can you take on Lady Streve for me?"

"Lady Streve! You mean the wife of——"

"That's the one."

The ten-second silence at the other end of the telephone line was as pregnant as Lady Streve, who was very. Sir Lionel Streve was one of the most important men in the Cabinet.

Sir Archibald thought he had better break into the silence before it became permanent. He said, "Anstruther," naming his assistant, "can handle my practice until I get back, but Lady Streve is going to be very upset. But if I could tell her I had persuaded you to take her on——"

The silence at Dr. Rosen's end was finally broken, "Yes, quite. I see. If you can persuade—I'll be glad to—as you say, she won't be very pleased."

"She's damn lucky you can take her. After all, we're all having to make sacrifices."

"Of course. Look here, did you say you were off somewhere? Lucky man."

"Lucky, my foot," growled Sir Archibald. "Of all places, Gibraltar. I passed through there once on a cruise. Filthy spot."

Again there was a silence from Dr. Rosen's end before he

repeated, "Gibraltar! Who the devil is out there to—— I beg your pardon, Sir Archibald."

"No, no, that's quite all right, old man, I feel exactly the same. The point is I haven't a clue. It's hush-hush. I couldn't tell you because they wouldn't tell me."

"They?" said Dr. Rosen.

"M.I. 5 fellow I've had in the office here for the last hour. Ever hear of a Major Clyde?"

"No," said Dr. Rosen truthfully.

"Long gangling sort of chap. Seems to know everybody. I told him it was absolutely, utterly, and finally impossible. Impossible for me to get away at all, and completely and blastedly impossible at this particular time. Then he applied the arm-twister. He said, "The P.M. wants it, Sir Archibald. The P.M. is vitally interested in this one.""

"The P.M.!" Dr. Rosen's shout of surprise rattled the diaphragm of the instrument. "Good God! You don't mean to tell me——"

"No, no!" said Sir Archibald. "This Clyde fellow said it was a matter of national importance. Offered to get the P.M. on the line. I couldn't refuse, could I?"

"Hardly," agreed Dr. Rosen. "I'll be happy to look after Lady Streve for you."

"Good man," said Sir Archibald. "They'll be pleased in the end. More your type than mine. They'll want it to go into politics if it's a boy. Good luck and thank you."

"Same to you," said Dr. Rosen, and knew not what he wished.

"Am I to understand, sir, that I have been dragged away from my practice in London, my life risked in a flying machine that appeared to be appallingly unsteady, driven by a man who sang and muttered to himself the entire time of the flight and was obviously unbalanced [as good a description, Major Clyde thought, of Howard Cranch in action as ever he had heard], and set down on this exposed promontory to attend the pregnancy and delivery of a monkey? And you claim at the behest of the Prime Minister?"

The questions put by Sir Archibald Cruft closeted in Major

McPherson's office with Timothy Bailey and William Clyde were asked not so much in anger as complete and utter disbelief that such a thing could be possible.

It was a moment that Clyde rather had been dreading. He could think of nothing else to say than, "Yes, sir."

"When you visited me in my office you led me to believe that I was to attend a human patient of national importance in whom the Prime Minister——"

Clyde felt better now. "I never said human patient, sir, I said to attend a delivery of the greatest importance to the country. The instructions of the P.M. were that no effort was to be spared. If you will remember I offered to get him on the line to have a word with you."

The recollection threw Sir Archibald into some confusion and unsteadied him in his intention to proceed from disbelief to towering rage, and Clyde saw that the worst was over. He said, "Look here, sir, I couldn't explain to you when I called on you in London for reasons of security; there was too much at stake. You might have talked to someone."

Sir Archibald felt a sudden pang as he remembered that he had indeed talked to someone. It was as well then that he had not known whatever this great secret was.

Clyde saw the sudden alarm on the specialist's face and, even more certain of his ground now, he continued smoothly, "But we can tell you now."

Briefly and succinctly, in a well-ordered sequence that would appeal to a scientific mind, he outlined to the great man the facts in the case and all that hung upon the delivery to Amelia of a healthy, active offspring, able to face photographers at an early age and interrupt by its presence the morale-shattering pattern of the decline of the Rock apes.

Sir Archibald, as one who had not been contradicted in the last twenty years and was inclined to be a trifle pompous and well aware of his position in medical society and quite pleased with it, was at the same time no fool, and Clyde's lucid presentation of the situation and the consequences that might possibly attend failure were obvious to him. It was not the superstition or the eventuality that the British might be driven from the Rock, Clyde emphasised. He was too clever to present this to a man of Sir Archibald's stature, but he did make clear that belief in such a superstition was damaging on Gibraltar to the point where the Spaniards might not be able to resist entering the war. One more powerful enemy could well be the straw that would break the nation's back.

Sir Archibald felt all his anger drain away from him, but not his doubts, fears, and anxieties. "But why me, man?" he queried when Clyde had finished his recital. "Why not a veterinary? There must be half a dozen good men available. Embury and Hoskyns are two of the best."

For a moment Clyde again experienced a pang of uneasiness. Why not indeed? And he realised that he had been perhaps carried away by his own enthusiasm. In his mind birth had been connected with a gynaecologist, and the habit he had formed ever since he had had the directive from the Prime Minister had been to accept nothing but the best in every phase of this operation. "Not good enough, sir," he replied. "This situation calls for the best brain, the years of experience, and the steadiest hand in the field."

Sir Archibald swallowed the compliment, enjoying its savour, but then said, "That's very kind of you, Major, but you over-looked one important factor: I have never delivered a monkey."

"Eh?" ejaculated the Major, startled by the gynaecologist's words.

"While I might be willing to admit," Sir Archibald continued, "that the husbands of a number of my clients undoubtedly re-semble baboons, gibbons, mandrills, and chimpanzees, and their wives have demonstrated facial affinities to the lemur, the loris, the bush baby, and the potto, to name some of the more delicately featured primates, the fact is that my practice has been entirely limited to the species laughingly classified Homo sapiens, while the anthropoids——"

"Does that make any difference, sir?" Clyde asked, and actually was unable to keep the anxiety from his voice. "I thought monkeys were like——"

"—people?" Sir Archibald concluded for him. "Not at all. For one thing monkeys don't call upon the services of gynaecologists to assist them at birth. It might be better if they did, for the incidence of stillborn babies amongst the anthropoids and primates is very high, indicating that they have problems unique to their species." He paused and as a new thought struck him quite suddenly he clapped his hand to his noble brow and cried, "What will happen when it gets out back in London that Archie Cruft was called in to midwife a monkey? And it will get out. I'll never be able to face them. Rosen and Oates and that sneering old bluffer Pedgely," he groaned. "My God," and then, "Look here, Clyde, I won't——"

"Sir," Tim Bailey put in, "might I——"

Sir Archibald turned his massive craggy face towards Tim and stared at him as though he had never seen him before, which indeed he had not since Tim had remained in the background taking no part in the conversation.

"It needn't get out," said Tim, "my wife—you see, we're expecting, sir—if you could possibly see your way clear to—to accept her as a patient—why then *that* would be the story which would get back to London. We could see to that, sir."

It was a straw. Sir Archibald examined Tim more closely now. "Who are you?" he asked.

Clyde reminded him. "Major Timothy Bailey, sir, OIC, that is, Officer in Charge of Apes. It has been his responsibility——"

"Is your wife here?" Sir Archibald asked of Bailey.

"Yes, sir."

"I thought all of the women had been evacuated from the Rock."

"She's a WREN officer, sir."

"Oh, I see. What's her name?"

"Felicity, sir."

Clyde put in quickly, "Admiral French's daughter, sir."

The stern countenance of Sir Archibald Cruft suddenly brightened. "What," he said, "not old Tubby French's daughter! I used to beat him at golf. Hits the ball with a twitch! I'd be pleased to see him again."

"Will you take her, sir?" Tim asked eagerly.

"Yes, yes, of course," Sir Archibald replied somewhat testily as though it had all been settled. "Tubby French's daughter, naturally."

"And Amelia?" Clyde queried.

Sir Archibald reflected for a moment while they all waited anxiously. "Well," he said, and left no doubt as to the manner in which the affair was to be handled, "as long as I'm down here looking after Tubby French's daughter, I might as well. Suppose I have a look at the patient."

Three sighs of relief exploded simultaneously and Major Mc-Pherson cried, "Splendid, sir! That's very good of you. I'll have Lovejoy take you to the upper Rock and show you Amelia."

Sir Archibald asked, "Lovejoy? Who is Lovejoy?"

"Their keeper, sir," Bailey explained, and Clyde added, "He's been with them for more than twenty years."

"Felicity will be very pleased when I tell her," Tim beamed, "and so will her father. It's more than kind of you, sir."

"Yes, yes," said Sir Archibald gruffly. "Well, let's get on with it then. Where is this she-ape and this fellow Lovejoy? I hope he won't be around all the time telling me what to do."

The Military Hospital of Gibraltar was a huge, sprawling affair of grey blocks with odd Victorian trimming in black, Moorish arches, and crenellated towers. The operating and labor rooms, however, were modern enough, with incubators, X ray, and all the latest scientific gadgets, and Sir Archibald pronounced himself satisfied with the equipment and the nursing staff as well. There was also a waiting room decorated in soothing tones which had once been set aside for expectant fathers, and it was here that the three Majors Bailey, Clyde, and McPherson, Sergeant Lovejoy and his bride, the former Miss Boddy, and Felicity foregathered anxiously on the day that medical science, coupled with mathematics, had determined that Amelia would produce.

Tim had been violently opposed to Felicity's presence upon this occasion. The arithmetic in her case had decreed that she was not due for another two weeks and Tim did not wish her exposed prematurely to those grisly exhibits that are always being pushed or carried up and down hospital corridors. Felicity had overruled him. In the first place she would not have missed the show for anything in the world, and in the second she felt it her duty to be present to hold Tim's hand. If the agitation the young man was showing at the preparations for the accouchement of Amelia was any indication, he was in for a bad time during the birth of his own child. At least Felicity could stand by for the former.

There was far too much at stake to risk chancing a natural birth for Amelia in one of the cages up in the apes' village, and besides Sir Archibald was unaccustomed to working in the wilderness or on the concrete floor of a monkey cage. He felt comfortable only when aseptically scrubbed, capped, and gowned in a proper operating theatre with a reliable anaesthetist, theatre nurses, and other help. Birth was a serious drama to him. At the moment of its occurrence it was he who was the chief actor occupying the centre of the stage and he liked an audience.

Sir Archibald appeared at the door of the main operating theatre for a moment, gowned but not yet capped and scrubbed.

Tim, who had been chain-smoking nervously, was on his feet instantly. "Is everything all right, doctor?" he cried.

"Do you anticipate any trouble?" asked Major Clyde.

"Oh, doctor, you will take good care of our Amelia, won't you?" pleaded Mrs. Lovejoy.

Sir Archibald had assumed his professional manner and soothing smile with his surgeon's gown. "We haven't even begun yet. In a Prime Ibs., as you know, the presentation is always a bit chancy. Still, I don't anticipate any difficulty. The monkey appears to be normal. We'll take every precaution, of course. Well, gentlemen, we shall know shortly. Don't excite yourselves. If I encounter any trouble I'll let you know. Not to worry, then." He turned on his heel and strode through the door leading to the operating theatre, like an actor exiting on a good line.

Chairs ran around the walls of the waiting room, and the six were perched on the edges of them. Through the open door they had a view of the long hospital corridor and the entrance to the operating theatre. As Tim had anticipated, they were missing none of those fearful comings and goings, openings and closings of doors, the carrying out of things hidden under cloths, probationers bearing trays, nurses arriving with syringes and medicines.

The time was nine o'clock in the evening. The nervously hurrying feet echoed in the otherwise silent hospital.

There was a larger bustle and stir as down the corridor, flanked by two gowned and masked nurses, an attendant wheeled a stretcher table. On the table was a box. Inside the box sat Amelia. She was whimpering softly. Mrs. Lovejoy half started up from her chair, and her husband laid a restraining arm upon hers and said, "Don't worry, there's nothing to it."

Major Clyde quoted, "Our birth is nothing but our death begun."

"For God's sake, shut up," Tim hissed at him in a furious whisper, indicating Felicity.

Major Clyde clapped a hand over his mouth and said, "Sorry, old man! Must be the strain."

Felicity was watching the procession in the corridor as it passed through the door into the operating theatre. She murmured something which to Tim sounded very much like "Into the valley of shadows . . ." but she was giggling and appeared to be enjoying herself hugely. Tim was able to stem his nervousness for a moment to reflect upon the miracle of the woman he had married.

From somewhere in the town a tower clock tolled the strokes of ten, the door of the theatre opened, and Sir Archibald appeared minus gloves and mask, his cap pushed on to the back of his white locks. Instantly he was surrounded.

"Well, sir?"

"Has she had it?"

"My poor Amelia!"

"Is everything all right?"

"For God's sake, Sir Archibald, say something. I can't stand this suspense." This last cry of anguish came from Tim, for it seemed to him that all the effort and work and worry he had put in ever since he had resumed the job of OIC Apes was now concentrated into one small pinpoint of time. It was almost un-

bearable that things were out of his hands and there was no more
he could do. The jury was out and that was that.

Sir Archibald blandly waved all queries aside. "Not yet," he
said. "We are still waiting. I have come out for a cigarette." The
three men in unison pressed smokes and fire upon him. Observing
him, Clyde wondered whether the gynaecologist was concealing
something from them. Tim was certain he was. The great man
did not appear to be entirely at ease. He drew in and swallowed
three long drags of smoke, then dropped the cigarette and stifled
it with the toe of his boot. "Well," he said, "I'd better be getting
along back inside. Not to worry."

Inside the waiting room heavy gloom began to settle. Tim
commenced to pace up and down and Felicity noted that at the
place where he was walking off his nervousness the carpet beneath
his feet was worn thin by several generations of feet similarly
agitated. She wanted to giggle again but refrained because her
heart was too full of love for him, and she reflected that she was
probably the only expectant mother in all history granted the
privilege of observing the birth agonies of a husband. Poor thing
—what would happen to him while she was occupied with her
own delivery?

Then they were all aware that the comings and goings of the
nurses and messengers began to increase in tempo. Doors banged
somewhat more loudly; feet scurried more quickly; and the almost unbearable atmosphere of mystery and tension was increased
by the one-way conversations which were funnelled quite audibly
down the long tunnel of the corridor from the switchboard located
at the end of it.

The operator appeared to be searching frantically for a Colonel
Wheeler. "Is Colonel Wheeler there? Calling Colonel Wheeler!
Dr. Wheeler is wanted in the operating theatre!" And then afterwards there was a search by telephone and minions for some elu-
sive and difficult-to-locate piece of equipment with a name which
sounded like thermosphygalamometer.

Colonel-Dr. Wheeler never showed up, but the thermosphygalamometer did, justifying its name by turning out to be a terrifying-
looking cabinet on wheels from which protruded tubes, arms,

clamps, and compressors, festooned with dials and gauges and columns of active and pulsing coloured liquids.

Major Clyde remarked, "That ought to do the trick if anything can."

Tim, regarding the monster as it trundled past them and vanished through the door of the operating theatre, groaned, "My God, you shouldn't be seeing that, Felicity."

But Felicity's eyes were shining with excitement as she cried, "But I am absolutely fascinated!"

The lower lip of Mrs. Constance Lovejoy began to quiver and tears came to her eyes. "Oh, oh," she moaned, "my poor Amelia. I never should have allowed it."

Sergeant Lovejoy, who had slipped far more easily than one would ever have expected into the role of husband and protector, laid a comforting hand upon her arm and said, "There now, Constance, don't take on so. She'll be right as rain. I never saw an 'ealthier specimen. It'll be no more trouble to 'er than layin' an egg."

But, if so, the egg was a long time coming, for quarter hours passed in agonising succession with no news from behind the closed door.

To Tim the waiting had become a double torment. For all of Felicity's gallantry and lightheartedness the passage of the thermosphygalamometer had shaken him badly, dramatising as it did the fact that birth, which ordinarily ought to be a smooth and natural affair, sometimes isn't. Waiting upon the delivery of this confounded monkey, upon whom so much seemed to depend, was like a preview and at the same time a travesty of what the production of his own child would be like; only then Felicity, his beloved Felicity, would be the silent victim hidden behind the silent door. It seemed somehow grotesque that she should be present during these alarums and excursions attendant upon the parturition of this monkey, and which would have been comic had not Major Clyde so effectively pointed up the seriousness of the situation. Win or lose, they were all embarked upon a project in whose importance they all believed and it had to be carried through.

Major Clyde joined Tim on the well-worn carpet strip and said, "Move over and let someone pace who knows how."

Felicity watched them gravely for a moment and then said to Major McPherson, "Aren't you going to join them?"

Major McPherson half started up from the edge of his seat in obedience to the suggestion, which showed how nervous *he* was. The four of them then burst simultaneously into roars of laughter which were stilled abruptly when the doors of the operating theatre opened, this time with swift urgency, and Sir Archibald Cruft appeared on the threshold. His white cap was askew on his hair and his surgeon's mask had slipped under his chin. He was worried, and his alarm at once communicated itself to the waiting group as Sir Archibald said curtly, "We're in trouble! There's a blockage."

"Blockage!" repeated Major Clyde. "What does that mean?"

"Can't you do something?" shouted Tim.

Mrs. Lovejoy emitted a wail of anguish and threw herself into her husband's arms, much to the Sergeant's embarrassment.

"She's not presenting properly," Sir Archibald explained. "She should have been bred much earlier. Special instruments are wanting. The only chance would be a Caesarean."

"Then get on with it, man," ordered Clyde. "Do it."

"What are you waiting for?" cried Tim.

Sir Archibald refused to be flustered. He was still very much in command of the situation. "We lose the mother if we do," he said. "Unfortunately, there is no other choice."

And suddenly it was comedy no longer, not even to the irrepressible Felicity, and for the first time she experienced doubts with regard to her coming ordeal which up to that moment she had faced with fearless gaiety and calm anticipation. She read the horror in her husband's eyes as the import of what the gynaecologist had told them struck home. He was faced not only with the problem resulting from his job but she knew that in his mind he was transferring this dilemma to himself—*which will you have— mother or child—I cannot save both!* Then it was true what people said. There was danger. Things could go wrong. Husbands were right to worry and pace. Nature was not all that kind and genial.

"Damn the mother!" snapped Major Clyde. "It's the kid we want."

Mrs. John C. Lovejoy extracted herself from her husband's arms, swollen with all the indignation of a foster mother and animal lover, to which was added the dignity of her recent bride-hood. "Oh no you don't!" she cried. "Don't you dare touch my Amelia! I'm going in there right now and——"

Desperation had left Tim momentarily speechless, and Felicity fairly ached with sympathy for him, coupled with the feeling of helplessness and a strange new kind of nervousness she had never experienced before.

The voice that brought them all to a kind of shocked standstill belonged to Sergeant Lovejoy. "Look here," he said, "what about letting me have a go?"

"You?" shouted Major Clyde, who for the first time since he had engaged in fighting a war felt as though *his* nerves might be about to go. "What the devil can you do when the greatest gyno in England can't——"

"It's my wife's hape, sir," replied Lovejoy, "and if it wasn't for me she wouldn't be in the trouble she's in. If I 'ad 'alf a crown for every one of them creatures I'd 'elped when it was in a bit of difficulty——"

Sir Archibald looked sharply at Lovejoy. "What's that you say? You've been present at births?"

Lovejoy snorted. "Like I said, if I 'ad 'alf a crown——"

"Never mind your half crowns, man," interrupted Sir Archibald. "Go in then and don't stand there gassing. Get into Colonel Wheeler's surgical gown and cap. The theatre sister will show you how to scrub. Hurry, man—in there!" and he pointed to the door of the operating theatre.

Lovejoy rose, marched to it with a firm tread, and went through. Mrs. Lovejoy looked after her husband as though she had just seen God.

Felicity uttered a plaintive little cry, half arose from her chair, and then sat down again with the most peculiar and frightened expression on her face. Quite suddenly there was something timorous and childlike in her looks and voice as she said, "Oh dear, Tim. I don't think I feel very well."

Tim plunged to her side in what amounted almost to a rugby tackle, landing on his knees with his arms about her. "Felicity darling, what's wrong? What is it?"

It seemed no longer absurd or ridiculous that her husband should be showing every sign of being reduced to dithering panic. She found that she was even glad. It was right that it should be so. She said, "It's—it's just that—I mean, with all the excitement and everything I think that——"

"Oh my God," shouted Tim and disintegrated completely. "Sir Archibald!" he bawled. "Quick! Get Sir Archibald!"

That individual, who was standing no more than two feet behind Tim, said testily, "Yes, yes, I can hear you, you needn't shout! Come on, my boy, pull yourself together and let me have a look." He pushed Tim aside, examined Felicity briefly with no more than a knowing professional glance, and said, "Ah well, here we are. And I must say I'm not surprised. I always thought you were wrong about the date."

At that moment the theatre sister appeared at the door and said, "Dr. Lovejoy is ready and waiting for you, sir."

"What? Who?" said Sir Archibald. "Oh yes, of course, I'll be along in a moment. In the meantime take Mrs. Bailey here to Room C and prepare her. Call Sister Thomas and Nurse Agnew. I'll look in as soon as I can."

He started for the door only to find his way blocked by Tim. "You'll do what? To hell with these bloody monkeys! You'll look after her right now! She's my wife! You can't leave her!"

Sir Archibald again managed to remain calm and controlled. He was still the leading actor in the drama, now a double one. He said, "Will someone take this lunatic off me and explain the facts of life to him? It will be hours yet before Mrs. Bailey will have any need of me. In the meantime——" he brushed Tim aside, stalked into the operating theatre, and vanished.

Major Clyde murmured, "Maybe the doors of history are being

thrown open again. What will happen when they find Gunner Lovejoy standing there?"

Within the glaringly light-blue painted operating theatre the question was being answered.

On the operating table on her back lay the miserable, quivering lump of fur that was Amelia. She was whimpering and trembling in every limb and her hazel-coloured eyes were filled with pain and terror. Over her bent the figures of two men.

If the purpose of a uniform is to make all men alike or designate the kind of service they perform, the surgical cap, gown, mask, and rubber gloves can swallow up the individual inside it more quickly than any other costume, and for the moment Sir Archibald Cruft forgot that it was one Sergeant John Lovejoy, a Royal Artilleryman and Keeper of the Apes, who was inside the garments and addressed him in the manner of a learned colleague, bandying Latin gynaecological phrases to the effect that the unborn infant on whom Major Clyde, and through him the nation, was basing his hopes of an important and successful psychological-warfare gambit had got itself skew-wiff in the uterus and because of several more unintelligible Latin and medical terms could not survive another three minutes. It was too late practically now even for a Caesarean section.

Sergeant Lovejoy, looking down upon the suffering creature, said, "Gord luv you, sir, you've got 'er wrong end to and topside up to be of any 'elp to 'er. I've seen 'em like this many a time. 'ere, let me show you, sir."

Swiftly and with practised hands he turned the ape round on her stomach and then drew up her legs beneath her, putting his arm down just above the top of her head. "When they're out in the wild, sir, they can get 'old of a branch or a bit of rock for purchase. Now you watch 'er."

Gratefully Amelia was already clutching the brawny forearm of the Sergeant and was moving her body in a kind of rhythm accompanied by shrill squeals.

"Now what I usually does," continued the Sergeant, "when they gets about this far along is I puts me thumb 'ere," and he suited the action to the words, "'olding 'er like this, pushing a little, and out she pops. There you are sir."

And out indeed it did pop, a tiny wet creature with fingers and toes that were almost transparent and a miniature face that was terrifyingly human.

"Well, I'm blowed," were the exact words of Sir Archibald Cruft, the great gynaecologist. "Dr.— I mean Sergeant," he paused in the eulogy he was about to deliver, for the Sergeant was staring down at the body of the monkey which had not yet relaxed and was saying, "'ello, 'ello."

Sir Archibald, too, scrutinised the beast. "Dear me," he said, "what's this? There's another one in there. Do they ever?"

"Not to my knowledge," replied Lovejoy, "but I 'ave heard of it once in ten thousand times maybe, or a million I read somewhere once. But then the second is always stillborn. They ain't got the staying power for it, sir."

"Well, this one isn't going to be," declared Sir Archibald Cruft with a sudden fierceness. "Here, help me. Show me what you did before. We've got to bring this little fellow out alive. The thermosphygalamometer, Sister."

The theatre sister wheeled the contraption over and now Sir Archibald proceeded to show how and why he was the great man he was. Working surely and deftly he fastened the various attachments in the proper places to stimulate the blood, oxygen, and sugar supply of the beast, bolstered her heart, took the strain off her pelvis, all the while muttering, "Damnedest technique I ever saw, Sergeant. Absolutely brilliant. We can adapt that to cases of——" and here he went off into another page-long harangue out of the medical dictionary. And now it was Lovejoy's turn to look upon the other man with approval for he understood enough about the physiology of the apes he had attended so long to be able to see what the surgeon was doing for her.

Amelia began to squeak and chitter again, and her small body moved. "Now then," said Sir Archibald, "where was it exactly you put your thumb?"

"Right here, sir, you can feel——"

"That's it," said Sir Archibald exultantly. "I might have

spared the Countess of Crite a nasty hour with this. Well—next time. Push, you say!"

"And out she pops."

And out popped the second, alive and identical to the first.

Sir Archibald gave a perfunctory glance and murmured, "Boy and a girl! What more could they want?"

Sergeant Lovejoy regarded Sir Archibald, his eyes above his mask filled with undaunted admiration. "By Gord, sir, you've done it! It's never been done before with an ape. Two for the price of one, sir. Major Clyde won't 'arf be pleased."

Sir Archibald was not ungenerous. "It's your technique, Sergeant," he said, "and when I write a paper on this I shall give it your name. Well, let's get on with it."

A short time later the door to the operating theatre was thrown open, revealing Sir Archibald and Sergeant Lovejoy, still gowned, with the theatre sister. The metamorphosis of Lovejoy was astonishing. He looked like one of those old-fashioned country surgeons. The face of the theatre sister had assumed that expression akin to the various Madonnas of the Italian school, for she was looking down upon two tiny objects carefully wrapped so that only their faces showed and cradled in her arms.

Sir Archibald's wonderful countenance bore the grand and illuminating smile he reserved for the occasion. "Twins," he announced proudly. "A boy and a girl."

"Not Felicity," quavered Tim Bailey.

"No, Amelia."

Major Clyde was up and upon them with a whoop and a holler. "Eureka in spades!" he shouted. "Amelia's done it! This will shake the horrible Hun to his heels. What we don't do with this bit of news."

They crowded around to look down into the tiny faces. Tim was both astonished and startled, for they did not look like monkeys but humans, or rather caricatures of humans.

Sir Archibald said to the sister, "Take them back to their mother now and see that they are kept warm. I'll look in again in an hour." And to Mrs. Lovejoy he said, "The mother is doing fine.

No complications. Nothing to worry about. Your husband is a genius, Madame. You can thank him——"

Major Timothy Bailey seized the great gynaecologist by his surgical gown and shouted, "What about my Felicity? Who the hell cares about a couple of lousy——"

Sir Archibald disentangled himself carefully. "Look here, young man," he said. "I have handled any number of fathers but you seem to take the prize. It will be at least another four or five hours before I can deliver Mrs. Bailey, so you had better save some of that for later, hadn't you?"

At this point a door farther down the corridor, marked Room C, opened and a young nurse came skimming quickly down the hall. When she reached the group she stood on tiptoes and whispered something into the ear of Sir Archibald, which appeared to startle the great man. "Dear me," he murmured, "you don't say. Well, well!" He turned to Tim and said, "I'll just go along now and have a look at Mrs. Bailey. Not to worry."

Tim put his hands to his head. He felt nervous, drained, exhausted, pleased, anxious, worried, frightened; his was such a turmoil of emotions that he did not see how he could bear the long wait. "Four or five hours," he groaned, "I won't be able to stand it."

"Look here, old man," Major Clyde said, "you won't hold it against us, but Mac and I are going to have to pull out—you know—give us the apelets and we'll do the rest. Well, we've got 'em now, all right. Felicity couldn't be in better hands."

Lovejoy, who had divested himself of his gown and his new profession, came and stood before Tim, a respectful and affectionate Sergeant again. "Sir, if you like," he said, "my wife and I will stay with you. We've just been through it in a way, so to speak, so we know what it's like, waiting."

But it was not four or five hours at all. It was no more than forty-five minutes later when Sir Archibald appeared, his face once more wreathed in his famous another-Cruft-baby-successfully-brought-into-the-world smile.

Tim, who had been hunched down in his chair, his head buried in his hands, looked up miserably for news of more delay.

"A most remarkable woman indeed," said Sir Archibald. "Never encountered anything like it before in a Prime Ibs. Had her baby quietly and without fuss in twenty minutes. Didn't even give us time to get to the operating theatre. Didn't need to. Astonishing girl. Wish they were all like that."

"Wha—what?" gasped Tim. "Did you say——"

Sir Archibald nodded. "A boy," he said, "mother and son doing fine. Come along, let's have a look at them."

Dazed, Tim followed in the wake of the stately pace of the great man to Room C where Felicity sat propped up in bed, looking as fresh and blooming as an English rose, and ten times more beautiful.

At the side of the bed in a bassinet was something red and squealing, which at first glance caused Tim to recoil from shock. It looked so much more like a monkey than a person. The presence of Sir Archibald was embarrassing and that of the red thing completely terrifying.

Felicity called to him, "Oh, my poor darling, you look awful. Have you suffered just terribly?"

There was no point Tim felt to hurling himself across the room, taking his wife in his arms, and comforting her for the travail she was supposed to have been through. She had never looked better or less in need of sympathy in her life, an unquestioned tribute to the Cruft technique. He turned his attention to the red object in the bassinet and nothing he saw there tended to diminish the panic engendered by the first glimpse. He now looked down into the tiny screwed-up countenance which so very greatly resembled those of the apes who had been his charge.

"But—but," he stammered, "the faces of the others were so *human.*"

Sir Archibald nodded sympathetically. His vast and impressive experience included dealing with an endless procession of disappointed and panic-stricken fathers. It was the first glimpse that did it to them. "I know," he said, "it's a bit shaking. However, I can assure you that within a week or so the features of the other little chaps will have turned properly simian while yours will have begun to get over his astonishment at finding himself in our midst and will have commenced, I trust, to resemble his mother. Well, I congratulate you." He turned and marched from the room.

"Tim," Felicity cried, "tell me, what has happened?"

Major Bailey was still badly rattled. "You—you have had a boy," he said, "there—here it is."

"Oh my darling," Felicity said and voiced all of the tenderness and understanding that women have for the ridiculousness of males. "No. I mean—Amelia."

"She—she's had twins! When—when old Cruft came out and announced it I thought——"

"Oh Tim," Felicity cried, now thoroughly moved to commiseration, "how perfectly awful for you. You must have gone through absolute hell. Oh, why is it so easy for us and so terrible for you? Come here, my poor darling, sit here on the bed and let me hold you and rub your head; you've been through a perfectly frightful time."

To his surprise Tim found himself sitting exactly where he had been directed and letting it happen to him. It was good; he had been horribly harassed; it was soothing.

But after a while positions were reversed and Felicity was nestled in his arms where she sighed and said, "Oh Tim, I'm so happy. I never thought it could happen to me, but it has. I have a real Cruft baby. It's absolutely perfect."

A spark stirred within Tim and was fanned to a sudden glow. "Dammit," he said, "it's mine. All old Cruft did was——"

"Say Abracadabra," Felicity concluded for him. "It's a Bailey baby."

"Yes, yes," said Tim with sudden and strange fierceness. "That's it." He got up and went and looked down in the bassinet. Was it his imagination or had the red object in it already begun to look slightly more human? And had it smiled?

"And thus," Felicity murmured to herself, "thank God, are fathers born as well."

Chapter 22

EPITAPH FOR TWO APES

Gibraltar 1962.

The British flag still flies over the Fortress; the cruise ships and passenger liners calling there discharge their quota of tourists with cameras slung about their necks; others arrive by air, touching down on the concrete strip that juts out into the blue bay of Algeciras; others still come by road down the winding coast line of Spain or burst from the folds of the brown hills to cross the border at La Línea.

By car and on foot they spread out over the Rock, to find it an engaging backwater outpost of an Empire which the processes of history have turned into a Commonwealth, with charming people, the best rate of currency exchange in Europe, cheap goods, and some breathtaking views.

Dry docks and dockyards are still busy; O'Hara's Battery at the pinnacle of the Rock, its cannon as obsolete as Nelson's twelve pounders and carronades, still pretends to menace the Straits. The ruins of the Moorish castle and the caves are worth a visit; the service and accommodation at the Rock Hotel are first class and no tour of Gibraltar is complete, of course, without a visit to the famous Barbary apes and their village on the upper Rock.

They haven't changed. They still pry into pockets for monkey nuts, sit on shoulders, pull hair, nip fingers, remove windscreen wipers from cars, and make off with handbags, cameras, binoculars, or anything one might be so incautious as to leave about unattended.

Another artilleryman—Bombardier Bychurch—is Keeper of the Apes, guide, and cicerone to the tourists who come to watch him feed them, and he has a tip-earning patter satisfying enough to the visitors, part of which runs:

"They're greedy little beggars, always on the scrounge. Mind you don't move too quick, ma'am, with him on your shoulders. They're nervous like and don't like quick movements. The apes have been here since 1763, looked after by the Royal Artillery. There's twenty-six of them here which is known as the Queen's Gate pack, and twenty-two around on the other side of the Rock called the Middle Hill pack. During the war when their numbers was reduced through sickness and privation the Prime Minister sent a special message saying they was to be kept up to strength and accordingly a number of them was sent over from Africa where they bred with the apes remaining on the Rock and them here is their descendants."

This is as far as Bombardier Bychurch's knowledge goes; he has, of course, no idea of the means by which this was achieved and the astonishing success scored by the counter-intelligence intrigue of one Major "Slinker" Clyde in the long ago of almost two decades past, a success far greater than he or any of the others connected with the affair had envisaged.

For when in June 1943 the announcement of the birth of twin apelets to a Gibraltar Rock ape was made, the impact was a double one. Not only did it attest that ape-wise all was normal on the Rock but it shook the scientific world as well and, carried over the international press wire, caused as great a stir as had the birth of the Dionne quintuplets.

The effect upon the Germans was exactly what Major Clyde had foreseen. They gave up. And themselves worshippers of science they actually carried the story in their own newspapers. The propaganda broadcasts with regard to the apes ceased immediately, as did their operation of buying up available Barbary apes in North Africa.

But this again had further unexpected and welcome repercussions. For the Germans had caused a boom in the macaque market and Arabs along the entire coast line from Marrakesh to Oran had been scraping them off the rocks and hauling them down out of trees to cart off and sell to the German agents who were paying practically anything asked for the brutes.

Suddenly and without warning the boom collapsed, the German agents with their gold, whisky, cigarettes, dollars, or whatever was demanded disappeared, leaving the traders stuck with whole crates full of the animals. It was now they remembered the primary British interest in the purchase of these beasts and legitimate commerce being anti-no one they returned at once to their original channels of this trade.

In a fortnight, and upon wings supplied by a chastened Group Captain Cranch, twenty of the finest specimens, male and female, of Barbary apes had been flown to the Rock to establish the quota solicited by the Prime Minister. He was informed that his orders had been carried out, and the newcomers soon adjusted themselves to the life of ease and luxury provided by His Majesty's Royal Artillery. The crisis was at an end and never again threatened.

As always when looking back over a war there are many turning points where one can say, "Here if this had not happened and so and so had not arrived in the nick of time all might have ended disastrously." What actually would have occurred had the Barbary apes been wiped out will never be known, but at least the prospect appeared of sufficient importance and danger to the leader of the British Empire to engage his attention.

But all this happened nineteen years ago. Gibraltar today is moulded into the somnolent blessings of peace, and all those involved in the affair scattered far and wide.

Major William "Slinker" Clyde returned to Christchurch immediately he was demobilised, where he was received by a grateful Master who asked him, "Well, how was it, Will?" to which the ex-Major replied, "Pretty silly, sir," and that was the last he ever referred to his wartime experiences. He attained a Professorship at his College and in recent years has turned to writing brilliant and erudite detective novels, under a pseudonym, which bring him a small fortune.

Felicity has never regretted her choice of mate, for her husband is the youngest Colonel at Staff College and a brilliant future is predicted for him. He can write D.S.O., C.B.E. after his name and he is used constantly on the Rock when some new officer is to be stuck with the post as an example that even such a doubtful office as OIC Apes can be a springboard to greatness.

Felicity, it might be added, has worn extremely well and at forty-two looks no more than thirty. She has put on a little weight, but Tim always liked her better that way. Her first-born, the boy Anthony Bailey, is about to go up to Oxford to pursue his studies under the eye of his godfather, Professor Clyde. He has elected science over the Army or the Navy and as a Crufter is certain to make his mark in that field. He has two sisters and a younger brother, also Cruft products.

Five years after the end of the war Sergeant Lovejoy reached the age of retirement and with his wife bade farewell to the Army, Gibraltar, and the Barbary apes. They returned to England and on a holiday visit to Hope Cove where they had first met they found that the guest house where they had stayed was up for sale. The combined savings of the Sergeant and the competence left his wife by her relatives enabled them to buy this property, carry out the necessary improvements and decorations, and bring it back as a successful year-round holiday hotel.

With Tim Bailey's extraordinary services being recognised with the C.B.E., it is only natural that his right-hand man Lovejoy should win the lower order of B.E.M., and this dignity was conferred upon the ex-Keeper of Apes in a subsequent honours list and celebrated in all the newspapers with extravagant stories and suitable photographs.

But John Lovejoy achieved far greater rewards in a pleasant and contented existence with his wife. They like and respect one another and he has made her a good, kind husband, and for this he has had a most astonishing and unexpected return.

It will be remembered that spinster Constance Boddy had made total abstinence on the part of the Gunner a condition of her yielding to him, and outside of the one rousing wing-ding, the last jamboree at the Admiral Nelson, Lovejoy kept his pledge.

Well, in these late and approaching twilight years Mrs. Lovejoy closes an eye. On Saturday nights Mr. Lovejoy steals away to The Crown and Anchor and has himself a couple with the boys. He takes Guinness and lime for old time's sake. And on his return home, even though his steps be slightly unsteady, Mrs. Lovejoy sees no evil, hears no evil, and speaks no evil—a truly remarkable and loving woman.

Howard Cranch is Air Marshal Cranch, solid with gold braid, medals, years, dignity, and the problems of the jet age. Packed away in a trunk are his costumes, his Chinaman's wig, his minstrel make-up, and his musical instruments with which he used to entertain. Memories, however, cannot be tucked away as easily as old clothes, and often he will look back to his days upon the Rock and the monkey flights, and at such times he is quite likely to substitute "well" for "good" and, when asked how things are, reply, "Well, well," in the manner of a certain Spanish Señor Blasco Irun of long, long ago.

The Brigadier retired to Surrey where he raises mushrooms with great success, selling them to such famous hostelries as the Savoy, the Connaught, Claridges, and the Berkeley, while Lord Cruft was gathered to his forefathers only last year, full of honours and the regrets of the new generation that theirs cannot be Cruft babies.

Sir Archibald before his passing was given a Baronetcy for his many and varied services to humanity, not the least of which was his describing and popularising what he named the Lovejoy Technique to be applied in certain cases of difficult delivery. He was also celebrated, and after a time was able even to joke on the subject, as the only gynaecologist who had ever successfully brought a pair of twin monkeys into the world.

Alfonso T. Ramirez, retired from the Navy Yard and suitably pensioned, still lives at Gibraltar where he is known as a rabid Anglophile and staunch supporter of the British against enemies past, present, and future.

The manner in which this happy transformation came about was the following: on a certain day shortly after the end of the war two special policemen attached to the Colonial Office appeared at his laboratory where he was working and summoned him to accompany them to Government House. Half fainting, convinced that all had been discovered, sure that he was being led off to interrogation, torture, and execution, Mr. Ramirez went with them, knees quaking, teeth chattering, sweat pouring from his pasty countenance.

He was taken to the office of the Governor, at whose desk reposed a box. Upon his entrance His Excellency arose and made the following speech:

"Mr. Ramirez: during the war you performed a considerable service to the Government and the nation, which has not been forgotten. Owing to the nature of that service, of which I need not remind you except to say that by using your intelligence and knowledge of certain species of apes you were instrumental in bringing about a conclusion greatly to be desired, it was not possible to reward you suitably at the time lest dangerous information be conveyed to the enemy. Now, however, it is His Majesty's pleasure to tender you this scroll in appreciation of your deed."

And suiting action to words the Governor opened the box and produced a beautifully engrossed parchment which detailed the fact that Alfonso Tomaso Ramirez had been of signal service to his country and had thereby earned its gratitude.

As is well known the Germans have a built-in forgetter, an apparatus that aids them not to remember past wickednesses. This Mr. Ramirez shared. The awarding of the scroll turned him from *phobe* to *phile*. Treugang disappeared forever. Besides, what had the Germans ever done for him?

Old Scruff? In any event he would not be alive today. The life span of apes doesn't stretch that far. However, he was denied old age. One remembers in the Golden Bough the boxer king of the Greek isle who had to fight every newcomer and kept his crown and his life only as long as he won. Well, it was like that with Scruffy. One of the imports from North Africa was bigger, tougher, stronger, younger, more aggressive, truculent, possessive, and malevolent. They had it out. Scruffy lost. He went down fighting, bravely, dirtily, gallantly, struggling to do his conqueror in as long as there was still the faintest spark of life in his great, grey body, and when it was extinguished his canines were still tight in the flank of the victor, who was himself not counted for very much good or use thereafter from the mauling he had received.

It is sad to be compelled to report that Amelia never got over the loss of Scruffy, for whom her affection remained constant, and she was found dead in a tree by Sergeant Lovejoy soon after Scruffy's passing. The autopsy reported something gastric and pulmonary, but both Lovejoy and his wife knew that she had died of a broken heart. And strange, though grieved, they were content to have it so.

There was then a most private subscription initiated, for which contributions were received from such diverse characters as the then Majors Clyde, McPherson, and Bailey, Sergeant and Mrs. Lovejoy, the Brigadier, the Colonial Secretary, and even, when he heard about the subscription and its purpose, the Governor.

From these funds was purchased a small bronze plaque let into the concrete platform of the lookout on the upper Rock, inscribed, "Scruffy–Amelia, 1945," followed by a single line of epitaph and accolade, "Thanks to Them."